Three Souls

By
Jacey K Dew

To the loves of my life, my children;
Emily and Jeremy.

I hope you never lose the magic
inside of you and your love for
adventure in life.

I love you forever and ever.

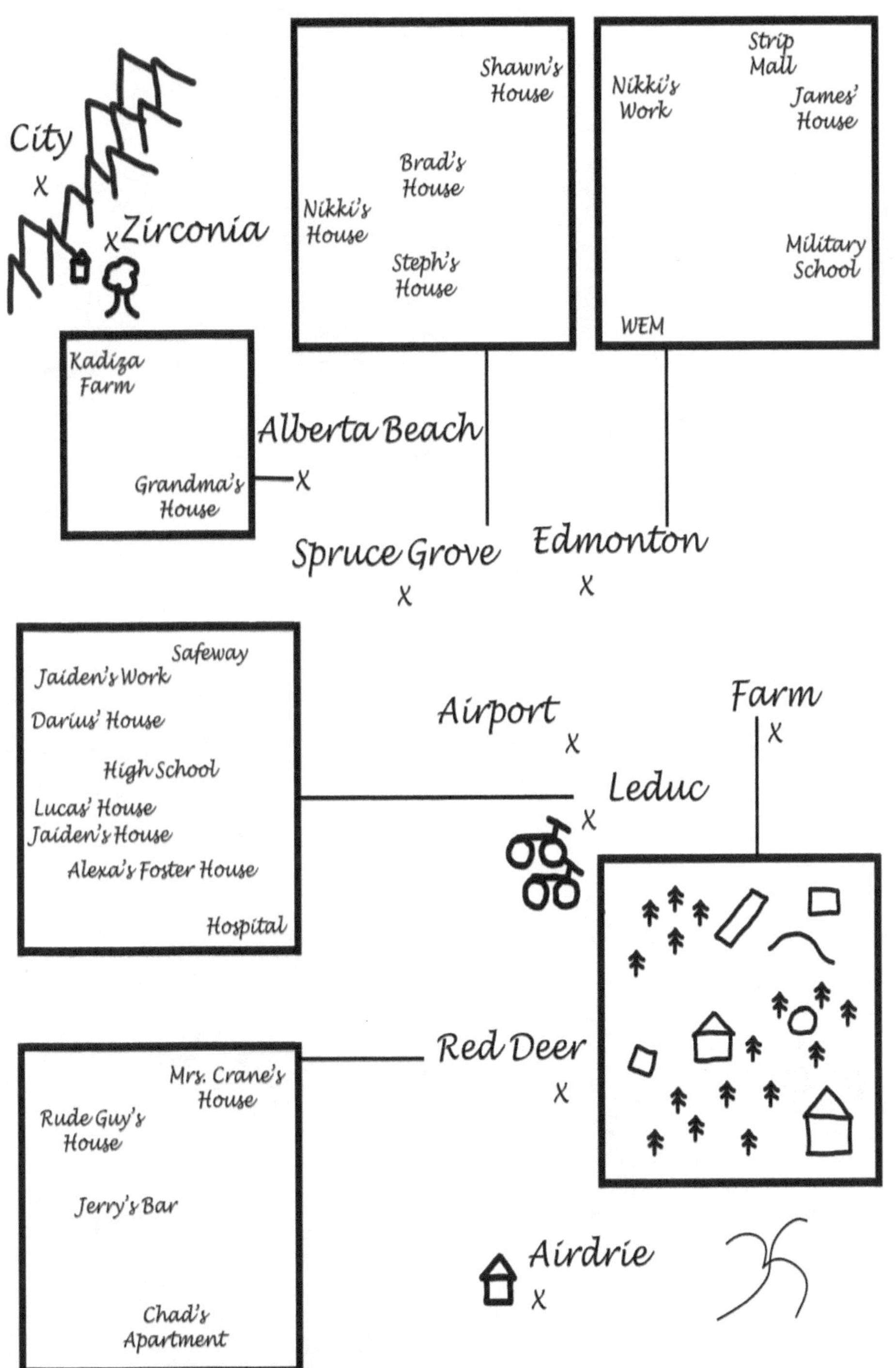

City
X
Zirconia
X
Kadiza
Farm
Grandma's
House
Alberta Beach
X
Spruce Grove
X
Shawn's
House
Brad's
House
Nikki's
House
Steph's
House
Nikki's
Work
Strip
Mall
James'
House
Military
School
WEM
Edmonton
X
Safeway
Jaiden's Work
Darius' House
High School
Lucas' House
Jaiden's House
Alexa's Foster House
Hospital
Airport
X
Leduc
X
Farm
X
Red Deer
X
Mrs. Crane's
House
Rude Guy's
House
Jerry's Bar
Chad's
Apartment
Airdrie
X

Looking back, I never imagined their lives having such an impact on me.

Or, how our lives were going to impact the world.

And, how exhausting it all was.

How impossible.

I almost wonder if it was all worth it. If everything would have been better without us.

If the world would have been better off without us.

If we would have been better off choosing different paths than the ones that we lived.

They probably would have died sooner, and not left nearly as much behind.

Maybe I would have died, and not been the only one left.

Their souls, these memories, are a cold comfort.

Chapter 1

Sick, fulfilling pleasure creeps into Darius' features. My boyfriend appears devilish and somewhat wicked. Piercing blue eyes lock onto his next victim.

The warmth on my shoulders fades as Darius stalks the oblivious boy. Matt doesn't notice Darius until after he speaks. Jumping up and away from the sudden sound.

"Hey Matty, where are you going?" Darius turns Matt sharply; his well-built body easily overpowers the smaller boy. "We haven't seen each other for a while and I think you're trying to avoid me." The intimidating male stands directly in front of Matt; their bodies almost touching.

Matt tries to say something, but my boyfriend's actions are working well to overwhelm his ability to run away or work his mouth properly.

He gapes for a few moments before Matt finally comes up with enough courage to speak. His voice catches in his throat. "N-no, I'm not."

I'm bored of this display of dominance but won't do anything to prevent, deter, or stop it. I wouldn't dare try.

"Why don't I believe you? You see," his voice deepens as he goes on, "I don't think you enjoy our little visits anymore. And, I don't like that." These interactions have been going on since before I've known Darius.

Darius roughly shoves Matt into the brick wall. I cringe inwardly as he winces. His back is likely getting scratched up from the brick.

Coach Renner chooses the right, or rather wrong, moment to come through the school's doors. He immediately recognizes the scene. I take the few steps needed to reach them and tap on Darius' shoulder.

Catching his attention, I nod towards the approaching coach. He loosens his grip enough for Matt to free himself and run away.

Coach Renner's movements hesitate slightly as Darius turns to square up towards the approaching coach.

The all-around coach of the small high school is, and rightly so, nervous around my boyfriend. Darius holds an air of danger around him that can intimidate anyone trying to oppose him. It helps that he towers over most and is built like a tank.

Though I've only known him a couple of months, I've gathered that one goes against him; that was part of what had drawn me to him in the first place. Nothing and no one can get in my way, or tell me what I have to do; when I have him backing me up.

"J-Johnston! Brenner! What do you think you're doing?" His voice cracks in the beginning but remains authoritative for the remainder. Coach Renner's familiar look, of something between disapproval and fear, stays through his walk to us. "You're going to risk tonight on this? You're lucky I'm the one that caught you. Don't pull any more of this shit and get to the locker room. Now!"

While he smirks at Coach Renner, Darius grabs my hand to escort me inside the school.

Coach jogs in the direction Matt went. I bet he's going to do damage control to ensure his quarterback can still play tonight.

A slight tug pulls my attention back to Darius. He leads me into the school and guides me away from the dwindling crowds and the halls. I follow him the opposite way we should be going to tuck underneath a tucked-away stairwell.

I let myself be turned and pushed into the wall. My eyes close instinctively as his lips cover mine; moving in harsh movements. I allow him to do as he pleases; wrapping my arms around his neck for support. He controls the moment.

The back of my head hits the wall as Darius forces his way into my mouth. I play with him a bit by rubbing my tongue against his. Moaning quietly as a heated bubbling grows inside me from the feeling of his hand sliding up my shirt; rubbing against my side.

The bell's shrill ringing barely registers in my head until, with one last forceful move of his lips, he pulls away and looks into my eyes. He pecks my forehead. Nails run along my side as Darius pulls his hand out of my shirt.

Opening my eyes, I find a lust-filled stare aimed at me. His hungered look unnerves me in some ways, but in others makes me feel wanted; special. The suit adds an extra level of dashing intensity.

"Let's go." Immediately, the cool wall on my back and the warmth from his body dissipates as each is removed completely.

Darius leads me to the boys' locker room. His teammates are audible from down the hall. Their hoots and hollers echo in the empty hallway until metal clicks against metal.

Multiple male voices sound like nothing more than loud mutters from behind the closed door; only every odd word can be made out as someone shouts out above the rest.

I hear the hard click of the door opening before I can see the movement of it. Miles' familiar face peeks around from behind the door; his natural smile changes slightly as a small twitch-like grin appears for only a moment when he spots us coming. His pointed looks, though intense, have a caring and comforting feeling to them.

Miles opens the door enough for him to slip through and then holds it open for Shale. Once they both are through the door, Shale lets it shut, with the same harsh click, and stands to the side. They've already changed out of their suits and into their gear.

"What took so long?" A slight knowing creeps into Shale's brown eyes. I ignore him in favour of the other one. Miles has the decency to ignore the obvious, and me.

"Coach decided to try to give us trouble for talking with Matty." Shale nods slightly. Understanding the undertones after Darius' trademark devilish grin appears. "I've got to get ready." He turns his attention back to me.

The arm around my waist tightens and pulls me against his broad chest. Darius' gaze holds me as he leans down for another hard kiss.

My eyes close from impact. It ends quickly and his arms release my waist.

Opening my eyes, I find an empty space where he had stood only a moment ago. I watch as he and Shale disappear into the change room.

"Alexa, how are you?" Miles' smooth, quiet voice calls me. Turning naturally at the sound of my name, I notice the concerned look on Miles' face. It takes a moment before I remember he asked a question.

Giving him a hard look, I answer while ignoring what I know he actually meant. "I'm fine, Miles. I'll see you at the game."

The slight nod of his head signals his acceptance. With one last glance at me, then he turns for the locker room door. Muffled noises roar then go quiet once more.

The stillness of the hallway is discomforting.

Turning on my heel, I hurry to the football field.

People have already started gathering for the final game of the year. This crucial game is not only for the first-place position in the division but also the bragging rights over the long-running school rivalry between the Bears and Tigers; I recite words from the earlier pep rally.

From what I'm told, it's the talk of the school and the city. I don't get it, but I'm going to support my boyfriend.

Our rivals, the Bears, have already started going through their warm-ups as I walk to my usual spot beside the bleachers. Standing here gives me shade from both sun and wind, while I watch Darius play.

I wrap my arms around myself, wishing I had something warmer for the chilled November air. It's going to snow soon; the type of snow that sticks around for the rest of winter.

I watch the opposing team's warm-up, as their coach shouts out commands. Their team barely starts running drills when loud cheers come from our bleachers at the sight of our team coming out of the school. They make a slight production out of the entrance. Our school's mascot follows the train of hoots and hollers of the louder football players.

Darius leads everyone onto the field to immediately start the warm-ups. Everyone knows the routine by heart and flawlessly pulls off every move. The cheers of the crowd encourage them.

The warm-ups last until the referee calls the Captains to the middle of the field for a coin toss. Darius and Shale win the toss and get to pick the starting sides.

Darius looks for me on the way back. He waves once before his attention returns to the team and game.

"Huddle!" His loud voice orders his teammates to gather.

Coach Renner gives a small talk to the team before they all yell, "Tigers!"

The team breaks off into two groups; one walks back to the bench, while the other jogs out to their pre-determined spots on the field.

People have been looking forward to this all week; half the school has shown up to watch. Pep rallies and posters have plagued all the students; so it's no wonder everyone is here.

Everything goes quiet, until a kick signals the start of the game.

Both teams look evenly matched; not that I would ever say that to Darius. Neither team is willing to let the other score points as the first, second, and third quarters pass with no touchdowns.

As a player and fanatic, the game would be a harrowing experience. As someone here to support a boyfriend and his friends, the lack of major action is boring.

With time almost out, Darius gets the ball. His helmet moves side to side but no one looks open. He throws high into the air.

Out of nowhere, Shale exits the bundle of players and grabs the ball. All the players react quickly.

Shale passes the ball behind to Miles then turns into a moving shield, until Miles grows an unrecoverable lead.

Right before the end zone, his sudden stop becomes the start of a suspenseful and confused silence. Unfazed by the silence of the crowd and the players running to take him out, Miles stands just before the line.

A realization comes to mind.

My eyes wander to the clock.

Three...

Two...

One...

An eruption of cheers turns my attention. Miles waited for the time to run almost-out to step over the line. His hesitation to cross into the end zone gives no chance for the other team to score.

Miles' touchdown will be the cause of the entire year's bragging rights and embarrassment of the Bears. People practically leap over each other to congratulate the team in all of the excitement.

In all of the chaos, I lose sight of the three guys. I raise myself on my toes, uselessly trying to get a better view.

The referee blows his whistle to try to calm the mass of people. The crowd is instructed back to the bleachers so the teams can receive their medals.

Both teams find their way to the center of the field; only one team bursts with excitement, while the other is solemn.

As the referee gives out the medals, an uneasy feeling comes over me. All my attention is drawn to a tall man beside me. An icicle draws up my spine in fear of this stranger. I move myself to the seat side to put a railing between us.

The trophy is passed around the team. Once they are finished celebrating together, all the players head back to get congratulated by friends and family. I wait for Darius, but he meets up with the tall stranger instead. Could that be his father?

Curiosity pulls me closer. I quickly try to examine the male from behind. Everything in the man's clothing speaks of importance; from the black dress pants and shoes, to the white button-up shirt, and the black sports jacket held in his arm. Everything about his posture and the way he holds himself speaks to his superiority.

I still can't shake the awful feeling he gave off.

The conversation between this man and my boyfriend looks to be one of business rather than a social call. Darius has his helmet off. I can see his frown and furrowed brow.

My ears trick me as I approach. The distance between them and me is close enough that I should be hearing something; yet not a voice reaches me. What would they need to talk about in such a hushed way? My ears ring with anxiety.

The stranger's back visibly tenses as I approach. He turns and looks through me. Darius finishes moving his mouth. He looks from the man to me and back again.

Darius surges forward and around the man. He turns me around quickly before pulling me with him. His arm around my shoulders keeps me from looking back. Chills creep up my spine. I know the man is staring at our backs as Darius quickly takes me away.

Looking up at Darius, I study his expression. The glare is still on his face. The man's reaction to me has riled Darius up enough for his eyes to hold anger.

Maybe his father is abusive. It would explain everything. I don't voice the thought. I don't think now is the right time.

Darius' tensed muscles relax the further he hurries us away from the man, but the vice grip he has doesn't loosen.

Darius pulls me outside the locker room so he can change. This time a different mood is created within the empty halls. The hallway seems to hold a slight bit of danger that wasn't there the prior visit.

Jerking open the door, Darius bursts into the room; the impending danger looks me in the face. His sharp features crease with anger. The attractiveness I typically find in him is gone.

He turns me around and pulls me in a smooth motion. Whatever he and the strange man talked about was something bad enough to change his mood drastically.

A shiver travels up my spine, my body tenses and relaxes as the jolt reaches my shoulders. It's not too unusual of a spasm after being outside so long in this cool fall weather, the more unusual is the cause of my shiver. Darius' arm around my waist is strangely cold after the kind of activity he just finished.

Miles passes us as we walk through the main doors. He hesitates for a moment as he looks like he wants to intervene. Darius cuts his look with one of his own.

Unspoken words go around me, just out of my grasp and

understanding. I know I'm missing something important.

Hoots, hollers, and honks fill the air in celebration; a clear result of the win. Vehicles slowly inch out of the parking lot as they avoid other vehicles and people. The stop sign is largely ignored by those speeding out to the main road.

The cold arm wrapped around me disappears as we reach the running black truck; my cue to go to the passenger's seat. The leather seat is hot to the touch. Warmth quickly seeps through my clothes, warming me from Darius' cold touch.

Darius turns the key and hits the gear shift with jolted movements. He white-knuckles the steering wheel. I buckle in the moment the truck starts lurching, as he makes quick starts and stops. The engine growls loud from the exertion.

Once we leave the parking lot, Darius wastes no time picking up speed to drive down the long stretch of road.

Darius cuts a couple of vehicles off. They honk their annoyance. I just hope the way is clear of police. The usual ten-minute drive only takes half the time.

He rushes into the garage; managing not to hit anything as he skids to a stop. Cutting the engine, the blond hits the button to close the door.

Apprehension runs through my spine as we leave the truck. The slight noise the door makes when I close it is nothing compared to the loud slam of the driver's side door.

Looking over the hood, I see Darius' head coming around the front. He wraps his arm around me without stopping or slowing his pace and opens the door for us. I feel almost like I'm a captive as he gently shoves me through the opening and by the firm grip of his hand that stays on my shoulder.

Not one moment through the door, a cooled body covers my back while pushing me face-first into an equally cold wall. A jolt races up my spine at the same speed a knot clenches and releases in my stomach.

One large hand buries itself through my hair before pulling tight. He pulls at my hair to bring my head to the side. The freshly exposed skin raises with goosebumps as cool puffs of Darius' breath caress the area. He alternates between firm lips travelling, of teeth gently scraping, and of his wet tongue lapping at my skin. The sensations inside me twist between pleasure, pain, and fear.

Darius moves his other hand from its resting place of my hip, slowly up my torso and under my shirt. Electric tingles follow his hand. My hands rest tense against the wall. Hastily, I raise my arm, quickly dismissing the feeling of something rubbing against my forearm, to wrap around the back of his head. As I bring his head closer I feel a slight curl in his lips.

A different sort of electricity fills the air, soaking in the moment, as the intensity rises. His body pauses, tense for a moment before his lips and teeth descend on my neck again, rougher this time.

His teeth latch as he quickly bites harder. The delicious painful pleasure quickly turns into just pain. A slight cry escapes my throat as my body tenses reflexively.

White-hot panic engulfs me. I need to get off this wall. His grasp is too strong. Pushing and twisting are useless. He's too strong.

"Darius. This hurts." I tell him. He doesn't let up.

A ringing starts in my ears. My heart clenches. Gasping for breath is a laborious activity.

Darius stops in a frozen grip. I let down my arm and rest it in front of me on the wall. His chest rising and falling with his quick breathing is the only sign that he hasn't completely frozen in time.

Moments feel like hours until he moves; lessening his grip on my hair and slowly bringing his hand out from underneath my shirt. The ringing in my ears stops just as suddenly as it started. A new sound reaches my ears. Whipping my head to the side I see Shale in the entrance of the hallway; still dressed in his football gear, minus the helmet.

"Downstairs." Shale's tone says the rest of the sentence for him; his hard stare is fixed on Darius. A quick, sharp breath is released from the male behind me, his hatred to the order clear. Shale takes no notice, however as he turns on his heels and quietly leaves.

"Wait here." Darius' voice is rough and hoarse. I have no interest in the wrath of this angered man. I nod my head once, turning around to look at him.

When angered, Darius has a wild, uncontrolled sense about his whole persona that isn't there normally; he's not usually like this. His shoulders are set back; his dominant presence is almost overbearing, and his stoic features set on the spot Shale just left. Darius doesn't look at me before following Shale to the basement.

Tension releases as he leaves. I rest against the wall; resisting the urge to fall to the floor. I close my eyes and concentrate on controlling my breathing. The air clears of its thickness and my lungs receive their proper oxygen. My fevered skin cools as my heart slows down.

I wait through moments before opening my eyes. Wiping tears away. My heart has somewhat calmed and my head clears as I can move my now functioning body off of the wall and fully onto my feet.

Darius' words override any notion of moving from this spot. Goosebumps creep their way down the lengths of my arms as the air feels warmer. I rub my palms against the skin of my upper arms.

A low growling of an engine tickles my eardrums. Another vehicle is pulling into the garage just as abruptly as Darius' truck had pulled in. Not a second later the engine is cut and barely a moment after a door is slammed.

Miles hastily barrels into the room, still dressed in his football gear. I take in his worried expression. He looks me over before relief flashes in his emerald eyes.

"Move," Kelly's voice demands right before Miles stumbles forward. Quickly he regains his balance. The taller girl is now in the doorway. She smiles as she spots me against the wall. She rushes over to me, quickly grabbing my wrist. "Good, you're here. You can help me. The boys want barbeque tonight."

Kelly drags me away before I can get out a word. She pulls me down the hallway, through the lower living room, up a couple of stair steps, and straight into the kitchen.

Darius will forgive me for leaving the spot so I can help set up supper. I hope.

Letting go of my wrist, Kelly opens one half of the fridge. We pull out everything we need for tonight and pack them into a couple of coolers.

I open the sliding patio door and walk out onto the deck. The sun's heat instantly warms my skin even in the cool air. There is no wind here to make it colder, which makes it bearable.

Kelly comes out carrying a glass-bottled drink I recognize from a couple of times I have drunk with this group. The label is decorated in a set of lines and curves in an alternate of red and black. The label on the side reads Fekete Vér in an old, gothic style of writing. I haven't tried it yet, maybe I will tonight.

I walk closer to her. She stands there with her eyes closed for a moment before she looks towards the sun; her hand shielding her eyes. For a moment the sun reflects in her eyes giving her light blue eyes a silver glow. She looks at me smiling, her normal mischievous grin before I realize she isn't quite looking straight at me but slightly over my shoulder. I turn to follow her gaze.

The three guys have come from around the side of the house, each carrying various items, and are headed towards us. They are no longer dressed in their football gear. All have changed into their regular styles of clothing; jeans and a variety of shirt styles. Shale's long black hair is pulled back into a low ponytail; out of the braids worn for football.

Shale and Darius go straight to the barbeque. They busy themselves with getting the grill going and the food cooking. Meanwhile, Miles sets up the table with the fixings needed for the hamburgers and a couple of different store-bought salads.

Kelly gets a fire started with wood and gasoline. She lights a match and tosses it in. In a whoosh, the gasoline lights up and disappears. I'm sure if I looked into the pit there would be some flame on the wood.

The tall girl saunters over to her boyfriend, giving him a quick peck on the lips before she looks at the table. Walking over there myself, I nod a greeting to Miles. Gazing back over to Kelly, she has her eyes on the table.

"Miles." Her strong voice catches his immediate attention. "You're missing a few things. You don't have the utensils yet and what about the spoons for the salads? You should have brought everything out at the same time. It would have saved you a trip and time." Miles nods his head once before retreating into the house. Not worth the argument.

Kelly turns to me. "I don't know how many times I have to tell that boy. You can get so much more done in a day if you don't have to spend the time doing things twice when you could very well do it only once. He's always walking to and from places more than necessary." She barely pauses with a quick breath. "Oh, did you see Carla's new haircut today? What was she thinking? That haircut is atrocious." Kelly continues talking about the daily gossip about anything and everything going on.

Miles comes back as I start to drone out what Kelly is talking about. As he sets the utensils on the table, I help him open the containers, letting Kelly believe she still has my attention by nodding and humming every so often.

A familiar hand settles itself on my shoulder slightly gripping and releasing. "Well, Kelly, as interesting as this conversation is, I need to steal Alexa for a moment. I need help with something." He doesn't wait for an answer. Darius grips my shoulder slightly to guide me into the house. Dropping his hand, he follows me through the door.

"What did you need help with?" I ask him.

"I can't find the bottle opener." Nodding, I start looking through the usual places for the bottle opener, the utensil drawer, the side of the fridge, and the drawer beside the sink. My search there is empty-handed.

Darius looks through some of the other drawers, while I look through some of the organizational holders on the countertop. I watch him. Waiting for an apology, some mention to what happened earlier, or why that man pissed him off, but he doesn't speak. He pretends that everything is normal. I wonder if I should bring it up.

Continuing my search, I move into the front room. A first glance search to the spotless room tells me it won't be in there.

"Found it." The voice suddenly almost frighteningly appears in my ear. Even though I didn't jump, my heart races at the unexpected appearance of my boyfriend.

"Where was it?" I ask him as I turn to face him.

"In one of the drawers." Darius holds up the bottle opener on his finger by the little chain attached to its sides.

One of his warm hands grabs mine. Pulling me closer he rests the hand holding the keychain on my hip. Letting go of my hand he slowly slides his own down my arm and my side to sit mirroring his other hand.

I look into his face and his eyes, and then he closes the distance between us. His tongue compels my lips to open almost immediately and enters my mouth. His warm tongue plays with mine for a moment and moves to explore the rest of my mouth. Darius' hands travel slowly, massaging across the small of my back then lower to grope my butt. His right-hand jumps to the back of my neck. Simultaneously, his hold tightens, crushing me to him in one swift movement. Harsh kisses feel bruising as he allows no room to back away.

He controls my movements, my body moves to his wants, rather than to my mind. The tight hold tenses and clenches for one last, drawn-out moment. Darius parts his mouth from mine and loosens his hold only enough for me to look him in the face again. His gaze pierces into me. "Let's go. The steaks should be about done."

Letting go of me and taking a step back, he then holds out his hand. Taking the offer, I grip his hand as we walk back outside.

Shale has four steaks off the grill. The last one he takes off and puts it on a plate; mine devoid of any hint of red meat. Giving the plate to me, he grabs his own from the side of the barbeque and goes to sit down.

I let go of Darius' hand and head over to the table instead, I pick up a set of utensils and look over at Miles as he scoops himself a spoonful of the potato and egg salad. I help myself to the other salad as I wait for him to finish. Putting the spoon back when I finish, I look up to Miles who is patiently waiting for his turn. Walking behind him, I switch him places to get some of the other salad.

Once we are both finished I follow him back to the three lawn chairs. Miles sits down behind Kelly on the one, as Shale sits on the second one and Darius occupies the last one.

When I settle, Darius hands me an already opened bottle of liquor; a lemon flavoured vodka cooler. I notice an already empty bottle of the Fekete Vér beside him on the arm of the chair, as well as one by Shale and Kelly. I wish he had opened one of those for me instead. It would be rude to refuse the already opened drink.

I take one gulp of the vodka drink inside. The familiar warmth almost burns down my throat, while a tingle runs through the back of my nose.

Chapter 2

Earthy mint smoke rushes from my lungs and momentarily darkens the air in front of me. One last breath from the brown stick finishes what I dare to breathe in before burning the filter. I put it out and drop the remainder in the butt tray.

Turning the corner of the building, I go inside using the propped open back door. The heat blasts at me. My fingertips tingle.

Not too far off down the hall, I walk into the staffroom and hang my coat up. I unwrap the decorative white and black knit scarf from around my neck.

The clock on the wall says it's 3:26, meaning the actual time should be around 3:30. My phone confirms the actual time is 3:31. That clock is getting slower.

My phone buzzes. Mom texted me. I touch the notification and it opens up another screen. *Pizza tonight?*

I reply to her, *Four cheese*, then put the phone back in my pocket. Time to get back to work. I walk to the front desk to relieve my substitute.

"You're late," Karen sing songs.

Not answering her right away, I look for the time on the phone closest to me; 3:32. Since I know that whatever I say, she won't care, I make something drastic up. "Sorry, my mom called me. She cut herself bad and is going to the hospital to get stitches."

"So what? You have to leave now?" She grinds out.

The thought tempts me to cut out of work early, just because of her shitty attitude. But, I think better of it. "No, she just wanted to let me know."

She rolls her eyes. "Whatever. I've got work to do." Karen gets up from my chair and goes back towards her office.

As soon as her back is turned to me, I glare at her and project my thoughts out to her. Calling her a Bitch. My hand twitches, itching to give her the middle finger. I restrain only because I'm at work.

A high ringing interrupts my thought. I sit in my chair and pick up the phone on the second ring. Without having to think, I start the speech they taught me on day one. "Thank you for call-"

His loud voice drowns mine. "I need to speak with Louis."

Keeping my sickly sweet phone voice professional, I say, "One moment please." I press the Transfer, 4, 7, 3, and 6 buttons. The phone rings and rings. His answering machine picks up, so I press the transfer button again and hang up the phone.

Swivelling in my seat I turn towards the computer; I shake the mouse to get the screen saver to go away.

Ring.

Pick up the phone, "Thank you for-"

"I need to speak with Louis. I don't want to leave a message. Can you page him?" This guy again. My eyes roll.

"I'm sorry, Sir. We don't have a paging system and it appears that Louis is not at his desk right now. If you leave him a message he can get back to you as soon as he gets back." I hold my finger over the transfer button.

"Well, then go look for him." I hike an eyebrow. This guy is starting to irk me.

"I'm sorry, Sir. I can't leave my desk. He might not even be in the building right now. He might be out on a call." I bite my tongue so I don't say something that could get me fired.

Seriously, he's not at his desk; leave him a damn message and he will get back to you. And, then on top of it, asking me to go searching for someone who might not even be here; the nerve of some people.

"The incompence of people these days." My eyebrow arches. Incompense? "You work there. You are in a line of customer service, so you have to do what I say. I want to speak with your manager." He yells out at me.

I poke Transfer, 4, 7, 6, and 3.

Fred picks up on the third ring. "You look like you're talking with an angry customer." He sounds a little too amused. I look up to his office. Fred is looking at me through the open blinds of his window, so I glare back and tilt my head. "Okay, I'll talk to him."

"Thank you." I press the transfer button and hang up.

Shaking my head at the guy on the phone I wish I could just let the conversation go. However, I need to figure out what he said.

Incompence? The incompetence of people these days?

Incompetence? Was he calling me incompetent? He tried to call me an idiot but he couldn't even say it properly.

Knock. Automatically my head turns to face the person knocking. Fred stands on the other side of the counter straight-faced. "So apparently, I should fire you for not being able to do your job properly."

"Oh, yeah?" I dare him to try, but I doubt he would.

"Yeah, however, he was a-" He looks around to make sure no one is going to hear what he has to say next. "-asshole and I have work for you. How do you feel about filing for the rest of the day? It'll get you off the phone and if he calls back you don't have to deal with him."

Turning back to the computer, I log off my name and turn back around to him. "Who's taking reception?"

"That would be me." Karen comes to stand beside Fred. She does not look impressed. I hide a grin. This feels like payback.

Fred leads me to the storage room. A few boxes are stacked on the floor. "I already pulled them off the shelves earlier. I was going to make Ann do it, but now you get to. Yay. I need you to scan these to the drive and shred the paper copies. We need more room back here and boss-man thinks it would be better to stay away from sending them to the offsite warehouse. Scan it into a folder under the shared drive; I don't care what you call it. Just tell me whatever it is later.

Scan each file separately so it'll be easier to find later. Name each file under year and company name. That should be about it. Any questions?"

"No, I've got it," I tell him.

"Well, have fun." Fred turns heel and walks back to his office.

Suddenly it's one of those situations. So much work to do, but no set place to start. I just grab the closest box to me. There is a printer right outside the door that I use to scan the first document. I start a pile on the floor to be shredded. The next file has a staple in it; so do the next few after it.

I don't want to wreck my manicure by trying to manually remove the metal clips. So, I endeavour to find a staple remover. The closest department to me is accounting.

Just around the corner of a cubicle wall, I find a surprisingly tear-filled face. For a moment I think about backing away however, Julie sees me.

"What's wrong?" She bursts and starts crying harder. Julie slides off her seat and crouches behind her desk. I'm the only person that could see her unless anyone comes into the cubicle area.

I walk over to her and place a comforting hand on her shoulder. She has tissues on her desk. I hold out the box to her to take one.

After a few moments and nose blowing, Julie calms down enough to start talking. "I had an account that I placed on hold because they haven't answered any of my calls or emails for the past month and they have ten thousand dollars outstanding over ninety days. So, I put the account on hold." Julie takes in a deep breath before she can continue. Fresh tears go down her cheek. "Then the customer called the sales rep and then he called me. He yelled at me because the company is linked to a very large national account and they're threatening to not sign the one point two million dollar deal because of this. There are, apparently, other issues with these invoices that I didn't know about. No one told me why they weren't paying. Nothing in the account suggested they were linked to a large account." She continues to talk and I just nod my head. It sounds like she's having a rough day.

Julie pauses, so I take the chance to talk and comfort her. "It sounds like the sales rep is having a bad day and is taking it out on you. There's no way you could have known. Don't worry about it so much. Do you need coffee or tea? I'm sure no one would mind if you took a break to calm down. You can make an excuse to go fill your cup."

She looks at me and nods her head. "That's a good idea." Julie stands up. Hugging me quickly, I don't get to react to the small girl before she walks away.

There is an awkward moment while I stand alone in this section.

Remembering why I'm here, I start searching through a desk drawer I think doesn't belong to anyone. I take a blue staple remover back with me.

The repetitive task helps the last hour of my shift to go by faster. Probably something about this job being so different from my regular one that makes it go by so fast.

Two boxes down. The remaining boxes will give me something to do tomorrow. I can then sort them all from the front desk.

The moment the clock hits six o'clock I get ready to leave. First putting on my jacket then grabbing my purse from my locker. And, I'm out the door shortly thereafter.

I walk to the end of the parking lot. My old white beater is one of the last vehicles here.

I press the unlock button on my key fob. The lock mechanism doesn't click, so I try again. Making sure I press the middle of the button hard with my gel nail. It unlocks after a couple of smashes to the button. I'll have to remember to get dad to take a look at my key fob later. He probably needs to replace the aluminum tape again.

Once inside, I place my purse on the passenger seat. I start my car and put on my seat belt. Placing the car into gear, I head out onto the familiar trip home.

It's days like this that I am glad for my half-hour ride home. It's nice to work on the edge of the city. The highway trip is long enough to work out some feelings in the music I blast but short enough that I'm not spending extra hours on the road each day.

My phone buzzes.

Are you coming to wings tom night? Steph asks.

I take my eyes away from the text to check the road and my speed; still in my lane going a hundred and twelve. It's only two over the speed limit so I'm still good.

I text her back. *Yeah. Where at?* With my eyes back on the road, I correct the steering wheel to put me back in the middle of the lane.

A sign reducing the speed limit signals the outer limits of town, so I take my foot off the gas. By the time I reach the speed limit change sign, I'm going seventy. I tap the breaks to make sure I'm going the speed limit by the time I reach the lights. The next lights turn red, so I stop quickly.

My phone buzzes again. Steph replied. *Mall pub?* Cars move around me. I look up. The light has turned green. I don't answer her back. It's only a couple of minutes to my house from here. I speed up.

Double-checking the speed on the dashboard, I touch the breaks a half a block down. Once I pass the radar truck that's always in the exact same spot, I put my foot back on the accelerator.

A couple of turns and roads later I park out front of my house. Turning down the volume, so I don't deafen myself tomorrow morning, I then turn off the vehicle. Turning on my phone, I respond with *K see you there* and press send.

I don't bother to lock my car, but I do bring my purse through to the backyard. A moment to myself before going inside the house. I put out the butt of the cigarette and put it in the can. I find my purse perfume and spray some on me. The smell of it should cover the smell of the smoke.

I really should quit one of these days.

Closing my purse, I then go inside my house. The first thing to greet me is the smell of freshly delivered pizza. I take off my heeled boots and jacket and put them in their proper places.

Mom and Dad are already at the table dishing out their plates and pouring their pop. Their heads are turned away from me, so they don't notice me until I drop my phone in the phone basket on the side table.

"Hey Sweetie, how was work?" Mom asks.

"Don't ask." For no reason, the pizza slice I grab gets a glare before I bite into it.

"That bad, eh?" Dad looks at me wanting more of an explanation.

Finishing the cheesy bread in my mouth, I tell them what they both want to know. "There's this bitch-"

"Language." Mom's interruption has a silent threat attached to it. I've never found out what the threat is, but I also don't want to find out.

"Sorry. Karen just gets on my nerves. She treats me like I'm an idiot and it's just because I'm the youngest person in the office. And, then there was this guy on the phone. He called me incompetent. Said I couldn't do my job properly and tried to get me fired. It didn't work but I'm tired of it all. I think it's time to start looking for a new job." The first slice went down a bit too quickly. I pour myself some pop while switching the conversation. "So, how was your day?"

Mom answers my question. "Not as interesting as yours. We had a safety meeting for half the day and the rest of the day was a write-off. Do you still have your resume updated? Maybe somewhere closer to home this time?" She nudges.

I finish the fizzy liquid in my mouth before throwing her own words back at her. "What was that, again? Beggars can't be choosers. It may be a long way away, but at least it's a job in a position that can help in the long run."

A piece of crust bounces off my chest and onto the table. "Aren't kids your age supposed to be rebellious of your parents and not listen to a word they say?"

"I'm sorry, what did you say? I wasn't listening." I pick up the crust and toss it back at her.

She catches the crust and takes a bite out of it. "That's better. We were thinking we'd have a movie night. What do you think?"

"What are we watching?" Finished eating, I grab a napkin from the center of the table and wipe the grease off.

"That's right! It's my turn to pick, isn't it? I'll go pick something out. You two can handle the clean-up for tonight." Mom gets up and walks over to the bookshelf holding all of our movies.

I stand up. Taking mom's plate and my own, I put them in the dishwasher and go back to the living room.

Dad is still eating the piece of pizza on his plate. "You done?" I point to the delivery box so he knows what I'm talking about.

He mumbles something with food still in his mouth, then nods. I close the box and take it straight to the fridge; placing it on a shelf.

I grab my phone out of the basket and put it back in my pocket. While mom picks the movie, I go up the creaking stairs; not much chance of sneaking out of this house. My room is on the right. I change out of my stiff office clothes for grey sweat pants and a matching sweatshirt.

Back downstairs, I hear the commercials playing. Just one more thing before I go to the living room; going through my purse I grab the pencil and yellow silk notebook inside.

Mom presses play the moment I sit down. No idea what movie this is however, right off the start, I get the idea that it's a romantic movie. One, because mom picked the movie, and two, because the girl seems to be a hopeless romantic.

About fifteen minutes into the movie and the girl has signed up on a dating website. She's gone on a few horrible dates then meets a guy that says and does all the right things and then meets a guy on the side of the road when she gets a flat. At this point, it's about the time that every romantic movie gets to the gushy filler. Nothing interesting should happen until the last fifteen minutes, so I open my notebook to the next blank page.

Pitiful society has come to such ruin.
Man against man and woman against woman.
We wage wars against brothers and sisters.
Because of what? For what?

Yelling, screaming, hating
Fighting, cursing, crying
It only hurts. For nothing.
From nothing.

There is no answer.
Wake up and do it again.
There is no end to it.
None but darkness.

The movie ends both on a sad and a happy note. Caroline ends up with the man that helped with the flat tire. The other man dies in a car crash. She loved them both, but death decided for her. It's a cruel twist for a romantic comedy.

I look over to my left. Mom and Dad both passed out at some point during the movie. The corners of my mouth lift briefly.

They're always doing that.

Both of them fall asleep during every movie we watch. It doesn't matter the genre. It doesn't matter if it's a movie they've never seen before, or they've seen a million times. It doesn't matter if they were interested in the movie or not. It doesn't even matter if we watch it right when we get up in the morning.

At some point, they will fall asleep. It might be five minutes in or it might be near the end. I think they're just always so exhausted, that just one moment of comfort causes them to sleep.

Dad's worse. He's always asleep by the first half and is never up beyond eight o'clock. We call him a party animal on the rare occasions he makes it to nine o'clock. I think the last time that happened was my eighteenth birthday.

Mom can run on two hours of sleep and four extra-large coffees. There have been some occasions that she's outlasted me; especially if we're playing board games. She's so competitive.

I watch them for a moment. There are no signs they'll be waking up once I've turned the TV off. The sudden silence is sometimes enough to wake them.

Sneaking off, I put my poetry book back into my purse, quietly go up to my room, and get ready to go to bed.

Knock. Knock.

Mom opens the door. She must've woken up while I was turning things off. "Goodnight sweetheart. Sweet dreams."

The same words each night. I say the last part with her. "Don't let the bed bugs bite."

She turns off the light and shuts the door. I crawl into bed. It doesn't take long for me to fall asleep.

Chapter 3

Water rushes by my feet as I bolt downstairs. The warm musty air is hard to breathe. Waterfalls spout from fresh soggy holes in the ceiling.

I round the corner into the laundry room. Opening the breaker panel, I turn off all the switches to ensure there are no accidental electrocutions.

Reluctantly checking my bedroom next, I can only imagine what I will find. The water is coming from the broken dishwasher, while my bedroom is the room below the kitchen.

It isn't as bad as I think when I open the door; despite the waterfalls and ankle-deep water. My bed is ruined by a waterfall running directly into the center of it. But for the most part, the bed, and clothing on the floor should be the only things that take great devastation from it.

Looking up I see something that looks unnatural and makes me take a few steps back. A bubble has formed in my ceiling from the water having nowhere to go, and the painted ceiling not wanting to break. I don't want to look at it anymore, so I shut the door, and trudge back upstairs.

The floors are dry now. My clothes dry instantly. I need to search for something. I know it's in the living room, but I don't know what it is.

Walking in, I find what it is; my mom. She looks like she is sleeping in our rocking chair. I'm standing in the middle of the room when she wakes up. She doesn't speak but starts rocking the chair.

Rocking into the wall each time. Harder and faster. Harder and faster.

Red spots splatter onto the white chair and walls. Pained, and horrified expressions twist her face as my mom looks directly at me, all while she bludgeons her head into the chair, and in turn the wall.

My heart hurts as I see all the blood; as I see her kill herself in front of me. I try to scream but nothing wants to come out. I close my eyes because I can no longer handle the blood.

The crisp air freezes my fingers and stings my face. When I open my eyes, I stand face to face with the exterior door to my house; anticipating a relaxing end to a hectic day at school. It all ends when my hand turns the knob, twisting, and pushing, only to find that it had been locked. My brows scrunching in confusion; our door is never locked. Brushing the confusion off, I ring the doorbell.

And again.

And again.

No answer.

My heart sinks.

Something is wrong.

The door to my house is never locked. We don't even have keys to my house. My mom always keeps the door open and unlocked. An eerie feeling crosses me as I see my dog standing in the entrance to the hallway. He keeps looking between me, and down to my mom's bedroom. In my mind and heart I know something is wrong; gravely wrong.

My heart starts beating fast, and my instincts click in before I can think. My legs carry me away from the door, and towards the back of the house. Panic clouds my mind as I need to find a way into the house.

The first clear thought comes to me. I grasp it, cling to it, and blurt it out to myself. "My window."

My window is never shut tight enough that one can't just open it. I have always left it cracked; just encase. Never would I have imagined for a moment such as this one.

I grab for the window and shake it open. Relief washes over me that it hadn't been frozen shut by ice. Quickly, I take off my jacket, throw it on the ground, and then my boots come off next. Without the extra clothing on it's easier to get in through my window. Sitting on my ledge I eye an area that is not covered by clothing or other items; dropping down into it. As I land on the floor a pain shoots through my foot up my leg.

Ignoring the pain I run up the stairs, and then race down the hallway. Mom's door is open. I catch myself on the door frame to put an instant stop to my run. The sight hits me just as hard.

My mom is scrunched, lying on the ground between the computer desk, and the wall. Curled, as if she had fallen from where she had been sitting. My voice comes out as a whimper.

"Mom." I take a step closer.

"Mom." Another step.

"Mommy." My voice cracks near the end.

I take notice now of more details; the pained expression on her face, how splotchy and purple-veined her arms look, but most of all, how still she is.

One touch to her cold arm just confirms it in my mind.

She's dead.

I wake in a jolt; gasping for breath. A few tears roll down my cheeks from a rush of dreams and memories I don't want to remember.

The alarm clock across the room finally registers in my mind. Throwing back the covers and jumping out of the bed, I turn the alarm off. I wait for a moment to listen for any noises upstairs.

Nothing.

Good. No one else was woken up. I wouldn't want my dad to find me awake and doing homework at this time.

Moving my thoughts away from the combined dream, and memory, I find the light switch by my door. A glance at my alarm says it is two am; right on time. Turning the lock on my door I unlock and open it.

The light switches for the basement living room are on the wall next to my door. I flip them on. Everything is as I left it an hour and a half ago.

I walk to the coffee table. Opening my agenda, I use it to guide me through what needs to be finished before I have to leave.

French – Paragraphs 1.5 hours 2:00 – 3:30

Social – Worksheets 1 hour 3:30 – 4:30

AP English Read Book – 3 hours 4:30 – 7:30

It's scary just exactly how good I've gotten at figuring out how long all my homework should take.

I finish and cross off the last of my list, just in time for my morning routine. I pack everything away until my backpack is overloaded with textbooks and binders.

My agenda is the last item I pack. I flip to tomorrow to see what's due. Quickly counting up the hours for tonight, I'm not sure how much sleep I'll be getting with this and whatever else might be assigned today.

I've wasted too much time thinking about it, not like it's going to help anyway. I put my agenda back into my bag. Making sure I've got everything packed, I put my book bag against the wall by the stairs, and pass into the room adjacent.

I have fifteen minutes before I have to leave the house. Quickly stripping in front of the mirror I begin tracking the changes in my body. I take out the notebook, pencil, and measuring tape from the middle drawer. Opening up my notebook, I flip to a page in the middle of the book.

Laying the notebook on the counter I step onto the scale. The dial zooms up and lands on the number one hundred fifty-two. I've lost another pound since yesterday. It'll be a good day today. Maybe I'll even eat something substantial to help with energy. I check my bust, waist, and hip measurements; each is down another inch.

A quick look in the mirror and I smile at my accomplishment. The numbers don't lie like a mirror can. The words are written on my body in black permanent marker from my mental breakdown the other night clearly states all the ugly words that, somehow, make me feel better about myself. To have them written out in the open helps me cope. Large words cover my stomach and thighs.

Unlovable Alone Freak Stupid Obese Liar Disgrace Mistake Nothing Worthless

I've lost fifty-three pounds, and sixty-two inches everywhere. I'm not a skinny twig, though I would say I'm skinny compared to where I started from. I'm not fat anymore; maybe chubby is a better word. Maybe my father will be happy with my body's progress.

I've spent too much time on this. I hop into the shower and quickly clean myself.

In a short three minutes, I turn off the shower and wrap a towel around me. Peeking out of the bathroom I make sure no one has come downstairs while I was in the shower. The coast is clear. I run across the way into my bedroom.

It's a race against time to dry myself and get dressed. I've only got my pants and undergarments on when my phone buzzes.

Mary texted, *Are you ready? I want to get a bagel.*

Yeah, I'll be right out. I answer back.

Almost blindly, I grab a black tank top out of my dresser and throw it on, then a black hoodie from my closet. Next, black socks. Running around makes me realize that I might need new pants soon, and a new belt too. Maybe, I'll just sew the sides of these ones to take them in. Either way, they're a bit too big now.

I can't help but think I'm forgetting something with having to rush so much, although I like to think I'm much too organized for that.

There isn't time to dwell either way, so I grab my backpack and go upstairs to the front door. Mary is already waiting there. I slip on my black and white Converse.

The door is already unlocked, so Jacob must have already left for work. I leave the house. Shutting, but not locking, the door behind me. "Morning." I sound a bit too cheerful for my taste but I can't take it back.

"Good morning." She says as she starts walking towards the school. I feel like a slob compared to her, but I could never take the time she does to get ready in the morning. Her hair is poker straight. From head to toe her outfit, make-up, and jewelry all match in some way. In a way, I would describe her look as being fashionably preppy, as opposed to my frumpy thrown on oversized clothes. The only jewelry I have on are my diamond earrings that never come out; unless I'm cleaning them.

We walk without saying much, well at least I do. Mary talks about what her bird and dog were doing this morning, and the trouble her brother got into last night from trying to drive her dad's truck.

When I was twelve, I would have never thought about stealing my parent's vehicle. I fear that Jacob would literally have killed me. I guess kids are getting more defiant as the generations go on. The notion makes me sound older than I am, as there are just three years difference between her brother and me.

I nod every once in a while or make an affirmative noise.

"Yeah, and then he hit that thing at the end of our driveway with the side thing, and he thought he could park it and no one would notice. My dad noticed immediately." She says.

"Hit that thing with the side thing, eh?" I say to bug her. Sometimes Mary has her very own 'thing' language. She will replace words with the word 'thing' if the exact word escapes her for a moment. "The lamp post with the side mirror?" I ask her though I'm sure I already know.

"Exactly. See you know what I'm talking about."

"Only because I've spent way too much time around you." I remind her. We've known each other and lived beside each other for, maybe, ten years now.

We enter the school through the cafeteria side. There must be a game tonight; all the football players are wearing their suits. I need an excuse to not go to the cafeteria, and my bag is getting too heavy, so I tell Mary, "I'm going to my locker first. I'll meet you here after."

She says, "Okay," as she walks away from me. Her sights are on the cafeteria to get one of the infamous bagels. How I wish I could have one of them again without the guilt.

My locker is straight upstairs, and to the left a little. I open up my locker and stuff all my unneeded books in there. I have Accounting, then Social, so I don't need much. I grab my Accounting booklet,

Social textbook, and my binder.

Closing up my locker I go back downstairs to meet with Mary. She is waiting in line still for her bagel, but at least it's in the receiving line, and not the ordering line; which seems to have gotten a big rush since I left. I go closer to her but then she disappears into the crowd. She comes back with two bagels in her hand. She shoves one at me. "Here, it's thanks for helping me out with my English assignment. I got a ninety-two on it."

"Thank you." There isn't anything I can do now, so I resign myself to enjoying this bagel. I just won't eat for the rest of the day; use this as my one meal today. I look on the side of the bag as Mary, and I go to the sauce table. She got me the BLTC, my favourite; bacon, lettuce, tomato, and cheese on a multigrain bagel. We take turns and dump the hot sauce into the bagel package. It's just not a cafeteria bagel without the hot sauce.

We go to an empty bench by the library and get as comfortable as we can. We've got a few minutes before we have to head to class. We eat our bagels in silence. I try to concentrate on not scarfing it down to my empty stomach. That wouldn't be very ladylike. What if someone was watching? Word could get back to Jacob, and that would be horrible.

I try to remember why I'm doing this again. I love food, I don't care about my body weight, but my father does. Weight loss is a bonus to anorexia. Maybe one of these days my father will see the weight loss, and stop making his weight comments. But, it's partly because my father doesn't buy food for the house, and partly because I'm trying to save all the money I make but mostly it's become the symbol of my control factor. Things have kind of calmed down a bit, do I really need to continue doing this? Or has it morphed into something else? A comfort to feel the pain, I suppose. Something other than the emotional pain is welcome. Have I come to terms enough with everything that I can to stop this, can I control my emotions enough without having to do a physical pain band-aide on top of it? No, I need to continue.

I try to remain emotionless, keep the smile on my face, but tears swell into my vision. Obviously, I can't quit. Especially, with that messed-up dream of a memory last night. I had thought I had exhausted myself enough not to dream anymore, but I can't be that lucky.

Do I miss my mom? Honestly though, I barely remember her. Even when she was alive, she wasn't around much. I more miss what my life could have been if she hadn't died. If she hadn't died, my father wouldn't have gotten a second wife. He wouldn't have gotten the son he always wanted. That changed more things than her death did.

The bell interrupts my thoughts. I finish the last bite of my bagel and get up. I toss my garbage into the can beside us. We have five minutes from that bell to get to our class and be ready for work. I pack up my binder, workbooks, and carry them in my arms.

"See you at lunch," I say.

She looks nervous for a moment, trying to think about what to say, but I already know without her having to say a word. "I-um Nara asked to hang out with me for lunch, and I said yes. Sorry." She looks very sheepish, and I can't blame her. Though I can't say I can blame her for hanging out with that group of friends. They're popular. It doesn't matter to me that Nara is the ring leader for most of the bullying I've received. At least, perhaps, if I say it doesn't bother me enough times then maybe eventually I will start to believe it. It's selfish of me to even think about telling her it hurts me that she goes to them time after time. When they have bullied me and threatened to do the same to her for just talking to me.

"No, that's fine. I'll see you after school for the walk home. See you." I wave goodbye and go off to my classes. Each one is boring or awful, but I manage to read the English book in my spare time and I get tomorrow's social booklet finished during lunch.

The bell finally signals the end of the day. I rush out of the school. The halls are buzzing. There's a football game tonight. So the rest of the students aren't trying to leave. School pride or something like that. I honestly couldn't care less about it.

My cell phone buzzes with a text from Mary. *I'm staying late for the game. I forgot about it.*

AKA, Nara probably invited her, and she wants to hang with her without telling me.

I text her back a *kk* and go to my locker. I see them before they see me. A group of people surrounds my locker. I recognize the faces of a couple of them but not all. "Excuse me. I need to get to my locker."

I feel like I've walked into a trap as they clear the way for me. My locker has some words written on it: Douche Bag. Bitch. Slut. "You know you're a freak, right?" He says to me. I don't recognize this one.

"Whatever, I need to get to work." I've dealt with this enough times. Don't make it fun for them. No emotions and they usually back off. It works. They leave.

I open my locker and replace my books with the ones I'll need for homework tonight. I close the locker door. I don't need the teachers seeing this so I wipe the waxy words away.

I open my agenda up and make sure I have everything I need to get all my homework done tonight. I might get a couple of hours of sleep tonight since I was able to finish a bit during school.

I go home only to drop off my heavy bag. I follow the familiar path through my neighbourhood, and down the alley. I take the shortcut through the treed area infamous for homeless people, druggies, and suicides, since I don't have time to go around. Walking across the road, down the alley by the reservoir, under the highway through the tunnel, across the field, down the row of stores, and finally, I get into the dollar store.

I go into the backroom to hang my coat up and adorn my apron. It's about ten minutes to my shift but I decide to start anyway. There isn't much else I can do. I go down to the other side of the warehouse. I don't find anyone, but I think I found our job for the night; there are six pallets full of boxes ready to be unpacked.

I go out the back door and look down the aisles until I find the boss. Tamara sees me right away. "A shipment came in today. You guys need to get them unpacked, and out tonight."

"Okay," I say. I walk back to where I came from. By the time I get back to the pallets, I see Kate starting on one of the pallets. She rips the plastic with her knife. "Hey."

She echoes back "Hey."

We don't talk as we each fill carts full of boxes from the pallet. We organize the carts and boxes so that each cart represents two aisles. As soon as one cart is filled I take it out to the floor. Soon enough the rest of the night crew arrives and gets to work. The day crew must have left, but they didn't give us any indication that they had done so.

We work hard to get the entire product dealt with by seven-thirty. Taking our much-deserved break from working our butts off, we sit in the back.

Kate suggests, "Hey I downloaded Apocalypse. Do you want to watch it? We have time for that, and then do a quick clean-up, and cash out."

I agree. We've finished all the work we would need to do tonight. It would just be general tidying from here on, but it's not that messy.

We sit in the staffroom huddled around an IPad, as the movie plays.

Five men are camping on a long weekend. The large forested area is filled with many cabins and hoarded by people drinking and having parties in the evening.

The main male character, Zane, just broke up with his girlfriend of five years. His friends took him out for a guy's weekend to get over her. As the evening progresses they drink more and more, while Zane nurses his beer. He decides to go to bed early.

As soon as he gets into the bedroom he hears screams. He runs to the door and sees people screaming, and running. Someone yells 'ZOMBIES!'

He gathers up his friends and barricades them into the cabin. They freak out. Zombies try breaking into the cabin. Zane breaks the back room window. His one friend, I can't remember his name, was killed by a zombie.

Zane and the remaining friends run. They veer off from the rest of the crowd and miraculously find a vehicle with keys in the ignition. He drives them out of the campground. Suddenly, an explosion goes off, and they get run off the road. The car gets stuck in a field. They get out of the car and start walking down the road.

A bunch of zombies chase them from their route, and down a side road. The zombies disappear as soon as they are headed towards the random industrial building in the middle of the field ahead.

Oh, I remember this dream; another ruined movie. Zane falls through the floor and finds out that it's all fake, and a part of a TV show. Rich people pay money to a network that mocks up a 'reality' series about people dying in an apocalypse. He rescues his friends and resolves to tell the world about the show.

They go into the building. There are many levels and beams. Zombies appear out of nowhere and chase the group. Zane gets separated when he falls through the floor. Zombies go up to Zane's still body and break character. They talk about how this kill isn't going to make it into the show since there are no cameras here. The next time the woman wants to be part of the first wave. When they leave he gets up and corners someone. They confess that it's part of a TV show. Rich people pay to see mock apocalypse scenarios. All the people die, but, oh well. He runs to go rescue his friends from the office. He goes through a door and gets them out of the warehouse. He explains what he knows. They say it's not right, and they resolve to let the world know about it.

The movie ends right at closing time. I help Kate bring all the tills to the back room. We close the door behind us per store policy.

We talk as we count the money and do paperwork.

"Where would you go on vacation if you could? I've always wanted to see Paris." Kate asks me.

I think about it. While there are quite a few ancient places I would love to see, I would rather a vacation be about no stress. However, that would involve zero contact with just about everyone I know. No internet, no phone, no nothing. I would need to be the equivalent of a hermit in the woods. "Camping anywhere."

"And then, the zombies attack." Kate jokes.

"I would love to be in a Zombie apocalypse. I feel like I would do very well." I say.

"Of course, you would." She's half-joking and half-serious about it. We've had many a conversation on the subject before.

There is a knock on the door. Trevor says, "everything is put away, and the mats are vacuumed. Can we leave?"

Kate thinks for half a second. "Yes, Jaiden can you lock them out?"

"Sure," I say.

I unlock the door and go out to the hall. They are ready with their jackets on. Anyone could have guessed Kate would say yes to them leaving. It's a regular occurrence when everything is done. I let them out of the store, and say goodbye. I lock the door.

I go back to the office and knock on the door. Kate lets me in. She's finished everything up in the couple of minutes I was gone. She tells me to go get my stuff, and get ready to leave.

I go to my locker and place my apron back in there. I put my coat on. Kate comes out of the office ready to go. She sets the alarm, and we leave the store. We say quick goodbyes, and I start walking home.

It's really cold out now. I think we are going to get snow soon. I dread the inevitability of having to make this walk when the weather drops to the minus twenties and minus thirties.

The walk home goes by fast. I walk a lot faster at night. It's too creepy, and potentially dangerous not to walk as fast as I can.

I manage to get home safely. I go straight to the basement and start on my homework. I have a book to read, worksheets, a social project, and an essay.

Chapter 4

Arriving at the school, Darius parks in the closest stall he finds. One of the problems of coming later is the parking stalls are mostly filled up. I don't mind. It only takes a few extra seconds to walk the farther distance.

Darius walks slightly in front of me as we approach the door. He lets go of my hand to throw open the door. I grab the door as it closes in front of me; I open it and follow him through.

Regaining my steps slightly behind him, we retrace our normal morning steps. We walk down one hallway, turn into another, and finally walk into the cafeteria.

Immediately spotting Miles sitting at the table in the corner, both Darius and I go to him. I take a seat. Miles looks at me with a curious look on his face. "You're looking a little green, are you alright?"

"I think I'm a little hungover." Correcting my posture and taking in a deep breath, I try to chase the look of being green away.

"Would you like some water?" He asks.

"No, thanks. I'm good." A slight smile and widening of my eyes, I hope is enough to convince him.

It doesn't work.

Miles pushes his seat back and stands up, all at once, in a smooth move.

He walks through one of the two open glass doors and talks to one of the ladies in the kitchen. She disappears around a corner for a second before reappearing with a bottle of water. Miles takes the bottle with a nod.

He walks back over to me placing the bottle in front of me. "Drink up. It will help."

I take a sip of the cold water before looking to where Darius should have been. Looking around me, he isn't anywhere in sight. I hadn't noticed him leaving, and he didn't say anything about leaving.

Did I do something wrong?

"He left just after you sat down. Probably had to go talk to a teacher or something. How's your head?" Miles asks.

Immediately, I resign from any attempts at bringing the topic away from my health; knowing that I wouldn't win anyway. "It's mornings like this that make me think that it might be time to join you and stop after one."

"You and I both know that's not going to happen. But, give it ten years and you might not even touch alcohol." Burrowing my face into my hands on the table, I shake my head. "Here, let me try something. Give me one of your hands." I raise my head.

The request, although weird, intrigues me enough to do it. Giving him my right hand, he takes it in one of his. He places my hand palm side down on his hand and then puts his other hand in between my thumb and pointer finger. Miles then squeezes the area right in between those two fingers.

My mind focuses only on the warmth of the hand under mine and the pressure in my hand. The two feelings combined start a sort of electric tingling. When he lets go everything stops and my mind focuses on my surroundings. The end of a shrill ring of the bell tells me it's time to go to class.

"Class time." He gathers a book bag he had hanging from the back of his chair and heads off swiftly.

Standing up, I turn to head off to my first class.

My head doesn't hurt anymore. What did Miles do to me? Something with pressure points, I'm sure. I should ask him about it later. He's all into the naturalistic health stuff, but as odd as it is sometimes, it may be useful if it cures hangovers that quickly.

Going down the hall and in through a set of doors, I go upstairs and through another set of doors leading into the girls' change room. Finding my locker in the second row I set about opening it.

Not remembering the actual combination, I turn the dial around to the numbers I think it is. The guess is fine, as the lock has leeway from excessive use. The lock opens and in turn, I take off the lock and open the locker.

I take out my gym shoes and then my gym clothes putting them on the bench behind me. Proceeding to change quickly as a couple of the other stragglers do the same. Finishing up, I put all my clothes into the locker and lock it shut.

Walking around the corner and through the door, I hurry down the stairs and through another door across the one that leads to the hallway. Coming into the gym, I see everyone gathered on the bleachers still chatting about whatever to their friends. With no coach insight, the normal order of everyone set up in a line alphabetically isn't there.

Looking around, I can't find Darius anywhere. I sit down on the bleachers and wait for either Darius to show or the coach to start the class.

All around me, people continue to go on with their conversations.

Every once in a while, however, I can feel people glance in my direction. The assumption that at least one conversation has turned to me is backed up with a whisper that sounds like my name. Each class, at lunch, every moment in school is filled with people who can't keep to their own business.

I look over to the direction where my name came from. The source of it could be one of four people. None of which, should be talking about me. Maybe they weren't. Turning back, I ignore them. Taking, instead, to biting my thumbnail.

The sound of the creaking gym door quietens most of the people. Its noise is the tell-tale sign that the coach is here.

Coach Renner walks up to the center of the mass of students with a clipboard in his hand. "Alright, let's get through this, run for five minutes, stretch, then we can play our last class of volleyball." The coach looks over the class. He runs through his class list; calling out names of people who aren't there or he doesn't see right away. He waves us to start orders.

People uproot themselves from the bleachers and start running around the outer lines on the gym floor. Following them, I get up and start running; more of a fast jog.

I go through gym class as though I'm just going through the motions. Darius was supposed to be here, but he's ditching today.

After changing back into my normal clothes, I head to the one place I can always return to; the art room. The teacher allows all students she has taught to return to her classroom at any time, as long as there is no conflict with other teachers.

I have it for the next class anyway, but it's nice to know I can join early after getting out of gym class a few minutes before the bell.

Walking down the art walk, I take notice of one of the newest paintings on the wall.

The painterly effect on the painting is the signature of an amazing artist I know. Checking the bottom right corner confirms my suspicion. The captivating wolf acrylic painting's artist is Miles. Each paint stroke creates a texture you can feel with your eyes. The attention to detail of the animal shows the passion and pure talent of the artist.

Continuing down the hallway I turn the corner and go into the art room. The space is abuzz with the people chatting away while doing their art.

I go around to the back of the room and from the acrylic paint brushes drawer, I grab all the different sizes and different bristled brushes I could need; along with kit number seven.

Stepping up the steep steps to the upper level in the room, I go to my table. The art piece I'm working on is waiting there. I set down my assigned art kit.

Miles works on another piece at the table next to mine. The bare starting of blocking in is the only hint to what the painting will end up being, and even then, it doesn't tell much. A couple of reference pictures sit in different places on the table. One picture is of an orange and purple sunset with rays of the sun coming out from behind the clouds. The other picture of a valley-focused picture with a city far off in the background.

Going back downstairs, I collect a few more items I'll need before heading back upstairs.

Placing everything down onto the table I set everything up how I like it. The same place for everything, every day. Everything is out of my art kit and placed to my right, the water is placed right off the top corner of my canvas, and the paper towel is to my left.

Miles lifts his head from his work after noticing my arrival. He takes the headphones out of his ears. "Hey, Alexa."

"Hey, saw your wolf painting. Amazing." I take a seat on the stool. The metal scrapes against the floor causing me to cringe, as I pull in closer to the desk.

Miles grins toothily. "Thanks. Your portrait is coming along great."

"Thanks." I look over to my canvas. A five-year-old redhead smiles at me from behind the white daisy. Her freckles pop against her light skin. Light blue eyes gaze into my own. The innocence behind the little girl is depicted in the almost finished painting.

At least, I think so.

"Are you going to Darius' today?" He asks while going back to painting.

"No, not today. I have to go to the house." The little girl I'm painting reminds me that I need to go to June's today.

"Going to check up on Rayleen?" Miles has gotten attached to the little girl after only meeting her twice.

I nod, realizing immediately after that he probably isn't looking at me. "Yeah."

"How's she doing?" A hint of interest touches his voice. I know he wants more than the standard one word response.

"Good. She's doing better in school and making friends. Still as bubbly as ever. She's getting so excited for Christmas already, even more so than her birthday." The simplicity and innocence in the girl charms me back into the familial need to protect her. She immediately attaches to me when I go to June's. I feel guilt suddenly, that I don't see her as much as I should.

"Christmas is exciting when you're that little." Miles reasons.

"True." I pick up a paintbrush and brush the dry brush slightly above the surface of the painting. Once I get the feel of the painting again I know what I need to do next.

Looking over to Miles I see him putting his headphones back in his ears. Going to do the same, I put the paintbrush down and pull my iPod out of my pocket. Unravelling the headphones, I turn the iPod, put the headphone in my ears, and press play. The creativity in the music kicks my creativity into action; an inspiration in another form of art.

Stroke by stroke, I create on the canvas. Blending the colours in a way only acrylic paint allows me to. The soft blends allow realism as much as a picture allows. I blend and blend directly on the canvas until satisfied.

Getting the right blends to match her skin tone with both highlights and shadows is difficult, and sometimes I accidentally miscalculate the colour. This happens now, and I clean off the brush and remix until I get it right. Detail blending and texturing the fabric and design of the dress. The flower petals are smooth to the sight.

The final details I meticulously paint in. The last lines are put into place. Looking over the picture and each time finding one last thing that needs to be fixed or added in. One problem with painting someone you know, there is always one last thing that needs to be fixed to make it perfect.

My right ear headphone is tugged out of my ear. I look to my side. Miles had pulled it out.

"Bell rang." He says simply. Cleaning up his station, he waits for me to clean up mine. I trash my paper towel, then saran wrap the plate. I dump my dirty water and wash the paintbrushes. Once everything is done, I put things back into the kit and put them all away.

Miles waits for me right outside the room. We turn the corner down the art walk. I look at some more of the paintings hoping to see something I haven't noticed yet. Nothing catches my eyes.

We turn into the cafeteria and walk to the corner table Miles had been sitting at this morning. Everyone is there already; Darius, Kelly, and Shale. I find a couple of people I don't recognize socializing with them.

The light brown-skinned girl has red-brown hair that wisps down in front of her shoulders and flows slightly longer in the back. Getting closer to her I notice a tiny stud in her nose. Scanning up her face to her eyes I find her staring at me. She looks through me with almost all orange eyes; baby blue circling them. She looks my way belittling me with her gaze. She takes her eyes off of me, so I follow her example.

Switching my gaze to the man, I look him over as well. His dark brown complexion. The clean-cut brand clothing and shoes, golden necklace and ring, and perfect posture speak of a more privileged background.

Darius walks between the parted couple and stops just in front of them. He separates Miles and me as we come within reach. Pulling me with him as he faces me towards the unfamiliar faces.

"Lexy, meet Sandra and Ram." Darius looks away for a moment. A slight ringing starts and stops very quickly. The moment passes and Darius seems to get a slight twitch in his eyebrow. "We're leaving. Things to do. Have a good lunch with Miles. I'll see you after school." He lets his arm down from my back and quickly kisses my forehead.

Like they had all been suddenly dismissed, the group walks out the double door exit. I turn to face Miles. He looks concerned, almost worried, as he watches them leave.

Moving suddenly, he goes to the table and moves the chair back to its original position. Miles takes his book bag off his shoulder. Drawing up the flap, and unzipping the top zipper. Miles reaches into the bag. He pulls out his lunch in a brown paper bag.

"Are you okay?" I ask as I take a seat right across from him. His brow is still scrunched.

He continues unpacking his food. Taking the top off the container with his sandwich in it, pulling an apple out, and taking to top off the reusable bottle to take a drink of the water inside.

He doesn't look at me as he says, "I'm fine."

"I don't believe you," I tell him.

The side of his mouth twitches upwards. He looks me in the eyes. "I'm fine."

I pick up my eyebrow. "Then, what was that all about?"

He huffs. Miles looks to his right and then to me. "Fine, I'm not, but I'd rather not talk about it. You'll find out soon enough but just leave it alone for now." I am curious however out of respect for his unusual assertiveness, I give up.

Looking over my shoulder, I look over to the quickly disappearing line. I quietly tell Miles, "I'll be back." Moving my seat back, I get up and walk to the back of the cafeteria line.

When I make it to the cooler, I look in through the glass and prey on what is left of the selection.

The tuna wrap and egg wrap don't seem too appetizing to me, and I had the veggie wrap the day before. A croissant filled with mustard, ham, lettuce, and tomatoes seems like the best choice. Sliding the window towards the other, I reach in and grab the sandwich.

Taking the sandwich to the lunch lady, I tilt the top towards her to let her see the type of sandwich. She immediately types the price into the register; knowing the price from her experience. I pay the lady with a five and get my change quickly. I squeeze my way through the students waiting for cooked items.

Going back to the table I sit across from Miles. Quietly, I eat one-half of the sandwich. Looking up at Miles, I search for something to say to him to get him to talk to me about what's bothering him.

Grabbing the other half, I concentrate more on looking around the room rather than at Miles. Still not giving up on finding out what's wrong with the male across from me, I look to what happened right before his mood changed.

He was fine in art class. It was just when we came upon the group. So, what was it about the group that made him so troubled? Could he have had a bad past with the two people Darius introduced me to? Could it be because Darius didn't take Miles with him and the rest of the group?

My thought process focuses there for a moment. The odd scenario plays in my mind. It is out of character for Darius not to include Miles in anything and everything.

What happened that made Darius not include Miles? Could Miles have done something to Darius? If so, what did he do? But, if that was the case, why would Miles be acting this way? Maybe Darius did something. And, who were those people anyway?

All these questions swim in my mind and I can't come up with the answers to any of them. The strangeness of it all causes more questions.

"Stop thinking so hard, I'm starting to smell smoke." I look at him dumbly for a moment before the meaning behind the words he spoke registers.

I give him a playful glare in light of him trying to lighten the mood. "Hey, that's not nice!"

"Whoever said I was nice? You know you shouldn't be listening to those voices in your head anymore they lie to you." Miles says before taking a bite of his sandwich.

It gives me a moment to think about what to say next. "I like the voices in my head. They are nice to me and keep me company when the other choice of company is annoying and uninteresting."

"Wow, they must not shut up at any point other than when you're in my company. I feel sorry for you." Miles exaggerates movement to make himself seem all-important. He sits with perfect posture, raises his chin, and pulls at the edges of his buttoned shirt to pull out wrinkles.

I laugh at his actions. This seems to bring his smile back into his eyes. A silent agreement comes between the two of us to not speak more on the previous subject.

I won't dwell on it for now, but I'll get my answers eventually.

Quietly we eat the rest of our lunches. The bell rings sooner than I figured it would. Still, there is no sign of any of the group.

Clearing up my garbage I take it over to the garbage bin. I look back at the table and am unable to locate Miles. Broadening my search, I scan over the entire cafeteria. I come up with nothing. Figuring I may have just missed him rather than him disappearing, I continue on my way.

For my more academic classes in the afternoon, I go to my locker and grab my binder, and science and social textbooks.

Chapter 5

I check my messages over again; thinking I might've missed a ringing notification.

"Waiting for someone?" I recognize that deep voice.

Turning around I confirm who it is. "Hey, Shawn."

He takes a seat across from me on the bench. The waitress is on him immediately. Her shirt is pulled down lower than I remember it being when she was dealing with me just a minute ago.

She asks him, "anything to drink?"

"Rye and coke." He doesn't look at her while he orders and she looks upset about it. Someone is trying too hard for their tip, or perhaps something more. She walks away. "How was your week?"

I take in a deep breath and sigh before I begin. "Work sucks as usual. I think everyone's been PMSing this week or something. Karen's a bitch, as usual, but she's been worse; if that's even possible.

And, there's been a lot of very rude people calling in this week. I had one asshole trying to get me fired because he wanted me to go look for someone that wasn't answering the phone. Another jerk started yelling at me after he made a speech because I couldn't help him myself and had to transfer him to A/R. Then, there was this-"

"Bitch, jerk, asshole? Nikki, sweetie, has anyone ever told you that you have anger issues?" Stephanie says from behind me.

I glare at her jokingly. "Shut up." She sits down beside me while

Brad sits beside Shawn.

She just smiles. "I love you too. Bad week?"

"Can I get you something to drink?" The waitress almost makes me jump. She sets down Shawn's drink.

"Pepsi," Brad answers her.

"Is Coke okay?"

"No. Can I get Iced Tea?" Brad sounds ticked off. The waitress looks at him confused at his attitude.

Steph takes the attention off Brad. She's used to the looks he gets when he refuses the other brand option for a similar drink. We all are. "Coke, please."

I gulp down a few sips of my beer and check the level in the pony. I still have halfway to go until it's empty.

"So, how was your day?" I ask no one in particular.

"Better than yours." Steph jokes. "No, it's just the same old thing. Work sucked, but I didn't get yelled at today, so that's a bonus. I'm thinking about quitting."

"Didn't you start that job a month ago?" I ask her. That would make, what, five jobs this year.

"Three weeks and I can't help it if I'm picky about my job. I'm not settling for something that makes me miserable." Steph serial dates her jobs. On one hand, I admire her because she's not settling for a dead-end job she hates. On the other hand, how can she stand not having a stable flow of money?

"So, what's next? Maybe you should try something out of retail this time?" I say.

"Yeah, I was thinking of waitressing. Maybe, Olive Garden. Sharon works there. She was telling me she makes ten bucks an hour, but she gets about a hundred bucks in tips every day. She only has to work, like, six hours a day."

"Nice, so that's like." Shawn looks up for a moment. He does some quick calculations. "Twenty-five bucks an hour. Fuck! Why am I going to University? Even after I'm done the four years, starting wage is twenty an hour."

"Hmmm, sounds like someone should drop out." Brad teases. "You're paying what ten thousand for tuition and textbooks per school year. That's forty thousand altogether. You're also only working part-time, so you can keep up with school work; so you're losing the difference between that and full time. And, you will also have to pay back your student loans for the next ten years. You're also not guaranteed to get a job immediately out of school in your field and-"

"Okay, I get it. So, how many job openings did Sharon say there were?" Shawn cuts him off. I think he's half-serious about his question.

The waitress sets down everyone's drinks. She had also got me another beer without me asking. I tell her, "thank you."

"Can we get a nachos pan? No olives and extra cheese." Stephanie asks.

"Anything else?" The waitress asks. She looks around at the rest of us.

"No, that's all. Thanks." I tell her.

"So, I was thinking. Tomorrow morning. We should ditch work and do something. Anything." Shawn suggests.

"We could go shopping? Go to the mall." Stephanie suggests.

After the week I've had, it takes nothing to convince me to play hooky. I'll call in and spend some time on my mental health. "Yes! Love it. I'll call in if you all will." I tell them.

"Maybe something closer to home?" Shawn suggests.

"No! Let's have a mall day! I don't see enough of your faces anymore." Stephanie insists.

"Let the girls have their mall day." Brad backs us up. We all give pressured looks to Shawn.

"Okay, fine, mall day. Everyone cancels work tomorrow for a mall day." Shawn says.

"I need to get out early because I'll have to pretend to go to work. Try to be at the mall for eight thirty – nine?" Steph says.

"Should meet at Timmies in Spruce first then?" Shawn insists.

"No point. The Timmies is open early here." Brad says.

We each agree in our own ways.

"So, we're actually doing this?" Shawn asks.

"Yeah, we're doing this." I look to each person for agreeance. I don't want to be the only person to call out sick for work, then find out no one else did.

The prospect of a mall day is exciting. We haven't done that in a while. None of our schedules seem to sync up well enough to spend much time together. It's not like it was in high school.

I miss how it was in high school. We'd see each other in odd classes, and for lunch. Always after school for at least an hour. Many days, we'd hang out all evening, if we didn't have homework to finish.

I constantly feel like I'm missing out on the lives of my friends. Big gossip I'm sure I'm missing out on. There are huge life moments I hear about days or weeks after the fact.

My head turns to the DJ's booth when the music turns up. Must be eight o'clock.

"Looks like we're losing the girls," Brad says.

"Shut up. Come get us when the nachos are here." I stand up and head to the dance floor. I don't have to look to know Stephanie is following me.

The dance floor is empty but that won't last once we start dancing. Others might join us. People are usually more likely to dance when they aren't the first or only ones.

I don't mind, in the meantime. It's a small dance floor; made by moving a few tables and chairs around. There isn't a lot of room for two people to dance, let alone twenty.

Chapter 6

Mary texts announcing she is outside my house. Time for school. We don't have much to say to each other this morning. We split ways as we enter the school as she cites that she has to talk to a teacher. I continue on my way to my locker. I keep my view tunnelled to the path I need to walk.

I realize too late that I should have gone another way when I notice the large group in my peripheral. Smile sculpted on my face, I don't let them notice that I noticed them. One of her little sheep, I don't know the girl's name, alerts Nara to my presence. I can see the whole group turn to watch me. I hear the word 'pig' muttered under someone's breath.

That doesn't bug me.

It's the laughter and the staring at me that unnerves me. I continue smiling all the way.

I remember lessons from my early childhood; reiterated time and time again. Never let anyone see they've hurt you. Never cry in front of anyone. Don't give them anything else to fuel the fire. Kill them with kindness. You are better than they are.

I deposit unnecessary books in my locker and collect the books I need for my morning classes. I go to the classroom.

The teacher isn't here yet, so I sit down in my assigned seat and open my book. The other students are all talking about their things in small groups.

The second bell rings, and the teacher still isn't in class.

Great, he's going to be late again.

Oh well, I can always do some homework. I decide to work on Social. Not that I have much of a choice with my selection of books here.

I pull out the workbook and textbook, and turn to the right pages to start working on them. It's easy enough to find the same word combination, and insert the correct word into the space provided in the workbook. I don't have time to read the actual words so I never do. It doesn't matter anyway, we rarely have tests in that class, and most of our marks are from projects and these workbooks.

I look up at the clock when our teacher finally makes it in. He's only forty-five minutes late.

I put away the social text, and pull out my calculus math book.

"Sorry I'm late, but do I have a story for you." His words don't make me confident that we will be working on any math today. He does this all the time. I have come to expect it, which is why my math mark has gone down to barely eighty percent rather than the high nineties. He doesn't actually teach us anything, and tells a lot of stories or gets off topic easily.

Once the teacher gets settled he continues, "So I had my car in the shop to switch my tires around yesterday. Picked up my car, and drove it around the block home. This morning I start driving here, and just as I stop at the lights my car sinks and crashes to the ground on my side. All I see is my tire rolling into the intersection."

The class is abuzz with people talking, and asking questions. Our teacher isn't in the mood for teaching, and neither are my classmates. We spend most of the rest of the class looking at pictures of cars and videos of car crashes.

In the last minutes of class, our teacher finally notices the time. He quickly assigns fifteen questions from our workbook, all the odd questions in the chapter. I write it down in my agenda, along with 1.5. Fifteen questions should take about five minutes each for seventy-five minutes, that's an hour and fifteen minutes. Adding another fifteen just in case it takes extra time.

Foods class passes by uneventfully making suckers.

The bell rings for lunch. I put my headphones in. The iPod is dead. I forgot to charge it last night. It doesn't matter that much, but at least it should stop people from talking to me.

It however doesn't stop them from talking about me. I pass by two girls who decide to call me 'stuck-up', and say 'she thinks she's better than everyone else'.

When I get to my locker, I feel a dizzy spell come over me. I have enough strength to get my locker open so I can hide while trying to overcome the spell. It finally gives way without anyone noticing.

I think I should eat something for lunch.

That won't give me much time to get any homework done, but almost fainting is cause to stop everything else and eat.

Five minutes for myself; crazy idea.

I find the healthiest salad and milk I can at the cafeteria. I plunk down in a corner to eat. I toss away the salad dressing after only using a quarter of it. The salad and milk go down easy, and I find myself feeling better by the time the bell rings to go to class again.

French class goes by with the class learning vocabulary for bedroom items.

I use the time to walk through what I need to say for my presentation in English class. My heart runs wild as I get anxious over the prospect of it. I'm glad I ate earlier because I'm pretty sure I would faint in the middle of my presentation otherwise.

When I get into English class I can see my project board on a shelf at the side of the classroom. I half believed that it might not have been there today; paranoia that someone would steal it to make me look bad.

The teacher goes through the daily motions and starts the presentations. We were each assigned a character in the book, and we're told to delve deeper into the character for the project.

I don't hear the other people's presentations. I keep going over my own. I think I have it down. Everything that I need to say I have been thinking over and over through the last couple of hours.

It does nothing to quell my mind over the nerves of having to do a presentation in front of everyone.

He calls my name.

I gather up my project while trying to steady my racing heartbeat. Settle the project on the ledge of the whiteboard. The project board looks flawless. If the grade was only based on the project I am sure I would get a hundred percent. Unfortunately, twenty-five percent of the final grade is based on the presentation.

I know this.

I turn around and start the presentation.

I don't know this.

I've forgotten everything. All that practice has been for nothing once again. This happens every time I do a presentation. I stammer and ramble through my project.

I know I sound like an idiot. I can feel my palms sweat and I shake. After what feels like forever I finally finish the presentation clumsily

The rest of the presentations go by with me stuck in my head. I know everyone had to of noticed how horrible I was doing up there. They were probably judging me the whole time.

I did horrible. I'm horrible at presenting. I'm the person who sits at the back of the class. I'm the person who will pick a job doing something by myself, maybe be my own boss and work from home. I will do something where I can speak to my strong suits, and not work every day being anxious and scared.

A dull ache in my head tells me I need to de-stress. As the doctor said 'you get stressed, then you get a migraine, so don't get stressed'. He had gone further to say that he normally sees this thing develop in forty-year-old CEOs, and I was the youngest case of tension migraine syndrome he had ever seen. He did look young so that might not have been as impressive as I thought it was at the time; I was brought into the ER after falling off a ladder at work due to blacking out at a particularly bad episode.

That was a fun day.

My stillness and thinking are getting the best of me. My eyes droop, and I can feel myself going to sleep. I strum my fingers against my leg to try to wake myself up enough not to fall asleep.

I can feel the effects of not having enough sleep.

How long has it been? I think I've gotten about three hours of sleep in just as many days. I wonder how long I have to go before I start hallucinating?

I have a social project due tomorrow, and math questions, I have a book to finish, a test on it, and a French worksheet. I don't think I'll get any sleep tonight either. Maybe tomorrow night I can get some sleep. I could always just skimp on something get the lower grade so can have some sleep.

No, that isn't a possibility. Father would kill me if I got a low grade, and I'd only be able to carve out an hour or so. So, I guess I just need to call in sick for work.

Once the bell rings, I race home to make the call. My pulse races as I press the last number. It only takes two rings before Judy answers. "Thanks for calling the Dollar store. Judy speaking."

"Hey Judy, can I talk with Tamara?"

"Sure thing, sweetie." She answers.

She puts me on hold. A minute later Tamara says, "Tamara speaking."

My heart drops to my stomach. "Hey, it's Jaiden. How are you?"

"Good." She says quickly. I wait for a moment but she doesn't return the pleasantries.

"Umm, I was wondering if I could have the night off. I haven't slept in a couple of days, and I've got about eight hours of homework to do that's due tomorrow, so if I hope to have any sleep tonight I can't go to work tonight."

She doesn't give it a moment's thought. "No, you need to come in tonight. Having homework isn't a reason to miss work. It's busy, and we don't have enough people."

"Oh, okay, yeah, no problem then. I'll be there. Have a great day." My chest hurts.

I hang up the phone. Tears come to my eyes. I need sleep, but I guess I have to go to work tonight. I gather my book bag. I need to leave now to make it to work in time. I place the bag strap over my head and feel the heaviness against my side. This isn't going to be a pleasant walk. I throw on my coat and shoes, and go out the door.

Father is walking up to the door. He looks surprised to see me. "Where are you going?"

"Work," I say. I add, "have a great day. See you later," for good measure.

I try walking away but he calls me back. "Wait. I'll drive you there. Get in the car."

"It's okay, you don't have to drive me. I'll be a bit early if you drive me there." I try not to bother him by having him drive me.

It really wouldn't be too bad to have him drive me. It would save me from having to walk in the cold air.

Then again, I would have him for company. Maybe it won't be so bad; I can be optimistic about it. It's a ten-minute car trip.

How bad could it be?

"Get in the car. I'm driving you." He says. "I'll be right back out."

He goes into the house. I assume he needs to grab something or go to the bathroom.

I get into the car and wait. And wait. I watch the time pass by. I have ten minutes to get to work or I'll be late, by the time he comes back out. He then turns straight around and goes back into the house. I try not to get frustrated with him.

What am I thinking; of course, I'm frustrated with him. He does this all the time.

He comes out and gets into the car when I have eight minutes until I have to be at work. Maybe we'll hit all the right lights, and I can still get there on time.

He leisurely pulls his fancy red car out of the driveway and seems to be going at a snail's pace to my work.

"How was your day?" He asks me as he tries to make conversation.

"Good. How was yours?" I ask to return the courtesy.

"Good," Dad says.

We stay silent for a bit. I don't have much to say to him. I decide to lay on the gratitude. "Thank you for driving me to work."

"Did you make me anything for supper tonight?" He asks.

The question shocks me, though it really shouldn't by this point. He doesn't have a clue. He's a narcissist; he wouldn't notice so long as it doesn't affect him directly. He hasn't given me money in four months to buy food for the house. "No, I didn't. We don't have any food in the house."

"Don't be snarky with me." He admonishes me.

I wasn't aware I had taken a tone; I didn't take a tone with him. That doesn't matter either way. There is no use in saying otherwise. An apology quickly falls from my lips.

"I'll give you money, and you can go grocery shopping tonight." He orders me.

"Yes," I say no more.

I give no sight of any fuming done internally.

By the time we come to the turn into the shopping area, I stop all my thoughts and calm myself. It would be bad if I give any signs of negative emotions. As it is, I am sure there will be something on my bed when I get home; probably another chocolate bar.

A smile on my face. Check.

Looking straight. Check.

Relaxed but proper posture. Check.

He stops the vehicle right outside the doors to the store. He puts the car into park and then reaches for his wallet. He hands me one hundred dollars and puts his wallet back. I put the money in my pocket.

"Thank you. Have a great night." I unhook my seatbelt, grab my bag, and let myself out of the vehicle. I wave at him goodbye and go into the store.

I can feel my cheeks go red for a whole new reason when I get into the back room, and my manager is in there getting ready to leave.

I say a quick "Hi." She says it back, and tells me that I'm on cash tonight; which I am sure is a punishment for my call earlier.

I grab my apron quickly and go out to the cash registers. I relieve Judy and watch most of the day crew leave.

There is a little line of three people. They only have enough items that they can carry so I know I won't need any extra help. When the line is free, and I am sure all the day crew is gone I will call Kate up to cash.

I see the familiar face too late; not that I would have been able to do something about it. I quickly think I should call Kate to cash immediately. But, I'm frozen.

Jacob stands on the other side of the counter. "What the hell is your problem? You ungrateful brat. How dare you talk to me like that? You need to respect me. Your mother would be rolling over in her grave if she saw you treat me like that."

"I'm sorry. I didn't mean any disrespect." I cast down my eye while I feel my cheeks go red.

He continues on his rant. He's angry, and I'm scared about what that means. He's scary when he's angry. Not that he's ever physically hurt me when he's angry, but he could do anything. I know he at least respects my work enough that he won't pull me out of the store.

Goosebumps raise when I remember the time I pissed him off in a coffee shop, and he force me into his car to drive me across town to an empty parking lot. The situation scared me enough to worry for my life but ended with him saying that he was glad I agree with him and get along with him so well, and he took me home.

"I'm so sorry," I say. I'm sure my face is red from embarrassment. I look at the people in the growing line; hoping that someone might help me. That would be too much to ask for, however. I just wait for him to finish berating me.

Eventually, between his yelling, and my apologies he always talks himself into me agreeing that he's right, and I'm wrong; whether or not I was right, and he was wrong. I take the submissive actions just to get him to stop yelling.

There is no use in fighting; it doesn't help anything to try even the slightest argument. If anything goes against his opinion it's wrong.

Eventually, he does leave. He was very happy that I agreed that my actions were abhorrent, and I would take care to never do it again.

I'm still not sure what exactly it was that I had done. Was it my body language, or my tone? Did I word something wrong? Is it because I didn't talk much during the ride over? Did I not show my gratitude enough for the one hundred dollars he gave me for groceries? Is it because I didn't say 'I love you' at my departure?

Many questions run through my mind. I can feel my anxiety going up, and, with it, a tension migraine appears.

I quietly go back to my work. Apologizing to the people in the lineup, while I scan the first gentleman's items.

"That was your dad?" The woman after him asks; breaking my thoughts. She's one of my regulars.

Dejected I tell her. "Yes."

"Don't be sorry. I'm sorry." She says to me.

Kate puts her hand on my shoulder. She pulls up my closed sign and puts it on the counter as I finish helping the lady. "Come to the back." She says to me. She looks at the rest of the lineup. "She can help you over there."

I follow her into the back she motions me to sit down in the staff room. "I'm sorry."

"Why are you apologizing? Stop apologizing. What happened out there?" She starts off angered that I would apologize for something that isn't my fault. I get it, however, I have gotten used to apologizing profusely for things that aren't my fault.

"I don't know," I tell her honestly. "Just my dad flipping out about nothing, again. I did want to talk to you about something." I go over to my bag and open it up. I pull out my textbooks and binders. "This is all the homework I need to have done for tomorrow." I show her my agenda on the page for tomorrow. "I was wondering if I could work on this tonight."

"Why didn't you call in sick?" She says.

"I tried. Tamara said I had to come in. Homework isn't an excuse for not coming into work." I say the last sentence in a mocking tone. "I've had three hours of sleep in the last three days because of homework, work, and school."

"That's bullshit!" She looks over her shoulder and quietens after that remark. "You work too hard, and we have more than enough people for tonight."

"Exactly." I know the schedule. There were five people scheduled for tonight. Everyone came in, and we only have four tills. Even if we got swamped there are more people than there are tills.

"One minute, I'll be right back." She tells me as she's walking away from me going to the office. She takes out the keys from her pouch and unlocks the door. In no time, I hear her voice over the speakers. "Fred and Trevor to the office, please." She comes back out of the office locking the door behind her. Opening the door I came through moments ago she then shouts out to Kayla who is at cash. "Can you come to the door for a moment when you're free please?" She leaves the door open for all three workers to come through.

It doesn't take long for Kayla to come to the back with the boys following shortly after her.

Trevor throws up his arms as he says, "Safety meeting! No one moves, and no one gets hurt." He says this joke every time we all get together for a meeting.

"Not quite. I want to make sure that it's okay with everyone that Jaiden is going to stay here in the back, and work on her homework." She moves out of the way so that everyone can have a good look at the binders, and textbooks I have on the table. "She tried calling in sick, but Tamara wouldn't let her. Tamara told her that she needed to come in tonight because we were short-staffed and busy. As you can see she's got hours and hours of homework to do tonight."

"I think the real issue we need to deal with is, who's going on a Timmy's run." Trevor crosses his arms and tries to make his face looks serious. He doesn't do a very good job. However, with agreement from the other staff members, I get the gist that they are okay with me working on homework.

Kate pulls out her debit card, "it's on me tonight."

Although I bought for everyone on the last run, I feel obligated to pay this time around. I reach into my pocket and pull out my debit card. "If you're going to let me do my homework all shift then it's on me. Do you remember the number?"

Fred takes the card out of my hands and puts it in his pocket. "Of course." He walks out with Trevor following shortly after him. We go for so many Timmy's runs that no one has to ask what anyone else wants. A Double-Double for Fred. A half French vanilla half coffee for Kate. A French vanilla for Trevor and Kayla, and, a green tea for me.

Kayla has disappeared out the door; I can hear her helping a customer. The phone rings from Kate's pouch pocket. She answers the phone as she walks away. "Thank you for calling the Dollar store, how can I help you today?" She pauses for one moment, waiting for the customer to answer her. "We are open from nine to nine every weekday, and nine to six on weekends." Another pause, and I hear her grumble. I hear her click the call button on the phone. The person on the other side must've hung up.

Kate doesn't come back into the room so I decide to get started on my homework. I won't have long until the boys come back, and who knows what distractions they might provide once they do.

I decide to pull out my math homework first. This should take a while, but provide stops between each question in which I can be distracted for a moment. I don't know how many times I will have to go to cash, or how many times someone may come back here to talk.

Math seems like the right choice when the boys come back. All four coworkers come into the back room, and it takes ten minutes before they leave again.

As the night goes on, I get through half of my math before it comes time for Kate's break. She comes into the back room quietly, opens her locker, and pulls out her supper. As quietly as possible she opens up the microwave, shoves her supper in, and heats it. She cringes each time she makes a noise.

I decide to let her off the hook. "It's okay. You can make noise." Her shoulders relax.

"So, what do you all have?" She asks me.

"French, Math, English AP, and a Social Studies project."

"Who do you have for English AP?" Kate asks.

"Mr. Scall," I tell her with a bit of a sneer.

She scowls at me. "Ouch, he always gives a tonne of homework. And, his tests are Hell." She must've had him when she was in high school.

"You can say that again. I've never finished one of his tests. Not even with the extra time." I confess. Mr. Scall lets you, highly recommends you, come in during the time before or after class. For my class, this means you can come in during the lunch hour.

"I finished them, sort of. I had a system. I went through the test and answered all of the questions that I knew the answer to, if I didn't know then I skipped it immediately. That almost takes all class, but I always made sure I had time left over to go back and at least guess at all the questions I didn't fill in. It worked, mostly." Kate instructs.

"Maybe I'll try that for my next test, it might help me get a better mark." The microwave beeps telling us her food is done. Kate grabs her food from the microwave and sets it down in the only place I haven't taken over on the table.

Kate tries her best to be quiet for the rest of her supper. I get a few more questions done before she leaves.

I don't expect to get much work done when the boys step through the door. They make a lot of noise but have decided to eat at McDonald's today. I don't expect them back before the end of their lunch; they will probably rush in about five minutes after their supper should have ended. The McDonald's is across the parking lot, a road, another parking lot, and inside the Walmart.

It takes me until eight o'clock, but I finally finish my math homework. I put my math textbook inside my backpack. I can at least cross that one item off the list. I'm grateful they let me work on that now. It took much longer than I thought it would.

My stomach aches from missing supper, I decide to appease it a bit by drinking the tea I got and gulping down the whole thing. It has finally cooled enough for my taste. For dessert, I go into my backpack and grab a piece of mint gum.

What to work on next?

With the time I have left I should work on my French homework. I wouldn't have enough time or resources to work on my English or my Social project.

I find my French homework in the stack, and grab the French to English dictionary. One very slow hour passes, but I finish it and put it in the bag. The stack is looking smaller. I pull out my agenda to calculate how many hours I have left.

Jaiden Kensington

English: 2

Social studies project: 4

I should have about six hours of homework left.

I'll be done here around nine-thirty. I'll need to go grocery shopping then. Go to Walmart, and grab the groceries. I only have a hundred dollars, and I don't want to spend a good portion of it on a taxi. It should take me about an hour extra for shopping and then walking home and putting groceries away is another half hour. That should bring me to five o'clock.

It looks like I might get two hours of sleep tonight, at least.

It angers me to think that without Kate, and my coworkers letting me work through work, that I wouldn't be getting any sleep tonight. I probably wouldn't have finished my homework.

I know I can't continue like this, but my work ethic and moral integrity won't let my school marks slide just because I need sleep. I think I've proven that out enough times this year, between working almost full time, going to school, and completing all of my homework. It would take me going to the hospital to be allowed some reprieve.

I just might put myself there.

I pull out the book for English. Whatever I read now, will shave off some time from what I have to do tonight.

I put away all the rest of my homework, and keep the book out. My stomach protests from being empty; save the green tea. I grabbed the mint bubble gum out of my bag as my cure-all trick. It usually helps settle my stomach, but it's not working completely tonight.

I'm on chapter fifteen of sixty. I have to finish this book before class tomorrow. My memory helps with the detail needed for the tests, that, and bullet point internet notes. But, nothing can prepare you for a test that asks you for the tiniest details like the colour of a pot mentioned one time in chapter three.

At eight forty-five I hear Kayla over the speakers, "Attention shoppers. The store will be closing in fifteen minutes. Please make your way to the tills. Have a great night."

Kate comes into the backroom moments later. "Can you help close up? The store is a mess, and we need to make sure that everyone is out."

"Yeah, no problem." I put the book down. I follow her out the door, but as she goes to the tills, I go to the front door and grab a cart. Starting in aisle one, I grab everything out of place and on the floor, putting back anything that belongs in this aisle as I go. I continue this for each aisle.

I fill up two carts. By aisle ten Kayla is making the final call. "Attention shoppers. This story is now closed. Please make your way to the tills, and have a great night."

I quickly finish the remaining three aisles. The boys have started sorting the other two carts into thirteen baskets; one representing each aisle.

I drop the cart off with them and start making a run around to search for customers. I find one in aisle five still meandering around. As I've done many times before, I walk up to the middle-aged man. Asking him, "Can I help you find anything?"

He answers, "No, thank you."

"Let me know if you need anything, and just to let you know we are closed now."

He looks at his watch, and says absentmindedly "I guess it is nine o'clock." He looks back at me, and says, "I guess you want to go home don't you?"

I smile, and say sweetly, "doesn't anyone at the end of their shift."

"I'll get out of your hair then. Have a great night." He walks away from me.

"Thank you, you too," I call after him.

I run away to see if I can find another person. They aren't all as accommodating as he is. I've had some nasty people in the past tell me to 'F' off.

There are some more people in the next aisle over, but they have grabbed Trevor for help, so I move on to the next aisle. I get to the end, and run back, just in case I have missed anyone. Trevor is still helping the couple find what they need, and the middle-aged man is now at the till.

Kate is waiting on Kayla's till to finish the cash-out. If I know her, and she's already gotten the other three counted, and written down in the book. She looks at the time impatiently on the till. She looks back at me, and I know she wants the number of people in the store I hold up two fingers. She scowls and makes another announcement.

In a slightly angry tone, she says, "Attention shoppers! The store has been closed for five minutes! Please make your way to the tills, and have a great day."

I grab two baskets and disappear down aisle thirteen. It doesn't take me long to put all the items back. I put the baskets where they belong near the entrance, grab another couple baskets, and proceed to empty another five aisles before I hear another announcement.

"Attention shoppers! The store has been closed for ten minutes! Please make your way to the tills. Have a great night."

Her voice is getting angrier, and angrier. No doubt she'll go talk to the customers directly in a couple of minutes if Trevor doesn't bring them to the front.

I empty a couple more baskets, slightly out of breath, and sweating from the effort. Part of me is reminded that I am doing the job of all three people but they also let me do homework tonight.

Another five minutes pass before the couple finally get through the till, and out the door. They made Kayla angrier when they come up to the till feigning that they didn't know the store had been closed. Trevor locks the door behind them.

Kate grabs the till out of the register and brings it back. I follow after her as per policy states that have to. Not that we care too much, and she has already done the first three by herself.

I get to spend the time watching her count the singular till, while I get to write a couple of numbers down in the book; another rule we break often. I know the supervisor position inside and out, without being a supervisor.

Five more minutes is all it takes for us to finish everything. We lock up the tills.

Kate makes an announcement, "are you done?" We stay quiet for a moment to hear the shouts of 'yes' coming from the store. People come running into the back room to grab all of their stuff.

I grab my book from the table and shove it into my backpack. I make sure I haven't left anything else on the table. Zipping up the backpack, I grab my jacket and go out to the front door.

The boys and Kayla follow after me, while Kate goes to set the alarm. She enters the code, and we all run out of the store walking the main doors behind us.

We each say our goodbyes; the boys walk off in one direction, Kate goes to her car, Kayla goes to her Jeep, and I walk off to Walmart.

It doesn't take long for me to gather up just one hundred dollars in food. I don't grab anything fancy, but the tally goes up fast. I make sure that I can carry everything for the whole walk home. I go through the tills and walk outside.

It just keeps getting darker out as I walk home. I could take the extra ten minutes to walk around but I decide to go through the shortcut. It's extremely sketchy, especially with this darkness. The whole time I watch the three-sixty degrees around me to make sure I am aware of my surroundings. To make sure that no one is following me.

I finally make it home safe, and with only a chill, but plenty of sweat from my heavy load. As I go through the doors, I can hear dad and Kendra arguing about something or another. Just what I needed to come home to, another fight. I don't think they notice me so I go quietly into the basement.

I unpack my book and start reading from where I had left off. After only two pages, I can hear footsteps pounding down the stairs.

"We need a mediator." My father says. I inwardly sigh.

I keep my page with my finger, close the book, and put it on my lap. Just what I need, to be the mediator between him and his young wife. "What happened?" I stare and nod my head at my dad so he knows to go first.

"I merely suggested she change her top to something more appropriate. She looks like a floozy with her bra hanging out." Appropriate? You're the one who married a woman a week after my mom died, and then went on to have two more marriages because no one can stand you. And Kendra is half your age.

"This is completely appropriate. My bra isn't hanging out. You can just see my bra strap a little bit." She tries to defend herself. But, I know with the strict traditional rules of my father's house that top would never pass. Especially, since she's also wearing booty shorts.

"Okay, there are two sides to this. Clothes are more about how you present yourself in something. Two people can wear the same clothes, and one will be classy, while the other one sleazy. Just because a bra strap is showing, which is common nowadays, it doesn't mean she's being a floozy.

This is something small that has just gone out of control. Dad, you can merely suggest that she changes her clothing by saying something other than 'you look like a slut'. Don't you think you'd rather wear, insert clothing item here? Oh, I like that red top of yours, why don't you wear that instead.

Mom, it's winter, not summer. What you're wearing is more appropriate for summer wear. That top would be perfectly fine with a pair of jeans or leggings. You have to remember that he is very traditional, and showing bra straps isn't traditional.

It's about compromising on both sides, and not letting it go way out of proportion. This should have never blown up into a huge fight like this because of something so small.

We're good?" Both of them nod so I pick up my book, and open it up to the page I was on.

They look at each other and go in for a hug. I start reading my book trying to ignore them as a hug turns into a kiss, and a kiss turns into a full make-out session.

It's completely grossing me out.

"You mind checking on your brother?" Kendra asks me.

I don't answer. I just get up, leave, and walk upstairs. I take my book with me. I guess I'm relocating to my brother's nursery. I can hear a belt being undone so I start running faster up the stairs.

I walk through the kitchen and down the hall to my brother's nursery.

Opening the door quietly, I peek inside. He's sleeping soundly; glad someone can. He doesn't stir at all as I pick him up, blankets and all.

I sit down in the rocking chair. There is a soft light that I turn on right beside me, so I can have some light to read.

It's a little bit more difficult to read around the baby, but I don't mind as I indulge myself in the unconditional, need-based love of a baby. I need the snuggles.

Chapter 7

Locking my locker, I turn and look down the hall both ways. I don't see anyone in my friend group. With how today went, I don't know where anyone might be. I decide to just walk home.

I'd prefer to avoid Darius right now; not ready for that confrontation. I debate whether I should even send him a text to let him know.

I walk quickly towards my targeted location. Slipping around the other students, I turn the corner and hit the bar on a side exit door. Not losing any momentum to the slight blinding from the sun.

My eyes don't adjust fast enough. In the next moment, I'm stopped by another body hitting into one half of my body and I get pushed back in the direction I came in.

"Oh Alexa, I'm sorry. I wasn't paying attention." Daniel, a teammate of Darius', spits out as he grabs my shoulders to steady ourselves.

"That's okay. I wasn't either." I respond. He lets go to rush off.

Returning to my walk home, I see Darius in his truck rolling down the passenger window; looking non-to-pleased. "Get in" His voice is stern. Unable to argue with his tone I get into his truck. "What were you doing with him?" I hesitate to answer that question out of confusion; a moment too long for Darius. "I asked you a question."

"He just accidentally ran into me. It was my fault; I wasn't looking where I was going." He puts his truck into drive. I can tell his anger is getting to him by how the truck jerks forward.

"He knew exactly where he was going. He did it on purpose." Darius jerks the truck then continues in a smooth roll.

I can't talk to him when he gets like this. No matter what, he is always right. Hoping to get off this particular issue, I change it to the one thing he hates most and my goal for the night; preferably before we are headed the wrong way. "I have to go to the house today. I need to check up on Rayleen."

"Why the hell do you always need to go check up on her? She's fine." He shouts at me.

"She's just a little girl and she's my responsibility. She's my family. Just take me home, Darius!" I sharpen my voice.

He hits his hand against the steering wheel. Pulling out of the school's parking lot, he turns to the right. He's driving the way to my house instead of his. He doesn't speak for the short two-minute drive.

Unbuckling the seatbelt as we come down the last few houses to mine, I get ready and jump out of the truck as soon as he stops.

Darius shouts at me as I start walking away. "I'll be here to pick you up in the morning. Don't leave the house until I get here." Darius quickly drives off after his comment and I watch him leave. I shake it off and go into the house.

No one says anything as I come through the door. A stale smell hits me before I remember not the breath through my nose. I leave my shoes on because of the stains that cover the ground.

Furniture is cluttered by the years of collection by the hoarding mentality of some of the people that live here. It's not garbage or anything of the sort, it's just a lot of items that could be done without.

The television is on. Walking around the separating wall, I look at the big man sitting on the couch. Dave looks at the television with a vacant look. His actions are automatic as he lifts the pop can to his mouth and tips back. The emptied can is set down on the table with a clang.

"Whoever's in the kitchen, bring me another pop. I'm thirsty." He orders.

June comes out from the kitchen holding a couple of cans. She seems slightly startled by the sight of me in the doorway. Bringing the dual cans to Dave, she turns around. She folds her arms and puts most of her weight onto one hip.

"So, you finally decided to show up. Did your boyfriend kick you out?"

I know it's better to damper my reaction. "No. I came to see Rayleen. And, I still technically live here." Passing through the kitchen, I quietly open the refrigerator. I grab a couple of apples to take with me.

I go quietly down the stairs and into the first door on the left at the bottom of the stairs.

The little redhead plays on the floor with the doll I gave her; combing its hair with a hairbrush. She jumps up as the door bumps against the wall; as though she's been caught in the act.

Her smile brightens as she sees me. Light blue eyes shine from under a jean material hat. Rayleen runs over to me. The slight impact of her weight is comforting. I hug her back tightly, picking her up at the same time.

"Hi, baby girl. How was school?" I prop her on my hip. Closing the door, I walk over to the bed. Setting her down on the bed, she starts her story as I sit beside her.

"Tommy went to the hospitable today. He got all sick and stuff but my teacher told us he is all better now. And I got to play in the sandbox. And my teacher told us that she has a surprise for us tomorrow, but she won't tell us what it is. I think it might be cookies but Sally thinks it's going to be a puppy or a kitty. Oh, and Tyler got another toy taken away from him today. Well, it really wasn't a toy. It was an eraser. He was pretending it was an airplane. He was playing when the teacher was reading us a story, so he deserved it." Rayleen's stomach growls. The little girl simultaneously looks directly at her stomach, brings her hands up to hold it, and makes a shushing sound.

"I brought you an apple." I prop up the apple a bit to get her attention on it. She takes it from me and bites into it.

"Do you know why I like apples?"

"Why?" I have to ask or she won't answer.

"Because, they make my teeth wiggly."

"Oo. Do you think you might lose a tooth soon?"

"Maybe." Her smile fades a little. "I missed you."

"I know, sweetheart. I missed you too. I'm staying tonight. We can do whatever you want." I promise her.

Her face lights up again. "Can we get slurpies?"

"I can go get us slurpies. If you want?" I don't want to have to ask June or Dave if I could take Rayleen. It's easier this way.

"Okay. Can you get me root beer?"

"Of course. I'll be back in about fifteen minutes." I give her a quick family kiss on the lips. I hug her before I leave the room. Opening the door right next to Rayleen's room, I walk through the unfinished laundry and furnace room, to the far room in the corner. Turning the sticky doorknob and giving a hard push on the door; causes me to lose balance as it opens the first push. Normally, I have to push at least twice.

The stench of cat urine fills my nose. Previous to my living in this room, June had kept her numerous cats in here locked up most of the time.

Feeling my hand along the wall, I find the light switch. Flicking the switch, the light doesn't come on. Trying it one, two, three times, nothing happens. Rolling my eyes, I open my door to its full extension. Walking a couple of steps away from my room I pull on the cord to the light by the furnace. The light flickers once but stays on after. Light streams softly into my room through the door but leaves almost half the room in darkness.

Going into my room, I go to the night table beside my bed. Opening the drawer, I pull out my picture album. The small album holds pictures of my older sister and her little red-haired baby girl: dated a little over four years ago. Stopping for a moment I'm drawn to look at the photos; as I am each time I pull out the album.

In addition to my sister holding Rayleen, the album contains nine other photos. All the photos date back five or six years ago. They mostly contain pictures of my family.

It's the two last photos that I linger on. The one was taken the night my family was taken from me. It was taken in the front room of the house. My parents, Kathleen, and her husband all dressed up in their comfiest attires, ready to spend ten hours on the airplane before they start their vacation. Bags are packed and ready at the door; smiles on all their faces.

The last photo is the one Kathleen took of Rayleen and me, taken the same day. She had stolen my camera to take a picture of me dangling the locket on my necklace in front of the girl. Her hand reaches for it as her eyes focus on it.

I look at the girl I was in the picture. The red of my natural hair shines with the light on it. My face is covered with a couple of freckles here and there. Not a trace of makeup is found. I hadn't started dying my hair black yet. A smile that reaches her eyes, makes the girl glow in the picture; myself completely unrecognizable to the person I am now.

Flipping that last page over I open the built-in folder and find a few bills in there, pulling out a twenty, I put it into my pants pocket.

I close the album, putting it into the drawer, and shut it tight. Going out of the room I close the door with a slight bang. Yanking the doorknob closes the half of an inch left; satisfied that my door is closed.

I pull on the light's string to shut it off and I walk over to the dryer. Climbing on top of the machine, then standing up, I open the window. Putting my hands on the ledge in front of the windows, I give a slight jump and use my upper body strength to pull myself the rest of the way up. I get my leg up on the sill and crawl through, watching out for the garbage and dog feces littering the yard.

I wipe my hands and knees off from the dust and dirt while crouching. Moving under the deck, I avoid being seen by anyone who may happen to be in the kitchen.

I run the short distance from the other side of the deck and around the corner of the house. I duck for another window as I make my way to the gate.

Lifting the hook out of the eye hook, I slowly let the hook down to rest. Aware of the spider webs that coat the gate, paranoia lingers that the spiders may still be somewhere on the gate. Watching where I put my hands, I give a small push to the gate. Holding it in place after it becomes loose, I listen for any sounds that would alert me to someone coming this way to check out any sounds I may have made. Not hearing anything, I continue to push the gate open, just enough for me to pass through without touching the rotting wood.

I close the gate; pushing twice to get it in its proper place. Reaching over the gate I find the latch and put it into the eye hook.

Knowing that at any point from here that any of the neighbours could see me and rat me out, I make a break for it; down the short walking path, across the alley, and down another walking path. Once out of the view of the house and the next-door neighbours, I slow down into a brisk walk.

A short three blocks away, I walk into a small corner store. Against the back wall are the slurpy stations. After filling two cups with slush, I walk over to the till.

The man behind the till greets me and rings through the purchase. I pull out the cash from my pocket and hand it to him. He puts the cash in the till then counts out and hands back my change. The change goes into my pocket; I grab the cups and walk out without any further pleasantries.

Walking home quickly, my speed increases from the brisk walk to a jog, and then once more into a sprint the closer I come to the house. Stopping roughly by angling back and sliding against the loose rocks on the pavement, I quickly peek around the corner of the fence; the coast is clear. I climb the slight slope. Reaching one hand over the gate, I fish and pull up on the now located latch.

Ducking down, I speed back the way I had come. Looking through the window I look to see if June is in the laundry room; she isn't there.

Opening the window, I crawl through enough to place the cups on the ledge to the side. Backing out, this time, I place my legs through first and sit down on the ledge myself. Closing the window behind me I look down at the floor and track the safest and quietest location to jump down. Placing my feet against the wall and moving my hands on each side beside me, in one motion I kick and push my hands back. Bypassing the dryer and landing on the floor, a slight pain in my feet is the only evidence of my long fall. It goes away just as fast as it comes.

Crawling back up onto the dryer, I grab the cups and place them on the dryer and crawl back down. Grabbing the drinks once more I go out the door and knock on Rayleen's door before opening it and walking straight in.

The redhead looks up to the door and grins knowingly, anticipating the drink she knows I'm bringing her. "Hey baby girl, I've got your root beer slushy." She cheers and repeats her thanks over and over enthusiastically.

I close the door behind me and walk over and sit on the bed. Rayleen gets up from the floor and hops onto the bed. I hand her the smaller cup.

The normally talkative girl is quiet for a moment as she scarfs down her sugary drink. I pause my actions for a moment as I ponder whether or not I should tell her to slow down.

Rayleen starts to slow down on her own towards the end of her drink. She speaks as soon as she finishes her last bit. "Can you colour with me?"

"Yes, sure." Rayleen hands me her empty cup, then jumps off the bed as soon as I agree. She runs over to her desk and sits on her chair; where she has a couple of colouring books and a pack of crayons.

I get off the bed. Walking to her desk I stop to stand next to her chair. She has one of the colouring books open to a picture of a mermaid and fishes. She's already picked out a red crayon.

"Can you colour her hair red?" She doesn't wait for my answer. Rayleen shoves the crayon into my hand. She picks up a green crayon for herself to use on the fish. I start colouring my portion.

I get three-quarters of her hair coloured when the ceiling shakes as three thuds are heard; June is stomping on the ground.

Since arriving here, June has stomped on the ground as a replacement for calling for us. The longer it takes to respond the louder and angrier the thuds sound. Supper is probably ready.

Rayleen jumps up from her spot and rushes up the stairs. By the time I catch up, she's at the table eating her sandwich.

June frowns when she sees me. "I just made an easy supper tonight. Eat quickly because you have a bunch of chores to do. Do the laundry, tidy the main areas of the house, and take out the garbage.

You need to catch up on the chores you've skipped out on for the past couple of days. This house better be clean by the time I wake up tomorrow morning or you'll get double duty tomorrow." June dismisses herself and walks away. I hear the front door creak and slam.

Her punishment for my misbehaviour seems to be always making me clean the house. The work keeps me busy enough to keep the evening boredom away, but cuts down on the time I can spend with Rayleen.

I curse at her in my head but know better than to not do the work. I don't want anything to backfire against me or Rayleen.

I scarf down my sandwich and get to work. Walking through the kitchen and down the hall, I stop at the first door I come to. After knocking on it, a preteen male answers the door. I look over the boy and into the only spotless room in the house.

"Andy, can I get your laundry?" I ask.

Chapter 8

I wake up, in an instant, when my alarm goes off. Grabbing my phone I turn off the alarm and call the office.

Making up my best scratchy throat, not difficult from drinking last night, I talk to Fred's answering machine. "It's Nikki. I won't be coming into work today. I've been throwing up all night. See you tomorrow."

Release.

Barely a blink of sleep later and the alarm is going off again. It's now seven thirty and I've got a text from Steph. *Are you still coming today?*

I answer her back. *Yes, just getting up.*

I get ready while listening to music. Once I get out to my car, I text Steph to let her know I'm leaving.

Us too.

Flipping through radio stations I find one playing a good song. As long as the good music keeps going then it doesn't seem that long to go anywhere.

Traffic slows to a crawl as soon as I get to Edmonton. There must be an accident up ahead.

I press the button and down goes my window. There is some honking in front of me. Something tells me that there isn't an accident. The closer and closer I get, the more I can see. There is a group of people picketing on the road. Some vehicles are slowly pushing through the people.

My phone vibrates. I pull it out of my pocket.

Do you see this? Crazy people. Brad texts.

I look back at the road. No one's moved. Looking around me, I spot Brad's truck a couple of vehicles back in the next lane.

My lane starts up again as a few vehicles swerve around the group. I open my window so I can hear them clearly. Two women break off from the group and come closer. The rest of them spread out to stop the people going around them.

"Repent now! The end is here. Demons are rising up and taking over the world." One woman shouts out.

A blonde woman goes up to the vehicle in front of me. She freaks out and starts banging on the window. The car jumps forward, tires screeching, as he runs through the line-up of people.

"Fuck!" I say when the girl runs towards me next. I don't know what to do. Panic courses through my veins.

My foot barely hits the gas pedal. In my panic, I only catch the pedal with a small portion of my shoe. My foot slides off. The car goes forward, but not fast enough.

Blonde's arms and face come through my window opening. Hands go to my neck.

Gas pedal. Pressing down hard, the car goes forward fast.

Choking! My hands, off the steering wheel, try to loosen her grip. She twists my head with her other hand in my hair.

A sudden bang and trust forward throw her out of the vehicle. I hit a lamppost. She screams, enraged, and leaps towards me.

In a blur, she's gone and Shawn is at my window opening the door. "Are you okay? We have to get you out of here."

My hands fumble for a moment with the seat belt. It lets loose. I grab my bag. Shawn takes my hand and helps me out.

The girl is on the ground, but getting up. She's furious.

Stephanie has the truck door open, we jump in, and Brad slams on the gas.

I must have spaced out for a moment. Steph looks at me worried. Her hand goes up to my cheek. Her lips move but only the last part I hear once I focus. "-okay?"

"I think so." Steph lets go of my face. My hands go up to the spots where the blonde's hands had just been. They hurt, but it shouldn't last long. "Shit, what the fuck is going on?" We pick up speed suddenly swerving. I look out the front window. "This can't be real."

I have no words. What just happened? Why did she do that to me?

My car.

I hope I won't get in trouble for a hit and run.

Under the circumstances, I would hope they'd understand I needed to get to safety first. I need to call insurance and file a police report.

All thoughts clear out when I see an impossible sight.

A lizard with wings lighting buildings, cars, and people on fire with its breath; a dragon.

The dragon's behind us now, as we turn down a road. A little way down, we turn into the parking lot of the mall and park.

"What are you doing?!" Steph half asks and half screams.

"Getting off the road. It's not safe out here." Brad answers her back a bit more calmly, but you can still feel the panic in his voice.

"And, you think it's any safer in there?" She yells.

"Who knows? But at the least, they've got cops, food, and shelter here. We can hide until it's safer. Do you have any better suggestions?" Shawn answers her this time.

The boys seem to be on the same page.

"Stop it! No fighting. We go inside and find the cops. Then, we figure out everything from there." I yell.

I don't want to stay out here longer than I have to.

We can figure out what's going on after we get to the police.

The vehicle is suddenly very quiet.

Stephanie is the first to open the door and get out. I leave and catch up to walk beside her. We get to the doors before the boys finally meet up.

Inside is completely different from what is going on out there. People are laughing and going about their regular business like nothing is happening.

No one is running.

Nothing is on fire.

No weird creatures flying around.

Brad walks like he is on a mission. He runs through the halls. When we turn the last corner to the police station he sprints the last part.

I miss what he says to them to start with, but when I come through the open door I can see they do not look impressed.

The one officer comes closer to us. I recognize this. He is trying to see if Brad's eyes are dilated or if his breath smells like alcohol.

The other officer looks a bit tense. Like he is ready to jump in if Brad tries anything.

I try to stop the list of questions before they even start. "We're not drunk or high. Turn on the news or take a look outside. He's telling the truth."

"What you're saying is impossible. We're going to give you one chance to explain yourselves before we arrest you. You're wasting our time for a prank." The closer officer says.

"This isn't a prank. We're telling the truth." Pulling my cell phone from my pocket, I Google 'Edmonton News'.

I go to the first site on the list. It goes to a local news website. Going through the list I find nothing about what we saw. Nothing about any other things happening out there.

No updates, period, starting from an hour ago.

I go back to my home screen and click on the internet and go to my socials. Immediately, I find everything I am looking for. I shove the phone in the direction of the officer.

He barely looks at it before saying, "get your phone out of my face, right now, or I will arrest you." We hear a scream coming from the halls. Both the officers run out of the security office.

It doesn't take long before they disappear from view. We hear them shooting off their guns.

Brad runs behind the counter. He's looking for something.

I go towards the door and look around the corner. There are so many of them. Creatures that belong only in the scariest of nightmares and horror films.

"Help me find the keys." He shouts.

"To what?" Shawn yells back at him.

"To the cell. What else?"

Turning around, I snap at Brad. "What the hell are you going to do? Lock yourself in a cell? It's a death trap. I don't think it would take much for any of those things to get through the bars."

Steph suddenly runs out the door. Forget about Brad and Shawn, I go after her. She can't be alone.

Running towards the main part of the mall she then turns, runs down the hall a long way, and opens a maintenance door. I catch the door before it closes behind her. There is a long winding hallway she leads me down. There are no more screams and no more people down here. She seems to know where she's going.

We run through an empty hall into another set of back ways.

Another hall and another back way.

My mind can't begin to imagine where she is going, and what she's thinking.

She finally stops at a large set of double doors and repeatedly hits a buzzer. Her breathing is heavy. I don't know if it's from the run or a panic attack.

I say her name quietly "Stephanie." She freezes.

Brad and Shawn stop behind me. I hadn't realized they were following us.

Opening my mouth to say something, a beeping interrupts me. The doors open only a moment later.

A brunette with pink highlights opens the door. From her apron, I can tell she works at the dollar store.

Stephanie rushes through the doors.

She stops.

"Stephanie?" The moment her name comes out of the girl's mouth, Stephanie's body goes limp. Only because she is so close to her, the girl catches Steph before she hits the ground.

In my panic, I almost trip over myself rushing to her. The girl puts Stephanie on the floor carefully. Her eyes open slowly.

"Are you okay?" The words come out of both our mouths, almost, at the same time.

"I'm hot." Her voice is groggy and faint. "Water?"

The other girl goes to a bunch of drink bottles in crates and grabs water for Stephanie.

"What happened?" Brad and Shawn come through the door. Shawn shuts it behind himself.

Brad goes to the other side of Steph and wraps her in his arms.

"She fainted." The girl hands Steph an open water bottle.

"Kayanna, do you have something with sugar in it?" It sounds like Brad knows her too.

"I'm fine. I think it's gone now." Stephanie tries to get up. Brad lets her after a moment of holding her in place. She looks a bit wobbly at first but steadies herself.

"So, what are you doing here?" Kayanna asks.

"Some crazy shit is going on out there. There are these things attacking everyone." Shawn announces.

"Right. Like what? Animals?" Poor Kayanna looks so confused. I don't blame her for Shawn's vague response.

"No, like dragons and demons and things like that." He clarifies.

"Right. You're crazy. Oh no! Demons are attacking. We must go run and hide." She mocks being scared then looks over each of us. "Are you high?"

"Why is everyone asking us that? No, we're not high!" I'm starting to get annoyed at everyone assuming we are high.

"Come help me; please." The heavily accented message comes over the speaker system.

"I have to go. Stay here." Kayanna says before punching a code in and going through the door opposite to the one we came through.

No one else moves to stop her. Are they just going to let her go?

I run and kick at the door to stop it from closing behind her. The door opens a bit from the kick. I go through and close it behind me.

"Wait. Don't go. It's dangerous. We need to get back into the back room." I try to tell her. There is a huge crash followed by a scream.

Kayanna stops in her place for a moment, before she goes closer to the aisle. She goes to the end and peeks around the corner very quickly. Turning around she waves at me to go back. I can see fear in her expression.

She doesn't have to say anything.

I rush back to the door, almost forgetting about the alarm as I turn the handle. At the last moment, I remember not to push it open. Kayanna comes up next to me and punches in the code.

I go through first. Kayanna shuts the doors behind her. She whispers "You weren't kidding. Fuck this shit. We have to get out of here."

"And, go where? Outside? Where the dragons are?" Brad asks. I can tell he tried to whisper but it still come out pretty loud.

"Shit. Fuck. Fuck. Umm?" Kayanna says at a normal level. She's not going to be much help in this. Her mind is too shocked from just learning about what is happening.

I try to get her mind off it. Focus on what needs to be done right now. "Is there somewhere safe we can go?"

"It's not like a locked door is going to help much," Kayanna says. Contrary to what she just said, she runs to the backroom doors and locks them. "There's a monitor in the office. We can watch them; see how many are in the store. There's a cage we use to lock up the store at night. It would be at least a bit of protection. If, we can get them out of the store."

The world turns black. I scream. Waiting, at any moment, for something to swipe its claws through me.

When it doesn't happen I reach for my phone. Turing it on, I turn on the flashlight and scan the room. Everyone is frightened but they are okay. There doesn't look like anything is in here. Just looks like the power went off.

"Well, there goes the cameras," Kayanna mutters.

"Are there any backup generators?" Shawn says.

"Not in here. There's some once you get out to the halls; for lights and whatnot." Kayanna moves away from us, towards the store.

"So, we should have a bit of light once we open that door." I point to the door behind me.

"Very little, if any. It would probably only light up the front of the store." Kayanna seems to have stopped near the door.

"Grab something to defend yourself. We need to get that cage shut." I say. Who knows what might still be in the store.

"I'm not going out there!" Steph screams. If something didn't know we were here before, they know now.

"It's safer for you to come with us. She's right. We need to get that cage shut and we need to stick together. Don't turn this into that moment in every horror movie that someone goes off on their own and gets killed." Kayanna plays dirty, even if it might be true.

I've had enough of this conversation. We need to get that cage closed immediately.

I scan the room with my phone light and find a small broom, a push broom, and the mop and bucket. It's better than nothing. Grabbing the small broom, I take the dustpan off and go to the door.

I turn off the flashlight on my phone. Readying the broom I open the door a crack. I can't see anything at this angle, but I listen for sounds from the demons. I'm not exactly sure what those would be, but I don't hear anything close either way.

I open the door quickly. Kayanna wasn't kidding when she said there would only be a bit of light. It is still almost pitch black down the back of the store, but I can see some light coming from the front of the store.

A light lights up behind me, I turn back. "Turn that off," I whisper.

"I can't see," Steph says back to me. She sounds scared.

Brad grabs her phone and shuts off the light. "Let's go." He says.

I don't have to be told twice. We all quietly, but quickly, go down the hall.

I'm not sure if our being quiet is even going to help us.

Just like Kayanna had done, I peek around the corner when I get to the edge of the aisle. I don't see anything but a dark puddle on the floor. There isn't anything in the hall either.

Kayanna walks up beside me. "I need to get to the other side. The cage is tucked into the wall over there. It's loud so we need to do this fast." She doesn't wait for a response before she runs out of the store and to the other side.

She opens a small door and starts pulling out a cage door. While she's running the cage back to this side of the store, I go out to help her lock it.

We wait for a moment after locking us in the store.

Nothing.

There's no movement outside and no sounds come from in the store.

A smile spreads across my face. We are safe for the moment.

The cage rattles behind me. I jump, turn and scream. It's a couple and a kid. "Please, let us in." The desperation in the woman's voice chills me.

I rush to the lock and let them in; locking the cage behind them.

I look around to see if there is anyone else out there. I see someone running. They look behind them and scream. Something is chasing them right down this hall. I almost yell at the person to come here, but the demon tackles them to the ground before I have the chance.

"Go." There isn't much of a warning I can get out before I run down the aisle we had come out of. Everyone follows in a panic. I put my back to the aisle and wait.

"Come on. Let's go to the back room." Kayanna whispers.

I don't want to get backed into a corner back there; with no cameras to see what's going on. No light to see what's going on around us. But then again, it's probably better we get some distance between the demons and us.

I'm the last one to get into the back room. Stephanie already has her phone's light on. I close the door behind me. Everyone is going through the aisles back here to the other side.

Everyone packs into the staff room. Kayanna closes the door behind me. We stay quiet; just listening for the longest time. Everyone gets a chance to calm down a bit. I pull out a chair and sit down.

What next? I think about it. We closed the cage and now we've shut ourselves into a small room. If there was something in this store with us, it would have killed us by now.

This is stupid. We need some light and who knows how long the batteries are going to last. We need the phones for other things.

What do they always say whenever there is a disaster? Watch or listen to the news for directions. Stay in a safe place. Prepare for everything. Conserve food. They should have something here. It's a dollar store. We should have everything we need to stay here for a long time.

I pull out my phone and turn it on. There's no service in here. Must be all the concrete surrounding us. "Anyone have service?"

Everyone pulls out their cell. Steph grabs her off the table. All around no one has service.

"Must be a bad reception back here," Shawn says before he tucks his phone back into his pocket.

"No, I usually get service back here, but I've got nothing," Kayanna says.

"So, what? They cut off our cells. Communication blackout? What the hell is going on?" Brad is getting angrier by the second.

"Keep your conspiracy theories to yourself. We've got no cell phones. There's nothing we can do about it. Our question should be, what do we do next? We can't stay in here forever. We need to get to a police station." I wonder what Kayanna thinks the police will do about this all. Guns only have so much ammo and who knows if it would work on those things or not.

"We tried the police here. They're dead now and we're left without protection. Those things are everywhere." Brad tells Kayanna.

Protection, we need to protect ourselves.

Thump. I turn my head a bit. Something crashes to the ground. It's faint. I don't know where it's coming from. Maybe it wasn't anything and I was just hearing things.

"Everyone, shut up." It works. Everyone falls silent. I wait for a moment. "We can't stay here forever. We need protection. There's an army surplus store upstairs. If we can get there we'll at least have something to protect ourselves with."

"Why? What's the point? They don't know we're in here. I say we stay here for a while. We have enough supplies that we could survive in here for a month without anyone knowing." I don't think Brad realizes how bad this could get.

"I'm with Brad on this. We do have things in here that we can use as weapons if we need to. We have everything we could need here, so why risk it for some army shit that's probably not even going to help us that much." Steph agrees with Brad.

"We should stay in here for now. They're right. No one knows we're here. But, she also makes a point. We do need better protection than a broom and, what, some kitchen knives. Maybe we should go in a few hours. It gives us more of a chance that they might have left thinking no one else was in here." The man, who I assume is the boy's father, tries to find a middle ground.

"Mom." The little boy pulls on his mom's arm to bring her down to his level. He whispers something in her ear.

She stands up. We all look at her expecting her to say something. She looks a bit embarrassed. "Does anyone have anything to eat? Tim is hungry and I'd imagine there are probably others too."

"Everyone usually goes to the food court for lunch, so we don't have anything in here. But, if we go out to the store there's plenty." I was hoping for a different answer from Kayanna. Now this means we will have to go out to the store sooner.

Tim's dad gets up from his spot leaning against the wall and comes towards me. "Maybe only a few of us should go out there. Less chance of us making noise. I'll go." He looks at Kayanna. "Do you want to come with us? You can let us know where to find things."

"Of course," Kayanna responds.

I open the door and go out first. Turning on my flashlight to make sure there is nothing out there. Sweeping the light over everything in sight; I don't see any demons.

"I'm Peter by the way." Tim's dad introduces himself.

We stop at the door. "I'm Nikki and that's Kayanna."

"Here." Kayanna hands me and Peter each a basket.

"Thanks. What aisles are the candles and matches down? And, maybe a radio? Batteries too; if it needs it?" I try to think of everything we'll need to last in the backroom for a while.

"Yeah, I'll take you to them," Kayanna says.

Kayanna opens the door. I listen for movement, while I wait for Kayanna and Peter to go through.

I follow after Kayanna. She walks down a few aisles before turning and pointing. "Candles and matches are down this aisle; left-hand side about midway."

I react first, going down that aisle. I expect them to come with me or wait for me, but Kayanna and Peter move on to some other aisles.

Right as she said, the candles and matches are in the middle on the left. I fill up my basket with both. It gets kind of heavy.

I hobble back to the back room. I set the basket on the floor. "I'm going to go help the others," I say. I don't know why, but I feel like I need to explain myself to the eyes watching me.

Dashing back out of the back room and into the store, I can hear some noises further down the aisles.

I stop. The other door to the backroom is darker than it should be.

It's open.

Didn't I close that? Maybe someone else opened it after.

"Kayanna," I call out.

I hear a small, "down here." It's from two more aisles down. She comes out before I get to her. "Was getting a radio."

"Did you open that door? Or maybe Peter did?" I don't stop looking at the darkness. I half expect something to jump out at us.

"No, and I left him down the food aisle." She pauses for a moment. "Not to creep you out or anything, but I remember it being closed before I went down that aisle."

Just what I thought, we aren't alone in this place. "Let's go get Peter and get back to the room."

Kayanna leads the way down an aisle. "Hey, we have to get back. We think there might be something else in here."

We all hurry back to the room. No one in the back seems to be worried. We close the door behind us and lock it.

I pull out a chair from the table and put it against the door. Peter sits down on it. He nods to me. An understanding between us, that he will be the one to hold the door. I assume he's trying to protect his family more than the rest of us.

It takes only a moment of silence before there is a knocking on the door. It scares us. The calm, quiet knock is strange. It should be loud and angry. There's silence on both sides.

I look around. No one looks like they know what to do. Fear has taken over. Peter looks terrified. No one wants to be the one to open the door; just in case. It could be a person. But, they would have talked; introduced themselves.

We take too long it seems as the next knock is angrier; such a knock I would expect from a demon. It shakes the whole room.

It stops once again. We can't just wait in here for it to break down the door and come inside. I grab the broom from earlier and prepare myself with it. Unsure of how much the demon may be able to hear, I get Peter's attention and mouth the word 'move' to him.

He gets the message. Standing up, he quietly takes his chair with him. The door, now free and clear. He stands at the ready to open it.

He holds the handle with his left and lifts his other hand. He starts with three fingers counting down; two fingers, one finger.

I brace to defend as he pulls the door open quickly. There is nothing there. It ran off. Was it just trying to scare us? No, well yes; maybe? I don't trust the darkness any more than what I can see in it.

"Close it," I tell Peter. He slams the door shut, locks it, pulls the chair in front, and sits back down.

Bang! Bang! Bang!

I jump. Three harsh knocks to the door surprise and scare us all. Steph screams and I can hear her get up and go somewhere. Tim is crying and cuddled up with his mother. Peter looks terrified and unsure if he should be sitting there or not. He grips the chair hard with white knuckles.

We wait exactly where we are. I don't know how much time passes. It feels like hours; though I am sure it is only minutes. Nothing happens.

One by one people busy themselves. Tim and his mother set about setting up the candles. Steph sets out some of the food and people grab what they want.

The sight of the flame, the stress, the habit, and the craving have me reaching for my lighter and smokes. Right before I touch my pocket, I remember I can't leave the room; with a child in it and I assume his parents don't smoke either. Out of respect, I put my craving aside. Still ready and tense, I lean against the wall; staring at the door while the others lighten the room and eat. I'm not hungry.

Tim gives his dad the radio. Peter tosses away the packaging. He pulls a tab out from the battery casing and fiddles with the back.

I jump along with half the room when a static noise comes from the little radio. Peter fiddles with the dial. It doesn't matter what station he goes to. Each is playing static. I expected the high-pitched scream of the Emergency Broadcast System, but I guess someone hasn't activated it.

He turns the radio off. It was worth a shot, however, we still have no idea what's going on out there.

Maybe now would be a good time to bring up the army store again. If we can make it, there is a set of glass doors we can break through.

"Umm, so, I have to pee." Kayanna breaks the silence.

"Well, I guess we had to open that door sooner or later." Shawn seems antsy. I think I remember him saying that he has claustrophobia. Being locked in a small room with a bunch of people is probably enough to set that off.

I grab onto the broom. Shawn gets Peter to get off the chair and go back to his family. The chair is moved out the way and in a quick moment, the door is unlocked and swung open.

Shawn picks up the chair to use it as a weapon; if he needs to. There is nothing more than darkness out there but I don't know if I would trust that the demon ran off. The last time we opened the door he was waiting for us. Who's to say he isn't doing the same thing again.

"Brad, get a light and shine it out there," Shawn orders a reluctant Brad. He pulls out his cell phone and puts the flashlight on. Shining the light to every corner he can reach from inside the room, then Brad moves towards the door a little more. Shawn tries to guard him as much as possible with a large, clunky chair.

They creep out of the room. Brad inspects the warehouse with his flashlight but nothing happens. Maybe the demon did runoff. They check the room beside ours.

"Bathroom's clear. I don't think it's in here anymore." Brad is a bit too optimistic for my liking. We need to be certain.

With the all-clear, Kayanna rushes into the bathroom with her light on her cell phone.

"We need to secure the store. Make sure it's safe in here then we should go to that army store." Peter is on the same page as me. Just because the demon isn't here right now doesn't mean it's left the store.

"Wait, isn't there a shooting range in this place," Shawn says.

"Yeah, but it's near the movie theatre. Do you really want to try making it there with a broom and a chair?" Brad reasons.

"There's knives in the kitchen aisle," Kayanna says as she comes out of the bathroom.

"Can you take us there?" Peter asks her. I assume she nods because Peter continues talking. "Great. We leave now. Whoever wants to stay can, but lock the door behind us."

For a brief moment, I think that maybe I should stay here, but I don't want to sit and wait to be killed. I'm the last one out of the room. The door is shut and I can hear the lock click.

Another click comes from my left. "What are you doing?" I ask.

"We need to make sure that thing isn't in here. We lock all the doors and search this room. Once we clear this room we only unlock one door and move to the store. Someone guards the door to make sure it doesn't sneak back in here. It's basic tactics." While Brad talks he grabs onto Peter's shoulders and places him in front of the door.

"Where the hell did you learn that from?" Shawn sounds a bit in awe and somewhat confused.

I can hear the smile in Brad's voice. "Video games."

"Whatever dude." Cue the smirk in Shawn's voice.

The rest of us make our way to the other doors. When they are shut and locked, we start our search of this room. There are a lot of places in here that one can hide, especially in the dark. Searching with our lights, we try to cover every inch of this place.

There are three aisles back here to go through and the space above the lunchroom. I go down the back most aisle. Sweeping my light down to the end. Nothing there. Up towards the rafters. Nothing. In amongst the boxes. Nothing, but there are spots up at the top that the light doesn't reach.

Walking to the end, I try to get the light to reach the space above the lunchroom, but again the light doesn't reach that area. Shawn meets me as I go around the corner.

"Hey, someone shine a light over here I can't see." Brad's voice comes from the first aisle. Shawn and I go over to him. When we get there, Kayanna has a light on him halfway up the shelves.

"What are you doing?" I ask him.

"I couldn't see anything up here, so I'm climbing up." He climbs up and stands at the top. He grabs onto a rafter to steady himself. Turning on his flashlight app he sweeps the light over the top of all the boxes. "I think it's safe to say that thing's not in here."

"Then, come down here and we'll go search the store," Shawn says.

It doesn't take long for Brad to make his way down. He brushes right past Peter to go to the door. I grip the broom harder as he unlocks and opens the door.

He walks out first, with the light sweeping across everything in sight. We follow after him. Looking around where our lights reach to double-check he didn't miss anything.

"Nikki, you should stay here and guard the door." He turns his head to Kayanna. "Where are the knives?" It seems like Brad knows what he is doing. I nod as they all follow Kayanna's lead down aisle twelve.

It would be difficult to defend myself with the broom if anything did happen to attack. I set my phone on the ground with the light shining up. It lights up enough of the area that I can see a few meters in each direction.

I can hear and see where everyone else is. They split up.

Soft light spots appear on the ceiling above different aisles and a beaming light comes towards me. Peter comes down the aisle in front of me, rounds the corner, and goes down an aisle a few rows down. Brad and Kayanna do the same as they reach the end of their aisles.

A small echo from the cage scraping makes me grip the broom harder. If the cage is scraping, that means that someone had opened it. That demon might be gone, but what if more came in?

They check all of the aisles before coming back to me in a group. I can now see the knives each of them grabbed. I pick up my cell phone.

"All clear," Shawn says. "Now what?"

"We should tell everyone else that we're safe, then go to the army store." Peter states.

"We don't need it anymore. We've got knives and this place is safe now. It's stupid to leave here to get more knives." Brad shuts down Peter before pushing past me to go into the warehouse.

I look at Peter who has one eyebrow raised at Brad's back. He's being stupid about this.

Behind me, I can hear Brad knocking on the door. "It's us. We're safe in the store. You all can come out now."

The door unlocks. The small light crack gets larger and one by one, they come out of the small room. Tim runs to his father. They embrace like they've been apart for years, not minutes. The mother joins in. Stephanie finds comfort in Brad's arms.

When all have calmed, we are left in a near circle. Looking at each other, in a deafening question of what's next.

Chapter 9

Shifting in my arms alerts me awake. Oh god, what time is it?

I look at the small clock on the wall. It's fine. It's only been one hour. I calm my racing heart. I can shave that.

When I hear yelling I know what stirred him. The fighting is escalating. I slowly put my brother back into the crib. He stirs a little so I put my hand on his stomach. The little comfort helps him fall back to sleep.

I think about intervening, but what good would that do? The fighting stops suddenly with a slap of the door. I imagine Kendra getting mad, and retreating into their room then slamming the door behind her. There is silence for a moment. It doesn't last long as dad has decided to not let Kendra retreat. More yelling. A door slams louder.

I hear a door slam against a wall. I throw my book to the floor and frantically run out before I register fully that Kendra is screaming my name in bloody murder. "JAIDEN! JAIDEN! HELP ME!" She screams.

I run out, and see Kendra on the floor with dad standing above her. I panic. Running into the kitchen and reaching for the house phone. I barely pick it up when dad blows up behind me. "WHAT THE HELL DO YOU THINK YOU'RE DOING? GET INTO THE LIVING ROOM! NOW!" I put the phone down and turn to do as he said.

When I get in there, I help Kendra onto the couch. We cuddle in a cowering way, while he paces in front of us. He starts yelling at both of us.

I only hear a word here and there. I'm so frightened I can't comprehend the words coming out of his mouth. He's very loud. I get the idea that much of his shouting is his normal rhetoric. He is Him, and we need to respect Him. Shame on us for being so disrespectful towards him. Yada, yada, yada, yada.

I don't know who is shaking more; me, or Kendra. Sometime later, I register my baby brother is screaming. Neither of us moves to get him. We're scared about what dad would do if we move.

He eventually stops his rant. "Someone shut that fucking baby up or I will!"

We both take the chance to leave. I go downstairs, book largely forgotten; for now. I grab everything I'll need for my social project, and lug the oversized poster board into my bedroom. I turn off the lights and turn on a flashlight.

I get lost in a storm of doing my homework. The whole time I worry dad will come downstairs. I keep my ears listening for anything above me.

At six fifty-five am, I finish reading the last words in the book I retrieved a few hours ago. I can't believe even with working through work that I still spent all night on homework. For a moment it doesn't seem worth it. I should just not finish my homework, and become a bad student. I'll get to sleep, while I still pass this course, well as long as I get at least a forty percent on my final. Unfortunately, I can't do that. It would be more stressful for me to not do my homework than to continue with no sleep and no life. My people-pleasing perfectionism will not allow people to think lowly of me; I jab inwardly.

I start getting ready for school by changing my clothes.

I hear footsteps coming downstairs. I just barely get decent by pulling my tank top down as Dad opens up my door without knocking first. He comes inside and sits down on my bed. I stare at him. "Are you okay?" He says.

"Yes," I respond.

"What are you doing?"

"Getting dressed," I tell him point-blank.

"Don't you have more than three words for your dad?"

Are you serious? He asked me questions, and I answered them after he barged into my room while I was changing. I still am changing. He's abrasive as a person but his antics have gotten worse in the past year. "I'm sorry. I'm getting ready for school. I just need to brush my teeth, and comb my hair, pack up my school work, and I can walk to school."

"I will drive you today. When do you need to leave?" He asks.

"In fifteen minutes," I say. I don't have to be there for almost an hour, but I don't want to be here longer than have to.

"Alright, I will see you in fifteen minutes." He gets off the bed and goes back upstairs.

I finish getting ready and pack up my stuff, and project. I go upstairs with it all and pack everything into the car. The project only fits with a bit of a curve. Fifteen minutes have passed.

I go inside the house and wait at the door. I wait and wait. I raise my voice a bit so dad can hear. "I'm ready to go."

"Five minutes." He shouts from his bedroom.

Ten minutes go by. I talk to him again. "I have to talk to some teachers and drop off my project. I need to go soon or I'll be late."

He freaks out. "I am your father you will respect me. I will be ready when I am ready."

I go on the defence. "Sorry. I can just walk to school."

The voice booms back. "No! Get in the damn car. I'm driving you to school. I will be out in five minutes." I've made him angry now. I'm scared again. Last night's events are still very fresh in my memory.

I get into the car. I'm anxious. I have to wait for him to drive me to school. If I relax I will probably fall asleep.

I should move out. Logically, I can't. I still need to go to school. If I want to get anywhere in life I need to go to school. Jacob is my legal guardian, and I'm only fifteen. I can't do anything without him calling the cops. I could submit to emancipate myself.

No, I really couldn't. It would ruin his name, our family name. I'm a Kensington. You act a certain way. You do not mar the Kensington name. But, I'm not really a Kensington.

Maybe I could've left with Kendra. She took off last night with the baby. She didn't leave any notes or anything. When I went upstairs to grab my book I expected to find my brother in his crib, and Kendra sleeping in the rocking chair. I instead found nothing. She wasn't out in the living room, so I looked for her car and found it missing. The diaper bag was also gone. She left me.

My phone vibrates. Mary's name pops up at the top of the screen. I pull down the screen to view her message. *I'm going to be late today. See you at school.* Whoops. I forgot about letting her know I was leaving now. It doesn't matter now anyway.

Dad finally gets in the car. He drives me to school. He only speaks once we get there. "I'm glad that we're are able to make up so easily, and we have such a connection." He gets out and goes around the car. I get out to collect my project, but he grabs me and hugs me. I'm tense through the exchange. The only time he's affectionate is after fights or when he wants something. He kisses my cheek. I want nothing more at this moment than to get out of his embrace. I'm disgusted by his unwanted affection. "I love you. Have a great day." He goes back to the other side of the car.

I take out my project and bag. I tell him. "Have a great day at work. I love you too. Bye."

I walk into the school with my enormous project. Thankfully my social class isn't too far away. I walk into the classroom and interrupt my teacher's quiet time.

"Good morning. Do you mind if I leave this in here until class?"

"Oh my god, of course. Here, lean it against the whiteboard." She rushes over to help me with it. She guides it onto the rail for the whiteboard. "Wow. You really outdid yourself with this one." She studies the project. She reads some of the information and opens some of the clock flaps. We make small talk about the subject. I might as well get out all the information I know now; show her I know the material before I forget it all in the anxiety of presenting it to the entire class. "You know I'm part of the school committee. I would love to keep this project when you are done with it. I would love to present it as a prime example of my student's projects."

"Yes, of course. Thank you." I have no idea what I would do with it if she didn't take it off my hands. Well, no, actually I know what I would do with it. It would go into the trash. I don't need it. "Well," I say awkwardly. "I need to go talk to another teacher. I'll see you later. Have a great day." She echoes back the last sentence but is thoroughly distracted by my project.

I leave the classroom to exchange my books and get ready for Accounting. I go straight to that classroom next. The door should be open, and I can rehearse my speech for my social project.

I get there and sit down. I open up my speech notes and go over them. I am one of a few students in the room. The others are chatting, and working on their worksheets.

"Please evacuate the building. Leave everything where it is, do not go to your lockers, and go out the closest exit. Go home." My English teacher runs in, and out of the classroom; just staying long enough to say those words.

Neither my bag nor my locker has personal items in them, but they do have things for homework due. I grab my stuff from my desk, then my locker, and then I do as she says. I assume something bad is happening, but not entirely urgently so. The last time I was in an evacuation it was because one of my classmates had lit the boy's bathroom on fire.

The school is abuzz but no one seems to be in a hurry to leave the school; typical high school students. Everyone thinks it's nothing big, so they dawdle and socialize. I think a little panic might be worth telling people what is actually wrong.

In passing I hear, "Mr. Fisher found a bomb in a bathroom."

Picking up the pace, I leave the school through the closest exit with a racing heartbeat. I'm on the opposite side of the school to where I need to be to go home. I get to the sidewalk. I hope if a bomb does go off, that I might be far enough away so it doesn't hurt me.

My head spins. The rush must be enough to use up any reserves I had. I need food. Good thing I got groceries last night.

The bomb, if there is one, hasn't gone off yet. No police, ambulances, or firemen are here yet. They should be.

The time our furnace almost blew up, the entire city's police force, ambulances, and the fire department was at our house in a matter of two minutes from the start of our call.

Either they are dealing with something more important or, well there really isn't an 'or'. What's more important than a bomb threat in a high school? I don't want to go there. I'm probably not going to like the answer.

I make it to my house. Dad and Kendra's vehicles are gone. I can be home in peace for a little while. I get excited at that prospect. I won't have to placate him. I won't have to worry about the noise I make, or whether I'm annoying anyone with my existence.

The bomb threat was a good thing. For me, at least. I can be home alone, eat, shower, and sleep. But first, I don't want to get in trouble later.

I go inside and call Jacob. It goes to voicemail. I leave voicemails at all his contacts. I leave a note on the table; that way if he comes home without checking his phone he won't freak out as much.

I go for a shower downstairs. I take time to have a long, relaxing shower. When I get out the mirror is steamed. I don't remember the last time that happened. I don't remember the last time I could manage a shower for longer than a couple of minutes.

I comb my hair and settle into pyjamas, then put the phone on the charger. Finding my iPod, I put my earbuds in. I turn on my calming instrumental music and lay down in bed. It takes no time at all before I start nodding off.

Chapter 10

A slight murmur gets louder until it registers in my unconscious mind. The twinkle of a voice is unwanted after sleeping for less time than I would have wanted.

Grumbling my consciousness to the little girl, she comes over to me and crawls into the bed. Her slightly cooler body chills mine and wakes me up a little more.

"Good morning. How was your sleep?" My voice is scratchy and cracking. I don't need to open my eyes yet, so I don't.

"Good, how was your sleep?" Rayleen's cheerful voice chimes in. Unlike me, she sounds as if she's been up for at least a half-hour; wide awake and clear.

Opening my eyes wakes me up completely. "Good, what time is it?" I sit up slightly and the little girl wraps her arm around me. Her body is now warmer just as it becomes time for us both to get out of the bed. Rayleen's hug ends as quickly as it started.

"Seven-thirty." We both get up from the bed. I grab yesterday's pants off the floor; I put them on and change into another tank top.

"Okay, are you ready for school?" I ask her.

"Yep." Rayleen gives me her goofy grin.

Footsteps come down the stairs. Only a moment later Andy appears.

"Hey." His greeting is motioned towards both of us. "Rayleen you ready to go now?" She nods to him. "Kay, let's go then."

Rayleen turns around and hugs me. "Have a great day. You too,

Andy." I tell them both.

"Bye." Rayleen runs off in a sudden burst of energy and Andy follows after her.

I should be leaving soon; rather Darius will be here soon.

I go up the stairs, through the kitchen, and down the hall. I go to the washroom. Finding deodorant in the back of one of the drawers, I put it on and put it back. Right beside it is a toothbrush, I grab it next. The toothpaste on the counter looks safe enough, so I put it on the toothbrush and brush my teeth clean of the plaque. I rinse it off and put it back. Grabbing a ponytail off the counter, I pull my messy hair into a messy ponytail. I clean up and reapply my makeup.

I go to the living room to wait. Looking out the window I see Darius' truck waiting for me. Taking a quick breath in, I let it out slowly and go to the door.

Walking out of the house, I jog more than walk to the truck. A soft click signals the unlocking of the doors. I let myself in and settle into the seat.

Before I can get my buckle done up, I am slammed into the cushion by the force of the truck moving suddenly. The scenery rushes past.

"Good morning." I try to break the tension that has built up over a quick second.

"Morning." Darius sounds like he is in a grumpy mood. Nothing is said for the next couple of minutes. I can't think of anything to say to him. Looking out the window, I watch the two entrances to the parking lot pass.

"Skipping today?" I ask Darius, but I receive nothing back.

As he continues driving, I continue crossing places off my mental list: his house, Edmonton, and the mall. Darius drives the truck out of town. I watch the fields pass me by; the trees are empty of the yellow, orange, and red leaves that filled it only a month ago.

The road changes from the smooth pavement to a rocky dirt road as Darius turns onto a side road. I don't see anything I recognize.

The road veers off to the right revealing two buildings; a metal garage and a log house. There are no other vehicles here however, I see some movement in the window of the house.

The moment Darius shuts the vehicle off, the door to the house opens. About ten people walk out of the house. Darius opens the truck door and steps out. I take this as my queue to get out as well. Many eyes pin onto me as I touch the ground and close the door. The scrutiny makes me want to retreat into the truck.

Darius comes over to me and grabs my hand; my ears start ringing when as he pulls me behind him. The crowd of people part as Darius pulls me through them and towards the house.

He brings me into the house. We go through the kitchen, dining room, living room, and passed a black bear rug tacked to the ascending staircase wall.

At the top of the stairs are a seating area and a computer with all the furnishings. The table in the middle of the seating area has papers strewn about.

"Stay here. I'll be back. Don't leave this house for anything." Darius demands me to listen not just through his words but through a tone that promises harsh reprimand if not listened to.

Darius pulls me to him for a quick kiss. He releases me with a smirk on his lips. "Make yourself at home." He heads downstairs.

Looking over the railing I ask, "Wait, where are you going?"

Darius stops walking and looks up at me. "Just need to run a few errands." He continues walking until he disappears. Moments later, the door creeks open and shut.

A dull tick-tock of a huge grandfather clock times the seconds in the complete silence that surrounds me.

Deciding to look around the room I was placed in, I find a quaint country-styled office area; a few stuffed animal heads are placed on a couple of the expansive tall walls coming from the downstairs living room and dining room. The wooden railings before the drop down have many plants hanging from them; none are flower-producing plants.

The office space is relatively clean compared to the paper-covered table. There are only a few papers placed on the desk and the other clutter is neatly placed in normal office utensils.

Curiosity crosses my mind to learn more about whose place this is and why Darius brought me here. The thought to go through the papers tempts me enough to sit down on the brown leather love seat.

I scan a couple of sheets; jumping my focus side to side. There's a symbol on each of the sheets of paper; like a five-point star in a square, but there are extra lines.

Deducing the sheets to be plans or schematics for something, I try to look for further details. The things I can see and read don't make any sense.

Finding a few more pages brings it all together for me. The words warlocks, werewolves, vampires, and shamans remind me of some sort of a role-playing game or video game or something. Though, the thought of Darius playing any of those types of games seems strange; maybe the people who live here play it.

Weirdos. Darius wouldn't play something like that.

Happy with my conclusion, I move on to preventing my boredom. Who knows how long it will be until Darius comes back.

I get up off the couch and go over to the desk. The computer isn't turned on, so I find the tower in the drawer under the desk and press the power button. The fan starts up. I close the door and sit in the chair.

I look around the upstairs quickly while the computer takes a couple minutes to start up. There's a couple bedrooms and a bathroom up here as well.

The older computer works hard to pull up the desktop. I click on the internet. Minutes pass and the screen is still white. Sliding the mouse into the corner of the screen to the icon of two computers, I see an X. Scrolling over it reveals a pop-up telling me that the internet wasn't connected. Feeling slightly embarrassed that I didn't check that first, I click and exit the program.

Going to Plan B, I go into the games section of the programs. I choose solitaire. Playing, whether winning or losing, multiple games occupies me for, what feels like, hours.

I play until someone comes back through the door. I close the program and shut the computer down. Miles shows his face as he comes up to the last step. He looks like a wreck. His hair is as wild as his clothes. On further examination, his clothes seem to be ripped and dirty in places.

"What the hell happened to you?" I get up from my seat and walk up to him.

Miles looks down at himself. Holding his shirt away from his body he sees the dirt and rips. "Long story. I need you to come with me. I have to get you away from here." The serious tone and urgency in his tense body are enough to convince me, but it doesn't answer anything; it just raises more questions.

"Miles, what's going on? Why do I need to follow you?" He starts going down the stairs, so I follow him.

"I'll tell you after we get away from here, but not before then. There's too much to tell you right now, and we don't need delays or distractions." I accept his answer for now.

He leads me out the door and around the house. I take note that Darius' truck is still in the parking lot; still in the same place. Is he going to get mad at me for leaving? We go into the forest. There is a small path carved from frequent travel.

Miles starts picking up his pace, and soon I'm jogging to keep up with him. The moment I start closing the distance between us, he picks up the pace until I am in a full run.

Sounds soon get blocked out with the pounding of my feet hitting the ground in sync with my heartbeat. The cooler air is drawn in quickly and wreaking havoc on my lungs.

After a while of running, I start to slow my steps. I can't go on. "Miles," I call out to the male running in front of me. I slow enough to walk. He stops a lot quicker than I do. "I need to walk for a bit." I slow my breathing down and get it under control with deep breaths in and out. I don't even run like this in gym class.

"We shouldn't stop." Miles walks beside me with a sigh. "I guess, while you catch your breath, I can explain a few things." I look up to him and nod to queue him to start his tale. "I guess it was bound to happen eventually, but it shouldn't have come around like this. Everyone just has a lot more grudges than we thought and unfortunately, it has led to up-rises everywhere.

The dark ages were not like what you've heard, but a time when humans gained control over the supernatural. A treaty was made that the supernatural beings left would go into hiding amongst the humans. Over the years they've gotten sick of hiding, of being myths, so now they're revolting and plan to take the world back from the humans."

I look at him. Though he looks serious, I see it as all a part of the game I spied on earlier. It all makes sense now. A giggle slips through, then one more, until I can't hold in the laughter. He has a very odd sense of humour at times. My eyes close as I can't stop laughing. My eyes start leaking and my stomach's sides start hurting. Soon enough, I control myself and stifle the laughter.

Opening my eyes, I look to my right. The spot is empty. "Miles? Miles?" Confusion causes me to crease my eyebrows. "Oh, come on; I'm sorry. I didn't think you took your game so seriously. You could have just asked me to play along in the first place." There was no answer from the forest. "Miles?" Leaves crunch behind me causing me to turn quickly. The girl from the cafeteria is walking towards me. "Sandra... Right?" I hope I remember correctly.

She nods. "Come, let's leave the boys to their silly games."

I nod to her and follow her back to the house. The way back takes a lot longer than it took to get there. It seems all the longer with the silence between Sandra and me. Her entire body is tense and guarded. She doesn't seem to want to talk with me, so I don't bother trying to make small talk.

The shed stands out against the forest. It's the first sign we are coming closer to the house. Looking closer at the back, I see a window awkwardly placed across the back. I can't see anything from this far away but curiosity bubbles of what could be in there.

"Sandra?" I break our silent walk to ask her my question. She nods and I take this as my cue that she is listening to me. "What's in the shed?"

"The boy's toys." Her short answer settles enough of my curiosity to not ask her more. My mind goes off into what kind of toys they might have: motorcycles, quads, and tractors perhaps. As we come to the door of the house Darius comes out.

"You weren't supposed to leave the house. It's dangerous out there." He looks angry.

I decide to get my apology in now before he says more. "I'm sorry. We just-"

"We? Who's we?" He looks over to Sandra as if he is accusing her.

Sandra answers him, "Miles. We caught him."

Darius looks like he's going to say something but he stops himself and neither talks for moments after. His expression turns more and more furious the longer the silence holds.

Finally, his face loosens to his normal stern expression. "Go inside." He moves out of the way.

Sandra walks through the door first. I follow after her and Darius closes the door behind us. I follow Sandra through the kitchen and into the living room. She goes down an adjoining hall, and I move to follow after her, but Darius guides me to sit down on the couch.

He sits on the footrest in front of me. "Why did you leave the house with Miles?"

I feel like I will be in trouble no matter what I say. "He asked me to go with him. He told me about the game you're all playing and then he just disappeared."

"Game?" He looks surprised. "What game?"

Now, I'm confused. He looks like he doesn't know anything; or he's pretending. "Whatever role-playing game he's playing. Something about supernaturals uprising against humans."

"Right." He stands up and stands over me. "You're never seeing Miles again."

"What?" Is this part of it? "What are you talking about? You can't do that!" I stand partially up straight before being knocked down; the left side of my face stings. Lifting my hand to my eye, I try to assess the damage, but touching it makes it hurt more.

"I'm sorry, but you made me do it. You have to listen to me. I know what's best for you. Miles is trouble. He's going to get you hurt." Darius reaches out to me and pulls me up onto my feet. He wraps his arms around me. "I'm sorry. You have to do what I say. I'm trying to protect you. Now stay here, I have something to take care of."

I can't say anything and he just leaves. This time I hear a sliding click of a deadbolt. I fall to the couch and sit almost completely proper. All this for some stupid game?

Then my head falls, and tears start burning in my eyes. The tears burn my eyes but don't dare to fall. I sit there for a moment nothing entering or leaving my mind; the moment just plays in cycles over and over in a never-ending movie. Soon enough key parts bold themselves and edit out the other parts. Eventually, the only thing I hear is his apology.

Getting up and off the couch, I walk heavily up the stairs. The room directly to the right is the washroom. I walk into the darkroom and turn on the light. Closing the door behind me and locking it. Going to the counter, I lean in close to look at my quickly swelling and discolouring face.

The dam in my eyes breaks and tears roll down my cheeks. The girl in the mirror's face scrunches up in pain. A weight holds down on my chest. I hold my breath when a noise dares to try to escape, and let it go in a shaky exhale.

Looking in the mirror bubbles up more and more tears. Having enough of crying, I look away from the mirror. Grabbing some toilet paper, I blow my nose and flush it down the toilet.

Swallowing the lump in my throat, consequently, lifts the weight on my chest.

Once calmed down enough, I dare to look into the mirror. The tears don't threaten to fall again, so I take a piece of toilet paper and run it under the tap for a moment. I wring out most of the water then open it up a little. Dabbing my face with the paper, I clean up the running makeup. Making sure to keep most of my makeup on, I make myself presentable.

The purple swelling around my eye has stabilized.

Deciding to look for something to cover it, I look in the drawers and cabinets hoping for some makeup. The top drawer on the right-hand side opens to reveal all the makings of a makeup kit. I set to work covering up my face.

Satisfied with the quick cover-up job, I put the makeup back in the drawer and wash it off my hands. Part of me is hoping that the person who owns the makeup won't notice. The other part knows that there isn't a way they would know.

I fill my lungs and purse out my lips on the exhale. Shaking my head in the mirror; I almost break down again.

Finally noticing my feet are on something squishy. I look down to the fully carpeted floor and all somber feelings leave me. That's weird. Why would you carpet a bathroom? How old is this house?

Unlocking the door, I take another look in the mirror, before opening the door.

I get taken aback when Sandra is waiting right on the other side. She looks me in the face. Her blue and orange eyes dart from the left of my face to my eyes. A slight twitch of her face; she's trying to hold back an expression of some sort.

Consciously, I turn my head slightly so that the left side of my face is less visible to her. I think she knows anyway.

Maybe the makeup is hers. No, the foundation is too light for her.

"Come," Sandra orders me. "You're hungry. Let's go get food."

As we go down the stairs, her hair moves back and for a moment I see a slight discolouring of the left side of her neck. Brown hair covers it again and the purple disappears from my sight; maybe it was a trick of the lighting.

We walk through the living room and dining area, before stopping in the kitchen.

Sandra sets to work on pulling a bunch of food out of the fridge: bread, lettuce, ham, mustard, tomato, mushrooms, cheese, and mayonnaise. She puts everything on the counter next to the fridge. The brunette pulls out two plates from the cabinet above her. I help her make us a couple of sandwiches.

Sandra takes both plates over to the table and places one on each side; taking her seat on the other side. I sit down at the empty meal place.

Despite my hunger, I hesitantly pick up the sandwich; eating the food slowly.

Three-quarters of my sandwich is gone when I notice Sandra is looking intently behind me. I set the sandwich down and turn to look over my shoulder. I hope it's not Darius.

Ram is walking towards us. He reaches the table and stops beside me. "How are you lovely ladies on this beautiful day?" The male pulls the chair out from the table and sits on it beside me.

"Good," Sandra answers his question first.

"Good," I answer him back so I don't seem rude. Looking away from him, I turn my attention back to what is left of my sandwich. I take a bite. I don't feel much like talking.

"So, I heard you're new here. That you only showed up a couple of months ago. Where did you come from before that?" Ram seems to have other ideas than letting me eat the rest of the sandwich in peace.

I finish chewing my sandwich and swallow the rest of the food in my mouth.

"Pretty much everywhere in the area. I've been in a lot of different foster houses for the past four years; just waiting until I turn eighteen this year." I tell him.

Ram looks surprised. "Why are you in the foster system?"

I tell him the same rehearsed story everyone gets. "My family died in a plane crash four years ago. My niece and I stayed home from the adult-only vacation. On the way there, the plane had crashed. There weren't any family members that wanted to take us, so we were put in the system. We've been lucky that most places haven't split us up."

Ram stays silent for a moment. Regretful for accidentally saying the wrong thing; just like everyone else when I tell them. "I'm sorry. I didn't mean to bring that up."

"No, it's alright. It happened a long time ago." I shoot a smile at him to make him feel better.

Ram smiles back. "So, how old is Rayleen?"

I don't remember telling him her name. Maybe someone else had mentioned it; Darius maybe. "Five." I remember her birthday is going to be right away; so, I add, "almost six."

"Ah, she's just a baby. They're so innocent at that age. Is she in school yet?" He asks.

"Yeah, she's really enjoying it. Well, more the socializing part;

typical girl already." I smile at memories of how she always chats about the people in her class, but never about what she's learning.

Ram chuckles. "She might be a handful when she gets older, but if she turns out anything like you, then she'll be alright."

"Oh, I hope she doesn't turn out like me. That's what I'm trying to avoid." I say honestly.

Ram sits down. "I don't think it would be so bad. You've seemed to have turned out okay. You're not in jail or into drugs, at least, and in today's society that's great."

"I guess so." I turn the conversation away from me, uncomfortable with the topic. "But, what about you? Where are you from?"

"I've been all over the world travelling for years. But, I guess you can say that I'm from Northern Africa. I can't remember exactly where, but I was brought to Egypt when I was young. That's actually how I met Sandra. I stayed with her family for a while." He trails off; telling me there is more to the story.

I try to pry a bit. "Really? Did your parents know hers?"

Ram shakes his head. "No. My parents didn't come with me. Her parents took me in because mine were gone at the time."

"So, you're like a foster child too then," I question.

Ram chuckles. "Not really, but I guess you could call it that."

I hesitate for a moment. "So, if you don't mind my asking, what happened to your parents?"

"They gave me up. I guess because they couldn't take care of me. But, they did eventually come for me." He smiles at the end of his sentence.

Sandra stands up abruptly. Her hands thump on the table and the chair screeches unnecessarily. "You know you might as well tell her what really happened if you're going to get all buddy-buddy with her." She narrows her gaze in on me. "You're playing in dangerous waters, my dear." Sandra looks back at Ram. "And you most of all. You know what will happen when they find out you're in love with a vampire's toy."

I don't know what I've done to upset her. Maybe she thinks Ram and I are flirting. Is she jealous? Are they dating and she's that type of girlfriend?

"Sandra, go take your chill pill," Ram says with an edge of a threat. The brunette runs up the stairs. A door slams moments later. "Don't worry about her too much." Ram pulls my attention back to him. "She has moments. Over the years she's developed some issues but if you've seen as many things as she has over the past five thousand years you probably would too." He hushes his voice. "Don't tell her, but I think she's jealous of you. She's had a bit of a crush on Darius the last seventy years."

"You guys are really into that fantasy game, eh? So, Darius plays a vampire? No offence but he's never seemed like the type to play role-playing games." I try not to offend.

Ram stares at me for a moment. He jumps out of his chair and rushes towards me.

I get out of the chair and try to distance myself. He stops. "Darius hasn't told you anything, has he? What was he thinking? We need to go upstairs. We'll explain everything."

Curious, I follow him upstairs. We don't stop at the games sheets. Ram goes up to knock on a door. "Sandra, open up." The door opens up. Ram pulls me inside and places me between the two of them. Sandra sits on her bed. "Darius hasn't said a word to her about anything. She knows nothing. Like, nothing nothing."

"Well, I guess that would explain a couple of things." Sandra walks up from her bed. She comes over to us both. Sandra pulls out a knife from her side.

I try to back up, but I walk into something hard.

Looking over my shoulder, I recognize the black t-shirt Ram was wearing. His arms come up to hold me in place. Looking back at Sandra I see the knife has disappeared from her hand. In its place, is a deep-coloured substance. Sandra comes up and in one movement my vision is covered, her blood is dripping down my face, and her other hand holds my head in place.

Trying to rip my head away from her, I whip my head from side to side. Ram's arms hold me in place; my struggling does not affect him.

My head starts feeling light and disorientated. My legs try to give out and I feel like doubling over.

Nothing.

Darkness.

A flash of bright light, as bright as coming out of a theatre at high noon on a summer day, blinds me. As the light fades gradual lines become silhouettes, and silhouettes become shapes and figures. Soft lights line the hallway.

My vision is moving down. I try to stop moving, but I don't. My legs will not stop. My head and line of vision change without my wanting to. It's surreal to be moving, but not be able to control any of my movements; like being trapped in a dream and knowing you are asleep. Without the ability to do anything about it, I let the body do what it wants to.

Looking within the line of vision, I search for details on my surroundings; trying to figure out where I am and what is going on. The creamy white walls stretch high and long.

Coming in and out of various doors are people and things. People and some of the things are dressed in modern-day outfits. The things look like monsters and mutated humans. I feel as though I am on a set for a movie, or at some high-budget Halloween party.

We come to a grand door that others have been disappearing behind. Arms, that aren't mine, come out and push the left door handle. The door opens into the room. Hordes of people are packed into the hall.

Weaving in and around people slowly allows us to progress through the crowd. The destination seems to be the stage in the front. The closer I get, the more I can see. On the stage are several royal-looking tall chairs.

I stop progressing closer. The view moves to look at Darius.

"You made it; just in time." He seems relieved and excited all in one. A smile that lights up his face in an unusual way, one I've never seen.

"Yeah, long story." Sandra's voice surrounds me. I hear it in both my ears and in my head; as if Sandra's voice came out of me, "Did I miss anything?" Am I in Sandra's body?

Darius shakes his head, "Nothing yet. Everyone I've talked to is in agreeance."

"Miles and Shale?" Sandra asks specifically.

His smile disappears, "Shale's with us. Miles will come around eventually. There's no other way." Darius turns to look at the stage. His posture is stiff and he seems agitated now.

"Darius…" The last letter drags.

"Leave it alone, Sandra." He pauses for a moment and looks over his shoulder. "They're coming."

The crowd jumps alive. Growing hollers, shouts, and roars arise all around; giving courage to others to do the same. In moments, the whole room is almost unbearable to stand in. I wish I could move so I can cover my ears. Before I can think it couldn't get any louder, it does.

Looking at the stage, I find two regal men sitting on the chairs. The one on the left I recognize. He's the creepy man that spoke to Darius at the football game.

I try to get a better look at him. His deep blue-black hair is tied in a low ponytail at the base of his neck. Ears come to a slight point adding to the other pointed, almost lined features on his face. His white shirt is partially open in the front showing off some of his angry-looking tattoos. The dark images cause a tint in shades under parts of the white shirt. The cut of the shirt falls along his chiselled form. His hand is gripped around the handle of a sword in a deep red sheath.

The other male looks over the growingly agitated crowd with a disgusted sneer. Amber eyes scan the crowd looking for something, or rather, someone. More casually dressed than the other male on the stage; they however share the same style. His nose upturns and nostrils flare the moment before a door to the left opens.

The crowd parts as a salt and peppered-haired man makes his way to the stage. He climbs the stairs and nods to greet both males on the stage. The man takes a spot on the chair in between them.

Before I can take a good look at the new arrival, a light shines behind me and my head turns. The light gains intensity as it nears the window high above. Red hues take their place on every crook in the room. Black envelopes my vision when the light gets to be too much to handle.

A crack of light enters my vision; it quickly shuts. A moment later the crack reopens, this time not stopping until the eyes are completely open. The red hue has dimmed.

My vision is turned to the stage once more, and the red light takes a form on top. Standing there is a body shape with giant fiery wings. Red intensifies for only a moment before cracking and spilling like lava around the form; gaining a solid shape as time goes on.

Deep red heels form the base of long flowing legs. A short black pencil skirt and blazer dress the body. Red accents all the edges on the suit. A ruby dangles from a black chain around her slender neck. Ruby lips form the serious look on her face. Eyes flash from red to orange and yellow matching the flame on her black hair.

She looks to her left at the male with the tattoos. Turning elegantly, she glides to the tall chair behind her and sits down. The three males follow suit. When the last of them settle in their seat, the room goes quiet.

The acoustics of the room allow the thick voice to surround everyone. The Russian accent is affected by an English influence; in the man with long hair framing his face. "We know of the unrest among many of the immortals and supernatural beings. We know some believe it is a good idea to return to the ancient ways; to rule the world and the humans. We are standing up here to tell you that this is a horrible idea."

The crowd roars in protest as he continues to shout. "It can never return to the old ways. The humans have advanced and have grown in numbers that far outreach our own. Those were the main reasons we lost the war and would be the reasons you would fail now. It's pure stupidity to rebel and break our treaty now. Those who would do this, would not have the support of every being.

You can't break the treaty because this new generation holds onto pride, have over-glorified lives, and are complete brats. You would be ending all that you know and squashing all the accomplishments your ancestors have been making since the treaty was made."

"Why can't we live with the humans in our natural forms?" A question is shouted clearly above the rest of the noise.

A strong feminine voice answers. "It wouldn't happen. The humans have lived so long without the truth; they would be scared and hunt us down. It would start a war. We should learn from the past. A pre-emptive attack would catch them off guard and we'd be able to kill or capture most of the humans. Give them no chance to retaliate."

The tattooed man next to her stands up. "Many races are in danger of being extinct. I say, we rise and take what should have always been ours." He pumps his fist into the air, and the majority of the crowd follows as they cheer.

The other two men look at each other with a look mixed with shock and desperation. They get up from their seats and the older man steps toward the male and female. "Seth, Aalayah, you can't be serious?"

Seth smirks. "Dear old James, you can't imagine exactly how serious we are. Either you're with us or you are our enemy. What do you say?"

James looks back to the male behind him. He nods and speaks. "I guess this means we are enemies now."

Seth rushes them as James grabs the shoulder of the man behind him. They both vanish through a set of doors.

His smirk of a smile never leaves his face as he turns, first to look at Aalayah, then to scan the crowd. Seth's arms rise. "Let's begin." He lowers his arms. "First, anyone who wishes to follow James and Niklas, you may leave now without repercussion. Just know you will be killed if you ever get in our way."

The crowd looks around. One person leaves, and this empowers a couple more to do the same.

Once the few have left, Seth speaks again, "Our best chance at this is for everyone all over the world to unite and attack all at once. Three days. Today we plan, tomorrow we travel and ready our forces, and the day after we reclaim our world all at once; taking down everyone who stands in our way.

We will never let humans rule our world again. We will hide no more."

My eyes open. I must've fallen asleep. An itching tickle jolts my hand to my face. Scratching around and rubbing my eyes causes something to clump. Makeup, I sigh inwardly. I'll have to redo it.

The sensation leaves after a moment. Rolling from my back to my side, I put my arm under my head as a pillow and bring my legs closer to my chest. Taking a brief look to find my clock, it isn't where it is supposed to be. Looking at my surroundings, I find an entirely different room. A silhouette across the room.

Chills creep like spiders up my spine. I pull myself to a sitting position and scoot backward. Memories surge forward.

"I'm an ancient priestess. You might call me a witch. My blood allowed you to see a memory from a couple of days ago.

Seth has since raised an army, and we're taking over. It's been twelve hours since the rebellion started and we're getting closer to having complete control. Demons have split into two sides; those who want things to stay the same and those who want change.

Darius is in charge of this region, and so far, everything has gone according to his plan. Well, except for Miles trying to kidnap you, but Darius is taking care of him." Sandra gets up in a fluid motion and walks over to the bed. I bolt for the open door.

I skip steps down the stairs. I watch for Ram but don't find him. Running through the kitchen, I go to the front door and exit the building.

The heart beats in my ears, thud louder than any other noises around me. I bypass the vehicles, knowing they are likely locked and the keys are nowhere near.

My legs take me to the forest. Maneuvering around branches, rocks, and bushes, I get about ten meters into the forest before I dare to look behind me.

Ram comes out of the house searching. I run behind the shed for cover. The darkness flows around me. A door and a window are in front of me. Before deciding to go through the door I pick up a corner on the tarp-covered window.

Soft light highlights my face. Pulling back, my eyes focus on the show inside. Miles is chained from the ceiling; blood oozes from wounds on his naked back. Horrified by the image, I freeze. Darius comes from behind Miles. A bleeding knife is held in his hand.

My body jumps, as does my mind, as a hand is placed on my shoulder. I gulp down a breath of air. Turning around quickly I don't recognize the two creatures. "Hello, Princess. You'll be coming with us, now." The one closest to me grabs me around my shoulders and under my legs. The ground pulls away and my stomach jumps to my throat, as the male pulls me with ridiculous speed.

The next time I feel the ground is in front of the shed. The other gentleman opens the door. My shoulder gets pushed, and I am shoved through the door into a crowded room.

Those in the room stop what they are doing, as I regain my balance. Darius comes away from Miles and closer to me. The glistening knife in his hand is lowered to his side.

"Alexa, how nice of you to join us. I heard Sandra showed you things. So, you must understand why we have to do this. It's us against them and we must punish those who try to steal you away from me to kill you." Darius tries to reason with me.

Sandra showed me practically nothing, but it did open my eyes to the possibilities of there being more to the world. "Miles wouldn't kill me. He's our friend. How could you do this to him?" I say as more of a whisper than at the level I want to.

"How could we do this to him, you mean? And he's our enemy now. He knew what it meant when he chose the wrong side of this war. Our friend is now our enemy. That's just the way it works." Darius walks towards me and sticks out his unoccupied hand. I hesitantly slip my hand into his, afraid of what might happen if I don't. The air is thick with danger.

Guided by his hand, he leads me to Miles. Stopping a meter away, I see the gruesome treatment Miles has survived through. Tears are brought to my eyes at the sight of him. Then, they are brought to my eyes for a different reason; pain in my hand as it's crushed in Darius' grip. I'll do what I have to to survive.

He lets my hand go. Bringing my hand into my other, I rub it to soothe the ache still there. Darius steps up to Miles, blocking my view of the strung-up male. Miles gargles a yelp in pain.

Darius moves out of the way. He turns and brings his hands up to Miles' head. One hand fixes on the top of his head and the other under his chin with the blade. "Look at her Miles." Struggling his eyelids flutter then open; pain-stricken eyes look at me. "You will never touch what's mine; ever again. She is on our side and she isn't leaving; she isn't leaving me. And, I will prove it to you."

He looks at me. "Miles was going to take you away. He would have held you over my head and would have killed you to get to me. This is a different world now, and you're going to have to get used to it. You're going to be changed and be my queen. You will have to get used to old friends being your enemies now. They will try to kill you the first chance they get.

Now you're going to have to do something for me to prove you can handle this. You're going to have to cut him." I can feel the colour fade from my face. Backing up slightly, I bump into something large and squishy. Looking behind me, and up, I look at the single eye of the massive being. "You don't have to kill him. Just make a tiny cut." Darius catches my full attention again. "He would do the same to you."

But, he wouldn't. My heart lurches forward, "I-I, no. I can't."

Darius' face flashes in anger in only a moment. Letting go of Miles, he is in front of me immediately. He looks me in the eyes intensely. "You will cut him." The voice I hear isn't what I'm used to coming from his lips.

He hands me the knife. Darius nods to me and moves out of my way, so I have a clear view of Miles.

I step forward. Once I'm within arm's reach of Miles, I take one more half step closer.

My hand reaches out towards Miles. Finding a bare spot on his stomach, I hold the knife there for a moment. A tear rolls down the side of my face. I mouth the word 'sorry' to him, as I ensure the knife cuts a shallow horizontal groove. More tears fall as the knife leaves his skin.

The moment the knife is a safe distance away, I drop it to the ground. My heart pounding from what I've just done to him.

Turning around, I jump as Darius' chest is suddenly in my face. I look up at him, tears rolling down my cheeks.

"Don't worry about it. It'll get easier. I'm proud of you." He looks diagonal over my shoulder. "Take her to the house. I'll be there in a minute."

Hands come from both sides of me to grasp my arms. Darius moves out of their way as the two gently push me to the front of the shed. They guide me through the door. I try to struggle enough just to get out of their grasp. Their grips get tighter and tighter.

Giving up, I walk straight towards the house. Taking a deep breath in and out, I try to relieve the pain in my chest. Tears continue to stream down my face uncontrollably. When we near the house, one of the guys lets go of me and walks ahead. He opens the door for me to walk through. Neither of them comes inside, letting the door shut behind me.

Standing at the front door feels awkward. I walk to the living room, making sure I don't see Ram or Sandra. Sitting on the couch, I wait. I don't know what else to do.

Silence allows the past few minutes to run through my mind. Thinking of cutting Miles sickens me; bile rising in my throat. It's different from any feeling I get when I cut myself. Whimpers and cries sound with my tears for the first time, finally being allowed to pass through. Drawing my legs up onto the couch, I lie down and hug my legs to my chest.

After moments, my tears dry up and won't fall anymore. My mind becomes blank and I sit up. Trying to breathe through my nose fails, as it is stuffed from crying. So, once standing up, my goal becomes finding a tissue.

Not wanting to go to the upstairs washroom, in fear of running into Sandra or Ram, I go to the kitchen to find a paper towel. On the counter near the stove is a roll of paper towels. Ripping a sheet off the roll, I blow my nose and toss the dirty tissue in the garbage under the sink.

Walking back to the couch, I sit on it. The moment I do, I hear the door open. Darius comes into view a moment later.

Standing up at the sight of him, I wait for him to give me a signal. He walks over to me and wraps his built arms around me; embracing me. I stand there idly only moving to position my head more comfortably against his rock-hard chest.

"I'm so proud of you, Love. You, are truly fit for this life." Darius pushes me slightly back so he can see my face. "And for that, I am going to give you a present. You'll want to wash your face first.

Sandra's blood is still all over you."

The goop I had scratched earlier, wasn't make-up, it was blood.

I rush to the bathroom to witness it for myself. Surface dried and crusted blood make for a nightmare of a reflection. The blood had pooled around my eyes, before falling like tears down my cheeks. My actual tears cleared away little of the tracks; here and there. The hand towel repurposes into a face cloth; to wipe away the horror.

Redoing my makeup helps me regain a moment of normality. It gives me a pause to recollect myself from the horrors of the last hour.

I return downstairs when I can do no more to waste time.

In a swift movement, I am picked up and placed in front of Darius. A slight pain from the moment of pressure causes my face to scrunch up a bit. His lips pushed to mine, his tongue forced inside my mouth, pushing aside the first pain. Darius pulls away as suddenly as he started. I'm twisted around to face the other direction.

"Sandra, you can bring her in now." He orders.

Small, quick footsteps are followed by larger, more drawn-out ones. A tiny red-haired girl comes flying around the corner. My heart drops at the sight of her.

"Rayleen!" Tears threaten to drop from my eyes once more. Crouching down to her level, I swoop her into a tight hug.

"Alexa, you're squishing me." On her words, I loosen my grip just a little. Standing at my full height, I examine the girl in my arms; making sure she has not one scratch on her. I sigh in relief when she doesn't appear to have been hurt at all. I look into her beautiful eyes.

"Guess what?" She asks me.

I know she won't continue until I ask her. "What?"

"I have a baby." Her smile stretches from ear to ear.

"You do?" I look at her in confusion. That is about the last thing I could have guessed she would have said.

"Yep." She turns as much as she can. "Sandra, what's it called again?"

"A griffin." Looking at Sandra, I finally notice the creature in her arms. A golden, grey, and white coloured creature sits balanced over

Sandra's forearm.

"And, Sandra helped me name her Crystal," Rayleen tells me.

Sandra sets the creature onto the floor. Crystal reaches her paws out and stretches like a feline. She comes closer to us. Rayleen struggles, so I let her down. The redhead walks over to the creature. Bending over to pick her up, Crystal jumps into her arms. Rayleen stands up and shifts her arms to get a better hold on her new pet. She turns to face me and comes closer.

Crystal looks like what the legends say a griffin should look like. She has a head of an eagle and a body of a lion; though miniature in size due to her age. At her size, the lion part of her looks like a body of a cat with oversized paws.

Fine feathers starting at her feline ears become finer and slowly form into short golden fur down her back. On her sides, tucked into her, are two feathered wings. Her tail tucks around her as she brings her beak around to tug at the tuff on her hair at the end. The griffin lets go of her tail and looks at me. Her ocean-blue eyes look into mine.

Opening her beak, a noise escapes; something between a squeak and a roar chimes into my ears.

Rayleen gives a short giggle. "That means she likes you. You wanna hold her?"

I look between Rayleen and Crystal. The creature seems too surreal to touch right now. "I'll hold her later."

Crystal makes the noise again, but it is slightly deeper this time.

She jumps from Rayleen's arms and runs to me; walking her front paws up to my legs. Her claws bite lightly into my skin. Bending over, I bring my hand down to Crystal's level. My hand flinches as the griffin moves her beak against it. She leans her head in to hint that she would like me to rub her head.

Her hairs are soft and thick. Using one finger, I scratch the side of her head. Strands of feathers feel stiffer; like stroking a finger through a hairbrush.

Crystal backs off my leg and turns towards Sandra.

The door to the outside opens. Shale appears to stand behind

Sandra. "Miles is gone. Kelly's scent was all over the area. They disappeared into the forest." I'm flooded with relief.

"Sandra, take Alexa and the child upstairs for the night." He turns to me. Grabbing my arm, he squeezes hard. "Don't leave the house, until I come for you."

He lets go of my arm after I nod my understanding to him. He's gone in a split second with nothing more than a slight breeze in his place. The door slams not a moment later.

Sandra bites her lower lip. Her face softens as she looks down at Rayleen. "Come on, Rayleen. How about we go upstairs and I'll tell you more stories." A motherly tone coats her voice. I'm wary of her after what happened earlier.

"Yeah!" Her voice gets loud in her excitement.

The woman smiles. "Alright then. Well. Shall we go up to my room then? Alexa, would you like to join us?"

Hesitantly, I agree to go; if only to make sure Rayleen is safe. Rayleen has already started running up to Sandra's room; apparently, she has been there, at least, once before. The griffin follows as a dog would.

Going into Sandra's room, I find Rayleen snuggled up under the covers on the bed. She made herself at home real fast. Crystal starts to rub into Rayleen.

"Come sit with me." Rayleen scoots a bit over. I sit beside her. The redhead leans against my side and I put my arm around her. I rub her back while Sandra sits at the foot of the bed. "Can I hear more about the princess?"

Sandra smiles, "Of course you can. What do you remember about the princess; so we can get Alexa caught up to speed?"

Rayleen looks up at me. "She's a princess. She looks like Sandra. She has orange eyes and brown hair just like her. And she lives in somewhere that's like a huge sandbox and there are rock buildings everywhere."

"Egypt, she lives in Egypt." Sandra lightly corrects Rayleen; holding back irritation. "She lives in a grand palace with a view of the Nile from her bedroom."

The little griffin plops down against Rayleen's side.

"Yeah, and she has lots of people around her doing everything she wants them to. She has a daddy and a mommy and other mommies too. And she has lots of brothers and sisters and a friend in her castle. She's got lots of pets too; like big cats, birds, and owls. Oh, and people made a big thing out of stone that looks over everyone." Rayleen is excited about the details she remembers.

"A statue. I think that's enough. I think she gets the picture now. Thank you, Rayleen. You did a great job; you remembered so much." Mostly orange eyes look into Rayleen's. "How about I tell you about how she met her best friend and the mischief they used to get into?"

Rayleen nods her head into my side. I feel her mouth open in a big yawn.

I smile at her. Stifling a giggle, I ask her, "Sweetie, are you going to be able to stay awake for the story?"

"Mmhmm," Her tired answer tells me she will probably fall asleep soon after the story starts. I look to Sandra and nod to her.

Sandra closes her eyes. "The princess was just a little girl, about seven years old when her father told her they would be getting new staff that day."

Double imagery lays over my eyes. I close them to shake and rub away whatever it is that clouds my vision.

Like the memory earlier, I see a perfect picture of what Sandra describes. This is different than before; more pleasant. There is no panic and no blood. I'm well aware of the memory taking over.

Opening my eyes works, but proves to be disorientating. I close them again and watch the memory.

Sandra speaks over the background noise. Describing what I see and providing translation, but she leaves some out in the version she speaks; likely for simplicity and Rayleen's sake. I fill in the blanks.

A male in his mid-twenties sits on a golden chair in front of a crowd of women and children. Weaving her way through the people, she tries to get a better view of her father.

"New workers will be arriving today. They are from far away. They do not speak our language but will know basic words so they can do

as we say. If they don't do as you say, inform one of the guards and they will take care of them. You are dismissed." He waves everyone off with one small movement of his hand.

One of the women takes the princess's hand. She is led out of the room and down a hall.

Rich colours adorn the room they go into. Colours are everywhere; paintings, fabrics, clothing.

The courtyard has a few of the other children playing already. Looking to the sides she sees a few darkly coloured people she had never seen before.

One boy catches her eye; he looks to be her age. His skin is dark with a reddish hue and he stands out even among the other slaves around him. She faintly hears her name being called. Breaking her view of the male, she searches around for the one who called her. One of her sisters is calling her to play with her and the others.

They play a game dancing in a circle around one of the princess' sisters until they were all dizzy. Picking up a papyrus ball they start running and tossing it to each other. Laughter brightens the whole courtyard. One by one some of the other children start to play other games, do each other's hair, and eat snacks.

The ball gets tossed over her head and into a hallway. "I'll get it." She jogs into the hall.

Going past a couple of people she tries to find where the ball had gotten to. Going around a corner she finds the boy from earlier. "Hi." She waits for him to say something; he doesn't. "What's your name? I'm Sakhmet." The princess points to herself when she says her name; hoping he will get what she meant. He looks at her confused. She points to herself again. "Sakhmet"

She points to him and tilts her head to the side.

He just continues to look at her. Giving up, she starts looking for the ball again. Before she gets past him he mutters something, "Raamiz."

She looks him in the eyes. He tries to look down at the ground under her gaze. Lifting his chin, she repeats his name as she misunderstands it, "Ramses."

A woman calls her name; she recognizes the voice as her mother's. Leaving the ball where it may have landed she leaves the boy to go to her mother."

Warmth rolls away from my side. Rayleen curls up facing away from me. I pull the blanket up to her chin. Looking back to Sandra, I find her eyes open. It explains the singular vision. I don't want story time to be over yet.

"So what happened to you and Ram next?"

She shrugs and shakes her head. "I didn't see him much for the next year or so. But when I did finally see him, it rocked me. Maybe I knew he was supposed to be important in my life.

Shortly after he had arrived, he was sent to go work with the labourers working on my father's tomb. When I saw him, he wasn't the same boy I knew. He was forced to grow up before he should have. It was normal back then.

In those times it didn't matter your age, if you were a labourer, your life was to serve, and if you couldn't do what they wanted when they wanted, you were severely punished.

The work itself was gruelling and dangerous. He has many scars covering his body from that one year alone.

It was the night of the fires that I saw him next." Sandra closes her eyes, so I follow her lead.

After dressing, two ladies sit me down. One starts to comb my wet hair and the other mixes together my makeup. Braids are affixed into my hair after it is combed thoroughly. My makeup is applied with careful hands.

Faint screaming echoes quietly into the room. The noise is unlike the cheerful screams of childish joy I am used to. One of the adults to my side tenses; the other does the same when she looks in the same direction.

The one woman walks away from me. Looking over in the one direction I see why; Ram is standing near the opening to the baths covered in a dark liquid.

When the woman gets to him she speaks something to him that I can't understand. He answers her in the same language. She brings him over to us.

"We have to go. We are being attacked." The woman speaks with a heavy accent, but the sentiment of the sentence is still striking to a child's heart.

The woman, still behind me, rushes to the room Ram just came out of. "Stop!" The woman reaches out as if this may stop the other woman, but it is useless. I blink and that woman is gone. Left alone with Ram and the other woman, I wonder what I am to do; should I go find my family?

A rough small hand grabs mine. His voice is just as rough, "Come." I look to him and then to the woman. She looks worried, but then she extends her hand to me. I get up off my seat.

The woman walks over to the opening in the wall. She hurries back over to Ram and me. She speaks to Ram and then to me, "We run, be silent."

The lady runs towards the opening furthest away from the baths. Ram gently pulls me to follow after her. I lose sight of her for a just a moment. Long enough to worry about losing her.

With the grip on my hand, I run faster than I ever have. Catching the woman again, she seems to have slowed down. She looks behind her and speeds up once she sees us there.

Twisting down different halls, of various lengths, to follow the woman; hopefully to safety. Each time we pass an open area, I cringe as I see more and more buildings destroyed. Spots of orange and yellow pop up everywhere, as the smell of smoke, fills my nose.

We follow the woman down a long length of the hallway. When she goes around corners we don't see her for ten counts at a time. She's always looking behind her to be sure we are still following.

She rounds the next corner and a shrill scream sounds from her. Ram stops us in our place. He swings me against the wall and puts his finger to his lips.

I hear a male's voice but can't hear more than a murmur. Something makes a swift whoosh while through the air. Closely followed is a thud and then a rolling noise.

Ram pulls me back the way we came.

Two hallways back and he stops again. He lets go of my hand and jumps up onto the edge of the half wall. I try to get up on the wall but can't jump high enough. The boy grabs my hand again and helps lift me.

He looks down. Sitting on the edge, he puts his arms to the left of him. Lifting off the edge he jumps down while holding himself to the wall. He stands on a ledge a ways down.

Trying to do the same thing I sit down, a lot more wobbly than he had been. Putting my arms to the side as he had, I try to force up the courage to scoot off the side. My arms tremble as I fear falling too far.

"Jump!" I take a breath and do as he says. Arms come up to make my descent and landing more sturdy. He turns to face the other direction. Placing one foot in front of the other he clings to the wall and walks towards the back of the building.

I follow after him. We only go a few meters before we run out of ledge to grip to. My arms are losing strength.

Ram slips off the edge to stop a foot down. Bringing his other foot down he starts climbing backwards down the rock. I watch him go past me and down a bit more.

Going to the edge of the ledge, I try to keep hold of it as I put my foot down. I don't touch the rock. My heart lurches in my chest. Knowing there is sturdy ground only a little distance beneath my foot is no consolation.

Hearing people running across the hall we just came from; footsteps, shouts, and screams. I steady my heart, let go of my grip, and fall for half a second. Catching my balance, I follow Ram's lead.

Eventually, we make it down to the sand. Familiar sand seeps all around my feet and my hand is picked up by Ram once more.

We run towards the river: passing the city by. The screams pierce through the darkness. As we near the front monolith, the relief that we will survive sinks in just as the realization that not many others will be so lucky.

Tears roll down my face. Ram doesn't let me return.

Reaching the Nile, Ram stops looking both ways and across it. "The closest city to us is just upriver from here." He looks a bit confused. I point against the flow of water.

The memory darkens. I open my eyes.

"We walked for a long time. At about mid-day, we finally reached the neighbouring city.

It was scorched just like ours had been. We found a couple of survivors, and they helped us since we were tiny children. We spent the next couple of years just trying to survive. We went to the next few cities until we were able to find someplace that wasn't ransacked.

Ram and I learned each other's languages. Eventually, I figured out his name wasn't Ramses. It took a while. Only about fifty years before he finally told me.

Anyway, I'm sure you have at least a couple of questions for me. Oh, like how I'm not dead yet. Well, that's more simple than not. We ended up getting into a fight in the middle of the night in a forest, and a trickster decided that it needed to meddle. Pretty much stopped time for us; we won't age until we learn to appreciate each other.

Apparently, we haven't done that yet."

I interrupt her with this fleeting chance. "Wait, a trickster? I'm thinking it's not just someone who's pulling pranks on people."

"Oh, no. A trickster is, I guess like a spirit, but not. They are spirits that have magic abilities. They like to meddle and don't have anything that holds them back: like feelings or consciences and such. Ummm… I guess if that kind of explains it at all. Anyway, so that's how we're still around."

"So, what happened after that? How'd you meet Darius?" One more question burns in my mind, but I hold my tongue to save it for last.

Sandra answers after a few seconds of contemplation, "Where should I start?

Ummm… well, Ram and I travelled around, saw, and did what we could around Africa and then around Europe.

By this time, we had attracted attention from other immortals. That only took them a couple of thousand years.

They reported us to the Council and we were hunted down.

Aalayah, she's one of the Council members on the stage and the fire elemental from my memory, drew up a ring of fire around us and well, basically recruited us to help them find others.

We had evaded them for so long, so we were put on duty to find those who were causing trouble or hiding with some of the others; well, after they trained us."

Light starts glowing from something in her hand. Quickly, it establishes itself as a flame. The flame floats up into the air. Sandra lifts her hand and points her finger. Moving her hand and finger she spells something out into the air: the fire mimics her finger's movements.

When she is done, she turns that word around by putting her hands around the word and physically moving it. Her name is spelled out in front of me. The heat from the flames warms my face. Sandra blows at the word and it goes out like a candle flame would. The smoky smell engulfs me.

"I perfected magic, defence, and some combat, while Ram perfected many forms of combat. Once we were done, we captured and killed many supernaturals causing issues.

And, that is how I met Darius. He is a baby as far as vampires go. It's only been about seventy years since he was turned.

No one knows who sired him, except for Darius, but he won't tell. It's kind of a crime to turn people into vampires, since the treaty, but it does happen.

Anyway, once we did track them down, the sire left Darius behind to save himself and we captured Darius. We took him back to the Council and Seth took him under his wing to get him trained properly.

The next time I saw him, he was travelling with Shale and they were being pulled back to be re-schooled." She must notice my confusion. "Basically, the Council's big idea to keep us immortals in touch with the times.

If you look like you can be in high school you go to high school and if you're older than that you have to go to college or do some sort of cultural thing.

It sucks, but I can see why they do it with how quickly things change in this world. They want to keep you in touch with modern people. Keep you knowledgeable and trained. Otherwise, you'd have a vampire decide to go into town after a two hundred year seclusion and draw too much attention to themselves.

You have to go every fifteen to twenty years and do a certain amount of hours; about six months' worth on an eight-hour day. There are a bunch of exceptions and rules, but I won't bore you with those.

I was supposed to go back for my re-schooling in three years. I was thinking about taking archaeology courses. Anyway, anything else you want to know?"

I try to absorb everything she's telling me. "So, Darius is a vampire, you're an immortal witch, and Ram is an immortal. What about everyone else?"

Sandra counts on her fingers as she lists them off, "Shale and Kelly are vampires, Miles is an elf, and well… I don't think you know anyone else. But, you'll be meeting everything that there has ever been a myth or legend about. Well, maybe not every because a lot have gone extinct since the old world but you'll meet a lot. You saw a lot of species in my memory."

"Speaking of that, what happened with that?" I gesture towards my face. I had been wondering about that, though I am not sure if I want to hear the answer.

"It's just a spell to let you see what I want you to see. In this case a movie of my memories. It won't last long if that's what you're worried about." Sandra tries to reassure me.

I wasn't, but now I am.

"But, I think that's it for tonight. I'm getting tired. You can stay here tonight and I'll go sleep downstairs. Good night." Demeanour changed, she gets up quickly and walks to the door. I asked a touchy question; I guess.

"Night," my word may have fallen on deaf ears. Looking down at Rayleen, I watch her very closely as I slowly get up off the bed. Walking around to the other side, I go to the window.

Looking out at eye level I see orange and yellow in the far distance; reminding me of Sandra's story. Visions of the destruction so many years ago translate to the city I knew. Buildings torn to pieces, houses on fire, and people dead on the street flashes through my mind.

I bring my hand up to soothe a tickle on my face. Pulling back my hand, my finger is wet. I wipe away the tears that have already fallen.

I look down to the ground. Seeing the shed shrouded in darkness sends pain through my chest, yet at the same time gives me hope. Hope that Miles really did get free and had not been captured again.

No one is walking around out there. Vehicles just sit where they were left today.

Turning around, I walk to the free side of the bed. Careful not to disturb Rayleen, I curl up beside her. Tears flow freely, while I keep any noises from being heard.

I wouldn't want to wake her.

Chapter 11

The racquet the rowdy boys are making is enough to wake the dead, or at least attract unwanted attention from the demons. It's been hours since our last sighting, but that doesn't mean they aren't still around.

Glancing down at the book in my lap and the pen in my hand, I try to go back to concentrating on what words I want to write. I haven't gotten a single word written down.

Frustrated with my writer's block, I shut the book and put it and my pen back into my purse. Feet walk into my view.

Peter sits down beside me. "We should go now. I don't want to be defenceless when they come back for us." He says in a hushed voice. I know immediately what he's talking about, so I nod. "Everyone's off doing their own thing. They won't miss us." Again, I nod.

We get up from the floor. The gate is right across from our spot in the aisle. We need someone to lock the gate after us. The perfect person walks by at just the right moment; a wonderful coincidence.

"Kayanna!" I whisper yell just loud enough for her to hear. Her head whips around in my direction. Walking towards her I say, "Lock the gate behind us. We're going to the army store."

She looks blank for a moment before she nods and walks us to the gate. Following her, I stop. Remembering I don't want to go out without some sort of weapon, I go back to the aisle and grab the broomstick.

Peter opens the gate; careful to not make much noise. He slips through, then waits outside for me. I pass him the stick and slide through the opening. Kayanna takes care to shut and lock the gate quietly.

I take the broom back from Peter. We look into the halls for any sign of a demon. Nothing. It seems clear. The dim light helps little. There are many shadowed areas which we are blind to.

I set a quick pace down the hall to a set of escalators turned stairs. Peter goes in front and looks up and ahead as he reaches the top.

So far, so good.

He goes to the wall in front of us and checks around the corner. Something tells me he might have some sort of combat experience. Maybe, he is a soldier or policeman? Or, maybe he just plays paintball on weekends?

The hall is clear again.

It's not far to the store. The gate is unlocked but closed. I'm a little hesitant about going inside. Peter opens the gate enough so we can get inside by only ducking. I grab at my cell and turn the flashlight on.

This store has most of what I want out in the back. I shine my light where ever I can, but it all looks clear. This may be easier than I thought.

Peter goes behind the counter and goes for the pocket knives in the glass cabinets. I hope he has the sense to grab durable ones, not the decorative ones.

I walk towards the back; shining my light as I go. An angry face appears in my light. Gary rushes towards me with a blade in his hand; I scream a little and drop my phone.

The blade is at my throat before I think of saying his name to stop him. "Gary!"

In the pitch-black, I can only wait. It's a good sign at least that my throat hasn't been slit. If he had wanted to kill me, he would have done so before I had a chance to scream. This wasn't a kill attempt, but one to immobilize me.

It takes a moment but the blade is removed. My phone is picked up and the light is directed to the ceiling.

"Oh, sorry about that. Can't be too careful." Gary huffs. His hand goes to my throat examining it. I can feel something wet slowly trail down my chest. I wipe it away and rub the blood against my pants. "It's not that bad. You'll live. What are you doing here? Where are your parents?" I feel instantly chastised.

Peter comes rushing down the aisle. "Are you alright?" He says.

"Yeah. Gary this is Peter. Peter this is Gary." I point as I say each name. "Is anyone else with you?"

Gary motions to the back with his head. "Judy's out back with a group. We were opening the store when we heard screaming. We ran a few people in here before shutting down. What were you doing here so early?"

"Just came out to walk the mall before shopping. We ran into the dollar store when everything happened. We've got a group there. My friends and his family. Came in here to grab some weapons." I tell him. "Do you want to come back with us? We have plenty of food, water, everything that we could need to last a while."

Gary doesn't waste a moment before taking me up on it. "Yes, thank you. We've already run out of food. Only had one granola bar between us all." He chuckles to himself. Turning around he goes into the backroom; to reappear moments later with a large group of people.

The only thing I can think of is that Brad is not going to like this.

Gary gives instructions to the group to grab anything they can carry. People quickly gather their items, most already decked out in armour.

I go for a samurai sword on the wall. The price is more on the expensive side, so I think it's safe to say it isn't a cast sword. Gary is too busy to ask.

Walking around to the outside aisle, I go through the armour. Finding a small woman's vest, I pull it off the hanger. The thick material should help protect me, at least a bit, more than my clothes. I try it on and zip it up.

Picking the sword back up, I make my way to Peter at the front of the store. There are a few people that have collected there. Gary rounds everyone up to the front. He doesn't say anything before he leaves the store. I quicken my steps to catch up with him. Peter is right behind me.

I take the lead; only slightly in front of Gary.

Kayanna looks happy to see us. She opens the gate loudly; no use in hiding or sneaking back in with all of these extra people.

We all make it inside the gates when Brad comes down from an aisle and furiously yells. "What the fuck are you doing? Shut the gate!" Kayanna, in the middle of doing so already, quickens her pace and locks it shut. "Who the hell are all these people? Who told you you could leave? Do you know the danger you could put us all in?"

His string of questions keep coming; his voice getting louder and angrier by the moment. The commotion draws out everyone from the aisles.

"Would you shut up? What's putting us in danger is how loud you're yelling right now. The only people we put in danger were ourselves and there wasn't anything out there anyway!" I scream at him louder than his volume had been. Walking up to him, I stop just about a foot away. Hoping the gesture would intimidate him into backing down.

He closes the gap more. "I can't have people coming and going as they wish. Every time you open the gate, you put us all at risk."

"At risk of what? You saw the damage out there. If anything wants inside I don't think a locked gate is going to stop it; especially with all the glass around the gate. It's nothing to break that and get inside." Maybe some logic will get through to him.

"You're not going to be happy until you've killed us all are you?" He shouts.

"I could say the same to you. You can't imprison us here and just expect us to be safe." I shout louder.

"Listen-" His voice rises slightly.

I yell as loud as I can at him. "No, you listen! For the small risk that something might see us, I brought back weapons, armour, and more people. What have you done in the last half hour? Ate candy and played with toys? We can't stay here forever. We'll need to leave at some point to find our families and find out what happened."

He goes silent at my words. He searches for something to say back, but can't find the words.

"Look, this yelling isn't getting us anywhere." Gary inserts himself between Brad and me; forcing us to back away from each other. "On behalf of my group I would like to thank you for giving us a chance to survive. However, this yelling and lashing out because you're scared, is not going to work. What's done is done. Now, leave it alone." Gary speaks firm, with authority. A silent threat seems to be in the background.

Brad glares from me to Gary. Abruptly, he shakes his head and storms off. He's just mad because he's scared. He'll calm down.

When I look back at Gary, he nods to me. I nod back to him in response.

"Is there somewhere we can put this stuff down?" It takes a moment of me staring blankly at him, before his questions processes thoroughly.

"Yes. Umm." I look around me searching for the best place. The backroom is small and dark. We vacated that in favour of more room. "Down Aisle 5. If you go down a bit, you can't see anything from the front." I think aloud. Gary takes this as my answer and instructs everyone to go halfway down the aisle.

Peter goes to his family, picking up his son and hugging him. His wife glares at him for a moment of scolding before turning affectionate.

Shawn has disappeared, probably followed right after Brad. Steph stands watching me and the action going on around me. She looks back and forth between us, and where Brad and Shawn had presumably gone. Hesitating for a moment about what to do, she then goes down the aisle after the duo.

Needing to do something other than just stand here, I decide to go to the gate. Looking, either way, to see if there is any movement out there.

Maybe it was a bit stupid to go out there. Suppose something had noticed us and decided to attack. What would Peter and I have been able to do about it? Even on our way back with Gary, none of us would have been able to do much. Those things are stronger and faster than us. They have pre-attached weapons in their claws and teeth.

Something touches my shoulder. I jump half in fright, half in surprise.

"Sorry," Gary says. He comes up beside me to look where I was. "Don't worry about him. He'll come around. I've seen fear do a lot worse to people." It makes sense, so I nod to him.

We stand for a couple of moments of silence to just listen. Noises from behind us quieten down a lot. "We need to go back out there," I say.

"Good. We'll let your friend calm down a bit first though. Wait a few hours to start a scouting mission. Come away from the gate now. We'll relax. Eat, bring up the mood, prep for any emergencies, rest, and worry about tomorrow when it comes." Gary lays out a plan.

"Okay," I say quietly.

"Your mom and dad? They weren't with you."

"No. They would have been on their way to work when things happened. We saw a dragon on our way here. I crashed my car because some people in the streets were going nuts. We panicked and just finished getting here. We thought the police would help, but they were useless."

"Hopefully they're fine. Your parents are great people. And, not just because they're my best customers." Gary nudges me with his elbow. We both chuckle at his joke.

One last look outside reassures me that there is no immediate danger of attacks. I lead Gary down aisle 5 and take a seat across from Peter and his family.

Salt and Pepper chips fall into my lap. I look up at Kayanna as she turns around and sits beside me. "Thank you."

I open up the bag, planning on nibbling on a few chips for something to do. More and more people sit down and soon we've got two rows of people chit-chatting back and forth about old jobs; things they hated and any funny stories they've got.

Dipping my hand into the chip bag my fingers come up empty. I pick it up and look inside. Nothing but crumbs are left. I put aside the disappointment that there aren't any left, to focus on adding to the conversation.

After a girl tells about a system they had to alert their non-working workers about any management that happened to come in unannounced. I jump in.

"One day, a few of us were in the back and suddenly two higher up supervisors came up behind Frank with duct tape. They taped Frank to his chair and I think we spent the next half hour watching him try to break free."

"What is it with supervisors and instigating things?" One girl questions. "I was working out on the floor one day when I had a question about how Wyatt wanted the display to look. I walked around the whole store and couldn't find him. Went to the office, he still wasn't there. I listened for a minute and I heard him talking to another worker. I went to the back of the warehouse and found out that Wyatt and another worker had spent the last four hours piecing together paperclips into a long string and they were hanging it from the ceiling."

The stories go on, but I get thirsty. Getting up, I go to the front of the store. There is a cooler full of drinks. Opening the sliding door I feel a bit of cool air. Grabbing four cokes I decide now, is as good as any, to see if I can get peace talks going.

I walk down the aisle to the back. They probably cornered themselves in the staff room, so I head there first. Turning on my flashlight, I light up the darkness. The staffroom door is open and no one is in there. Where would they have gone? Walking around to the other side of the shelves I go to the back door; it's locked.

I go back into the store by the closest door. I leave it open, shutting off my flashlight. The group of rowdy people has gone quiet. They look at me and I can see why; Brad, Steph, and Shawn came and sat over.

We must have missed each other by mere seconds.

The closer I get, the silence becomes more and more awkward; probably because of me.

The best thing I can do is just keep walking. I stop by the trio, hand out the cokes, and keep on walking, until I sit back down beside Kayanna.

It seems to be enough to break the ice. People go back to their chatter. I look over to see Brad staring back at me. Opening my pop I do an air 'cheers' in his direction. He returns it with a sheepish smile.

We're good.

Chapter 12

Waking up is blissful. I feel amazing after a nice long restful sleep. My room is dark. I must have slept into the evening. I look for my clock. It's out. Blindly groping for my cell phone I find it and turn it on. It's six thirty-eight. I detangle from my iPod. I unplug my cell phone and nestle it in my hand.

I navigate to the light switch. The light won't turn on. It confirms to me that our power is out.

I don't hear anything upstairs, but that doesn't mean anyone else isn't home. I click the power button on my phone. To my surprise, there are no phone calls or text messages; until I notice the No Service notification at the bottom. I have no internet bars either, but that's no surprise with the power out and no mobile data. The question is why don't I have service? I turn my phone off and on, but it doesn't help. Maybe my phone is broken. I turn it back off. I don't want to use up the battery while the power is out.

I put my phone on my dresser, and decide that it's time to face dad. He should be home by now. I grow anxious at the prospect.

I quietly go up the stairs. Stopping at the top, I wait and listen. I don't hear anything, but that doesn't mean anything. He could still be here. I go into the living room. No one is here. I look for cars to confirm this.

Nothing looks disturbed from when I had been here earlier today.

Well.

What do I do now?

My stomach growls with impeccable timing. I didn't eat breakfast or lunch today, so I'll have something now. I walk to the kitchen and stop when I catch a billow of smoke out the window. That's the direction of the school. I go out through the patio doors.

That's not coming from the school. My direction had been off. On the deck, I can see multiple plumes of smoke rising into the sky. I hold my breath for a moment. The slightest high-pitched screams reach my ears.

What is going on?

I go back inside when chills run down my spine from my neck. Are we under attack? War, maybe? Or maybe a terrorist attack? It makes sense and would explain the bomb. Bomb the children; bomb the future of the country.

I run downstairs and grab my phone. Pressing the button to turn it on, I wait for it to be on, and turn on the mobile internet; risking the extra charge. There isn't any internet there either. I don't know how that could be. I should have access to the internet. Although, if I were the people taking over I would cut off the internet. Kill the internet, or rather shutting off access to it for everyone I'm attacking would be extremely beneficial. It would cripple most people. Could take out a whole area through downing a tower.

Stop.

I'm not even sure that is what's going on here. Maybe, there's just an arsonist on the rampage. Maybe, something happened to a power cable. Maybe, they've made a mistake with my phone plan.

That all would be too much of a coincidence. I pick up the house phone; it's dead too so I put it back on the stand.

What do I do when terrorists are attacking the city? Stay in place, and hope help arrives? I should go to the countryside. Terrorists don't attack random dense wooded locations where there aren't any people normally. If Jacob is alive he will come back here to collect me as soon as he can. I think, and, Kendra is probably never coming back. She has the means to leave this abusive relationship in the long run. Unfortunately, she'll have to deal with him for the rest of her life because of their child. He's going to make her life awful to get custody. He's got too many influential people wrapped around his charismatic finger.

I go into the pantry and grab a ramen noodle package. It's not the healthiest thing, especially with all that sodium, but it doesn't require any cooking. I break the noodles in the bag before I open it up. I don't want to have dirty dishes hanging around so I keep the noodles in the bag. I shake half of the flavouring package over the noodle, and start eating the broken noodles using my fingers to pick them up. I go into the living room, and sit on the couch to eat.

I wish I had the means to leave him. What I would need is a witness protection program for people like me. I need a clean break. Get me a new life, and maybe I could be happy. I have a little less than a year until I turn sixteen, and can legally move out on my own. I wish there was a way to get my inheritance now. It would make things so much easier. If my multi-millionaire father even gave me just one million dollars I would be able to move out no problem. Start a life with no problem. I deserve at least one million dollars with all the things I've had to put up with.

I'm crazy to care about him, and his reputation. I mean, he's not even my blood. I'm not even a Kensington by blood. That detail is so important to him. He certainly doesn't act as a father should, and doesn't deserve to be called dad; not that that word even means anything more than just a title.

Maybe I'll get lucky and he'll be dead. I wouldn't miss him. I've hoped enough times for his death through the years, maybe this time I'll get lucky. I'd take that over the millions.

Am I even in his will anymore, or did he change that when he got his precious son?

I take a deep breath in and release it. I need to stop this thinking track or else I'll have another tension migraine soon enough.

I finish my supper. I put the bag into the garbage in the kitchen. I should be productive in this downtime. There isn't much else to do right now but clean and do homework. Or, rather, there isn't much else to do right now that dad wouldn't think productive or worth my time. The house needs a good cleaning and I have things to finish for homework. If there's even going to be school tomorrow.

I gather the cleaning supplies together. There isn't any water that I'm willing to spare, so I decide to use cleaner as my water. I start my way from one end of the house to the other. Without distractions, I finish late into the night.

There isn't anything else I can do without light. I lock all the doors and check all the windows. I go down into my bedroom and change into my blanket fabric pyjama pants, and a hoodie. I think I should find the sleeping bag, but I know it's buried; I would never find it in the dark.

I do homework by candlelight until it's all finished up. The air is noticeably colder now. The captured heat has been slowly escaping.

I just get under all my blankets on the bed. Dad normally turns the temperature down to nothing at night anyway, so I freeze when I have less than four blankets on the bed on a normal winter night. At least it's not too cold yet.

Hopefully, this doesn't last too long. Could I survive a long stay alone, without an iota of normal cushy life?

I revel in the idea. Of course, I could. I have that survival book from my survival kick in the sixth grade. I have my knowledge of the ancients to back up the knowledge from my different interests of the different societies a couple of hundred years back and older, and more; from multiple times in my life I decided to study them. I've studied many things over the years. I have the means and the knowledge.

The thought that I might be by myself for a while excites me, but not enough to stop the sandman from coming and sneaking me away into dreamland with a smile on my face.

Chapter 13

A hand on my shoulder wakes me. My heart races from two realizations; Rayleen isn't beside me and someone else got close enough to touch me while I was sleeping.

Behind me, Sandra smiles cheerfully. "Good morning!"

I turn back and bury myself into the pillow. Groaning, I state a rhetorical question. "You're a morning person, aren't you?" The mood changes of Sandra are enough to make my head spin.

"Yep, now rise and shine. Breakfast is ready and waiting and Rayleen's washing up and getting hungry. We all are. So, if you don't get up now, we might just eat your share." Sandra grabs the covers and pulls them away from me.

I sigh when my stomach growls at the wrong moment. Sandra giggles after obviously hearing my stomach protest.

"Fine, I'll get up." Dragging my body up off the bed, I get up and greet Sandra face to face.

"I have to use the washroom. I'll be down in a bit." I tell her.

"Right, I'll meet you downstairs." We walk out of the room and split at the washroom. I relieve my bladder and wash my hands.

Grabbing some toilet paper, I dip it into the cool running water in the sink. I wash the raccoon effect off my face; making sure to leave the makeup that stayed in place on my face. I touch up a little bit with the makeup in the drawer.

Satisfied, I head downstairs.

Rayleen is sitting at the table with her back to me. I sneak up to the chair, her attention occupied on Ram bringing her a plate of food.

Approaching her chair, I bring up my hands and go in for the pounce. "Hi Alexa," chimes the little girl in front of me.

"Ah, come on, there's no way you could have known I was there. Who gave her the hint?" I look at Sandra and then at Ram.

Ram's smooth voice defends both of them. "We didn't give her any hints, I swear. Maybe you were just making too much noise."

I counteract that statement as I sit in the chair next to Rayleen. "I could have sworn I didn't make any noises."

"You did!" Rayleen tries to assure me. "I heard you flush the toilet and you stomped when you came down the stairs."

Reaching over to her sides, I tickle her on her ribs. She laughs. Squirming in her seat, she tries to pry my hands away from her.

Taking pity on her, I let go and return to my proper place in my seat. Now that I've stopped, Ram sets down a plate of food in front of Rayleen; pancakes covered with chocolate sauce, strawberries, and whipped cream.

My eyes widen a bit. "So after all that sugar you're feeding her, you're looking after her today; right?"

He chuckles. "Nope sorry, that's your department. I have a few things to do today; Darius wants me to see what I can collect about how Miles escaped last night."

Ram brings me my plate. I stare at it before picking up a fork and taking my first bite. It's very delectable. "Thank you, it's very good."

"You're welcome," You can hear the smile and pride in his voice.

"Ram's a very good housewife-" Sandra's input is quickly cut off by the male she's speaking about.

"Hey, that's not nice. And, the only reason I had to become a 'good house wife' was because you would have killed us by now with your horrible cooking; if you can even call it cooking." Sandra sticks her tongue out at Ram as he gives her a plate.

Rayleen and I finish our breakfast before Ram sits down to eat his own. I get up from my seat and take Rayleen and my dirty dishes to the dishwasher.

I look out the window. The deck is the only man-made thing I can see from here. Beyond that are grass and trees. A beautiful, natural view distracts me for a couple of moments. Views like this can't be seen from the city.

Something moves in throughout the trees. Focusing on the shadowed figure as it comes closer, I determine it's a deer. It cautiously comes out of the trees; grazing on the grass and bathing in the sunlight. A breeze picks up. The ears on the animal perk up and twitch a couple of times. It stops eating and brings its head up.

In a split second, and a deep red blur, the animal is gone.

Leaning on the counter, I try to search for the deer and what took it. Both have disappeared.

"What are you looking at?" Jumping at the sudden womanly voice in my ear, I put one hand to my chest; as if the action could slow my racing heart.

Turning my head to Sandra, I tell her what I saw. "Something really big just swooped down and took a deer."

"What did it look like?" She comes to the counter and looks out it.

"I didn't see much. It was just a red blur." I try to think of anything to describe it but can't.

She looks outside a little more. "Really, already? That was fast. It must have been a dragon."

"A dragon?" Sandra nods her head in confirmation. "Really? Those exist too? How the hell did you guys hide dragons all these years?"

People are one thing. They can learn how to disguise themselves over the years; the ones that don't already look human. But, dragons are huge. How do you hide something that big? An animal with a mind of its own, that can fly large distances.

She laughs at my reaction. "Easy, all you need is to buy a couple of islands and build giant birdcage type thing on each one, and then create a no-fly zone around the island.

Oh, and get people in very high and exclusive places. We've had to do a lot over the years to keep everything a secret, especially as the world started inventing computer technology and satellite imagery. It's not as easy as taking out an entire town anymore."

"Excuse me, girls. I need to get to the sink." We both move so Ram can put his dishes away.

"Did you want to take that shower now?" Sandra asks me.

"Sure," I say.

She takes my hand and pulls me out of the kitchen. "Ram, watch Rayleen for a bit."

"But," Ram tries to protest but stops as he realizes it would be useless. I'm sure Sandra glared at him and that probably had something to do with it.

Sandra takes me upstairs to the washroom. Going inside, she pulls open a drawer in front of me. "This drawer's yours. It should have everything you need; makeup, hairbrush, toothbrush, toothpaste; everything. If there are any other colours you need feel free to use some of my makeup; it's in the drawer above.

Darius had people bring your clothes from his place over; they're in the guest room, next to my room.

That should be all you need then, have fun."

"Thanks." I start to follow her out of the room but stop and go to the guest room. Not only are my clothes here, but the same dresser is too. I pull out a change of clothes for the day; jeans, and a spaghetti-strapped shirt.

Going back to the bathroom, I close and lock the door.

Stripping from my clothes, I go to the shower and turn it on; waiting for the temperature to be warm before I go inside to take my shower.

Once I'm done, I get the clean clothes on; the jeans take a bit of work as my legs are damp in some spots.

Wrapping my hair with the towel, I leave it there as I go to put my makeup on. Going through the drawer I find all of what I need; unwrapping the new items and setting them out on the counter. Now that I know this is here for me, I don't feel bad about using them yesterday.

I look up to examine my outfit and face in the mirror. Immediately,

I notice that the bruise that should have been there is not. Finding it weird, but not questioning it. I am just thankful that Rayleen didn't see it when it was there.

Testing the liquid foundation colour against my skin, I determine it matches before I cover my face in it. I brush a loose yellowish powder on top of the foundation to prevent a shiny look. I apply black mascara on my upper and lower lashes until the fine hairs are covered.

Deep blue shadow lines the top of my higher lashes, spreading on two lighter shades for a base and highlight to my eyelids, I then blur the layers together to get a smooth procession. A light pink staining gloss goes neatly onto my lips.

Looking over my face, I check for anything I may have to touch up. Not finding anything to fix I step back from the mirror to examine the look all put together.

A couple of frantic knocks beat on the door. "Umm… Alexa are you dressed?"

Immediately, I become suspicious of the question and her tone. "Yeah, why?"

A pause is my answer. I open the door to make sure she is still there.

She hesitates. "Umm… well, Rayleen was playing with Crystal and then Crystal had to go to the washroom outside, and Rayleen begged me for her to go with us, and I only looked away for a moment because I saw the same dragon you did earlier and then I looked back and both Rayleen and Crystal weren't there anymore-"

My heart beats faster and I start to panic. "What? Which direction were you looking in?" I slam on my shoes.

"Left, towards the entrance." At her words, I leap down the stairs. Running through the living room and the kitchen, I swing open the door. Jumping the four stairs to the ground turning on a dime, I run around the deck area.

I pass Ram facing the other direction, a little distance away; he's calling their names out.

Scanning the area around me as I run, I try to find any hint of where they may have gone. I fear what may happen to her; whether a dragon may have picked her up, or some other beast may have put their claws on her; briefly a thought of what Darius may do if he finds Rayleen and I have gone this far away from the house.

My thoughts are scattered as I search frantically.

The trees open up and immediately I notice something moving on the hill a ways away. Focusing as I get closer, I see it is Rayleen. A smile creeps on my lips knowing nothing has happened to her.

"RAYLEEN! RAYLEEN! RAYLEEN!" The little girl stops and turns around the second time I call her name. She waves at me from the top of the hill.

It takes me a minute to maneuver in between the barbed wired fence and make it up the hill. I hug Rayleen as I get to her.

"Why did you run off? Sandra said she was looking after you and then you disappeared." I remember halfway through my sentences to not be too harsh sounding in my tone.

"I was chasing Crystal. I'm sorry. I didn't mean to scare you." Her eyes start to water and her lips puff out as she starts pouting.

I hug her. "It's okay. Just don't do it again. It could be very dangerous for you to run off now-"

"I think we should show her exactly how dangerous it could be." I jump at Darius' sudden arrival behind me. "There are things out there that will kill you or eat you. Old friends are now enemies and will try to kidnap you. The same goes with you, Alexa. That's why you weren't supposed to leave the house." My ears start ringing. Darius' lips are moving slightly but no noise is coming from them.

Rayleen covers her ears and whines.

"Are you okay?" I kneel to inspect what could be wrong with her. She stops suddenly, uncovering her ears and looking at me for an answer to what happened.

"I was calling Shale," Darius explains. "Vampires can communicate with each other by talking in a higher pitch than what most humans can hear.

Children can hear the high pitch and sometimes when concentrating hard enough, they can make out some of the words. However, the older the human gets the less likely they are to hear anything; due to the everyday damage done to the ear. So, while a child can hear us a middle-aged human may not hear a thing; a human of your age might hear just a high pitch ringing."

Shale comes from where I had. He runs faster than I've ever seen him run before. When he stops, Shale stands beside Darius.

Darius orders Shale. "Take Rayleen back to the house. Alexa, I'm going to show you around the farm."

"Can I come too?" Rayleen's big voice pipes in for her defence. "I'm bored. And Crystal doesn't want to be inside either and I promise I won't get into any trouble."

No one says anything for a moment. I look at Darius. "That's up to Alexa, I guess."

"I don't see why not, as long as the things we see are age-appropriate for her." I try to make sure that Darius gets the point that I don't want her seeing some of the things I have already been introduced to.

"Alright, so I guess Rayleen is staying for the child-proofed version. Shale we won't be needing you after all. You can get back to what you were doing. Oh, and please tell Ram and Sandra I would like to speak to them later in private." The undertones of his sentence sound a bit threatening.

I can't help but feel guilty about getting both of them in trouble; it is partially my fault and I feel guilty for Rayleen's part in it as well. My only hope is that they don't get into too much trouble for it.

Shale's look in his eyes dampens my hopes. "Are you sure you don't want Rayleen coming back to the house or at least have someone extra around in case something happens?" He looks to me for help.

"Darius, maybe he should come. At the very least, it's one more person to try to keep up with the amount of energy she has."

Darius nods his head almost reluctantly. "You can stay." A silent victory and thanks is exchanged from Shale to me. "And I guess since we are already here; I'll show you why the griffin cub was headed over here. It's just over the top of this hill." Darius takes my hand and leads us all to the top of the hill.

Coming to the peak, an old barn shows itself with each step. The greyed wood is broken and torn apart in a couple of areas. Scorch marks are burned into the grass in brief lines. The ruined destruction of a nearby newer-looking building lays about fifty meters away from the old one.

Crystal breaks away from Rayleen. Taking a running jump, she uncurls her wings out from her sides and opens them completely. She fumbles when she tries to flap her wings and takes a second jump; keeping off the ground for no more than three seconds. Her third attempt has her gliding to the bottom. The little griffin trips as she lands; rolling to a stop after a couple of three-sixties. Not missing a beat, she gets back on her feet and continues as if nothing had happened.

Trying to catch up with the small creature, Rayleen runs down the hill. Crystal ducks into an opening in the wall. Rayleen halts as she hits the wall; cushioning the blow with her arms. She goes onto her hands and knees with the purpose of following her pet.

Lifted into the air from around her waist, Shale prevents her from disappearing into the hole. He says something to her that I can't hear and puts her down a moment later.

The little redhead grabs hold of his hand and drags him to the door. He opens it for her and follows her inside.

The moment the door is opened, it's like a seal had been released, loud noises ring clear as day. This sound is similar to the one I had heard from Crystal yesterday, except more confident, loud, deeper, and it starts as more of a roar than a mew.

We follow after the pair through the door. The silhouettes of the creatures become more clear and defined as my eyes adjust to the darkness.

Five grown versions of Crystal go about their business; ignoring us as we come in. Gawking at them, I faintly think that they aren't as big as I thought they would be; remembering the sizes they are depicted in movies. Their true body size is only that of what a real lion would be. Massive feathered wings bulk up their width.

Others are in the barn as well. They look human as they go about their duties. A man is cleaning out a stall with a pitchfork, and another grooming a griffin with a brush. The only woman is picking out meat in a bucket and tossing it into the mouths of hungry griffins. Her bloodied hand goes in and out of the pail without hesitating.

The woman turns around first. Seeing her eyes makes me realize she isn't fully human, or human at all. Slit yellow cat eyes examine us before she gets back to feeding the animals.

"Crystal went to see her mother. We'll probably find her over there." Darius points to the one in the corner lying down; her attention on something out of our view.

Rayleen heads over there and I follow after her.

Halfway there a male, that had been grooming one of the griffins, steps in my way and stops me. "Don't go over there. A mother always protects their young, because he-" He glares with black and brown eyes at Darius' direction. "-took one of her babies. She'll be more cautious and protective than ever before."

The female walks calmly over to the mother and Rayleen. "Little Miss, please don't go any closer to the griffin." Rayleen turns to the female.

Crystal comes out of the stall and rubs herself on Rayleen's leg.

I can see the griffin's mother tense up. Her body moves into a defensive position; a warning growl rumbles in the air. Rayleen bends over and picks up the attention seeker.

Both the mother griffin and the female pounce at the same time. In a blur, Rayleen disappears. Shale pulls Rayleen out from behind a wall and comes back towards us.

The mother griffin roars her anger and readies to pounce again.

Darius picks me up and escorts me bridal style out of the barn; Shale follows with Rayleen. Setting Rayleen down the moment we get outside, he turns around and slams the man door shut. Bracing against it, while it shakes and almost busts from the griffin ramming into it.

After a few minutes, the banging stops, and Shale cautiously lets go of the door. He waits a couple more, just in case she tries for one last ram.

I don't want to think about how the griffin attendants may have fared from the attack. I can only hope they are alright.

I look Rayleen over from our distance apart. She doesn't look like she has any marks on her, though she might have something sore from Shale's quick movements. The griffin in her arms is licking her arm gently.

The arm under my legs drops. Reaching the ground, I catch my balance.

I turn to face Darius, "I think we should get away from this place." Looking over to the other buildings I see many possibilities to explore. "Maybe one of the other buildings would work. As long as a repeat of this event doesn't happen, it should be fine."

Shale's voice answers me instead of the male I had intended. "I don't think that would be a good idea. Maybe, if we went to the pond instead. There shouldn't be anything there that will freak out; if we even get to see anything other than a nice view." He looks to Darius for approval.

Darius nods and starts walking away. I start to follow him.

A small hand grabs onto mine from behind me. Rayleen walks happily along with no sign of any traumatization from the recent events. She plays with Crystal, as the little griffin follows after her like a puppy.

Shale comes up on the other side of me. I ask him. "So, what is in those buildings?"

He takes a moment to respond. "This used to be an old slaughter farm before we took it over." Shale stops his explanation at that. He does not need to continue because my assumptions and imagination take over. The buildings are probably filled with slaughter equipment, blood everywhere, and the stench of rotting death.

"Mm-kay, so definitely nothing we want to see. Thank you for getting Rayleen out of there." I tell him sincerely.

"You're welcome, it was no problem." He smiles.

We walk back up the hill. Everyone keeps their silence. Heading back the way I had come, we stop before we get to the road between the trees. Darius leads us to the left.

We walk along a fenced-in area. It looks like an area they would have kept the livestock in. We head down an unmarked path that opens up in the trees. Deep green and browns surround us. Crunching is heard and felt beneath our feet as we walk on top of the fallen leaves.

I step over a fallen tree limb and stop momentarily to help Rayleen over it. Crystal jumps up, barely making it up most of the way. She uses her claws to pull herself up the rest of the way.

We continue through more trees. Off a little way, I can see the pond once we get closer.

It's just a regular pond: murky water, croaking frogs, and water plants.

To the far right, leaning over the edge, is a scaly creature. Its long crimson neck is tucked down and drinking from the water.

We get as close as we dare. Setting Rayleen in front of me, I crouch down embracing her, and rest my chin on her shoulder. There is something peaceful and awe-inspiring about watching this magnificent creature. Something I have only felt an inkling of before when watching animals in a zoo.

Two horns top the head. Scales, like a reptile, adorn its entire body except for its wings. The wings look like they would resemble more of a bat's wing if they were stretched out rather than tucked into its sides. A long tail curls around and lies on the ground. Claws and long tendon-like fingers are all I can see of its legs.

The dragon stops drinking and looks up; raising its neck to be level with Rayleen and me. It stares at us. I stare back mesmerized by the creatures' gaze.

Looking down and continuing with quenching its thirst, the dragon seems to prefer to ignore that we are here. I stand back to my full height. Just as I do, the dragon stops drinking again. This time it backs away from the pond a couple of steps.

Lurching forward, it unfolds its massive wings and takes off. Sweeping across the pond and veering sharply up; disappearing over the trees. It leaves behind a mist of pond water cooling our skin and dampening our clothes.

Rayleen's facial expression is filled with wonder. "What was that?"

"A dragon, more specifically, that was an American dragon.

They're very-" Shale gets interrupted.

"I think we've had enough sightseeing for one day. Shale take them back to the house." Darius instructs. "Don't let them leave again."

I ask him, wondering, "Where are you going?"

"Hunting, it's about time I have some fun, and I need to feed." There is something sick about the way his eyes light up and his mouth twists into a grin.

"But, I wanna see more animals and I want to stay outside some more." Rayleen whines to Darius.

"No! You will go inside and you will not whine and no complaints." Darius snaps back.

Anger and protection rises in me. "Darius you can't-" I'm cut off when he is suddenly in front of me.

"You will not tell me what to do! As for the brat, I let you have her, so I can take her away from you. One more outburst and she will be gone." He motions to Shale. "Prepare her. When I come back, I will be changing her."

He is gone a split second later. Branches move to show the route he went.

"Let's go back to the house." Shale puts his hand on my shoulder, a gesture I'm sure is meant to comfort me in some way. It doesn't help me feel any better. "Wet clothes get cold quickly."

He turns and walks away.

I look down at Rayleen and the tears that are brimming in her eyes. I sigh at the sight of her and the reason why she got that way. I bend down to her and pick her up. She buries her face into my shoulder.

Making the ride as smooth as I can for the upset little girl, I jog to catch up with Shale. I walk behind him the rest of the way to the house to save myself and Rayleen from any concern he may have.

Along the way I find her body losing its tension. Her breathing evens out. These signal to me that she is falling asleep; if she isn't asleep already.

We are just breaking through the trees when Ram spots us. He shouts something behind him and moments later Sandra comes out of the house running. I have to switch Rayleen's support from two arms to one.

With my free arm, I lift my pointer finger to my lips in a motion to keep Sandra quiet long enough to get her attention on the sleeping girl.

She stops in front of us. "She's sleeping?" Sandra whispers while she points at Rayleen. I nod. Just as quiet she directs her next question at Shale. "So, how much shit are we in?"

He looks back at her. "What do you think? Darius is furious and wants to talk to you both in private later."

"Ooh shit." The sentiment said by Sandra looks to be felt by Ram as well.

"Do you think you can look after her for a few minutes, without losing her this time? I have to talk to Alexa." Shale jokes. No one laughs so he says, "too soon?"

"A little. I'm sure she'll be hungry anyway. It's about lunchtime." Sandra speaks cheerfully and confidently, but she looks hesitant.

Either way, I need to talk to Shale just as much as he needs to talk to me.

I bring up my one arm and pat the sleeping girl on her back. She moves only slightly. Swiping my thumb against her cheek brings her to full wakefulness. Drowsy eyes look at me, "Sandra and Ram are going to take you and Crystal for lunch now and I'll be there in a few minutes. Shale and I just have to have a little talk."

"Okay." She turns as much as she can in my arms. "What's for lunch?" I put her down so she can go with them.

While they walk away, I can hear the small talk between the two of them. A little ways away, she calls for Crystal to follow them.

I watch them walk out of sight before turning to Shale. "So?"

"Darius is going to change you into a vampire tonight. It's probably going to be extremely painful. Once reborn you're going to be Darius' queen and rule with him over his region." He says bluntly. "Any questions?"

I stare at him for a minute. "Yes, why is everyone so blunt about everything?"

He chuckles. "Because, this is our life, it's what we're used to. Someone being supernatural, or getting turned into one, or being cursed, anything of the such is normal to us.

Anyway, would you rather we all lie to you or take a long time to tell you something, or would you rather we tell you straight up and you get to spend all the time we would have wasted asking questions?"

Thinking about it, either way, I have to hear about it anyway. At least when he's straight to the point I don't have to weed my way through an information overload. "Yeah, I guess so. So, where's my choice in all of this?"

"You're dating Darius.

That was your choice.

Don't worry, once you become a vampire and you get the hang of everything, he'll let you have a say in some things." Shale speaks as though he knows this as fact.

"And, what if I don't want to become a vampire?" I ask curiously.

He shakes his head. "Tough, you're going to become one anyway so you might as well go along with it. What would be so wrong with it? You gain so much, increased strength, hearing, vision, taste, feelings, touch, you age slower. Why wouldn't you want that?

The world we are making isn't going to be a friendly place for humans for too much longer. So, you are better off turning into one of us anyway."

His reasons and rhetorical question sound like a fair deal but what he said after that sparks my interest. "What are they doing with the humans?"

"Many demons eat humans or some part of them. Once they've had their feast, they will calm down, and there will be some order. After that, humans will have little to fear; for those who are left at least." Shale sits down on the grass.

I sit down beside him. "What will happen to Rayleen?"

"Nothing for now. She's too young to turn. No one wants to be a kid for fifty years. And, as long as you don't piss Darius off, he won't dispose of her.

Once you turn though, he would have a harder time getting past you to get to her. So, I guess that's another reason you should just go along with it."

I take some time to ponder on what has been said so far. His reasons are good, and it doesn't seem like being a vampire is like anything from stories. None of the vampires I have known so far have been bloodthirsty or monsters. They have been fairly human-like.

"Is it anything like the movies?" His confused looks tell me I need to elaborate a little more on my question. "How someone is turned into a vampire?"

Shale rolls his eyes. "Well, that depends on which version you go with. Most of them have partial truths to them. Others are completely wrong.

Vampire's teeth are sharp, strong teeth. Eye teeth protract a bit; more and more with age. Saliva takes on a venom type quality with numbing properties in it.

You'll have to ask Sandra about that if you want to know more. She's a whiz on the actual properties and biology of every supernatural out there.

The blood is what contains the vampiric pathogen. I guess you can say it acts, kind of, like a virus once it gets into your bloodstream. It multiplies by feeding on the dead or dying cells in your body. Eventually, it takes over and you become a young vampire. It changes more and more, the longer you've been a vampire."

I stop him by putting my hand up. The information is confusing. "Wait, so you can be a vampire without dying? I thought that you had to die to become one."

"Sorry, I guess that would be confusing. We have movies to blame for that one. Almost all the shows these days require a human to die to become a vampire.

The vampire cells get into your system. They feed off of dead and dying cells. Soon enough your body is filled with these cells. The cells change you as they gain in numbers and basically kill the human in you.

It is true that if the vampiric cell is introduced as you are dying that you can become a vampire quicker, however, it is also riskier because you might die before you change and heal; which just makes you dead.

While changing you might notice little things; you might not get a papercut when you otherwise should have, you'd be gradually more sensitive to sunlight, things like that. It gets better or worse as vampirism takes over.

Your skin becomes a little tougher, but also will light on fire if you go into the sun.

Good enough explanation? Sandra could explain this so much better. She's old. She knows everything. She's had to explain these things a thousand times; it was literally her job at one point."

He pauses for my answer. "Yeah, it's fine. So, what actually works to kill or hurt a vampire?"

"Pretty much most of what you've heard doesn't work. Holy water, crosses, dead man's blood, garlic don't do anything unless you're allergic. The sun, stakes through the heart, well mostly anything through the heart, incineration, and decapitation do.

We don't turn into bats; that was an unfortunate incident with an animus."

I stop him before he can continue. "Animus?"

"An animus is a human-based supernatural that can transform into animals. Not to be confused with a shapeshifter.

Animus can only transform into animals, sometimes only one or two, and usually carry a trait from their transformations. It's rough on their body; painful to watch.

Shapeshifters can transform into anything and anyone; they don't get any changes from their transformations.

Any other questions?" He asks.

I think about it and remember him saying something earlier. "Yeah, you're out in the sun right now, so why aren't you on fire?"

"Special sunscreen, products, and contacts. It's really simple but it works. Technology has only gotten to this point in the last century.

Before that, however, we just went out at night.

Anything else?" Shale asks.

"Not really." Not a moment after saying this, a question races through my mind. "So, what will Darius do to me tonight?"

That question was never fully answered. He said it would be painful, but it didn't sound like it should be painful.

"That, I guess is kind of like the movies. He'll feed on your blood, mostly because he hates to see human blood go to waste, but partially to quicken the process.

He could cut his tongue to cover his fangs in blood before the bite. He might have you swallow some of his blood. He might also cut you and himself, and mix your blood openly. Maybe some unprotected sex. Maybe a needle injection.

Shortly after, if the infection was successful, the vampirism should take over and you start the transformation." It seems quite simple for, what he makes seem like, a possibility of vampiric infection.

He stands up. I'm not ready for the conversation to be over, but he seems to be.

"How long until I change completely?" I ask him quickly.

"It's hard to say because it's different for everyone. It's kind of like getting drunk; administration of vampirism, your metabolism, size, how much blood was drained, and weight all determine how long it takes.

My guess would be about a day before you'd start noticing things." My stomach protests the amount of time that has passed since my last meal. "You need to eat. Go inside. I think you know enough for now and I need to get going. I have some things to take care of."

I agree with him for now. Over the past couple of days, I have been told a lot of information and changes. Yet, I still feel entirely clueless. It feels like he's left so much important information out of our talk. I want to know more. I need to know more.

"Well, thank you for the talk." The moment becomes awkward, and I avert my eyes and turn my head towards the house.

Looking back to say my goodbye, I find I don't have to because he is not there. He's running towards the forest beside the shed.

I walk to the house with a pit in my stomach, and go inside to find Rayleen.

Chapter 14

My eyes open for the tenth time this night; it's getting annoying. I try to go back to sleep. Lying still on the hard floor is uncomfortable and probably the reason why I keep waking up.

I sit up in the make-shift bed, fumbling in the dark. I hit my cellphone. Grabbing ahold, I figure out the top from the bottom and hit the button to turn the screen on. It's 9:06 am. Somehow, with going to bed early and waking up a million times, I've managed to sleep for twelve hours.

My battery is low. I only have twelve percent left. It still has no service, so I turn it off. There's no reason to keep it turned on. I should have turned it off last night, but I hadn't thought about it.

Down Aisle 6, I find breakfast in a box of some cereal I've never heard of before, but I know enough that it's a knock-off brand.

Following the path of candles and flashlights to the staffroom, now looking more like a base of operation, I sit down in a chair while Gary finishes giving instructions to Judy.

"Good morning, Nikki. I trust you had a good sleep." Gary sounds very chipper.

"It was okay," I say between mouthfuls of cereal. Looking down at the table, I see there is a bunch of pieces of paper surrounding a crudely drawn map of the mall.

Gary sits down across from me. "We've got packs made for the scouting missions. First aid kits mostly; just in case. We shouldn't need much else out there.

We'll go out in three groups. One group each for left and right. The other group will go upstairs. We cover all the bases." He points to each section as he says so.

Gary quickly scouted outside yesterday. He said the world went to shit. We'll need to hunker down here while we wait for help. We decided we need to make sure the mall is secure, and see if there's anyone else around.

"We should lock all the entrances and exits. Search all the opened stores." I suggest. There's no use in doing all of this if the demons come and go after we leave.

"Yes." Gary thinks for a moment. He writes down Group 1, Group 2, and Group 3 in a line. "Any suggestions on how we break them down?"

We don't need to complicate things. "I'll go with Steph, Brad, Shawn, and Peter. Mary, Tim, and Kayanna stay safe here. You break up the people you had upstairs in half."

Gary writes my name down for Group 1: pirate ship. He puts Judy for Group 2 and his name under Group 3. "That should be it. Alright, there is no use in delaying this." He grabs the paper, gets up from his seat, and comes around the table.

I set the cereal box on the table and follow him. The moment we set foot out of the warehouse he shouts, "Everyone to the front gate." He does this twice more on our way there.

Everyone has already beaten us to the front. I can see that everything we will need has been moved to the counter. The first aid packs and all the weapons. They must've been busy.

Gary gets right to splitting everyone up from his group. He semi-privately tells Judy what to do, then gathers his half and leaves.

Taking cue I walk over to my group; conveniently standing together. Brad looks irritated but isn't arguing. I wonder if Gary and he had a conversation to make him agreeable, or if a good night's rest helped.

"Kayanna, Mary, and Tim are staying here. Let people come in when they come back. Keep the gate locked otherwise. Everyone else, you're coming with me towards to pirate ship." I don't wait to see if they are following before I grab a pack, a flashlight, and my samurai sword from the counter; attach it through my belt and leave. The extra weight on either side of my hips feels weird.

The gate clicks shut behind us as we go down the hall. No one says a word. I can only hear the noises we are making with our footsteps, and those of our other groups.

The whole mall seems to be quiet. Perhaps the demons attacking thought no one would be at the mall that early. There weren't many of them. It would mean that the demons are familiar with our schedules and habits. They may be more intelligent than I originally thought; possibly not bent on pure destruction and blood lust alone.

But, this might also explain why we aren't hearing anything. They could be intelligent enough to stalk us. I stop my thought process there when a shiver goes up my spine.

I make sure to look in every direction; scanning with my flashlight in an up and down motion. So far, there haven't been any open stores. We come up to a four-way crossing.

"Peter, come with me. We'll go lock those doors." I point to the right. "Brad and Shawn lockdown Bourbon Street, and Steph make sure nothing tries to sneak past here." Immediately after splitting everyone up, I go down towards the exit I assigned myself; not wanting to give anyone a chance to argue.

Now in a smaller group, I feel a bit less secure. Compensating for it, I pull the sword out of the scabbard and ready myself for an attack. Peter does the same. I'm not sure if it is because of the same reason or if I freaked him out by drawing my own.

Getting past the store in the middle of the walkway there is only a short walk to the doors. What I see through the glass makes me stop in my tracks. My jaw drops on its own will.

What we experienced on our way to the mall was only the beginning. The devastation must have continued long after we escaped the outside.

Black smoke rises from smouldering buildings. Cars had been tossed around like toys. Some lay on their sides and others are upside down. I try to count the number of cars out there and compare them to people we have found. There should be at least double the number from this parking lot alone; even more, considering the number of parking lots this place has.

Going through the first set of doors and to the second makes the whole thing more real. I can't help myself as I push open the outer doors. I put the sword back in the scabbard and the flashlight in my pocket.

Reaching into my back pocket, I grab a cigarette and lighter. Automatically taking one out, lighting it then putting everything else away. The action calms me in just the right way. The taste and smell clear out the dirty gasoline smoke from the cars and whatever else might be mixed into the air.

A bit more focused now, I try to look a bit further. Everything is eerie calm and quiet. The calm after the storm and hopefully not the calm before the storm.

This may be a bit more serious than we had originally thought. I would think by now we would have heard something from the army or at least the police.

My cigarette is done too soon, but from the look on Peter's face, I should go back inside. I drop the butt and step on it. Going inside, I don't say a word to Peter. I need a moment to process everything before I do any explaining.

We figure out the locks on the doors and proceed to lock every door on both sets of the inner and the outer doors. We go back towards Steph, on the other side of the middle store. She looks relieved to see us.

The boys are making a bit of noise as they make their way back to us. It sounds like they are horsing around, so I don't see a reason to worry about it when I hear a short yell and someone's flashlight goes flying.

Brad makes it back to us first, shortly followed by Shawn rubbing his shoulder. Both have stupid grins on their faces. I roll my eyes, but can't help but smile.

Shawn pushes Brad towards the direction we need to go. I pull the flashlight out of my pocket and catch up to Brad.

When the area opens up, I realize just how big of a job this is. We don't have enough people to cover everything if we don't all go separate ways alone.

Brad interrupts my thoughts. "You girls stay here. We'll go look around. Peter, go that way. There's an exit down there. I'll go down that way and get the exit to the left. Shawn, you get all the food court and the Brick exit. We'll come back and towards the waterpark together." Brad tries to do the same thing I did just minutes ago. Order people around then leave, so there aren't any arguments.

"Brad, there are two exits over there." I point towards the back left; where he had Peter going. "The one by the music store and the one for the hotel."

He stops and turns around. A partial glare is still in his eyes until he realizes his own mistake and that I'm not completely disputing what he decided.

"Stephanie go with Peter and split up for the exits." He decides then leaves.

Steph looks at me apologetically. I wave her on and smile to tell her it's okay. I pull out my sword and ready myself. There is so much area to cover; just from my position here.

Footsteps above me stop my heart for a moment before I hear Gary's voice right after the stomping around.

Walking forward a bit, I get in a position to see the people above me. I shine my light up there. It only takes a moment for Gary and a few other people to lean over the railing. A couple of flashlights blind me. I put my hand up to cover the light.

"Nikki? That you?" Gary asks.

I answer a short, "yeah."

"Where's everyone else?" He moves the flashlight off of me. I can finally see again, though not without dots in my vision.

"We had to split up to cover the whole area."

"I'll send a couple of people down to help you out." His head disappears for a couple of moments, only to return. "Have you had any trouble?"

"No, nothing so far. You?" I return the question.

"No, we've added a few people though." He says. Maybe the ones who were attacking moved on after they attacked.

I turn my attention to the footsteps approaching. There must be about a dozen extra people. Looking back up at Gary I say "I thought you said a couple."

"Okay, maybe a few more than a couple." He backs away from the railing.

Looking back to the group, I feel they are waiting for instructions. "Hi, I'm Nikki. Umm." It is probably best to split them up by sections, then send them off in different directions; just like the ones Brad set out. I get closer to them and put my hand with the flashlight out the split up a section. "You go down that way." I point down where Peter and Steph had gone. Splitting up the remaining people in half, I point to each way Brad and Shawn had gone. "You go down there and to the right and you through the food court and to the right." As a last moment thought, I tap a couple of people on their shoulders as they go to walk past me. "You two will stay here with me."

The tense edge is slowly disappearing as I hear people talking and laughing through the echoing room.

It doesn't take long before people start returning in their large groups.

Gary yells, "all clear," from the stairs. What people had remained upstairs, now follow him down.

"Us too. We've just got to clear the water park." Steph pipes up. "We should probably also go through the maintenance halls. You can't get in from the outside without a key, but something still could have gone in there from the inside of the mall."

Gary looks to me "You want to take the water park and we'll take the halls?"

"Sure." I stay put, while Gary gathers a group together.

He leaves me with a couple dozen people and my original group. "Alright let's go."

It feels like we're playing a, more dangerous, game of follow the leader. No one seems to want to do anything until I lead the way; all except for Brad, who sticks right beside me.

We go down the escalators. It feels a lot colder down here, probably because this is more of a basement-type area.

Once I shine my flashlight to the entrance, I see a bit of an issue with wanting to go through the waterpark, but probably a blessing in disguise; locked gates are keeping us out.

"Hey, this door's unlocked." A guy says before he goes into the gift shop. So much for that idea.

We corral through the door and out through another door leading to the area behind the gates. Automatically, we split off into the change rooms.

I chuckle to myself as the guys go through the men's room and the girls go to the women's change room. Of course, people would still stick by those rules, when there isn't anyone to catch them and give them trouble for it.

No one goes to the family change room, so I go to that one. Brad races me in there, once he figures out where I'm going.

With my sword still in my hand, I put it on guard in front of me. A couple of people follow in after us. I flick my flashlight into stalls and between the rows of lockers. It doesn't take long to make our way through and out to the traditional waiting area.

People out here already are going out to the different sections of the park. I go to the right and head towards the large pool. It's light enough from the sunlight that I turn off my flashlight and put it into my pocket.

I look up. It's going to take forever to search this whole place. There are too many hiding places. It'll be exhaustive to have to climb all these stairs and trek the slides down.

Some movement to my left catches my eye. There is something over there; for sure. I see some more movement which confirms it.

Heading over there to investigate, I tap Brad's shoulder and get a few peoples' attention. Without talking, I call attention to the Tiki Hut; where I saw the movement.

As we get closer, I can see two people. There is a girl behind the bar and a guy sitting on a barstool. The girl notices us first and lets the guy know. I put my sword away. They're not dangerous.

He spins around. "Hey sup peoples. Welcome to Tiki Hut casa de Tyler. Sit down. Relax and enjoy yourselves. Babe, get our guests a round of drinks." The girl sets about grabbing glasses and filling them with alcohol. I'm sure they are both already drunk.

"Well, this place is clear if you haven't been eaten by now," Brad says before plopping himself down at the bar and grabbing one of their glasses. He starts handing the others out as they are filled. I take one from him.

Matt's eyes are glazed over and his dull stare tells me how drunk he is. Tyler raises his cup, once we all have our own. "A toast. To the end of the world. Let's get shitfaced and enjoy ourselves until we die." I take a drink at the disturbing toast. "Whoo, now, here are the rules. There's a ten drink minimum. If you aren't so drunk that you're puking your guts out, you need another drink. You puke, you clean it up, and don't do it in the pool. Don't drown because this lifeguard's off-duty and most of all, there are no rules. Do whatever the hell you want."

I look around to try to see people's reactions to this. Most people look cheerful and ready to embrace it. I don't know quite what I want to think about it.

On the one hand, if it is the end of the world, I wouldn't mind some fun before I go. However, if it isn't quite the end of the world yet, how am I going to survive with a hangover?

The mood is catching as people embrace Tyler's rules. It may not be so bad to have a few drinks and some fun. We'll be rescued soon, right? I take a sip of straight rum.

My shoulder is tapped. I turn around to find Peter with a straight frown. "I'm going to go get my family."

Oh yeah, we should go get the others and tell Gary too. Whoops. "I'll come with you."

I set the glass down on the closest table, untie the first aid pack to leave it here, and follow beside Peter.

Once we get to the main pool, I remember the doors leading to the main mall. "Hey, let's go out there." I point to the balcony exit.

It doesn't take long before we're there. I can hear the cheers behind me. I'm kind of disappointed that I have to leave and miss out on the fun. I know everyone's going to be half-cut by the time we come back.

Peter unlocks the gate to the balcony and I unlock the door to leave the waterpark. We head back towards the dollar store. I pull out the flashlight and turn it on. The halls seem darker than they were before. My eyes are no longer adjusted to the dark.

Remembering back to the winding halls Steph guided us through earlier, I think it might be a bit more difficult to find Gary than it sounds. Kayanna works here, so it might be better to wait until we find her first. Peter can take his family back to the waterpark while Kayanna and I can go find Gary.

Peter sets our pace. He must be anxious to get back to his family as we slowly keep speeding up. I am glad for my long legs, as I can keep up with him easily.

It only takes us a couple of minutes to get to the gate. Mary is waiting for us. She looks relieved to see us and lets us in immediately. She tackles Peter with her hug.

A shout of "dad," comes from down an aisle. Tim runs out with Kayanna following shortly behind him.

I catch her as the others have a little family moment. "Everyone's at the waterpark, so we're all going to head over there. But, I need your help first. Gary and some others went into the back hallways to make sure nothing was back there. I've seen how twisted it is back there and I was hoping you'd be able to guide me through."

"Sure. I only know bits and pieces but I'll help." She says.

"Is that true, dad? Are we going to go play at the water park?" Tim asks. Excitement fills each word.

"Yes, but the slides aren't working so we'll just be swimming and going to the jungle gym," Peter explains.

"What are we waiting for? Let's go!" Tim grabs both his parents' hands and starts pulling them out of the store and towards to right.

The little boy is super excited to be going to the waterpark. I hope he won't be too disappointed when he gets there and finds out how little there is to do without running water and electricity.

Peter stops and looks at me. I know what he is going to say, so I beat him to it. "Go to the park. We'll meet you there once we find Gary."

"Good luck." He says as he walks away.

"Thanks," I say, though I'm not sure if he hears me. Once they are clearly out of the way, I close and lock the gate. "Let's go out the back."

Kayanna nods. "Do you know which way they went in? Upstairs? Downstairs? Not everything's connected back there."

Oh shit. That's why Steph had us going in and out. "No, I didn't. It would have been close to the big food court." I hadn't thought of watching where they went in. I assumed it was all connected.

"We should just leave a sign on the gate telling them to meet us at the water park. We could search for hours back there and still not find them. But, at any point, someone could come back here and see the note. Plus, they knew you were going to the water park, right? So, they might even go there first." She reasons.

This would solve a few issues and let me party with everyone else while they're still sober enough for me to catch up quickly. She's right anyway; there isn't much of a chance that we'll find them back there. Who knows, they may have even split up too. "Let's do that. You have paper and a pen?"

She doesn't say anything but pops open the cover on the till and grabs some till tape. There is a pen on the counter that she writes a quick note with. It doesn't take long for her to find the tape and stick the message to the gate.

While she does that, I grab my purse from the aisle. Kayanna unlocks the gate and steps out. I follow after her. She locks the gate behind us. Looking at the note, it's been crumpled a bit, but anyone will still notice it.

I lead our way in silence, lit up only by my flashlight. It's a tense silence. Even though we've already cleared the mall, something can always break in. Or, who knows, it could have evaded all of us. All it would've had to do is hide in a dark corner, inside a store, or even in the maze-like halls. Then, go somewhere we already searched.

I feel like a thousand eyes are focused on me from the darkness. As I get more and more paranoid, I pick up my pace; Kayanna has no choice but to speed up as well.

It doesn't take long until the hall gets brighter. The glass walls let in a lot of light from skylights in the waterpark. We enter through the glass door. The puff of the warm air isn't noticeable as it has been in the past. That warm humid air inside the waterpark is becoming as cool as the rest of the mall.

The cold is going to become a huge problem soon. Worse, as the weather outside gets colder and colder. Winter has barely started. This shouldn't last that long though. The army will rescue us soon enough; right?

Joyous hoots and hollers remove all of the seriousness of the moment. Maybe Tyler was right; this is what we all need.

Kayanna and I walk to the Tiki Hut. Almost everyone we see along the way has changed into a bathing suit. The cold not seeming to bother them.

I wonder where they got them from; where I can get one? I don't want to have to go out to the main stores to grab one. Was that one bathing suit store open? I don't think it was.

Will we get in trouble for looting? No, maybe? If it was necessary for survival. They might make us pay it back. If they care after everything that's happened.

A pile of bikinis and swimming trunks answers my one question; at least partially. I still don't know where they got them from. Oh, maybe that store downstairs.

There are a few bathing suit stores in the mall. Would they of had enough time to raid one of those stores. I suppose they could have. I pick up a yellow top and bottom.

Kayanna sits down at the bar and pours herself a drink. I walk up and set my purse down on the counter. Eyeing the bottles, I put down the bikini and grab the vodka. There are many used shot glasses everywhere. Lining up a few, I fill them.

I nudge one over to Kayanna. She takes it up. Clinking them together we say, "Cheers," at the same time. I toss my head back and gulp the burning liquid. The taste sucks, but it feels great.

Kayanna is just drinking now. I give her another. This time, I pay attention. She taps the glass against the bar before shooting.

"Why do you do that?" She looks confused. "Tap the counter."

"Oh, I guess it's a Cheers to the bartender. A thank you, sort of."
She shakes her head. "A friend used to do it, so I had started too."

I pour us another round. "To the end of the world," I say.

She echoes back, "to the end of the world," as she hits her shot glass
against my own. The vodka gets better as I go. The more I drink, the
better it tastes.

Before I get too far gone, I should change. Then, maybe, go for a
swim. I pick up the bikini and decide to walk somewhere close by to
change. There is a food shack close by. That would offer enough
cover.

There isn't anyone over here. When I get to the gate, I go in through
the door, and behind the food serving station; where I will be hidden
by the counter. A quick look around, assures me no one will see me
change. Just in case though, I change fast.

Taking my clothes with me, I go back to the Tiki Hut. A few people
have joined Kayanna at the bar. I drop my clothes on the table and get
in on the next round of shots.

Chapter 15

Six days. I cross out another day on the calendar. It is now six days into the takeover, and still no sign of anyone I know. Still no sign of the army. However, there have been signs of the attackers, but that too has lessened over the past couple of days. I still don't know what's going on, but it can't be good. I tried to go to school on the first couple of school days following the attacks, but I've given up. It's a ghost town out there, but worse. Bodies littered the ground. I tried my close neighbours, but no one was home.

I shudder as I remember a moment from my nightmare last night. The humanoid creature's mouth lurching for me. The pale green skin lit with a flashlight. Red-eye, euh, I can't. My nightmares have gotten bad, in frequency, and ferocity. I remind myself, they are just nightmares.

Back on track, I can't believe that no one's come to get me yet. Maybe they're dead. I can't help the smile on my face. They're probably dead.

Everyone I've ever known is probably dead, is it sad that I find that relieving, freeing? I should feel guilty that I am wishing them all dead, but I don't.

The devastation of the end of the world is my ticket to change things; to free myself from a more cruel life than the one ahead.

Sadly, I would rather explore this life than deal another day in what was normal just one week ago. It's sad that I have been driven to such a point in my life that I am happy at the prospect of never having to see anyone I knew ever again.

Maybe now, I can just be me. Who am I? Who am I going to be?

The answer is a big blank. I can't imagine who I am, and who I will be. I've never gotten a chance to be me; excluding these last six days, but even that was underlined with the thought of my father coming back for me. The thoughts of all my expectations.

I guess I might have to find other people eventually. I don't know how long the salted meat will last. We don't have much for non-perishable items left either. I'm already out of fruit, and vegetables.

Who will I be if I come across people? Can I be like Ashley? Crazy outgoing, she's a people magnet. She's one of those people that can make a friend anywhere. She does wild things I had never hoped of doing. Can I be like Chris? Charismatic. The type of person who can talk anyone into anything. He always gets his way with everyone because he knows just the right thing to say. Maybe I could be like Kayla? Athletic, smart, and driven.

I stop. I could never be one of those people. They are them, I am me; whoever that might be. I have a tonne of baggage. I'm an introvert. I have a lot of issues: zero confidence, zero self-image, zero conversational skills, and a hundred trust issues. I don't even know what a normal person should act like, or how a normal person should be treated. Heck, I didn't even know that it wasn't normal to be afraid of your father until like a year ago. I didn't know that it wasn't normal for you to not have physical contact with people beyond what was necessary or manipulative.

For all of my life, I've been told how to act in front of different people. You act this way in front of grandma, you act this way in front of teachers, and you never mention that thing to Mr. Hall. Don't even think of talking to schoolboys, because that will lead them on, and you'll end up disgraced and pregnant before you finish high school. But, no one's going to want to marry you anyway. You'll be an awful wife to someone someday.

If I'm ever going to be someone else, I would need to erase my past. Can I get elective amnesia? Keep my basic knowledge, but forget my personal memories?

No. I'll just have to deal with it. It should be easy to figure out who you are when no one knows who you've been; when you know you'll probably never see those people again. Even in the past few days, I've never been more myself.

I've found out that I like to be by myself. I prefer my own company to that of anyone else's. I love being alone. Though I know that's not great as a survival plan, so it won't last.

I love to learn, but I already knew that. How many other people do I know that can say they've read an encyclopedia front to back, not to mention that I've read ours at least six times? How many people search information for hours on different topics that catch their fancy that day or week or month?

I have some things to do now. I put another log in the fireplace while wishing it was summer. I swear it's going to snow any day now. Maybe I should go south. It would get warmer the further south I go. In any case, I'll need to travel somewhere, and soon.

I've got my sleeping bag, and it's good for minus forty Celsius. I think I could survive a Canadian winter, but it would make it easier, and less bone-chilling to go south. If everyone is dead, there isn't anything left here for me.

I grab my hiker's bag. I'm really glad I convinced my dad I needed to go on a school camping trip a few years ago for school credit. The different camping tools I got then, are going to be handy now. I never liked that I was a rich kid before, but now I am thankful that he didn't bat an eyelash at some of the camping 'necessities' I convinced him I needed. I have a flint, Swiss army knife, solar-powered flashlight, and a water bottle with a built-in purification filter have all been the most helpful the last week.

There are still some leaves in the opening of one of the compartments. I leave them in there. I search the bag for anything else that might have been left behind, but I don't find anything. I need to think this through logically. How much can I carry for any large length of time? What is necessary versus convenience, and wants?

If I go anywhere, I will need what I've been using. I've been switching out clothes every day, but if I am going for light travel then all I need are the clothes I'm wearing, plus a few more layers. Maybe a couple of extra outfits for my bag.

I need a first aid kit. Many of the items in there are multipurpose too. I can use peroxide and iodine as water purifiers in an emergency. The gauze could be used as a weak rope to bind something. I find rubbing alcohol too. I put them all in the bag. Not a moment later though I take them out, and put them on the floor next to the bag. I might want to organize this a bit better.

I gather items from around the house. Anything I might need; Matches, fire starter stick, candles, crayons, camping dish, and utensil kit, salt, granola bars, a chocolate bar, tin foil, duct tape, survival book; the list goes on.

I grab enough items to fill every compartment. The thing weighs a bunch, and I could never outrun anyone, but otherwise, I would survive. I drag the bag into the corner of my closet.

It's a shame that there isn't enough light to light up my books or I would read more. I'd light up something, but I need to conserve everything I have, and someone could see.

I don't need light to work out. I guess I can do another today. I half feel, half see, my way to the side table where my wrist and ankle weights are. I strap them to each appendage. The extra weight is only about twenty pounds total, but after a while, it feels heavier. I walk to the cleared space in the middle of my room. The routine is ingrained in my head. Cross, cross, uppercut, uppercut. Over and over. A while later I change to punch, knee, punch, switch, repeat. Over and over.

Over and over. The same circuits over, and over again. I eventually exhaust myself. I don't think it will take any time to get to sleep. I remove the weights.

I take off my boots and crawl back into my sleeping bag. I have a feeling I will be spending a lot of time here.

There isn't much to do but go to sleep. I hesitate at the prospect of another nightmare, but I really can't help whether I have one or not. Not unless I exhaust myself to the point of no longer dreaming.

Chapter 16

While putting my dirty dishes away, I realize darkness has fallen while we were eating dinner.

I turn around after I feel a tug on my shirt. Rayleen stands behind me with a pout on her face. "I'm bored, and Crystal just wants to sleep." Her tone matches the exaggerated bored look on her face.

Amused with her antics, I humour her dramatics. "Crystal is just a baby, so she needs to sleep a lot. I guess, if you're bored, we should do something about it. So, what would you like to do? Keep in mind, it has to be inside this house."

"I don't know." She whines to me.

Sandra comes into the kitchen. "Sandra, are there any board games in the house?"

She pauses and looks up to her right. "I don't think so. Not that I remember seeing, anyway. How about you play hide and seek? You're still young enough for that right?" She directs the last questions to Rayleen by looking at her.

Her little face lights up. "Yes! Do you want to be It first?"

"As much as I would love to, I'm afraid it will just be you and Alexa playing. Ram and I have to go out. We've got work to do." Sandra pretends to pout.

I close my eyes and put my hands over them. Starting to count out loud, "one, two, three… You better start hiding or I'm going to find you and then you'll be it." A small playful shriek comes from in front of me and could only belong to one person. Footsteps start running out of the room. "Four, five," I uncover my eyes because I know by now she shouldn't be able to see me. Looking around briefly I see Sandra and Ram had escaped as well. "Six, seven, eight, nine, and ten. Ready or not, here I come."

Not in a hurry to find her, I walk leisurely into the living room. I look through the room thoroughly; looking behind couches, curtains, and the television stand. She isn't in this room.

I only heard one set of footsteps up the stairs. With Sandra's disappearance, it could have possibly been her, so taking that chance I decide to explore the main level a little more.

There is a hall between the stairs and the kitchen; I walk down there. There are three doors in the hall. I open the first one and am greeted with darkness. I flick a light switch on the left and see another stairway in front of me. It goes straight down to a wooden platform connected to two other stairs that go to the right and the left. Quickly deciding she wouldn't go down there, I turn off the light and shut the door.

The next room down the line is a bathroom. It takes a quick look behind the curtain and the door to realize she isn't in there either.

Next, I check the bedroom. It is the master bedroom in the house. I'm surprised that it isn't the room Sandra would have chosen. It is about twice the size of her room. Tossing away the fleeting thought, I get back to the task at hand.

Once I clear the room, I leave it. Looking to my left, out of the room I see the front door. Remembering there is another room near the door I go towards it. Turning the corner, I find a small laundry and freezer room. There are absolutely no hiding spots that aren't right in the open. Looking it over quickly just in case, I determine she isn't there.

As far as I know, that is all there is to this level in the house. That leaves the upstairs or the basement. Still figuring that I should rule out the basement, I head to go upstairs.

Checking over the living room quickly, I make sure she hadn't changed her hiding spot while I was in the other rooms. I haven't caught her moving yet, but in the past, I have caught her in spots I had already checked before.

I go upstairs, being careful to quieten my steps as I go. The urge to surprise her bubbles up in me suddenly.

Checking the bathroom up here, just as quickly as the one downstairs, I come up with the same verdict. I look behind the couch and under the desk up here; still no sign of Rayleen.

The only two rooms left are Sandra's and the guest room. I check through Sandra's room quickly, feeling awkward that I am in her room without her or her permission.

Figuring that she should be in the guest room, I go in there and shut the door. A musty smell fills the room, as though this room is never open. For a moment, I think about opening the window. Forgoing the action to the thought, I start searching the room.

I check out every nook and cranny of the main part of the room before I look in the closet. Moving some of the clothes aside to get a better look I determine that she couldn't be hiding in there. I turn around. Then remembering that I should close the closet I turn again.

The little girl I was looking for is standing right there. I jump from the surprise. Grabbing her, I take her over to the bed and throw her onto it. She laughs as I jump onto the bed beside her. Her giggles turn to shrieks of laughter and cries telling me to stop tickling her.

Crystal jumps up on the bed and squawks at me to stop my assault on Rayleen. So short of a time and the griffin is already protective of the little girl.

I release the child when Crystal looks like she is about to pounce on me. Rayleen backs away from me. "I scared you good, didn't I?"

Crystal bounds over to Rayleen. She forces Rayleen to pet her by rubbing her head into Rayleen's hand. Not stopping even after Rayleen starts petting by herself.

I playfully glare at the little girl. "Just surprised me; that's all."

She points her finger at me, "Alexa, you're not supposed to lie."

Thrusting my hands up to my shoulders in defence I tell her, "I'm sorry, yes, you did scare me. So, how about another round?"

She grins from ear to ear, "Okay, you're it."

Rayleen jumps off the bed and tries to get away. Crystal follows after her.

As she opens the door I shout after her, "Hey, it's your turn to be it."

The redhead holds onto the handle on the other side. "Nope, you didn't find me last time. I found you, so you're it." She shuts the door before I can argue.

I sit for a moment waiting for what should be a good amount of time to pass before I go looking for her. Because of the shut door, I can only guess where she had gone this time, not that that has helped me much in the past.

Going into Sandra's room again, I check the same spots again; leaving the room in record time. I look into the bathroom checking to see if it was left the same way I had left it. It is, so I move on.

Going down the stairs, I check the living room. I notice a light coming from the basement. Thinking, 'gotcha,' I grab the doorknob and open the door.

The stairs creak as I walk down them. Noticing the backs of the stairs aren't there, I get a childish chill creeping up my spine; the feeling that someone is going to reach out and grab my ankle makes me speed up my descent and jump the last couple of stairs to the platform. Quickly, I turn to look at the space behind the stairs and relief slows my rapid heartbeat as I see nothing and no one there.

I look around. From my position, most of the basement is visible to me; save for the contents of the room behind the doors on opposite sides of the room.

It's a pretty average basement for one that is used mostly for storage purposes. Cold concrete surrounds me from floor to ceiling. The entire wall behind the stairs is filled with boxes, totes, and randomly placed items. There is a Christmas tree in the corner. All of its decorations and lights have been left on it.

On the other side, there is a small attempt at making this space livable. A singular couch sits in front of an old-fashioned fireplace. Walking over there, I look to see if she is lying down on it, but no such luck.

My heart stops at the sound of quick little footsteps behind me. I can't tell where they came from exactly, but when I turn around what

I do see startles my heart again. Taxidermy animals, both full bodied and just the heads, sit against the side of the stairs.

Moving on to the storage area, I can't help but feel eyes on me. The hairs on the back of my neck stand on end. Something in the back of my mind tells me that I should just leave the basement and call that I give up, but I ignore it. Looking through the storage items I make sure she isn't hidden somewhere in or behind things.

The footsteps make me turn around again. This time they sounded and felt closer. Before I can even realize it my legs have already started moving and I run like my life depends on it. Half tripping up the stairs I can't get out of the basement fast enough.

Closing the door behind me, I lean against it.

My cheeks enflame when I realize how much I let my childish fears get a hold of me and control me. Especially when I try to think of rational reasons for the noises; a mouse could have made them or even residual noises from someone walking upstairs.

Deciding the latter is going to be my choice I push myself off the door. I hear noises again but this time they come from upstairs.

I bolt upstairs hoping to catch her while she is moving. She might have gone back to her last hiding place, thinking I wouldn't check there again, so I go into that room and close the door like the last time.

The window is open, unlike last time. She must have opened it because of the smell. I smile from feeling I am on the right track. I open up the closet, looking more thoroughly this time, and determine that there is no way she could be in there this time. I close the door.

Coldness slaps down on my mouth. A feminine body envelopes me and holds me still; struggling doesn't work as her body keeps me in a vice grip.

"Shut up and stay quiet and I'll let you go." I hadn't realized I had been screaming until she said something about it. The second thing I realize is that I know the voice speaking to me. I stop.

Trying to nod doesn't work because of the hand over my mouth, but she lets me go anyway.

I turn around, "Kelly."

She doesn't let me say anything after calling her name, "Shhh, we have to go. We've already got Rayleen and the rat, so let's go."

She surprises me. "What do you mean? I'm not going anywhere. Where's Rayleen?"

Kelly backs up from her shock. "What the hell?" She looks shocked and confused. "Are you kidding me? With the way he treats you and how terrified Rayleen is of him. I know what he made you do to Miles, that isn't something you would ever do on your own. And, he hits you. No one should go through anything like that. He's abusing you. Why-"

I lash out immediately, "Darius isn't abusive. He just gets angry and sometimes the cast-off gets turned in my direction. But it's okay, he immediately apologizes and he means it. He treats me like a princess the rest of the time."

She raises her eyebrow at me. "Wow. I'm not letting you get Rayleen back as long as you're with him. It's not safe for her, and it's not safe for you. Look, you have two options: you can come with me willingly, or you can stay here without Rayleen."

"I'm staying here and you're bringing Rayleen back." I counter.

"How can you so calmly stand there and say you're fine with everything he does. All the destruction and deaths." Kelly shakes her head at me and then looks away.

"It had to happen so the world could change. They are casualties of war. There are always casualties of war." I try to argue. What is she talking about? What did Darius do?

"But there didn't have to be a war." She waits a moment. "How do you rationalize the humans in the blood farms?" The what? "You don't know. Darius ordered any human left walking the streets to be put into farms so that they can extract blood and feed off of them whenever they want.

Look, I don't have time to argue with you. Are you coming or not?"

I weigh my options. If I don't like what I see I can always come back. "I'll go, on the condition that you will let me come back here when I want to."

"Deal, now let's go." She smiles at me trying to assure me.

I know the distance from this floor of the building. One misstep ending in a fall would result in at the least one broken bone, if not death at the worst. "And just how are we supposed to get out of here?"

"Piggy-back of course. Now hop on." Kelly turns around ready for me to jump on.

I put my hands on her shoulders, not wanting to just jump right on without a warning to her, "Ready?"

"Yep," at her mark, I jump up. Situating myself on her back feels as though I am trying to hold onto a slightly padded statue.

As soon as I stop moving she takes off in a jolt. I dig my fingers into her shoulders instinctually to be sure I won't fall. It comes in handy to keep myself up when we hit the ground. Already I don't know how long I can do this. Her grip on my legs hurts, and will no doubt make them fall asleep soon.

As I open my eyes, I see trees racing around me. My stomach is slowly returning from my throat.

Kelly speeds us through the forest. She's fast but not as fast as I would imagine a vampire could go; more like a super fast-human runner. She doesn't stop when we break through the tree line; her speed increases from the lack of resistance and obstacles. I wonder how fast she could go without carrying me.

She follows the road. There are no vehicles anywhere; no sign of any life anywhere. Off in the distance, I can see dark clouds above where the city should be; orange and yellow highlights lick the bottom edges.

Stopping abruptly feels like slamming into a concrete wall. My breath is exhaled out but my throat closes and refuses to open.

Hands go out from under my legs leaving me no support. Falling to the ground on my hands and knees opens my throat back up.

The first breath is drawn in so quickly I choke on the spit that gets sucked in with it.

My throat burns with each cough. Getting it under control I stand up to face Kelly. My cheeks are inflamed from the embarrassment of the situation. She doesn't seem to care much because she just turns around and starts walking towards a motorcycle.

She gets on and turns on the engine. I get the idea and climb on the back. She puts on the only helmet. Wrapping my arms around her, I can only hope to live through the ride. She takes off slowly but quickly gains speed.

The closer we get to the city the more destruction there is. I start to see life when we race onto the road headed into the city. Kelly slows when people run screaming from the hospital. Moments later a couple of green child-sized human-like creatures emerge and leap on top of one of the people running. Chilling screams die as pointed teeth tear chunks out of the neck.

One of them looks up at Kelly and me, the meat still in its mouth. "What is that?" I yell. My stomach rises to my throat but this time is different; it comes with a vile taste in my mouth.

She stops the motorcycle and twists. Kelly opens the visor to talk to me. "A goblin. They're loyal to Darius and are doing his bidding. He told them to kill so they're killing."

She doesn't miss a beat and takes off at a faster speed once again. Images flow past me. I have to concentrate to see anything.

They look like fleeting photographs of the disaster area of a horror movie. Monsters are everywhere eating, chasing, and ripping people apart. Any people that are still in the streets are looting from stores and houses, killing each other, or running away.

My heart stops with one particular image as my brain tells me it was him. Darius, with his back turned to us, with his head down. A twitching arm held out to the side from the hold he has on the person.

Seeing enough horror movies, adding the knowledge that he is a vampire, tells me exactly what he's doing to the person. Wanting to hold onto the picture, I so badly want to prove that it wasn't Darius. I try to look further back. I get no more than that one glance, but it told me a lot. Looking ahead I try to figure out where we are going.

Something wet and cold slides down my cheeks. I grip harder. Going faster than we had ever before, nothing is clearly visible anymore through my tears. We go fast; probably over the speed limits.

Despite Kelly blocking much of it, the wind takes a toll on my face and arms. The chill makes me shiver and I have to wonder how long I'll be able to hold on after the prickle sensation in my hands goes numb.

Grey and orange give way to green and darkness. Eerie quiet has replaced screams and sounds of destruction.

Kelly slows down quickly, but still controllably. She stops finally at the entrance doors of the building. Getting off the bike, I rub at my arms trying to soothe the bite. My arms are red even through the darkness.

I've only been here twice before but the building is recognizable as the International Airport. She pushes through the door first then holds it briefly for me to get through. The normally bustling halls of people are now empty.

I follow Kelly because she knows where she is going. I don't recognize my way at all. It doesn't help that it only has the backup lights turned on.

We finally enter through some doors and into a room with light in it. "Alexa!" My name is shouted by a familiar voice.

Kneeling on one knee, I catch the little girl. I stand up while hugging her close to me, much like I had only the day before. This time I have no intention to release her anytime soon. Crystal rubs up against my leg. I can feel her purring through the jean material.

Our tender moment is frozen when I notice one of the other people in the room. Miles stands from his seat when our eyes catch. He tries to reassure me with a small smile, but it does nothing to the pure nauseating feeling I get from seeing him after what I did.

He walks closer to us.

At first, he stands a respectable distance away, but soon that doesn't seem to work for him. The ginger male comes closer and reaches his hand up to rest on my shoulder. His thumb sweeps across the skin on my neck. Miles' actions take away the horrible feelings waging inside of me and leaves a peaceful feeling in its place.

"Elves have a nature-based power. Drawing energy and giving it back to the earth and all of its inhabitants: plant-based, animal, human, and many supernaturals. Through this energy, we can do many things; like healing. That's how I was able to heal my injuries so fast and the hurt you felt. The reason of which has been forgiven and I don't want to hear any more of it. Now Miss Rayleen, now that Alexa is here, will you go to bed?" The little girl in my arms looks to me searching for an answer. I in turn look at Miles. "She's been yawning the whole time she's been here and she has almost fallen asleep sitting up multiple times while waiting for you."

"Well, then I guess you should be getting to bed now." I switch my commentary from Rayleen to Miles. "Where would be a good place for her to go?"

Kelly answers for him, "I can show you. It's not far." Nodding my agreement, I follow her lead. Miles says his good night and Rayleen and I wave back to him. Kelly leads us out of that room and into the adjoining one.

This room looks like it was the staff common area. A fridge, counters, cabinets, table, and chairs make out the main components of the room. Up against the one wall are two worn leather loveseats.

Letting Rayleen down, I put her on the couch. She lays herself down and curls up facing the back of the couch. Crystal jumps up and lies in the crease her legs make. I don't say anything to her. Her ease in falling asleep tells of either her comfort level or her exhaustion.

The room we're in is relatively warm compared to how cold the November air is outside. As all the excitement of the day slowly goes away, I realize my skin still prickles from the temperature of the room.

Kelly comes around from behind me with a blanket. It's grey and scratchy. She opens it up and I help her cover Rayleen in it, making sure she is covered enough before I kiss her temple.

Kelly and I leave the candle-lit room and back into the last one. The room had been filled since we were gone. Not wanting to disturb the conversation, I reduce the amount of noise I make by manually easing the door shut.

Looking to Kelly I try to catch an idea of what I'm supposed to be doing; whether to stand here and listen or to leave. Kelly flicks her wrist twice and points to the door on the other side of the room. She starts walking in that direction and I follow.

The whole room freezes. When I look around, I find all the eyes are fixated on me. An awkward feeling passes through me. I continue walking, trying to ignore them. Walking past some of the creatures I receive glares, snarls, and growls.

A stunning lady in a baby blue, skin-tight, one-shouldered dress draws herself from the crowd. Blue-black hair is pulled back into a bun.

I look slightly down at her to catch her eyes. Her eyes are as black as the deepest depths of the ocean. "How can you show your face here?"

"Ariela!" Kelly reprimands her.

"No, she's been behind enemy lines while half the world dies. The sight of her disgusts me; sleeping with the vampire in charge of the destruction in this region and she's fine with it." She sneers at me.

"Let's not forget that your sister is also on the enemies' side." Kelly counters. Ariela's eyes lighten to a deep blue. I remember the woman from Sandra's memory, and I can see a familial resemblance between the two.

"That's purely her choice. Aalayah has always been a self-centred bitch concerned only with winning and how she can be the most popular. It's all about Aalayah. Please, we all act on our own and all have our own minds. She made her choice, she's making her mess, and she will clean it up."

"Aalayah is a little misguided. She'll turn around and come back to us. She always does. She just needs to get down and dirty, before she comes crawling back to where she belongs." A tall woman puts her hand on my shoulder. Flecks of green accent her dirt brown eyes; warmth flows from her eyes to her smile. "Now, I believe you were on your way somewhere." A gentle push on my shoulder sets my body in motion, but one last comment makes me pause for a moment. "And Alexa, don't be like my sister and need to learn things the hard way. You're smarter than that. Listen to the people around you." Her motherly tone scolds me then she waves me off.

Following my original path to the door, I can't shake the eyes on me. Kelly opens the door for herself and holds it for a moment. I slink through.

"Well, that was awkward. I wonder what they would do if they knew you were planning on going back to him. Actually, that might be fun to see." Kelly muses to herself. I don't answer her or say anything; though my heart wants to protest. I bring up my middle finger to bite the nail.

Rounding the corner, I stop while Kelly keeps going.

Hundreds of people lay on the floor. Blood seeps from everywhere. Make-shift bandages are stained red with the blood. My lungs fill deeply with an intake of air. Letting it out, I try to lessen the pain that has returned there. Jogging, I catch up to Kelly to stay in step behind her.

We walk in between the bodies. My eyes jump from face to face and wound to wound.

"This is our hospital, though it's turning into more of a morgue. Most of them will be dead by morning thanks to your boyfriend and his fun." Kelly practically wrenches a knife in my heart as she goes on about the terror Darius is in charge of.

I want to scream at her to stop.

I get it now.

One of the faces I recognize. Stopping mid-step, I try to examine the person more carefully. The lady in the barn from earlier today lays battered on a sheet. Her only ailment seems to be small scratches on her face and shoulders.

"What happened to her?" I ask one of the people attending to the wounded. The male elf, by my assumption through his similar looks to Miles, comes over. He puts a hand on her cheek.

Not even a moment after he does, her body springs up and she lands directly in front of me. I step back from her sudden proximity.

"Traitor, what's Darius going to do once he finds out?" Jowls form from her mouth. Her teeth sharpen and fur grows in an instant.

Backing up from the changing body, I trip over the legs from another on the ground; breaking eye contact for only a moment. In the next, a deep feline growl is aimed in my direction before she takes off like a cheetah.

The able-bodied people in the room charge after her. She dodges everyone until all are out of sight. The chase continues further on beyond my hearing range.

A quick check around me confirms I am the only up-right person in the room. My mind is torn in two; either I can stay here until someone returns, or I can go try to find someone to the conference room.

My choice is made for me when I feel the same awful presence from the football game. My searching eyes locate him quickly, lurking in the shadows.

I swallow the growing lump in my throat. Trying to sound as confident as I can, I confirm who he is. "Seth, right?"

Stepping out of the darkness, I catch the end of his nod. "Leave the child here, they will protect her. You'll come with me and I will explain to Darius of your kidnapping. If you choose to stay, I will kill you. Hmm, maybe I should just kill you anyway. You've made Darius soft. It might be to my advantage to rid him of you." Shale comes into the room. He looks me over before changing his focus and nodding to Seth. "But, that can come later. Shale." Seth turns direction to disappear around the corner in a blur.

Shale is beside me in the same motion. "Don't be alone with him. It's not safe." He whispers the warning to me at a volume I can just barely hear; maybe he didn't even say it at all. Shale guides us out of the building. Rayleen's safer here.

The ride begins again; this time we drive back in a car. I keep my eyes closed for the duration. In the darkness, I can pretend for a moment that horrendous acts are not taking place all around me.

The trip back is a lot shorter. Whether Shale travelled a different route or he drove faster than Kelly, I can't tell. Possibly it could just be my imagination that it took shorter too. Maybe we didn't go back through the city. Maybe it's because I'm not freezing my arms off.

Immediately after we arrive, I'm ushered into the house. The feeling of the house has changed. After the quick trip to the world outside, everything has changed.

Shale shuts the door behind us. Sandra comes to meet us from the kitchen. "You're back. I'll take her from here. She's had quite the day I'm sure. We'll let her get some rest before Darius changes her. She's going to need her strength for it." Something about the tone in her voice is different. She takes me by the shoulder and rushes me away from Shale. Sandra doesn't give him a chance to protest or approve. "Why don't you head to the barn and help them take care of things there?"

Sandra takes my hand. I am directed through the kitchen and upstairs. Sandra practically shoves me into her bedroom. "Stay in here. The window is bolted so you can't get out and no one can get in. It's safe for now at least." She sits down in her chair, "so?"

My mind draws a blank as it is busy looking for signs that she might snap again. "So, what?" Of course, my scars feel this is the right time to itch. It takes both hands, one on each thigh, to soothe the itch; though only slightly.

"What happened?" Sandra asks.

"She just got back. Give her a moment before you grill her." Darius walks into the room. Arms wrap tightly around me from behind. I can't help my heartbeat from racing as flashes of Darius killing the person in almost this position, run through my mind.

His hold immediately loosens and pulls back to grip my shoulders. My world spins as I do. Stopping when I face him, his hands focus my face directly on his. Darius' gaze drills into mine. When my eyes burn slightly I realize I haven't blinked; when I try to I can't. My body has frozen in fear. "What side are you on; mine or theirs?"

Compelled to tell him something I try to tell him I'm on his side. Opening my mouth to say his, but it doesn't come out that way. "I don't know."

"Then, you're on their side." Sandra turns to talk to Darius. "I knew this would happen. The moment they took her, they filled her mind with lies. Who knows, maybe they altered her thoughts or memories. You don't need her anymore. She's a liability."

Sandra walks up and puts her hand on his shoulder. Her alternate tone has returned and is more venomous than before. "I'll be a much more suitable queen than she could ever be and you don't even have to change me. We could put her in the farm; she'd have some use then." She laughs deep from the back of her throat. "Or, we could just feed her to the hobgoblins. They'll skin you, open you up, dig through to your bones and eat you while you're still alive, and once they are done with you we'll give whatever's left to the dragons; if there is anything left."

Terrified, flight instinct kicks in; trying to break loose and run away. I struggle in Darius' grip on my head. He shakes his head at me. Cold hands release themselves and my legs move into action.

Sprinting out of the room, I distinctly hear laughter coming from, I half jump and half run down the stairs. Rounding the corner, I run into a chest; the air is knocked from my lungs by the force.

Darius grabs hold of me and drags me towards the basement. Adrenaline pumps through me, but it does me no good right now. Any hits and kicks I land only serve to hurt me more than him; grabbing onto furniture only moves it and holding onto the corner of the wall only hurts my hands. He has no problem opening the door with me in one arm.

"I'm terribly sorry it had to end like this. I wish it could have been better between us but we're just two different people from two different worlds. But don't worry it's me, not you." He laughs at his joke. "No, no, it really was you. Goodbye, have fun."

Just as he finishes his last two words he pries my grip off of the door's crown moulding and tosses me like a doll down the stairs.

I reach out; trying to grab onto something, anything.

My heart seems to stop as the wall gets closer. My left forearm catches onto a wooden brace for the ground-level floor.

My direction and speed change. Slowing me down and bringing my upper body to a slight turn; enough so when I crash into the concrete wall the back of my right shoulder connects first.

Sharp pain, cracking, another hit and another and another. Cold floor rubs down my cheek before I finally come to a halt.

I had shut my eyes tight in the ordeal. Not that it matters, when I open them nothing is visible.

Blood goes to my head.

Pain drowns my hearing.

Every breath burns down my throat.

Moving causes all the more pain, but my brain tells me I need to move.

My hands are first; my left forearm sears. Dragging my legs off the stairs they seem to have nothing more than prospective bruises. I don't think they have any breaks; though I would bet my left arm is broken.

Once on level ground, I start to pull myself together and slowly stand up; using the wall to help me up.

The burning in my throat increases when I choke on saliva. Wet coughing strips my throat and tears run down my cheeks. The resulting headache tops everything off.

"Fucking hell." I try to attain my bearings once more.

Mapping out the room in my mind. I fell down the same side I had walked down. My hands go out in front of me; searching for the couch.

Each step further into the darkness takes a piece of hope away until my hands grasp fabric. A moment of elation is dampened by a noise. Rustling on the far side of the room, then tiny footsteps. Mice, I hope. Hobgoblins, echoes in my thoughts.

Running my hand along the back of the couch to the other side; my hand runs into something sharp. It's gone in an instant.

Hesitating at first, I release my security to venture out, this time in search of the wall; beyond that should be door number one.

Small laughter creeps behind me to the left. On the right, I hear breathing mid-height; coming from the couch.

Rushing as much as I can, I find the wall. Going left, I search for the wooden texture. Only a couple of meters away I find that too.

Noises come closer; something made of glass crashes to the floor, a piece of it bounces off my heel.

My hands desperately grasp for the doorknob. The first couple of tries I miss it completely. My left hand's fingers find the other side of the door. Running my pinkies down the edges with my other fingers fully sprawled.

My right thumb hits the metal knob. Wrapping my hand around it I turn it. Something small hits my pant leg and holds on. My hand releases the doorknob in my surprise. Tiny claws prick their way up to my back.

"Fresh meat," is roughly whispered in my ear.

"Kill her." Reaching my hand around to my back I feel my hand touch skin. Clenching the creature, I rip it from my back and throw it across the room.

Another one steps onto my foot and teeth dig into my shin. Shaking my leg, I try to get the creature off. Successfully I shake it off, but it feels like a chunk of my leg was taken with it. Turning back, I find the doorknob more quickly this time. I waste no more time and open the door.

An automatic light comes on just outside. In the excitement of the chance of freedom in my grasp, I trip over something and scrape my hands in the landing.

The small creature leaps onto my leg. I turn over to get it off, but it shrieks and leaps off of me. Red eyes retreat into the darkness. Three pairs of eyes watch me. They seem to be waiting for something.

Not wanting to figure out what that is, I quickly get up. Looking at my surroundings I see grass and trees to my right.

Heading that way, I figure out exactly where I am. Around the corner of the house, I can see the shed in the moonlight. The opening to the path in the woods is somewhere along this tree line. It doesn't take long to find it.

The woods are dark, but the light of the full moon seeps through the foliage. My crunching footsteps are the only noise I can hear. I listen intently for anything that might alert me before another creature finds me.

Hiking through the trees, I can't tell what time it is or how far I have to go. Slowly my heart and mind calm down. Every step I take I can feel twinges of pain all over my body.

I slow down to examine the wounds I can see. Scratches, welts, and bruises seem to be everywhere. My left forearm has swollen immensely; though no bones are sticking out so that's a good sign. Blood drips from each open sore.

"What happened? You look horrible." My heart races and I jump a foot off the ground. His voice sounds familiar to me, yet he shouldn't be here.

Stopping when he comes into view. "Miles," I whisper.

A pit develops in my stomach and rises up my throat. My head gets light and fuzzy. Weights pull down my eyelids.

Chapter 17

Did the world end yet? It feels like it ended.

My mouth feels fuzzy like a carpet has grown in there. My head hurts a bit and I feel like I've been hit by a bus.

I don't remember what happened last night. The last thing I remember is partying at the Tiki Hut.

My eyes open to blackness, a relief, since I'm sure any light would just make my head hurt more.

I have towels wrapped around me and something soft, but leather feeling underneath me. Like foam covered in leather, but not a couch. I'm still dressed in my bathing suit, but I have an army jacket and pants on too.

I'm freezing.

Feeling around, I find the edge of the thing I'm on. It's only inches from the carpeted ground. I sit up and find the ground with both my feet. No socks or shoes, so I am happy that the ground is carpeted; my toes are already ice.

Groping everything in reach I try to find something, a candle, my phone, a flashlight. Anything that could help me see, but there is nothing. How did I find my way in here, if I didn't have any light?

Standing up, I put down careful footsteps away from the cushion. I hold my hands out in front of me to make sure I don't walk into anything.

It takes a while, but I finally grab onto something hard.

A bookshelf!

Am I in Chapters? I must be.

They have cushions in the way back, in the children's section.

Great. Now, I'll have to find my way to the front of the store with a million obstacles in the way. Bookshelves and tables and books are everywhere.

I let go of the shelf in front of me. Going around it, I go on into the darkness. Hopping bookshelf to bookshelf; I get pretty far.

Finally, looking into the distance I can see a bit of light. My bet is it's coming from the skylights over the boat. It must be daytime. Letting go of the current bookshelf, I make a straight line for the light.

I run into a table. My thighs sting with pain from the jab. Books fall to the ground when my hand accidentally bumps them off.

Before too long, I can get myself free of the store and into the light and the extremely cold ground. I don't know where anyone is, but they obviously aren't in there, or they slept through all that noise I made.

I jog to the last place I remember seeing everyone, to immediately find some people sleeping on the beach loungers. Why didn't I do that?

I go through the glass door. It's getting colder just about everywhere now. After a detour to the bathrooms, I follow faint noises to the Tiki Hut.

"Welcome back from the dead. Where did you go?" Tyler makes a big drunken show of his words. The way he eyes me up and down makes me gritty and slimy.

"I woke up in Chapters. I don't remember anything else, since we started drinking yesterday." My shoes? They're on the floor by a table to the left. I slip them on. It's a huge relief for my feet until they start stinging painfully.

"Oh Sweetie, we started drinking two days ago." Do I know her? She seems vaguely familiar. The round glasses are familiar.

Wait. Did I blackout for two days?

"Yeah, here have a drink, get rid of that hangover and clear your mind." Tyler goes to hand me a beer, but I think better of it. I blacked out for a long time; too long.

"I think I'm better off with water or pop. I don't feel that great." My head aches, and now my stomach is starting to protest as well.

And, there are the questions that nag at me from a night or two forgotten. Looking around I try to spot something that is still full; something that isn't alcohol.

I can't find anything. Did we drink straight alcohol the whole time? That might explain why don't remember anything.

Oh, there's one empty pop bottle.

"Good morning." Steph comes up behind me and hugs me. "Want to go find food with me?"

"Sure." We walk off together to the main food court. The Chinese buffet that was open still has a few drinks. We take those and try to break into some of the other restaurants, but have no success.

We decide to walk around until we find something, figuring that we will end up having to go back to the dollar store.

I heard some rapid footsteps behind us. Rushing to us. Brad and Shawn descend upon us. Brad hug tackles Stephanie from behind, while Shawn taps my shoulder as he leaps in front of me.

I scream a little in surprise. "Hi."

"Hey." Shawn answers.

"What are you lovely ladies up to?" Brad asks.

"Walking the mall. Just like old times." I joke.

"Trying to find food," Steph answers at the same time.

"Have you tried Bourbon Street yet? It's so cold in here, some of the fresh stuff might still be fresh." Shawn says.

"Sounds great. Let's go." I answer. It sounds like Shawn has already figured it out with experience. The fresh stuff is better than the odds and ends junk food I've been eating. We make our way to the restaurant alley.

"So, where did you disappear to?" Shawn asks me.

"I woke up in Chapters. I'm not sure why I was there. I don't remember much from the last day." I reveal.

Steph switches the subject as we approach our turn-off. "I wonder what's going on out there? The end of the world should have happened by now."

"Not necessarily. Maybe they're biding their time." Brad answers, but I don't think that's it. "Maybe we should rethink it all; less end of the world and more of a global takeover." Brad puts into words where my thoughts had been headed. "They're what? Demons? Monsters? Animals? They would want a world they can live in after this is all over."

"They would need us for what? Food or slaves. Either way, they need us to live, for now." Steph adds on.

"How long has it been? Four days? Has anyone been able to talk with any of our families? Maybe, they're looking for us. We should try to find them." Shawn says. "Think about this going on for long while."

Brad continues. "We should go. Get someone to let us out for a day or two. We can find out what's going on and see if we could find our families. They could still be alive."

Now I feel guilty. All of us have been partying when we should have gone to look for families. Shawn is the first person to say we should go see if our loved ones are safe.

"We shouldn't tell anyone else. We can't go all over Edmonton looking for everyone else's families especially when we have to get to Spruce. And, if everyone has their own vehicles, we would never be able to come back here. A bunch of vehicles leaving here, are going to cause too much of a scene for someone not to notice us, and what? They pick of vehicles off one by one as we all try to leave." Brad makes a lot of sense.

"We can trust Gary. He'll let us out and back in. No problem. We go now, while everyone is drunk or hungover." I say. "They won't miss us."

Brad starts walking back the way we came. He turns around when he notices that no one is following him. "You said now, so let's go."

I open my mouth to argue that I didn't mean this second now. We were trying to find food, but I can't think of a reason why we shouldn't go right now. "Where's Gary?"

"Over by the boat with Peter's family the last time I saw him. One year sober. He said it would take a lot more than the end of the world for him to start drinking again." Shawn says.

I grab my sword and follow behind Brad to the boat; everyone follows us. When we get there, Brad already has Gary's attention.

Gary looks like he knows exactly why when he looks at Shawn. He's the one who had brought it up, so maybe he already had a conversation with Gary about it.

"Gary," Shawn says. "We're going to leave now."

"Alright." Gary doesn't get up from his seat. Peter and his family don't seem shocked either.

"Do you mind locking us out and letting us back in?" Gary is already getting up before Brad even finishes.

"Of course. You're taking your truck?" Gary walks over to us and motions at us to guide the way off the boat. Brad nods.

We walk in silence back to Bourbon Street. It doesn't take us long. We unlock a door and walk outside. A quick look tells us nothing is happening; no noise, nothing in our sights.

"How long should it take?" Gary asks. He looks at his watch.

"Half hour there, half-hour back and two hours to go through all our houses and maybe a bit extra time if we run into problems." Shawn figures out loud.

Gary figures out the time on his watch. "If you aren't back by nightfall, stay somewhere safe overnight. Don't risk it. Leave at sun up. I'll be checking up every hour or so for you here. Good luck."

"Thank you." Each of us says. Gary goes back inside and locks the doors.

Everything looks normal as far as we can see. I know that the moment we get out onto the roads, it will be all but.

We get into Brad's truck. I take the rear driver's side seat. Brad doesn't wait for us to get settled, he pulls away immediately after the last door is shut. The vehicle doesn't make a screech from the tires, but I'm sure they were very close to it.

He goes to the closest exit to the roads. Brad pulls to a stop. I can't see the whole picture, but what I can see is vehicles piled up; dark stains on the ground and smoke.

All of our windows slide down. We listen for any noise, anything to let us know if there is anything still happening where we are.

Slowly this time, Brad pulls forward. I keep my eyes glued out my window the whole trip. After a while, the images just pass by. I don't register anything in particular and Brad was driving as fast as he could handle. I don't think the whole trip between the cities took ten minutes.

My home town looks normal, but more ghost town-like. There's no one around. Not one sign of the devastation in Edmonton.

Maybe it's more localized than we thought. Something that only happened to Edmonton. Maybe, Spruce Grove was just evacuated.

I can always hope for the best.

Shawn's house is first. It's the closest house to this side of town. He lives in a new cookie-cutter house; in the new area of town. After a few twists and turns, we finally pull up out front.

Brad parks right out front. Something we normally wouldn't do because Shawn has a fire hydrant right out front of his house. The zone covers the entirety of his road parking area. After the first three times people got tickets, we started parking across the street, so now his neighbours get mad at us.

Shawn calmly gets out of the truck but everyone else stays. I'm not sure whether we should stay or go. He'd probably be faster if we all stay. But, there are a lot of different things that could be waiting for him inside.

He unlocks the door; I guess that might be a good sign. None of the windows look like they are broken. He should be fine. I roll down my window some more to make sure that if he yells for help, we can hear.

Shawn goes inside and shuts the door behind him. I watch the house. Looking for anything that doesn't belong; some sort of movement through a window. How long should we let him be in there before we go to check to make sure he's okay?

Brad tries the radio again. There's nothing but static on every channel he tries. Even through the satellite radio channels.

The door finally opens. Shawn comes out carrying a duffle bag and pulling luggage behind him. He shuts the door and brings the bags to the back of the truck.

He climbs back inside and buckles up. Everyone waits on him to say something.

"Drive." He tells Brad. When Brad doesn't immediately do so, Shawn gives up a bit more information. The answers to everyone's questions. "No one was there, so I grabbed a few things and got out. Drive."

Brad turns around and drives on. It's his house next. We drive away from the new area of town and go to the older neighbourhoods.

Brad, Steph and I live somewhat close. Ten minutes' walk tops to get to either of our houses.

We turn right before the school and go down a block. Neither of his parents' vehicles are here, so I'm betting they aren't either. Brad pulls the truck over and turns it off. He leaves the keys in the ignition.

He does the same thing that Shawn had; he goes into the house alone, and after a few minutes he comes out with a large bag of stuff. Brad loads the bag into the back and gets back in the driver's seat. He gives Steph a grocery bag of chips.

Brad rustles a bag in his hand. He holds the open bag out to us, "Chips anyone?"

"Thank you," I stick my hand in to pull out a handful. Shawn declines, so Brad puts the bag down.

He starts up the truck again and drives the few blocks out to the trailer park where Steph lives with her parents.

Steph hesitates for only a couple of seconds to get out of the truck. But, she goes for it. She opens the gate, goes across the deck, around the railing and up the stairs. She walks right into the trailer; her parents never lock the door. She leaves it open.

I search through her windows to make sure nothing goes wrong. Her scream is faint. Brad moves first. Leaping out of the truck. Shawn and I follow right after. My heart races. Someone should have gone with her. We were stupid to let her go in alone.

Brad gets caught at the gate. I almost run into him. He reaches around and unlatches the lock. He swings the gate open with enough force that it hits the side of the fence.

We get through the door and go left. A quick look to the right shows an empty kitchen. Through the living room and down the hall they pass the closed doors and go straight into Steph's parents' room.

Steph's dad lies on the bed. I gag. The smell and the sight hit me at the same time. His chest has been ripped open; inside him looks too empty. There is blood everywhere.

I can't look anymore. I go to Steph. She's frozen in place staring at her dad. I move in front of her to block her view. She just stares right through me. I think she's in shock.

"Brad, get her out of here. Go back to the truck." I tell Brad. He picks her up and carries her out. Turning around, I try not to look at the body. "Shawn." He doesn't answer, just keeps staring at Steph's dad. I try a little louder. "Shawn." He looks at me. "Let's get out of here. We'll grab a few things for Steph and go."

I close the door behind us. If we need to come back here because we missed something, then at least none of us have to see that again.

"No! I'm not leaving!" Steph screams. Shawn and I run to the living room. We get there just in time to see Steph fall out of Brad's arms and hit the ground. She quickly recovers and latches herself onto the couch. "I'm not leaving." Brad tries to make her let go, but he just receives an elbow to his nose.

Walking over to her I put my hand on Brad; silently telling him to let me try. I sit down on the ground in front of Steph. "Why don't you want to leave?"

"My mom isn't here. I can't leave until she comes back." She tries to reason.

Her mom and dad would have been together at the time of the attack. If whatever it was that killed her dad didn't take her mom, then she ran off and could come back here.

We need to leave here but I know she isn't going to leave as long as there is a chance that her mom might come back. "How about we leave a note? Tell her where we are and to come find us."

I stand up and go into the kitchen. Finding a scrap of paper on the table and a pen in their junk drawer. I bring them to Steph.

She lets go of the couch to grab them. She crawls over to the coffee table and writes her note. I look up from her. Shawn and Brad are looking at each other. They look upset.

Steph stands up and walks out of the house. Brad grabs the letter and shoves it in his pocket.

"What the hell are you doing?" I yell in a whisper, so Stephanie doesn't hear.

"We can't leave a note. Her mom's not coming back, but someone else might. We can't have the wrong people finding us." Brad walks away, placing finality to the discussion.

Shawn walks up to me. "You know he's right."

"Maybe, but there's a chance she could be alive and come back."

He doesn't agree. "If she's alive. Would you come back?"

"We did." I point out.

"And so far, my parents are dead, Steph's dad is dead and who knows if Brad found his parents dead too. Let's just grab her things and leave." He turns and goes towards her bedroom.

"I'm sorry." I apologize. He hadn't said anything. I didn't know.

Shawn busies himself, walking around the room. He settles on the dresser; opening a drawer. It's full of bras and underwear.

He sighs and sits down on the bed. "I have no idea what to pack her."

"She has a luggage set in her closet. Take the smaller one and grab some food. Whatever isn't going to go bad soon. I'll deal with her things." He looks grateful for the escape.

Shawn goes to the closet and takes out the luggage. He finds the one I spoke about and takes it out towards the kitchen.

I grab the other one and lay it out on the bed. Taking care in packing each item I find; a mix of sentimental items and her favourite clothing. It doesn't take much to fill the bag up. I make sure to pack her scrapbooking album right on top of everything.

I zip the lid shut and lift it off the bed. It's heavy. Pulling out the handle, I roll it along the floor behind me.

It's getting dark outside already. I don't think we'll be going back tonight. It can't be too late, but it's winter.

Shawn's not in the kitchen, so he must have left already. I leave the house; closing the door behind me. It takes some effort to get the luggage down the stairs and off the deck. Shawn meets me at the edge of the property and takes it from there.

Brad and Steph are in the back seat. She's crying now, and all I can see of her is her brown hair. Her face is tucked into Brad. The shock of it all is over. I hop into the passenger seat and Shawn takes the driver's seat when he's done loading the bag.

Brad hands him the keys. I don't bother to put on my seat belt. We go down two blocks, out of the trailer park, take a left and down one block and we're at my place.

I grab my purse and get out. I hear someone shut their door after me. Going into the gate to the backyard, I unlock and open the door. One moment of silence. I don't hear anything. Shawn comes up behind me.

"I'll take upstairs, you take downstairs," I tell him. There is enough light to still see up here, but I don't think he'll be able to see much in the basement. "We should have brought flashlights. Maybe, we might have one in the junk drawer." I go to our island and open the drawer. It takes a few moments and moving everything around before I finally find a small keychain flashlight; at least it is something.

I turn it on and give it to Shawn. He goes down the stairs. Three thuds and a small grunt of pain are familiar. I giggle at the memories of just about everyone that has ever been in the house, falling the same way down those stairs. I guess I should have warned him; again. Those stairs are slippery. "Are you okay?"

"Yeah." He sounds like he's not too sure about it, but I think his pride might be hurt more than he is.

I check out the living room next. There's nothing there, nothing out of the ordinary. I go upstairs. The bathroom is empty. Left to my parents' room or right to my room? Parents' room; might as well get this over with.

The door is open, so I can see most of the room. Nothing out of the ordinary so far. I walk further in. There's nothing in here. My room is next. I open the door and give it a quick sweep. Wait. Didn't I make the bed? Maybe I didn't. I shake my head.

"All clear!" Shawn yells from two floors down, probably from the bottom of the same stairs he fell down.

I take one more quick glance around the room; still nothing. I leave and meet Shawn in the kitchen. "Same. Hey, I was thinking we'd spend the night here. I don't think we'd make it back before the doors are locked for the night. What do you think?"

"Yeah, that would be a good idea. I was thinking the same thing. It would be the safest choice." Shawn agrees with me.

The familiar sound of the gate closing lets me know that someone's coming. I look out to the truck, but I only see Steph.

We hear Brad before we see him come around the small wall. "Are you almost ready? We should go. It's getting dark out there."

Shawn looks at me, then back to Brad. "We should stay here tonight. It'll be dark before we get back. Gary will have locked the doors and got back to the boat, and I don't want to find a place for the night while it's already dark out."

"We'll make it back before then." Brad wants to get back to the safety of the mall.

"No, we won't. It's winter. Blink and it's dark outside. Give it ten minutes and it'll be pitch black out. It takes longer than ten minutes to get back to the mall." The boys glare at each other and for a moment it looks like they're about butt heads.

Brad backs down first. "Fine, we'll stay." He leaves to go get Steph.

I relax. Hungry now, I go to the pantry. I stare at it, not able to decide what to eat until Brad and Steph are in the house. I guess it's a dry cereal night again. I never really noticed before how little we have for dry or canned food.

I grab a box and place it on the counter. For a moment, I think to grab a bowl, but I decided against it. There isn't much in the box anyway.

I pick the cereal back up off the counter. Opening the flaps, I stick my hand in the plastic bag and pull out a small handful of the sweet cereal. Tilting my head back, I drop the cereal into my mouth.

Box in hand and still munching on the cereal, I walk into the living room.

I stop just past the stairs. Stephanie is in Brad's arms sobbing quietly. Brad looks up when he notices me. He gives me a look that says to give them a moment. This might've been the best option for us all. Give Steph some time to mourn in a familiar and comfortable environment. Without people who couldn't care less.

I nod and back out. It may be early, but it might just be best for me to go to bed, or at least hide in my room. I walk up the stairs to the second door on the right; my room.

I close the door behind me. Wishing I had a light of some sort so I could see my way around. It's still not too bad. I can see the bare outlines of the major furniture in the room.

I walk over to my nightstand and place my purse on it. A few steps away, I place the box of cereal on top of the dresser. I pull out a change of clothing to change into something more comfortable to sleep in; something way warmer than the scant clothes I have on now. The clean clothes feel a lot better than what I had on.

While sweat pants seem to be warm enough to last me through the night, I think I may need a sweater to cover a tank top. My arms are already chilly.

I go a few steps to my closet and open the one door. It's a lot darker inside and I can't see a thing. I reach in and tried to feel for the right type of cloth. Following my fingers along the row of hangers I hit something that feels like a hood.

Holding it up in the light so I can see it; it's my warmest hoodie. Unzipping the hoodie, I pull it off of the hanger, tossing the hanger to the side and pull on the hoodie.

I walk back to the bed. Pulling back the covers, I slip in and settled down. For a moment, I close my eyes. In the comfort of my own bed, it's easy to believe, to pretend, that none of the past few days have happened. That my mom and dad are downstairs watching some TV show; that I can turn on my lamp beside my bed and just write some poetry.

Whatever poetry I would write, would be about some stupid thing that happened at work that day or maybe something that happened with my friends. Something dramatic for whatever drama I was facing. Or, maybe something flowery for the end of a wonderful day.

I would listen to whatever music or conversation was on the radio. Maybe turn on my humidifier to fill my room with the citrus scent.

I roll over and hug my pillow. I bury my face in it and take a deep breath in. It smells of home and my flowery shampoo.

I guess I can do one normal thing; I could try writing some poetry. I grab the notebook and pen out of my purse. I open it up to the next blank page.

It's a bit dark, so this entry may not be the neatest.

I think about what I want to write, there's so much that's happened it's hard to pick just one.

Devastating fire wipes away
Wipes it all away
Nothing is as it was
All that is left is was
Time passes and wounds heal
What was left has time to heal
The seeds will grow
The people have to grow
Once was will never be
The new world will be.

The time it takes to get the words out, depletes my light.

I yawn and yawn again. With no light, and exhaustion settling in, I decide to turn in for the night.

Going through my nightly routine, as much as I can, without any water. I make a note to pack my hygiene items tomorrow; they feel much better than the dollar store replacements.

As I settle in bed, I imagine my mom's voice in sync with mine. "Good night sweet heart. Sweet dreams. Don't let the bed bugs bite."

The words act as a comforting hug. The feeling helps me lull into a deep sleep.

Chapter 18

Where is she?

I can hear a commotion. They must've found the others. For some reason, I don't care. I have to find her.

The hallway is mostly dark, but I can make out many doors on each side of me. As I go pas, the numbers written on the doors get bigger, and bigger, and bigger. I don't know where I'm going. I don't know if I'm heading in the right direction. But I have to find her.

Someone steps into the hallway from a room. Just what I was hoping for, but was not expecting. I'm not sure who was more caught off guard, but I react quicker.

He seems surprised as I push him up against the wall. I'm surprised when I see it's Shale; a guy from school. Though, I shouldn't be surprised. He did hang out with Darius a lot.

"I'm sorry." He says to me. I wasn't expecting that.

"Where's Dominique?" I ask a bit too quietly and out of breath; not as intimidating as I would've hoped.

"She's gone." He tells me. "Into the forest. She escaped an hour ago. They've probably already eaten her."

"Who?"

"The trolls, the goblins, take your pick of anything that's in the forest."

"What direction did she go? Do you know?"

He shrugs. "Up the mountain. We have the south covered. Nothing and no one comes or goes that we don't know about. We would've seen her if she used the roads."

I let him go, but use caution because I don't know if he's going to try to kill me. There is always the chance, but I don't think he will. Not everyone in this world is a killer; not everyone on their side is a killer.

Hopefully, this is a situation where if he wanted to kill me he would have tried something already.

He goes for something in his pocket. The metal pieces clang against each other. He tosses the keys at me, underhand so I can easily catch them.

"Go down the road, and to the right. Not too far down, and park the truck. You might still see some of the people that are there. I just dropped off a load. She'll have gone that way. You'll find her in there. I wouldn't bet on her being alive though."

I run back down the hallway the way I came. Some people are fighting in the entry. More are fighting outside the doors and along the road. No one notices me; however, I noticed the truck to the left.

I sprint to the truck, the doors are unlocked, and jump in the driver's door. Miles knocks on the door, so I open it. Ready to tell him what is going on, I spout it out before he gets a chance to say anything. "I know where Dominique and Rayleen are."

He shuts the door and runs around the front. I can hear him yelling. He opens up the passenger door and climbs in scooting all the way over to me. It doesn't take long for another man to pile in. I can feel the back of the truck hopping up and down. Like someone is getting into the back. After a couple of moments, someone hits the window; signalling for us to leave.

I don't know how much time I have, so I start the vehicle and drive away. It doesn't take me long to get up the hill and find the road I need to turn right on. About a half a block down I see a couple of people just entering the tree line.

I stop the truck and get out.

People pile out of the truck while I scan the tree line. Somewhat ignorant people get out of the truck and walk across the road. I try to see if I can find the people who just left. Walking further and further down the road. I finally get a glimpse of someone.

I move closer to the tree line. Walking a bit down the hill into the ditch. Unconsciously, I realize there are people right behind me but I don't care.

I concentrate on the group of five heading towards me. They are covered in blood; I'm not sure how much is theirs, or how much is another's.

Suddenly, they disappear. A short scream from each of them sounds before being stopped and turned into gurgles. The people behind me start to run towards them.

About five meters in, the two who had entered on my right stop; such as one would, if they had been punched in the gut. As they keel over, a line appears at the midpoint of their backs. Right before the separation between their top and bottom half.

Did they just? Were they cut in half?

How?

"Stop!" The middle-aged man yells at everyone." Go back!"

There are shouts and hollers coming up the road. As they round the corner I know it is part of the rebellion catching up with us. There isn't much of a choice. Either we can try to run down the road, face them, and fight, or go deeper into the forest; I don't think they'll follow us.

There are a lot more of them than there are of us. I decide to take my risks with the forest.

I now know of two places not to step. Taking a deep breath I make a beeline into the forest; running past all the people coming out.

There are some shouts after me, but I ignore them and keep running. When I am too far into the forest to be stopped, and taken back I slow down. Turning around I see a bunch of angry faces, but none of the rebellion has followed us this far.

I turn back to the direction I had been running in, and continue walking. I may not know where I'm going but a straight line seems as good as any.

Metal jaws snap shut. A sickening crunch, and the wail from a guy behind me, and to the right. It sounds just like something out of a horror movie or, perhaps, a noise of a wounded animal being caught in a trap.

I turn around, and immediately wish I hadn't. Daniel is poised on the ground with a smaller bear trap, meant to maim, trapped around his leg.

The middle-aged man goes to help him. Somehow he releases the bear trap from his leg. Daniel whimpers as people help him up. The troubled new girl from school, Alexa.

We trudge on, a bit more careful until we get to a clearing. Two people are hanging above a woodpile. I turn my head to the right, someone fell into a hole. Horrified yelps tell me it isn't worth a look. I finally get to the people. She's here, and so is Rayleen. I help her down gently as others cut her down. I hear a roar behind us.

A troll is running for us. I cut her legs loose. She's conscious, and it only takes us a moment to get her up. The troll swipes at me and misses. But he goes for Dominique. In a swift movement, he breaks her neck.

That was weird. My dreams have been an odd mix of reality and myth lately.

Why do I keep having dreams about that man and some people I'd never hang out with from school. One person in it all stands out, Dominique.

I haven't thought about her in a while. I guess I should maybe think about finding Dominique, and the rest of that family.

They did talk about the Apocalypse Plan. To Grandma's house we go when the world goes to Hell. It's as good of a shot as any. I'll go there, and find them. The family was nice enough that they would take me in. They immediately counted me as one of their own once they found out I existed.

Or, maybe I should just stay here. There's no one here. No people equals no drama. But, survival would be easier with others around to share the work. And, her family seemed amazing. Nothing like my own.

Uhg. I put my glasses on and crawl out of my sleeping bag. I'll have breakfast, and get on the road; survival logic wins. I'll take Lucas' extra car. He won't mind. He's probably dead anyway.

I have cereal and water for breakfast. I want to stay in my little bubble, but I knew it couldn't have lasted forever. I go downstairs. I undress only to redress in as many layers as possible. I roll up my sleeping bag and attach it to my bag.

Footsteps above my head make me duck in my surprise. Who is that? Should I go see? I doubt it will be anyone friendly. Society is supposed to break down after only three days.

"You check the house, I'll grab the food." Someone calls out.

I hide my bag. I'll come back for it. It's too clunky for a quick escape. I climb on top of my desk and open my window. I crawl out in a practiced motion.

Keeping low to the ground I creep around the side of the house. I peek through the gate before I slip to the other side. An unknown truck is running out front with no one inside; things are piled in the back; looters.

If they are going house to house I have a fifty percent chance that they still have to go to Lucas'. There is a good chance they will find me if I don't hurry.

I race to his front door. The fake rock holds the key, and I get inside fast. No broken windows and the door is locked. They will be here next.

I go to his key holder. That's strange. Both of the vehicles' sets of keys are here. Maybe Lucas is here. Or, maybe not? His shoes aren't here. That might not mean anything. I take both keys.

I don't have time for this, but I run through the house. I whisper 'Lucas' as I go. He isn't here. I make my way into his garage. I pull up on the emergency cord to lift it. I take his cheaper car, the black one. It is an automatic car. I would never take the red one. It's an expensive sports car with a shifter. I wouldn't make it anywhere. I'd stall the engine so many times I'd break the car.

Someone appears in the doorway as I start up the engine. She looks like she's wearing a mask and an expensive Halloween costume. I process the purple skin and rib-like bones coming to a point on her face before she runs towards me. I step on the gas. The car jolts forward. I almost run the girl over, but she gets out of the way just at the last moment.

I look in the rearview mirror and see a group of five crowding the girl. They watch me drive away.

This can't be real. It's just freaky real costumes.

It's hard to accept that the smouldering surroundings were a mostly peaceful city just a week ago. I feel like I'm watching a movie from every angle.

I avoid most of the inner part of the city and soon look at the peaceful countryside. Snow starts to fall. It dawns on me that I might not have the gas to get out there. Or I might have enough for the ride straight there, but nothing for me to get lost with.

Well, let's hope I don't get lost. I just have to make sure I go exactly the way I was taken there first.

I try to remember that, and follow the memory as best I can. When I make it to the Alberta Beach sign I smile. It was a long way, but I was able to at least make it to the right area. I think it should take only about another five minutes, and I'll be there.

Left. Right. Right. First house on the right. Bingo. This is it.

I look at my gas gauge; just in time as it's pretty much empty.

I pull into the driveway. There are a bunch of vehicles here. I guess I chose the right place, but I don't recognize most of these vehicles. Grandma and grandpa's truck is the closest to the house.

I stop my car and get out. It's eerily quiet. They have three massive Rottweilers that should be greeting me, or at least be looking out the window and barking.

I walk the line of cars and trucks up to the main entrance. I turn the doorknob, and the door opens. I walk in. The house is warm. One of the reasons they chose this house to be the Apocalypse House was because they can heat the whole house with their fire stoves. Grandma and grandpa's boots are here, but why haven't they come to greet me yet. Maybe they're sleeping?

If the stove is on, they should be in the kitchen.

"Hello?" I wait a moment. "Grandma, Grandpa, are you here?" I wait in silence. Someone should be answering me. I settle the keys in between my fingers in my right fist. If I need to they should buy me a moment to get back to the car.

I walk around the corner, and down the hall towards the kitchen. As soon as I walk into view, I have guns and flashlights pointed at me. I don't know any of the people I can see.

They're going to shoot me.

"You don't look like their granddaughter. So, who are you?" A man's voice says. There aren't any pictures of me around, and none in the family portrait tree, so these people wouldn't know.

"I'm adopted, sort of." That's sort of the short truth. They told me that I'm granddaughter the last time I was here, but I'm not by blood. "Where are they?"

"Out." He says.

The way he says it makes me feel uneasy. "Can you please put your guns down? I swear I don't have any weapons on me."

There's a very tense moment before he gives them a signal to lower the weapons. I can tell though, that before I could move, any of them could shoot me still.

"Give me your car keys." He says. I immediately hand them over. I have no choice. If I hesitate at all he may take it as resisting, and they all still have their guns near enough that I wouldn't live very long if he decides I should die. "What's your name?"

"Jaiden, and you are?" I stick out my hand for a handshake.

"Paul." He goes in for the handshake. I make sure that I do a girly grip; something weak to make sure he doesn't take me as a threat.

"Nice to meet you." I smile sweetly at him. He has a dark stain on his shirt near his neck. "Are you injured?" I point to his neck. Showing concern for him should make him let down his guard further.

"Werewolf got me."

I laugh a little at his joke. "Like, one of the Rotties?"

"No, those vicious things are locked up in the garage. They're probably dead by now. A werewolf did this to me. We've got two of them locked up in the bedroom upstairs."

"A wolf?" The people in the room look around at each other. Others look bewildered. "Werewolves aren't real."

"Have you been living under a rock or something?" He frowns at me.

"Close. There was a bomb threat at my school last week, and they sent all the students home. I saw a few buildings blow up from my house, then bunkered down in my basement for the last week waiting for my dad to come home. He never did though, and then some people broke in this morning, so I ran, and came here. I thought we were under a terrorist attack."

"Follow me." He goes out of the kitchen the way I came in. I follow after him. He goes up the stairs and leads me to the bedroom. "It was a terrorist attack, but the attack came from demons." He opens the door.

The smell hits me first. I know it's excrement. Paul must not be letting two captives out of this room at all.

This is inhumane. I get locking them up, even making them stay in the room, but they shouldn't be living in this filth. There are two of them. They look completely human to me, but Paul says they're werewolves.

Paul does something to the female, and the male reacts. I see it for a moment, the human face morphs briefly into a muzzle then back. Paul pulls away before the male can grab him. I see his knife gleaming drops of red. He stabbed her.

"I don't understand. Did I just see? How did you manage to capture them?" I ask. I make sure that I only have a straight line of a smile. I don't want Paul to see how much this disturbs me.

He motions for me to leave the room. We go back downstairs. He guides me into the kitchen. "I lied to you. I apologize. They killed your grandparents, some of our guys too. We captured them shortly after. We need them to tell us where the rest of the pack is. We'll get our revenge, and kill every last one of them."

"Okay." So, he's bloodthirsty. He said he locked up the vicious Rotties. I'll need to check them out soon, but the Rotties wouldn't have caused them problems if they knew them beforehand, or even if they meant no harm. Once the Rotties are introduced to people, they don't bother them at all. If you're a stranger, on the other hand, especially if you cause harm to someone they know you need to watch out. The first matter is the couple upstairs. They don't have anyone guarding them. I wonder if I could get a chance to be alone with them; verify the story. "Would you mind if I go, and clean up her wound? If she gets an infection and dies her partner will never tell you what you know. If they mirror their animal counterparts they are fiercely loyal creatures."

"If you want to I won't stop you. I'll come with you to protect you." I don't think that's what he really means. He's just met me. He doesn't know me. Of course, he isn't going to leave a stranger alone with his two captives. He probably thinks I'm one of them.

You're the last person I want with me. "If you don't mind, could someone else come with me? I fear that they won't respond too well if you come back with me. Probably think you're going to stab them again, and probably wouldn't let me do the first aid."

Paul mulls it over for a minute but sees it my way. "You're not going to find anyone here they will be comfortable with. We've all taken our turns interrogating them."

I cringe inwardly at the term interrogate. I know he means they've all taken a whack at the prisoners. "Maybe someone can wait for me in the hall. If I scream rush in and get me?"

"If you scream it's because they're killing you, and we won't have time to rush in, and get you."

"Why would you care anyway? You just met me. If I die you'll mourn more about having to clean up my dead body than you would mourn my death."

He snickers. "That's true. Go do what you need to do. I have work to do. I'll send Harry with you. Go collect what you need."

"Thank you." I smile at him with my sweetest smile; the one that shows my dimples. I bow my head a little before I walk to the bathroom. I need to keep in mind that they won't take it too kindly if I use items they deem necessary. Opening up the medicine cabinet I see that won't be an issue. There isn't anything left in here.

I look under the sink. There isn't anything in there that will be useful. I go into the boot room. I climb up on top of the dryer. On the shelf up here I find the rags, and material slated for garage rags.

"What are you doing?" A voice says to my side.

I jump and scream a little from the sudden appearance, and a bit from my guilty, treacherous thoughts. The shoebox of rags falls on me, and for a moment I think I am going to fall off the dryer. I catch my balance with the help of the shelving. "Oh god." I look at the man and grasp my chest. "You gave me a heart attack." I take in a deep breath, and let it out loudly. "I was grabbing rags to clean, and bind wounds. Are you Harry?"

"Yes." He holds out his hand to help me get off the dryer. I know he's trying to be chivalrous, but it doesn't help me out any more than what putting my hand on the dryer would have. I let him help me down anyway.

I clean up the rags that had fallen out of the box. "I just need to get a few items out of the pantry and kitchen."

"Like what?" Harry says.

"Vinegar and salt. A little bit of water; just enough to dilute the solution, and, a bowl." I tell him. The kitchen items will do well enough as a disinfectant.

"No water. We need all the water we have." Harry gets defensive.

"Okay, no problem." There goes that thought. I don't have enough power to dispute it. The solution should work well enough without water, but I'll need more vinegar to dissolve the salt. Hopefully, it's not too acidic without the water to dilute it.

I take the rags with me to the pantry. Harry watches me like a hawk. I thought maybe I could grab a granola bar for them, but I don't think I could manage to grab it without him noticing. I could be in big trouble if he caught me. Besides, there isn't much in here left for actual food.

I grab only what's necessary. The next time I look at Harry he has a shotgun in his grasp.

We make our way upstairs, and into the room. They look me over warily; Harry even more so. I put my collection on the floor. Settling on the ground, I mix up the solution in the bowl.

I look up at the duo. "Hi, my name is Jaiden. I've mixed a solution of salt and vinegar to create a disinfectant. Would you let me attend to your wounds?" The male's eyes are off me, and on Harry. I glance over, and see him with the shotgun pointed at them with his finger near the trigger. I can only assume from my position that he's also got the safety off. I don't know what these two might do, so I leave him be for now. I collect the bowl and the box of rags, and move close enough to them to touch them.

I kneel with one knee, and one foot on the ground. It will be easier to jump away if I need to. From my position, Harry can't see my face, and I take this to my advantage. "Can you please roll up your shirt so I can see the stab wound?" She does as I asked, and I get to work cleaning the area around the wounds. It's bleeding slightly when I get done cleaning it. Her skin is a little pale. I wish I could have grabbed her some food. There is a lot of blood here, and I don't imagine they've eaten since they were imprisoned.

I make sure I don't move my head, but look up. In the quietest whisper possible I ask, "Did you kill my grandparents?" Her face softens momentarily. She blinks hard once and then glares at Harry. Does that mean no?

I wait for a natural break in the process to look at Harry. He still has the gun aimed at them. I don't think he heard me. "Could you please stop aiming that gun at me? Or, at least take your finger off the trigger. You're making me nervous."

He doesn't say anything, but he does move his finger out of the trigger hole. I set back to work. I should have grabbed a needle and thread. On second thought, I don't think I could handle that. Or, rather I don't want to have to handle that.

I finish by binding a long rag around her waist. "Do you have any other wounds? Anything that might need disinfecting?"

"No." The male says gruffly.

"Thank you." The female says.

"You're welcome." I start cleaning everything up but stop. I give them a rag, and leave the bowl with them. "You should use this on any minor cuts you have. Wash yourselves with it. Make sure you don't drink it. It would dehydrate you."

I get up; gather the rest of the supplies. Harry kicks the bowl over as I walk away. He finally puts the gun down when we leave. I go to the kitchen and put everything in the pantry. Harry is still watching me, but the gun has disappeared. "Harry, would you mind if we go to the garage? Paul mentioned that you have the dogs locked up in there, and I would like to see if they're okay."

"I'm not going with you. I don't think you'll find anyone to go with you. The dogs are probably dead anyway."

"They're harmless if they know you. If they're still alive I could introduce them to all of you, and you'll be fine. It's possible they're alive." But, they wouldn't hesitate to attack if any of you try to harm me.

"How would you get them out? They'll attack the moment we open the door." He says.

"Open the door, and jump back. They'll recognize me when they see me." I say. At least I hope they will. Who knows really?

"You can't go alone." He sighs. "I'll go with you but I'm bringing the gun."

"Yeah, bring the gun. If anything happens you can protect us." I hope nothing goes wrong. Harry takes the lead out to the garage. I find out that he keeps the shotgun on top of the fridge.

We get to the man door. I don't hear anything. Harry opens the door a crack. It takes a moment but a large nose shoves through the crack. She growls, and barks. Harry tries to shut the door, or keep the door where it is; I can't tell. What I can tell is which dog this is. "Missy. Missy. Hey girl. It's Jaiden." She stops barking but is still trying to get through the door. "Heel, girl. Sit." She does as I say, so I tell Harry, "You can open the door now." He opens the door a touch more, but he runs back about five meters and readies the gun. Missy comes out and excitedly rubs her nose into me. I'm glad she recognizes me. I spy two still bodies in the garage. "You can put the gun down." I talk to Missy now. "Hi, girl. Everything's going to be okay." Even from my angle, I can see she's emaciated. She tries to jump up to put her paws on my chest. "Down girl. You aren't allowed to jump up. Want to go inside the house now? Come on."

I lead the way with Missy shortly behind. Harry follows way behind us. We go through the house to the kitchen. People are alarmed until they see that she has no business with them. Missy goes straight for the food dish. It has some hard food in it, but not enough to make her full after days in the garage. I grab the bag of kibble from the pantry and fill up the water dish too. No one argues with me. Probably too scared of the dog. Good.

I put the food back. Not really knowing what I should do next, I go into the living room, and settle on the window seat. People either go about their business, stare at me or stare at the dog; there is no in-between. I wish I had my cell phone, then I could bury myself into something on there, and not have to think about the eyes on me.

Any escape plan is dashed. We're too far from anywhere for it to be reasonable for me to walk.

Missy finishes eating and comes straight over to me. She hops up onto the window seat, and quickly finds a spot to lie down. She makes sure to nudge her head onto my lap. I pet her, and scratch her head; particularly scratching behind her head.

"How did you do that?" Paul stands across the room.

I look up at him. He's across the room. I stroke her head to calm her when I hear her growl in his direction.

Now that I notice it, I realize people have put space between us, and them. "Sorry?" I say. I'm sure I know he's asking about why Missy isn't eating everyone, but I want to make sure.

"That dog attacked us the last time we saw it." He says.

"Of course she did. She's a guard dog, and she didn't know you. She's a sweetheart once she gets to know you." I kiss her head for good measure.

"I'll take your word for it." He walks away into the kitchen then down the hall.

People leave me alone after that. I just sit with Missy. I get hungry, but I don't dare say anything. I know I missed lunch, and I get the idea that I'm missing supper when it gets dark out. The pantry didn't have much in there.

Finally, others start going to bed. I learn they have people on guard at all times. I think about going to bed but I'm wired. Paul eventually comes around to toss a granola bar and blanket at me.

"Make it last. We don't have much for food around here." He says before he walks away. I put the granola bar in my pocket, and unfold the blanket. I'm warm enough with all my clothes, and jacket on, so I lay myself down on the window seat, cuddle Missy, and throw the blanket over both of us; mostly over Missy.

I don't plan on eating the granola bar. I've been eating pretty well for the last week. It's pretty well agreed upon that a person can survive more or less eight days without food, and water; more if they have water. We can make water through the snow.

I'll just save it for later; perhaps even give it to the couple upstairs. Speaking of which, how long have they been here? For that matter, how long has this group been here? It can't have been this whole last week or else Missy, and the couple would be worse off. If I had to guess, I'd probably say a couple of days.

The question is what do I do now? Do I steal away in the middle of the night? Do I stay knowing these people probably killed everyone that was here at their arrival? Do I rescue the people upstairs? Is it an option to become part of the group? Are they genuinely bad people, or are they doing what they misguidingly think they have to?

Do I even get a choice? Can I leave if I wanted to? Or, are they going to keep me here until they know what to do with me?

Questions fly through my mind. They help me stay awake as the night goes on. I'm too scared to go to sleep; I might never wake up. I lightly pet Missy's head. Missy will protect me.

Chapter 19

The lids covering my eyes are heavy and take some work to open; further work to keep them open. My blurry sight focuses as I stare at the ceiling in front of me.

A stained-glass chandelier is the first object I see clearly. With my eyes awake from their dead sleep. I move my head slightly; sitting up straight

I notice the shirt I'm now wearing is a brown long-sleeved shirt with a high neckline. Without drawing back the covers I can feel the jean material covering my legs.

Looking around me, I get a good look at the contents of the room. Antique, nineteen-fifties and creepy are the words that come to mind in the room. Rustic furnishings match those of the nineteen-fifties era; lavishly decorated wooden furniture including the four-post bed I'm lying in, a desk, a wardrobe, and a decorative cabinet filled with porcelain dolls. Painted eyes stare at me; making an uneasy pit lodge in my chest.

Tiny footsteps scurry across the floor. My heart leaps and pounds in my ribcage from the reminiscence of the events last night. A twinkle of a squeak under the bed drives me into a paranoia-induced state of action.

Quickly getting up into a standing position on the bed, I look over the edge. Nothing is visible so I jump from the bed. Landing a meter away on the floor, I make haste to continue out of the room, shutting the door behind me the immediate moment I step outside the door.

"Are you okay?" Miles' voice startles me once again.

Turning quickly to meet him; with a red tint to my cheeks from my embarrassment. He sits in an armchair with a book in his hands.

I try to cover up my embarrassment, "Umm, washroom?" He points over to the room next to the one I just came out of. I rush into the room and almost slam the door shut in my hurry.

I relieve my bladder to candlelight. I try to flush but the water doesn't fill back in the bowl.

Going to the sink I wash my hands with anti-bacterial sanitizer. I assume the sink won't work if the water won't run in the toilet.

Looking at my reflection in the mirror confuses me for a moment. My face is completely bare of all traces of makeup. There isn't even any eyeliner or mascara. Being completely natural looks strange to me and gives me a sense of being naked.

Looking through a couple of cupboards I cannot find anything I can use for make-up.

Giving up, I decide to go back out the door. Pain shocks through my toe as I bring the door back into my foot. Moving my foot out of the way I open the door the rest of the way and hobble out.

Sickness swells from my stomach upwards. Blood rushes from my head instilling ever-growing dizziness; feeling fainter and fainter by the moment. The floor calls to me. I slide down the door and lean my head on my knees.

Miles is beside me in a second.

"Alexa, are you okay?" He reiterates.

Making sure I won't throw up despite how I feel before I answer him, "Head rush."

Miles takes a seat beside me. His hand starts stroking my head and back. The soothing feeling, I'm sure with the help of his healing, almost immediately fills my stomach and head.

His hand stills when I lift my head to look at him. "Thanks."

"You're welcome." He says quietly.

Breaking eye contact with him, I take a look in my immediate location. Using a wooden chest beside me, I pull myself up. Standing perfectly still, I test moving my head for any lingering faintness.

Miles stands up beside me, ready to steady me if needed. "We should get you something from the kitchen: a cookie, juice, something with sugar in it to get your levels back to normal. You've been out for days and had lost a lot of blood. You looked like someone had taken a shredder to you. What happened?"

I couldn't have been out for days. That's impossible, but I guess with what happened. My thought trails off as memories flash by. My eyes burn from tears threatening to fall. "Darius... I don't know... He changed... He threw me down the stairs in the dark... I think Sandra said they were hobgoblins. They were down there. They were going to kill me."

"Darius has always been easily influenced and power-hungry. Sandra has always been able to manipulate him. Those two together is a bad idea. At the very least, you weren't killed." His hand squeezes my shoulder in a comforting gesture. "Come on, let's go downstairs. See what the crazy old man is trying to entertain Rayleen with now."

"What are you talking about?" I don't know if I like the way he said crazy old man. "And, who is this crazy old man?"

"Well, the last time I checked they were trying to teach Crystal common dog tricks." We head down the stairs. When the stairway splits Miles leads me down the left stairs. "James, he owns this house and he's the latest representative for magic folk in the Council." The stairs open up into the foyer. Another left brings us past two sets of stairs. One goes down and another goes upstairs. I stop for a moment to examine where the one going up could lead to. From what I can see the stairs lead back to the split-off we came from. "James can be a little quirky about some things. These stairs were originally made for servants because they weren't allowed to use the same stairs as their owners. Therefore, James believes that unless you are a servant you shouldn't be using their stairs. It's a respect thing on his part. But just a warning, don't use those stairs unless you want a lecture."

A smooth male's voice carries from the room beside us. Through the opened wall above the counter, I can see the back of his head.

Following Miles through the arched doorway I find Rayleen, James, and Crystal surrounded by various books, cushions and miscellaneous items.

The room seems to be a library, but it also has a dining table and chairs. The various windows in the room are covered in a material meant to let some light in but keep the outside world from seeing the inside.

Rayleen seems to be so fascinated by what she's concentrating on that she doesn't notice we have come into the room. Standing near the entrance we just watch her concentrate on a marshmallow on a glass plate.

Crystal is the first one to notice us. She jumps off her perch on the chair. As she gets closer to me she starts a purring noise while chirping every couple of seconds. Reminding me of a cat, even more, she rubs up against my legs, winding herself in and around my legs. Once she tires of that, front paws make their way up my right leg.

Looking back to Rayleen offends the small griffin. She digs her claws in slightly and loudly growls and squawks for my attention. The boom of her voice alerts the other two to our presence.

"Hi." Rayleen smiles from ear to ear.

"Hi, apparently someone doesn't like being ignored." I look down at the griffin. Picking her up, I rub her back to quell her noises. "What are you doing?"

"Trying to cook the marshmallow. Mr. James is teaching me how to do things with my mind." Rayleen goes back to concentrating on the marshmallow.

James gets up from his spot on the floor. He walks over to me. "Very nice to meet you, I'm James. How are you feeling?"

"Better, thank you," I answer his question.

"Good, good. You know you have a very special niece. I believe she has the potential to be a great sorcerous." James looks back at Rayleen.

Miles steps up, "She's only five years old, don't work her too hard."

James puts both his hands up in a defensive position. "I have no intention of that. Just helping her focus on the powers she has. I wonder though, Alexa, if you might allow me to check to see if you have any magical abilities?"

The skeptic in me says that it wouldn't be possible for magic to exist, but from the events over the past couple of days, logic has taken a back seat. I nod for him to continue.

James brings both of his hands up towards my head. "I just have to touch on both sides of your head where your frontal lobes are."

He does just as he says. Closing his eyes prompts me to follow. Where his fingers are touching I feel a ticklish tingle flow. The feeling spreads in strings throughout my head, then retracts where it can from.

I open my eyes to find him looking at me.

James takes his fingers off my head, "Unfortunately, she appears to have gotten that part of her from her father. I'm sorry to report that you have no magical abilities whatsoever. There is absolutely nothing abnormal in your past, you're one hundred percent human.

So boring, oh well. It's not like you can help it." He turns to Miles. "Lunchtime."

James walks past me. I can't help but feel insulted by his words. Looking at Miles I see the look of amusement on his face. The elf shrugs his shoulders.

Deciding it might be better to wave off the insult, I just shake my head. Miles' smile gets bigger before he follows after the wizard. I set down the griffin in my arms.

My attention diverts to the little redhead concentrating on the marshmallow. I watch her for a moment. Her face is scrunched and her body is tense. The hope in her eyes shines through, despite her efforts.

Walking closer to her, I crouch down beside her. "Rayleen, James is going to make us lunch, how about we get you cleaned up, hands washed, and you can try this again after you eat something."

She doesn't answer me. When I open my mouth to say something to her again, she says, "okay."

Rayleen gets up from the floor, heads into the kitchen, and disappears from my sight.

Standing, I motion Miles to come to me. Once at arm's length I ask him a question, concern plaguing my heart and mind, "Did something happen to Rayleen? She's not herself."

Miles looks away from me, "When you were taken from the airport you left behind a battle.

I don't know what happened to her, but I do know that something had scared her in the lunchroom before I had a chance to get to her.

It didn't help that she probably saw more than a child ever should when we were escaping through town. I told her to close her eyes, but you know kids. Either way, she was scared enough to change her entire demeanour, and she won't talk to anyone about it.

I've tried a few things but nothing so far has eased her mind. I'm hoping you can talk to her later."

"Of course." Images race across my vision. Memories from my trip through town were enough to give me nightmares; amplifying this experience through the mind of a child could petrify her.

I nod, though it is futile because his gaze isn't on me. Raising my hand to his chin, I move his head to face me. His eyes turn to focus on me while I do this.

"I'm sure you did all you could, it's not your fault at all. If something was going to scare her, it was going to scare her and whether you were there or not wouldn't have made a difference. By the sounds of it, this is going to be something she is going to have to get used to." I try to reassure Miles.

"All cleaned up? Perfect, I'll get you to help me." James assumedly speaks to Rayleen in the kitchen.

Miles and I exchange glances. Walking past him I go to inspect what we might be having for lunch.

Standing at the edge of the kitchen I freeze in place. The fridge doors are wide open and food is flying out of it; straight onto the counter, where it stops and settles into a spot. My eyes widen in awe and wonder as James looks at the cupboard, just as it swings gently open. Four sets of plates, bowls, and cups float out to a couple of designated areas: the cups on the table, the bowls near the stove and the plates with the food on the counter.

James closes the fridge and cupboard with a look as all he needs from them are in their places. "Rayleen would you like to pick out a soup from the cupboard?" The middle-aged man motions towards the pantry on the other side of the room.

Rayleen looks through the cupboard taking her time deciding what she would like.

James continues his work on our lunch. He lays out the plates in a row. The plastic tab breaks free of the bag surrounding the loaf of bread. The end unravels and slices make their way out of the package. Two slices land side by side on each plate. Numerous items continue to pile onto the bread, each new item levitating with only a look.

Perfect sandwiches are cut and completed. James lifts two plates, "Alexa, Miles, would you both please take a set to the table. Thank you."

Walking to him first, Miles takes the plates from him. I do the same right after. Following suit, I go to the table and place the plates down.

Turning, I quickly dodge a glass coming towards my head. A jug of juice bypasses me, following the glass.

Going back into the kitchen, I see James turning on a camping stove. The flame lights up and turns blue. Shooting up from the burner, the flame swirls around the pot and bubbling pops come from the pot. The distinct cream of mushroom soup aroma wafts through the kitchen.

James pours the soup by hand into four bowls. Setting the pot onto the cold burner, he turns the hot one off. He grabs two of the bowls and brings them to the table. Miles takes the two left and does the same. James acknowledges his courtesy with a nod.

"Let's eat," James states to all in the room. He takes a seat at the head of the table, and Miles at the opposite end. Gesturing to Rayleen for her to sit on the closest seat to her, I walk to the other side of the table and sit there.

Curiously, Rayleen sits and waits for a couple of moments before starting to eat; like she had been waiting for something. I start in on my sandwich first. The steaming soup, though mouth-watering, has a high probability of burning my mouth. The sandwich is restaurant worthy in flavour.

Gratuitous for the food, I finish the mouthful and tell James as such, "Thank you for the food. It's delicious."

"You're very welcome. I guess you could say it's the secret ingredient, not love, but magic." He chuckles at his little joke.

I just smile to be polite, and then continue eating. The table quiets down to nothing more than the sounds of a clinking of the dishes, slurps, and crunches.

Rayleen finishes first. She slightly tidies up her mess. The left-over sandwich is set into the soup, and the bowl is placed onto the plate. The utensils and napkins are placed into the bowl as well.

This unusual behaviour is noted but may be James' doing. He seems to have taken a liking to the little girl and could have possibly taught her something about proper etiquette. From what I've seen of the old-fashioned house, his behaviour and beliefs, it's highly plausible.

James, the last to finish lunch, clears his throat. "Now that we have Alexa with us, and we have quelled our stomachs, I believe we should get down to the serious business. I have sent Kelly with a message for the rest to meet us. They should be arriving right away."

He stands up. Everything on the table rises above our heads and floats into the kitchen.

Rayleen gets up and walks out of the room with James following closely behind her. Through the hole in the wall, I can see them both go downstairs. Miles has already started on his way; leaving me behind still at the table. I look to Crystal who is napping on a pillow on the floor.

Feeling that I should follow after them, I stand up quickly and almost run to catch up.

Slowing to a walk to go down the stairs, I watch my steps to be sure I don't fall. Instead of numbers of people, the basement is empty save for a furnished living room, James, Rayleen, Miles and myself.

James has stopped close to the far side of the room. He and Rayleen face and stare at the concrete wall. Coming closer I can see a crack in the wall growing, dust falling behind it. The crack forms an arc and comes back down. Scraping fills the room as the portion cut from the wall comes forward.

James peeks behind it. "It's clear." He shouts to us before he disappears behind it. I'm the first on the go after him this time.

Reaching the thick cut out from our doorway I briefly wonder how much that piece must weigh and get a slight sting of jealousy knowing that it's possible Rayleen may be able to do something like this in the future.

Behind the wall is a dugout tunnel of dirt, and at the end of the tunnel is a small light. I follow the light the source of which I find comes from a ball of light in James' hand. The tunnel stops underneath the winding roots of a tree.

He turns and speaks to me, "Ashlynn has already spoken to all of the wood nymphs to allow us passage, but for posterity's sake I would still like for you to be tested by the nymph who this tree belongs to. All she needs is a drop of your blood and to smell you. Through that she will determine if she likes you; if she does you will be allowed passage into every tree she calls home."

"And, if she doesn't?" The question flows through my lips before I need to think about it.

"Let's not dwell on that." He looks up at the roots. "Here she is."

Looking up, I slightly jump. A humanoid creature made of only bark forms from the thick roots. It doesn't waste any time in coming down to my level; never separating from the root it came from. Swirling around me it loudly sniffs at me.

"Slowly hold up your hand," James instructs me.

My hand reaches mid-height before the nymph grabs for it. A prick in my hand startles me and I come very close to shaking her off. Just as quickly as she had invaded my space she is gone.

My fear grows when the roots start moving. Heading straight for me and everyone else they wrap around us and lift us off the ground. They raise us up, my heart stops as we should have hit the ceiling of the tunnel; instead, we go through and are placed onto a floor.

We stand in the center of a round room. Sunlight streams through the leaves spotting the open ceiling. Everything thing in sight is made of only wood. Some of the same creatures from the board room in the airport are in front of us.

The tall brunette stands out from the crowd. "It's about time James. Now we can get this meeting started. For those of you who are new, James will explain to you what we know. James."

"Thank you, Ashlynn. The entire world has been affected by this takeover. It seems there was a lot more support than we had originally thought. We are extremely outnumbered and it's going to get worse before it gets better.

Now, we must start small. We are the rebels, recruit all the humans and supernaturals that you can. Convince those in hiding to join us and kill those who stand in our way. Send out word through only the most secure channels you know to any members of your clans and bring them here. We need more numbers before we can take over this region and keep it." James looks to Ashlynn for her to continue.

"As James had stated we need more beings in order to accomplish the bigger picture but in the meantime, we need to figure out how we are going to survive long enough to even have a shot at this," Ashlynn says.

"You're a fucking elemental, why don't you and your sisters just wipe away every traitor." Rasps a one-eyed, grey-skinned male.

"Over the years, our powers have weakened tremendously. They've polluted the air so badly Aleena has developed breathing problems, Ariela is almost perpetually sick over how much poison and filth is in her water, and I've grown weak because every time they cut down a tree, every time they build another concrete city I lose a part of me. Aalayah is so furious because she has watched us all fall due to human cause and that is why she is helping the traitors.

And, if we decided to wipe everyone out, we would wipe everyone out." Ashlynn's voice goes threateningly low and she balls her hands into fists.

Miles tries to get everyone back on track. "What we need are supplies. And, those of you that don't know how to fight, you need to be taught."

James takes hold of the conversation. "I've separated everyone into groups.

Group one contains me, Miles, Kelly, Ashlynn, and Alexa. Group two will contain Spencer, Owen, Aiden, Ava, Addy, Logan, Hannah, and Landon. Both our groups will be attaining new territory, recruiting beings, and getting supplies.

Group three Gio, Nia, Taylor, Gavin, and Rayleen. You will be the defensive team. You'll be in charge of fortifying our defences and coming up with strategies. As well as that, you'll be the healers and whatever we need for the home base."

Ashlynn moves to the center with us. "Group two, I believe we should get you started on the territory surrounding us.

Group three will go to James' and start thinking about strategies and preparing for the worst.

Our group will go out to the strip mall two blocks from here and try to secure supplies. It may be a daunting task, but in the end, I believe we can have peace. It will take a lot of work, blood, sweat, and tears but it can be done.

Now off you go. Make sure to return before nightfall."

Most members of groups two and three walk out, disappearing into the walls, but one of the girls stays behind. Nothing seems extraordinary with this one. She looks completely human.

The brunette walks towards us, stopping in front of Rayleen. "Sweetie, would you like to come back to the house with me?"

Rayleen looks to James for her answer. He nods. Then she looks to me for my approval. I don't feel comfortable leaving her with a total stranger, however, given that James seems to know what he is doing.

I nod.

Rayleen looks to the lady and takes her hand. "Okay, let's go." They walk through the wall a couple of steps away.

"We're screwed." Kelly blatantly states. James laughs at her. She tosses a glance in his way over her shoulder. Turning to face him completely she continues, "What? It's true. We have seventeen people against the entire world. We don't stand a chance in Hell right now."

The middle-aged man just smiles at her and shakes his head. "If you haven't noticed we are in Hell. Anyway, what do we have left to lose? Nothing, but our lives. So, at the very least why not have a little payback before they take that too."

"Well aren't you two cheerful. You know we do actually have a chance. Think of it. If we are to be able to convince enough people to double our numbers; there couldn't have been more than one hundred beings at the farm. That means there is one of us for every three of them. That I would say is very good odds. Especially, if we can convince some of them to change sides, or even free anyone left alive in the slaughterhouse." Miles optimism shines in his voice; an uplifting notion for everyone.

The last words will haunt me forever; I'm sure. Could he be speaking of the slaughterhouse we had walked past yesterday? If so, that would mean there were people in there dying, while we were completely oblivious to their existence.

My chest is heavy with guilt, I feel like an idiot for trusting Darius and Sandra.

I can't take this anymore, so I say, "We can't change the past. So what are we going to do from here going forward?" All four beings in the room look at me with shock.

James nods and smiles at me. "You're right. We can't change the past. We can only learn from it. I don't suppose you've ever used a weapon before?" I shake my head in the negative. "Alright, so we'll get you a dagger for now. Unfortunately, we'll have to do some training in the field before we can teach you anything, but sometimes it's better that way. I've got a dagger for you back at my house. Nothing fancy but it'll work for now."

"So, James, you get Alexa the dagger, then we meet outside the front door and head out to the supermarket to grab supplies. By the time we come back, it should be nightfall and we'll see the progress of everyone for the day." Ashlynn takes the final words to summarize and finalize everything.

James is pulled down through the floor by the wood nymph.

Everyone else walks to the wall and goes right through it, but I hesitate. My head still not being able to wrap around that I can walk through this wall when I should be hurting from smashing my face. I put my hand up to the wall and gently put it through. Walking through seems like no problem after that.

Ashlynn, Kelly, and Miles wait on the other side staring at me. They each wear a grin that makes my cheeks burn red. I look away from them and to the re-emerging James at the front door of the house.

He comes straight to me and holds out a dagger in a leather sheath. The handle forms a T and is made of metal. There is one green jewel at the end of it encased by the metal.

"Thank you." I grab the dagger and cover from him. Having nowhere to put it, I hold it in place by the belt on my pants.

Ashlynn's feminine voice breaks through the silence, "Be on guard, it'll be a couple of minutes walk from here. Alexa stick with one of us. If something happens we should be able to protect you." She starts walking.

We all follow her. Up one block then a left, and one block more. The supermarket is visible in the long line of the strip mall. Everything seems too quiet. No lights, no cars, no people in sight.

The front doors don't open as we walk to them. The electricity that had run them no longer flows. Ashlynn puts her fingers in the crease and opens them up. She does the same with the interior doors. From what I can see the shelves look bare and only a couple of items remain. Looters must have already come through here doing the very same thing we are.

"James, you brought the bags, right?" The brunette asks.

"This would be a perfect time to mention that if I had forgotten them." James' sarcastic tone echoes through the empty store.

Ashlynn wipes the smile off her face. "Oh, shut up and just give me a bag."

"Yes Ma'am, and I should mention too there is a flashlight in each one. Please take those out before you fill it up." He reaches into the pocket of his jacket and pulls out a handful of miniature bags. Once they touch his hands they grow swiftly to normal size. The bag is one of those reusable bags you get from any store.

He hands each of us one bag.

Ashlynn walks off down the first aisle she comes to. James and Kelly each take off on their own, leaving Miles and myself.

"So, I guess that leaves us." Looking inside it, I see the flashlight at the bottom. I grab it. There is a button at the end. Pressing it turns the LED light on. "Let's go." Smiling at this, I try to get rid of my awkwardness.

We walk to the end of the store. Miles tosses a couple of items in his bag as we pass them on the way.

The very last aisle contains hygiene items. We walk down that one.

Miles throws everything left of the shampoo and conditioner he can find, while I toss a couple of soaps into mine. I quickly notice the bag isn't getting any heavier. "What's wrong with these bags?"

Miles laughs at my expense. "Nothing's wrong with them. James charmed them. As more items fill the bag they shrink and so does the weight. You can put as much in them as you want. But a fair warning everything becomes concentrated in the smaller form, so just don't open anything while it is still in the bag because you might not like the results."

Taking his word for it I start throwing everything that is left on the shelves in the bag. We grab conditioner, toilet paper, female hygiene products, much to my embarrassment on that one, toothbrushes and toothpaste before we decide to go to the next aisle.

After many more items are thrown in there I finally start feeling the bag get a bit heavier.

The next couple of aisles don't contain too much. Most things food-related were swiped to the very last item.

It is eerie to be in a store with so little on its shelves.

The first aisle with some food left contains candies, chocolate and junk foods, but in a pinch, those are at least better than nothing.

We get halfway down the aisle and Miles finally breaks our silence. "Kind of feels like it's Halloween and we're trick or treating."

Smirking at his humour, "Yeah, the only thing we need now is the corny spooky noise track with animal sounds, ghost's howling and screams." We pack away a few more bags of candy and chocolate bars. A feminine scream echoes in the dark. "I was kidding."

"Come on." Miles takes the lead as we run in the direction of the scream.

It takes all of ten seconds to find a girl at the mercy of everyone else. The ground has risen through the floor to cage the girl in. A gun lies on the floor a few feet from Ashlynn and James.

"If you're going to kill me then just do it already." She spits at Kelly, but it falls short.

"I'm not going to. You're human so I'll excuse you this time and explain things. There are two groups of 'monsters' out there; those who would eat you, or the good guys trying to save you. Try to guess which one I am? Now, are there any more of you vermin scurrying around here?" The distaste in Kelly's voice is venomous in the end.

Miles steps up and puts his hand on Kelly's shoulder. "She, of course, means that in the nicest way possible." He shoots a charming smile at the girl.

"There's no way in Hell I'm going to tell you anything. But you better leave, before everyone comes back for me. We've already killed some of your kind." She tries to put up a strong front; however, she doesn't seem to be thinking before she talks.

Kelly calls the girl out, "You realize you just gave me my answer, right? Humans, really, and we're trying to save their hides. Why?" She lets out a huff of breath.

"Kelly," Miles says the name of his girlfriend. His underlying meaning is said in the singular word; be nice.

"She tried to kill me." Her eyes roll and her smile turns sickly sweet. "I'm, oh so terribly, sorry. Would you and your gang like to come with us? We'll treat you with food, shelter, a shower, and safety. So, what do you say? Stay here and eventually be picked off by whatever demon happens upon you or come with us and have a chance at surviving?"

Ashlynn breaks the moment by laughing, "Kelly, my dear, you need to work on your people skills."

"I was just defending myself. I wouldn't have actually hurt her. You didn't have to do that." Kelly points to the cage around the girl. Now I wonder who the cage was really for.

Ashlynn ignores Kelly and walks up to the dirt jail bars. "Hi sweetheart, I'm sure you've gone through a lot of hardships over the past couple of days. I'm certain you've lost a lot of people you cared about: your parents, brother or sisters, best friends.

I know you're in a lot of pain.

We can offer a sanctuary for you and your friends. We're building a fortress. We have plenty of supplies, and other people human and supernatural. We're trying to survive this war just like you are."

"Alexa? Where's Darius?" My name being said causes my head to turn instinctually. A football teammate of Darius' comes out of the shadows down an aisle. The first thing I notice on Daniel is the dry, caked-on blood; the highest concentration of it on the neck of his shirt.

I faintly register that the girl says something, but what it could have been, I couldn't say. Focusing on the emerging group I answer his question, "Gone, he's ruling the demons that have taken over."

"Of course he is. What are you guys trying to accomplish?" Daniel asks.

Miles comes to my side, "We're trying to survive for now. Later we're hoping we can take this world back from those like Darius who are just trying to harvest and rule over humans."

"So, if we join you there might be a chance I could be a pain in his ass." He smiles near the end.

Miles returns his smile with a smirk. "It's possible."

"Then we'll join you." Daniel decides for his group.

"-but" Matt tries to disagree with Daniel's decision.

"No buts, all of us are human. Don't be stupid and think that we possibly have a chance of living if some stronger demon comes to kill us." Daniel cuts Matt off. Matt stays quiet. "Now, do you mind letting Amy go?"

Not a word is spoken but the dirt loses its solid shape; turning soft and falling as dust. Amy carefully steps out of the circle of dust. She starts heading towards the rest of her group, then stops. She looks at Kelly and distances herself.

"We should head back. I think we've caused enough of a ruckus to draw attention for one day. We shouldn't push our luck." James heads to go down an aisle beside ours.

Daniel stops him. "We'll go grab our stuff and meet up with you at the front." Daniel's group goes down the back and through a door. The rest of us go down the aisles and to the front of the store.

It doesn't take Daniel and his group long to meet back up with us. James looks out of the glass window. Looking left and right, I can only assume he is checking to see if it is safe to go out there. Stepping back from the window he walks straight outside.

We follow him out there. There are a series of crashes and bangs off in the distance. A whoosh and a rumbling like a plane come from the same direction.

Our group, now doubled in count, make our way back to the house. The noise and destruction continue and grows more numerous as we get closer to our destination.

None of the sounds are close enough to worry about right now, however, it is still close enough that I can hear faint screams.

A chill rips up my back. I get a couple of looks from those beside me, and I'm sure those behind me as well; I ignore their questioning gazes and continue walking as if it had never happened.

We reach the house and James walks up to it. Although there is a doorknob he puts his hand in the center of the door and pushes; resulting in the door opening for him.

He holds the door open for everyone. As we file in, he instructs us, "Please set your bags down in the room you had collected the supplies for and start unpacking. Those without a bag help those who do unpack. The sooner you can get this done the sooner we can start on supper."

Many pile into the kitchen to help James and Ashlynn unpack the food they collected. Miles, Daniel and I go upstairs to the bathroom.

The bathroom is beside the room I had come out of earlier. We squeeze into the relatively small-sized full bathroom. Although, compared to the number of people we are brought back, we didn't collect much. However, we did collect more than should be able to fit inside this cabinet.

"How are we going to fit everything in here?" I ask.

Miles opens up the cabinet under the sink and puts the bag inside. He then closes the cabinet doors. "You have to remember you are living in a wizard's house now. Almost everything in this house is charmed.

Basically, everything is not as it seems.

It takes a while to get used to the wondrous things a wizard can do. Well, you had a bit of a show earlier with lunch, and then the bottomless bags, and now the cabinet that sorts and packs itself." He reopens the door and takes the bag out. He hands the bag to me. "Take a look."

I look inside the bag first as he hands it to me. The only thing I can see in it is the food and candy. Looking into the opened cabinet I see it full of everything he had picked up. The back seems to have no end.

"So, I just place the bag inside and wait and the drawer will take out everything that belongs in it by itself?" I question him.

"Essentially, yes. Of course, it's not perfect every time. I suspect there are certain things that James wouldn't have thought of adding to the list when he charmed each cabinet, drawer, closet, and fridge in the house, but for the most part, it makes the job a lot faster and easier. Here let me do it for you." Taking his cue, I place the handle in his outstretched hand. He places my bag into the cabinet.

Daniel takes the moment of silence to speak the questions plaguing his mind. "So, what are you?"

Miles snaps his gaze to Daniel. He takes a moment, just staring at Daniel before he answers him simply, "An elf."

"And you?" His question now directed at me.

"Human." The small room closes in with the awkward silence that follows. I open up the doors and pull out my mostly empty bag. Closing the door, I then look back to Daniel. Breaking the silence, I turn his question around on him, "And you are?"

"Uh, human."

"Well, now that we have that established, is there anything else you would like to know?" Miles directs his question to Daniel, who shakes his head in the negative. He looks like he's sweating from being put on the spot. "Then we should probably head downstairs; put the food away so they can get started on dinner." Miles tries to move Daniel along.

"Right." Daniel turns around and leads us down the stairs we had come up. He follows the path everyone else had taken.

The kitchen is empty and everyone is in the dining room. Different smells waft through the air. I can't tell what most of the smells are from but the basic idea of it tells me that supper is ready.

Daniel walks into the dining room, while Miles and I drop the bags off into the pantry. He walks away after closing the door, so I assume to do the same.

The dining room is filled with people. Some are sitting at the table, sitting on chairs and stools around the room, or on the floor. There are a lot more beings than there had been earlier. The group we had brought in and the beings I assume the other group had found.

Night has fallen. James has a couple of lights set up around the room; mostly gas lanterns and flashlights.

Many appear beat up and worn. Not to the level those had been at the airport, but they have had a rough few days.

Everyone has a bowl full of soup, and every bowl has a different kind in it. I follow Miles to the table. He sits down at one of the empty spots, and I take the seat beside him. A can of chicken noodle soup is in front of my bowl.

I look around the table for the can openers. There is nothing there.

Looking to Miles for help on what I should do next. His bowl is full of soup and he has started eating. He notices my gaze and looks at me.

He finishes the food in his mouth. "Hold the can over the bowl."

I do as he says. I look over at him. I see beyond him, James looking over at me. The can gets lighter. The soup is in my bowl. The bottom lid hangs by only one section still connected. I put the can on the table. My soup starts boiling in the bowl, then settles.

I look to James, "thank you." Turning back to Miles I ask, "How do you remember all these things?"

I pick up my spoon to start eating.

"I grew up knowing about these sorts of things. Don't worry once you've been exposed to this world long enough you'll know everything." Miles takes a bite of his soup.

While eating, I open up my ears and listen to the conversations going on in the room. The table seems the quietest with only James and Ashlynn asking Rayleen about her day. The little girl talks about how she and Nia checked out the house and drew some ideas on how to protect the house.

Moving my attention, I listen to those behind me. From the bits of sentences, I can hear many are telling stories about different situations they had gotten into; whether today or in the past I don't know.

One of the males voices his battle with a couple of goblins. They had come out of the shadows while he was searching a house. Five of them had come at him at once. He used his dagger to kill a couple of them, but his dagger was knocked out of his hand. He couldn't reach it so he used some of the objects in the house to kill the two that had been left.

A girl this time speaks of her terror with some giants. She hid behind a tree while the giants picked up cars and threw them in all directions. She heard screams and explosions but didn't dare to move from her spot or look until they had gotten further away.

Another tells of her horror of finding corpses of a family all in the basement of the house. The parents were thrown haphazardly across the room from the children, while they looked like they were just sleeping.

She wonders what kind of twisted rebellion they think they are in. They are being wasteful by just leaving the bodies where they die.

The woman goes on to tell the person she's talking with, that originally she had thought the rebellion was a good idea but once she had seen that scene she knew for certain she made the right choice when she picked her sides.

The stories I hear make me glad I had only experienced what I had. My experiences seem little compared to some of the things I hear. For what he had done to me, I hate Darius, but in a way, he had also saved me from a lot of horrors and probable death.

Finishing what is in my bowl, I set my spoon down.

James stands up, "No rush to finish but for those of you that have, please place your dishes on the kitchen counter and continue on your way downstairs. We will have a meeting to discuss what we have accomplished today. Before we start the meeting, be sure to pick a speaker for each group to state what you had accomplished."

He picks up his plate and heads into the kitchen. Many take this as the sign to start doing as he had said.

I continue to sit to avoid being knocked over by the crowd.

Many different species of beings pass me. Some I have started to recognize by experience, some from assumption through movies and stories, but others I had never seen or heard of before. Other people look human, but I assume they're not.

The crowd lessens and those left at the table get up.

Walking to the kitchen I set down my bowl on top of a pile and drop my spoon into the sink.

Following the tail end of the crowd, I go downstairs at a slower rate than I would have normally gone.

I expect to see everyone piling into the tunnel for the tree again, however, everyone takes a seat in various areas of the room; on the floor, the couch or leaning against walls. They have brought the lanterns and flashlights down and set up some candles around the room; giving everyone an orange glow.

The focus point is on James sitting in an armchair on the left side of the room. Kelly leans against the wall James opened the door in earlier. Miles heads off towards James. I stop in an awkward pause torn between whether I should stay with James or go to Kelly.

Deciding not to go to the center of attention I walk around others to stand beside Kelly. I mouth a 'hi' to her, and she nods back.

Turning around, I lean against the wall beside Kelly. The room is silent as James starts this meeting.

"From the looks of it, we've had a very successful day. Our group gathered some supplies, which you have all been made aware of already, and we gained a couple more allies. Addy's group gained much ground and even more allies. Nia, would you mind standing and discussing your progress." James stands up and holds his hand out in the direction of one of the girls sitting on the couch; as if he is helping her up.

A golden blonde-haired girl holds her hand up; as though she accepting his help up. She stands up like she did get help up.

Her voice is soft and feminine, yet loud. "We've established a couple of defences; bolstering James' on this house and we have started defences on the ground gained. The immediate surrounding area is already protected.

We will start housing many of you in the houses tonight.

We have charmed different items in the houses to open the paths between the basements of the houses. Until all of you know exactly what all the items are we will be placing them all on a table in the basement. James?" She nods her head and sits back down.

"Thank you, Nia." I flick my eyes to James again as his voice gets my attention. "Addy, your group and anyone new will find a place in the houses first. So, Nia if you don't mind showing them what they need to do after we're finished here?

Tomorrow, Addy if you could take your group out, I would like to expand into the blocks headed northwest and take over the strip mall we gathered supplies from today.

Tomorrow the rest of us here, will continue on defences and start on gathering weapons and armour.

In the evening, we will start training those who don't know how to fight. Even just the basics will help tremendously. I believe this is where the meeting will end for tonight. Get to your sleeping arrangements." James stands and I watch as a door opens in the wall and some walkthrough after Nia touched an old bronzed mirror. Many grab a light to help light their way.

Ashlynn walks over to the couch. She leans down and picks up Rayleen. From her limp form, I take that she is asleep. With a red-haired head resting on her shoulder Ashlynn takes her upstairs.

Miles comes over to Kelly and I. Kelly pushes herself away from the wall and takes Miles' hand. She turns him around abruptly and pulls him behind her up the stairs.

With most of everyone gone, I decide to go up to my room. I take a left-over lantern on the coffee table. I follow close behind Miles; up the stairs to the main level, then around the corner and up the other stairs. Kelly and Miles continue up one more level and I stand outside the bedroom I slept in earlier.

Creaking on the stairs behind me catches my attention and causes me to turn. James follows me up the stairs. I notice the thin, old book in his hand. The cover is ripped off. The next page is yellowed and creased at the corners.

"Here," he hands me the book. The paper feels rough from the ages.

"It's a book on the basics of different types of supernaturals. Of course, it doesn't touch on everything, but it's the most straightforward and it's alphabetical like a dictionary.

At the least, if you hear a name, you can look it up and find out what you want to know." He takes a step back. "It's been a long day. If you'll excuse me, I wish to retire to my bedroom now."

"Of course, thank you." I nod and look down at the book in my hand.

"You're very welcome. Have a great night." He walks off to my right. James walks into a room and shuts the door behind him. I wait in silence for a moment.

Looking to my left I see the armchair Miles had been sitting in earlier reading his book. Figuring it might be a good idea to look up a couple of beings in the book before bedtime.

I set the lantern on the table and I sit down in the chair. A bit of dust fills my nose. A tickle appears that makes me scrunch my nose, but the sneeze never comes.

The symbol on the page looks familiar. I recognize it though I've only seen it once. It's the same symbol that was on those papers at the farmhouse.

Thumbing open the first page, I look at the next. I adjust the angle and bring it close to the lantern. James's name is scribed on the next page. The thick paper turns easy from use.

In the beginning, there were only the four elementals born from Mother; Fire, Earth, Water and Air. The four siblings lived harmoniously together for millions of years, as they controlled the four elements which rule the natural world.

One day a fight broke out. The Earth and Water Elementals confronted their Fire Elemental sibling for destroying their elements with her fiery devastation.

The Fire Elemental drew the blood of Earth. It fell to the ground, landing on a wolf. The wolf transformed into the original werewolf.

Seeing the kind of creatures they could create with a drop of their blood the siblings created more of the first supernatural beings.

If a drop of their blood can turn a wolf into a werewolf, then could it turn me into something more powerful?

I thumb through the pages for a few beings I've met already and others that I've heard of in the past.

Chapter 20

Mom and Dad,

I'm alive. I'm at the mall. Come find me.

I love you.
Forever and Always
XOXO

   *Nikki*

I stick the notepad back on the fridge. Hopefully, my parents will come back here and find the note. If there is one place they would look if they come back here it would be the fridge. We always leave notes on the fridge to let each other know things.

I know, on some level, that I shouldn't leave a note for them. As Shawn said, we don't want the wrong people finding out where we are. But, I can't help it.

Grabbing my luggage and backpack, I follow after everyone else. They're already packed up in the truck and ready to go.

Shawn jumps out to help me toss the luggage back into the back. I think for a moment before deciding to throw my backpack back there too. There isn't enough room in the cab for us all and my bag; comfortably.

I crawl into the back and buckle up. I now know how Steph could react the way she did. I want to stay here; for even just a bit longer. We could pull away and my parents could walk through the door five minutes later; a near miss with possible devastating consequences.

I watch the house as Brad starts the engine and pulls away until my house is no longer in view.

My eyes tear up and a few manage to fall down my cheek. I wipe the wetness away, but I can't wipe the feeling away that I may never see my parents again. Whether they are alive or not, I may never see them again. I decide once and for all that my parents are alive and out there somewhere. So are the rest of my family and my friends. Everyone I knew is out there somewhere. They're alive unless someone can prove that they are dead.

I turn back around in my seat and let Brad take us back in a deafening silence. Each person is, alone with their silence, mourning our losses.

There's no doubt, this trip has changed a lot. The world didn't end and we're still alive. This is an invasion; a war zone.

We don't know how long this is going to last. Rescue isn't going to appear on the horizon in tanks and planes.

Brad pulls into the Bourbon Street entrance. He parks where the taxis usually sit. Immediately, Gary comes out to greet us. As soon as I'm clear of the truck, he grabs me for a big hug.

"Welcome back. I'm so glad you're all okay. You'll need to tell me all about it." Gary is smiling from ear to ear.

I open my mouth to try to say anything. Shawn beats me to it. "We should probably get everything to the boat. Did anyone notice we were gone?"

"No, no one noticed," Gary says. That's good.

Shawn hands Gary my backpack then the smaller bag from Steph's house. Shawn hands the rest of us our bags. They follow right behind Gary back into the mall. It's dark in here. Brad is the last to come in. He sets his one bag down to lock the door behind him. He does the same when he gets to the second set of doors.

Quietly, we all follow Gary down Bourbon Street and around the corner towards the boat. When the Water Park glass separation can be seen, I try to see if anyone can see us. I reason since I can't see anyone they can't see us either. I can't remember if I can see through the glass from inside the pool area.

We make it back to the boat without any trouble. Gary waits for us to put down our bags and sit comfortably at a table. Shawn and Brad sit on either side of me. Steph is settled on Brad's lap. "So, what's it like out there?"

No one wants to talk; we just look back and forth between each other. No one wants to be the one to burst the ignorance bubble.

I finally say, "It looks like the end of the world out there. There's no one out there anymore. There's not going to be any rescue anytime soon."

"Don't be so depressing." Tyler's voice surprises all of us. "We just need to have a good time, until the army rescues us. It won't be too long. I'm sure you're just exaggerating. Just grab a drink and party with us." Tyler and a few others make it onto the boat. I stand up and walk closer to him.

"So, I'm exaggerating what exactly? You didn't go out there. You didn't see what we saw. It looks like a bomb went off everywhere. Buildings are on fire, cars flipped, bodies and blood everywhere. Some of our families are dead." I try to defend myself.

"It's the end of the world, what did you expect? I'm sorry your families are dead but you're the ones who wanted to go out and find out for sure. It's your fault. Just stay here going forward and everything will be okay." He has a very small view of what is happening.

"No, it's not. You didn't see what we saw. We need to start thinking about survival, not partying all the time." I try to break through his narrow thoughts.

"Oh, don't be so serious." Tyler is being ridiculous. I'm sure he's still drunk. That might have something to do with it; it could just be his personality. Maybe, he's already given up trying to live and is just trying to drown himself numb until he dies.

"We need to start preparing. Figure out how much food we have and how long we can stretch it. It's going to get cold soon. We need to gather blankets and coats to stay warm." Gary puts his two cents worth in. I'm happy someone is finally trying to help me out.

"Relax old man. We're not going to be here long enough to even think we're running out of food. But, if it makes you feel better, you can do whatever the hell you want. We're going to have fun." Tyler leaves with a couple of people. This isn't the last time this conversation will come up; I fear.

I don't have anything to say back to Tyler. There's nothing I can say to get it across to him that this is serious. Nothing I can say will force him to want to try to survive. Maybe once the booze runs out they'll figure it out in sobriety.

I turn back around, thinking that I will just go back to sit down at the table. But, everyone is looking at me. They look like they're expecting me to say something.

So, now what?

"Sooner or later they have to figure it out. Everyone is going to deal with this differently. Besides, they didn't see what we saw out there. And, they certainly aren't going to stick around long enough to discuss things with us. We need to plan for the long run. They'll come around eventually." I go back to sit where I had been before Tyler's interruption and continue. Most everyone goes back to their spots. Stephanie now sits beside Brad. "We brought things from our houses that might help us, more comforts from home so…" I lose my thought. I don't know where to continue.

Gary clears his throat and gains everyone's attention. "I think we need to prepare, if we have to leave suddenly as well. It could be just luck that they haven't really attacked us yet." He gets us back on track.

"They could've thought that there wouldn't be many people here yet. Why attack a nearly empty building?" Shawn says.

"That's just it too. We didn't have any trouble out there. There's the devastation but otherwise, everything is a ghost town. It was eerie." I add.

"Are you suggesting those things are intellectually smart?" Brad pipes in against Shawn.

"Of course. You saw the way it cornered us in that room and waited until we opened that door?" Shawn says. Gary looks a bit excited at this new discovery.

"Predator smart and actual intelligence is something entirely the different." What Brad says makes sense. Shawn also makes sense. We were all here before the mall should have been open. What I want to know is where were they hiding? Obviously, they all had to come from somewhere. And, what exactly do they want? "We shouldn't waste our time with questions that we can't answer. What I want to know is how to kill them? As he said, they haven't attacked here yet, but it's only just a matter of time."

"It's got to be like the horror movies right? They're straight out of the movies. We're going to need silver bullets, stakes and garlic." Peter says.

"What do we do with any that come in here for shelter, those that don't want to harm us?" Shawn asks a question that I hadn't considered. I hadn't considered it because we were working on a theory that they were ravenous beasts intent on killing us, not that they were intelligent beings with a choice.

"Don't be stupid." Brad ridicules Shawn.

"I'm serious. What if they're like humans? There are some good ones and some bad ones." Shawn continues his thought.

I decide to help Shawn out on the chance that he's right. "He's right. First, we make sure they aren't going to kill us, then we offer shelter."

Shawn looks thankful to me, but Brad gets furious. "Hell no! They're all out to get us. I'm not letting any of them close enough to me to find out if they're good or bad. You saw it out there. They're all bad or else some of them would be fighting with us."

"If we're suggesting they have intelligence like humans, then you also have to accept that there could also be good and bad supernatural beings. The good ones could be just as scared as you are. They could be hiding because the supernaturals that are killing humans are also trying to kill the good supernatural beings too." Shawn argues.

"Why are you taking their side?" Brad stands up from his seat.

Shawn doesn't look like Brad's intimidation is fazing him. I do wish he would stop egging Brad on. We could have ended this conversation by now and moved on; figuring it out if the situation happened.

Shawn debates internally for a moment before he frowns and takes in a deep breath. "I'm an elf. I'm one of the good guys." Brad lunges towards him. I don't know if he forgot I was in the way, or what. But, I act like a barrier between them.

"Stop! Brad!" I push hard. Knocking him off his balance and onto the floor of the boat. Gary grabs onto Brad and holds him in place. Brad's attack forces me to pick sides through my uncertainty of the confession. "Shawn is your best friend. You've known him for four years and he's never hurt any of us. So relax, and hear him out."

My interest is peaked. He doesn't look like an elf. He looks human; like Shawn. Maybe elves look exactly like humans.

I give Shawn the platform to say his piece. Eyeing him up and down with the new knowledge. There's nothing abnormal about him. No large pointy ears; though he does have that slight point. Something he explained was an abnormality caused by exclusively side sleeping as a baby.

"The myths and legends are true; somewhat. Movie monsters are real. But, we're not all mindless and blood thirsty. We're people too. Some got angry and decided to attack. It's a revolution based on oppression thousands of years in the making. But they're going about it wrong. They didn't think humans would accept our existence without it going bad for us so they attacked." Shawn says.

"Is it just here? How did no one know about you people? How many of them are out there?" Gary asks his round of questions. Shawn puts his hand up to stop him.

"The war is all over the world." Shawn begins to explain everything. "There was a treaty made in the 6th century for supernatural beings to go into hiding. Humans were gaining numbers, we got overtaken. Since the treaty, we've all hidden; some in plain sight.

Any gaps in human records are little uprisings; well most of history is written wrong either way. But, with the technology nowadays this one is not going to be hidden." He shakes his head at the confusing turning in his thoughts. Jumbled mess spewing out of simplified information. "You'd be surprised at how many humans are actually supernatural beings in disguise. Ones that can blend in naturally, or those who wear makeup or get surgery to look human."

"So infiltration then destroy." Brad's body gets tense. I get ready to interfere if he decides to attack Shawn again.

"No." Shawn is offended. "We were just living our lives as best as we were allowed. Not all of us wanted it this way. Like I said, just like humans, there are good ones and bad ones. The bad ones are giving the rest of us a bad name. The rest of us, were perfectly fine living just the way we had been. We're just as much victims of this as you are. If you haven't noticed, I've been by your side this whole time. My family is dead too. My friends are dead too."

That finally seems to shut Brad up. His body loses its tension. Gary releases his grip but stays cautious. Brad slowly turns around and walks off the boat. I'm torn between going after him and letting him go. He could do something really stupid, or he could be going to clear his head.

I expect Stephanie to go after him, but she doesn't. She looks torn between staying with us and supporting her boyfriend.

"Let him go. He's just got to calm down and he'll see. What are we doing next?" Shawn tries to get us back to what we were originally talking about.

I want to continue talking about him. He drops that he's an elf, and then just wants to continue talking about other things. I'll respect that; for now. Eventually, my curiosity is going to require some questions answered. But, I don't think he was prepared to let his secret out like that.

I'll give him some time, but I don't know how I feel about it yet and I don't want to overreact. I try to stuff down the betrayal because I know it's not reasonable. If elves were a secret to the world, then of course he couldn't tell me. But, how much did he know about the war? Could he have had us prepared and had us safe at home with our families?

"This doesn't change anything. We survive. That's it. We do what we can to survive and make it through this alive; all of us. We need water, food, warmth and anything else to help us survive. This isn't temporary. We need to survive a long time. We're going to need to survive the winter." I finalize.

I look Shawn in the eyes. Shawn's never hurt any of us, so there isn't any reason not to trust what he says; not to trust him. He's still the same person I know and love and trust. He's just also an elf. I remind myself. I nod and tighten my smile briefly. He smiles in return; we're good.

Chapter 21

Half the day has gone by. I've hit a slump in energy, but it isn't anything I'm not used to. I didn't sleep much at all last night, but I will tonight. If not because of not sleeping well last night, then from the work I've done today.

I had decided last night that I would make myself useful; that I would give them a reason to keep me around until they trust me. I believe I've done exactly that with my survival knowledge.

I can figure them out in the meantime and figure out what I'm going to do about it.

These people are pretty useless. No wonder they had to go to extremes to survive so far. Not that I sympathize with them, but I do understand.

"Jaiden!" Paul yells to me. I look up where he stands at the back door. "You're on watch with me."

"Okay, I'll be right there!" I shout back at him. I take the pieces of wood I'm carrying to the garage and put them in the pile right inside the door. Missy follows shortly behind me everywhere I go. The large dog only zooms in front of me right as I try to go in through the door. She almost knocks me over. Paul's arm reaches out to steady me. "Thank you, I don't think she realizes how big, and strong she is sometimes."

"Right. Come on then." He lets his arm fall, and he brings me upstairs to the other bedroom. They have this room set up as a lookout. The window in the front can be used to hop onto the roof over the kitchen, and living room. The window in the back looks out onto the forest. Missy settles down on the floor near me.

"Do you know how to use this?" Paul holds a handgun out for me to take.

I clumsily take it and fumble around with it for a moment. Trying to hold it out and away from my body. "No, I've never used one before. This is my first time holding one; seeing one."

He smiles; amused. "I can tell. It's not going to hurt you just because you're holding it."

"It might." I've heard of people getting skin ripped off from having their hand in the wrong place while firing it. Hair triggers could go off at the slightest unintentional touch if there isn't a safety. I don't think the information would help me in feigning any of my innocence.

"Hold it like it's not going to bite you, or you might get hurt." He moves to the side of me and moves my hands into position. "Here's the safety. You need to hold that when you pull the trigger. Make sure when you have the safety off, but you aren't firing immediately, that your finger isn't in the trigger slot."

"So you don't accidentally shoot when you don't want to." I reason.

"Exactly. Also, make sure you never point the gun at anyone you don't want to shoot." Paul adds.

"Okay."

"And, make sure that where you keep the gun; you aren't accidentally going to set it off. The safety can get pressed in your pocket, and all it takes is a hair movement of the trigger to go off."

That doesn't seem very safe for a safety mechanism.

"I think I'd rather not have the gun, thank you." I hand him back the gun. Maybe not be the smartest idea safety-wise, but I think it might be more trouble keeping the gun than not having a weapon at all. It would give them a reason to watch me more. Someone might shoot me thinking I was going to shoot them.

"Keep it while you're on watch. You might have to shoot something." He hands me back the gun. I take it reluctantly.

"Hopefully, I won't have to use it."

We settle down in the middle of the room. Paul makes sure to look between the two sides. I try to make it look like I'm doing the same. In between switching sides, I look around the bedroom. There are quite a few weapons in this room. I guess they are using this room as sort of an armoury. I know they must have gotten all these weapons over the last week because my grandparents only had a few shotguns and a crossbow.

"Tell me more about yourself," Paul asks me. He sounds very serious. He's testing me.

It dawns on me, that the gun might've been a test in and of itself. If I had shown proficiency, would he have thought me too much of a threat? He could easily kill me and no one would care.

If I had tried to kill him, a house full of people would be here in a moment to kill me. I wouldn't make it out of here alive.

"There isn't much to tell. I'm an honour roll student. I'm in grade eleven. I-"

His eyebrows furrow before he cuts me off. "Wait, how old are you?"

"Fifteen." As soon as the word leaves my mouth his face flashes through many feelings; shock, disbelief, horror, and more. I add awkwardly, "I skipped a grade."

"Shit, seriously? I thought you were in your twenties. You're a kid. Give me that gun." I hand the gun over to him. "You act so old. What were you doing driving? You're not even old enough to have a license."

"I've always been told I act older than I am."

"I believe it." He looks me over for a moment. "Where are your parents?"

"I don't know. They never came back for me."

Paul sucks in a breath through his teeth. "I'll need to tell them." He says to himself. "If any of the men come on to you, send them to me, and I'll deal with them." He wags his finger at me.

"Of course." I smile at him. The look he sends back to me is comforting and fatherly. My age immediately gained his protection, and perhaps his trust. Sometimes being young has protective perks.

A few minutes pass. We go back to silence and looking at the forest.

"Do you know how to fight?" He suddenly asks.

"No. Never. I'm a goody-two-shoes. Never been in a fight. I wouldn't know what to do at all." I know I don't look like much. I'm short; only five-one, and a half. My height immediately puts me at a disadvantage. I don't look like I work out or play sports.

"You look like you'd get blown over in a breeze." He jokes.

"I have been." I joke. Maybe not blown over completely, but I've been knocked off balance because of a huge gust of wind. He laughs at this.

"Don't worry too much. We'll take care of you. I'll protect you." Perhaps this place, these people won't be entirely bad; maybe.

Chapter 22

Lifting my head quickly, my heart races until I realize I had been woken up by a little hand on my arm. My second realization of the day: I fell asleep in the chair last night while reading.

"You know, you're not supposed to sleep in a chair." I reach out to her head and shake my hand; slightly messing up her hair. Rayleen giggles and tries to get me to stop. I take back my hand to use both of them to straighten in the chair. Moving pulls the muscles in my shoulders and neck.

"I know that. I fell asleep while reading. Apparently, I was more tired than I thought." I try to explain to her.

Moving the book to the small table beside the chair, I let Rayleen help me to stand. "James asked me to get you for breakfast. You wanna help me wake up Miles and Kelly too?"

"Sure, do you want to jump on the bed to wake them up?" I ask.

"Yeah!" She runs up the stairs, I'm sure as quietly as she can in her excitement. A piece of the little girl I knew has come back. She seems to have put what happened to her behind her.

I shush while following her, but it doesn't help. The stairs are old, wooden, and creaky as I walk up them. I doubt anyone trying could sneak up these.

I'm only a second behind Rayleen getting to the upstairs, but even with that, I can still tell we interrupted something. Kelly stands with a scowl and her hands on her hips directed at Miles; who looks equally irritated.

"James says to come downstairs for breakfast. I was going to wake you up by jumping on your bed but you're already up." The end of her sentence tells of her pout in its tone.

Miles turns and walks to Rayleen. He picks her up effortlessly. "Sorry we've been up for a while, maybe next time you can wake us up. How about we go downstairs and see what delicious food James has made us today?"

"Okay, let's go." The pout is gone and her voice is filled with joy again.

Turning tail, I go back down the stairs. Breaking off from their path I go into the bedroom with a short, "I'll be down in a minute; just going to change."

Opening the cabinet, I try to find something that I would actually like to wear. There are a lot of dresses inside the two swinging doors; many look about as old as the rest of the antiques in this room. I close the doors and open the drawers. Finding a couple of bits of modern clothing within the drawers I grab jeans, a black t-shirt, and a zip up black sweater to wear. I find a couple of tags on the clothing, so I rip them off and dress. Going to the washroom next, I get ready further.

Ready and dressed, I feel refreshed. I go downstairs through the kitchen trying to find where everyone went to. The dining room has a few voices coming from it. Everyone is at the table and they all seem to be done eating already. There is only one empty seat with a covered plate on it; assuming it's mine, I go sit there.

Ashlynn speaks first, "Good morning."

"Morning," I reply to her; smiling and nodding. She goes back to listening to James and Gio discussing back and forth.

Uncovering the plate, I find a peanut butter sandwich, a couple of slices of an orange and a glass of water. I eat the food and focus on what James and Gio are saying.

"-need anyone to help you?" James continues from whatever else he had been saying.

Insulted, Gio smacks his fist down on the table and points to James. "No, I work alone. I can make all the weapons we will ever need as long as you get me the supplies."

James holds his hands up trying to calm the cyclopes. "Yes, not to worry. We'll make the trip after breakfast and ask the dwarves for supplies."

"The dwarves, eh?" This new bit of information changes his whole demeanour. He hides a newfound giddiness. "The raw materials will work well enough. The sooner I get the materials, the sooner I can start making the weapons we need." Gio gets up from his seat and walks out of the room.

Finishing my breakfast, I put the cover back over my empty plate and glass.

"Now that we're all finished, I believe we should get started on today's work. Alexa, I assume you were able to catch up a bit from our conversation?" I nod. "Good. Ashlynn, Rayleen, you and I will be using the trees to travel to the mountains to see the dwarves. We need supplies to make weapons. They will bring us no harm, but I will warn you they are proud, crude, and always dirty." James stands up and motions for us to leave the table.

"Why aren't Kelly and Miles coming with us?" Though directing the question at James, I half expect either Kelly or Miles to answer me. Why are Rayleen and I going, for that matter?

"Because I'm a vampire and, well, let's just say they don't like us. Anyway, Miles and I are going to see someone we've got on the other side about the information they've collected." Kelly stands up and pushes her chair in.

Rayleen's eyes brighten in wonder. "Like a spy?"

"Exactly like a spy." When the voice comes from behind her rather than from Kelly, Rayleen snaps her gaze onto Ashlynn. The Earth Elemental gently taps Rayleen on her little nose.

"We should probably get going while it's still early. It'll give them time to get things together for today. Meet me outside in the tree once you're all finished." James says as he walks out of the room. His hint of impatience gets through all of us as we hurry off to follow him. Falling into step after James, we go out the front door.

Getting half used to strange things, I barely flinch this time when walking through the tree. We don't stay long, James picks up two bags in the center of the empty room.

We follow James through the other side of the tree. Croaking frogs and chirping birds sound from around us in the near distance. Massive trees, lots of bushes and flowers live in this immediate area. Looking all around me I can see various peaks of mountains. By my guess, I would think we are about halfway up this mountain. I wonder how we would be able to travel through the tree, but I don't think the answer would be all that quick and easy for James to explain; or for me to understand.

James takes us through some of the trees. After a few moments, I start to see a structure that doesn't belong in the untouched wooded area. A small log cabin gets more and more visible as we get closer.

Close up, the cabin looks unused. Spider webs hang from the ceiling to the side of the house and the wood is rough and greyed. No lights are on inside.

James knocks on the door six times causing the doorknob turns enough to allow the door to open slightly. He pushes it open the rest of the way and cautiously walks into the dark room.

Looking behind me, Rayleen is holding Ashlynn's hand and is walking very close to her. She looks a little frightened. For a moment, I'm jealous of Rayleen's ease to use Ashlynn for comfort.

Walking into the darkness slowly gives my eyes enough time to adjust enough that I can see there is very little in the cabin. I can make out the outlines of a bed, table and chairs, and a wood stove.

James stops near the back wall. He squats down and lifts connected boards from the floor. As he does, soft orange light comes from under the boards. James goes down first; level by level with the bags in one hand.

Once his head is no longer visible, I go to do the same. There is a ladder made of wood to help. Two torches hang from the walls of the tunnel on either side of me, providing the only light in the area.

Ashlynn helps Rayleen until the little girl has a firm hold on the rungs of the ladder. Ashlynn follows last. As she comes down, she closes the boards over the hole.

"Hands up and bare all weapons." A gruff voice calls from the darkness in front of us. The sound echoes on the walls. I hold my hands up and make sure Rayleen is doing the same. James holds his hands open in front of him. "State your namesake and your cause."

"I am James Ellesworn, representative of the magic folk in the Council. With me I have Ashlynn; the Earthen Elemental, Alexa Brenner and her niece Rayleen, humans. We have come to consult with your King and Queen regarding a business proposition." James' voice is calm, firm and confident.

Silence greets him as a response and I can hear the movement of footsteps coming closer. I couldn't begin to estimate the number. It all stops suddenly and there is a clearing of a throat. "You brought a human child with you." The slightest hint of a reprimand in his voice. A couple more seconds pass before we hear him speak again. "We will bring you to the King and Queen." Out of the darkness men with long beards encircle us.

I get pushed from behind by one as tall as my chin height; enough to make me stumble forward but not enough to make me fall. I grab a hold of Rayleen and hoist her up to carry her. She clings to me in a backwards piggyback.

Even with my eyes adjusted to the darkness, I can still only see a couple of feet in front of me. The frequency of torches is not enough to do any good for me to see anything well. Stout men edge in light, but remain in darkness.

We walk, being guided by the dwarves, for a long time. Every once in a while, my ears pop with the change in altitude. We are led on paths going up and down, left and right; winding in a way I'm sure I couldn't follow to get back out again.

A crack of bright light in the distance grows as giant doors open. Orange light brightens the tunnel hallway little by little.

We are guided into a hole in the mountain. Carved out of the rock are condos and pathways. Doorways and windows are also carved into the rock, with wooden coverings. Lush plant life creates a confetti of green sprinkled everywhere.

A giant bonfire in the center is the focal point at eye level. Above, I glance at lights blanketing the roof of the cavern like thousands of glow in the dark stars on a ceiling. That's what's making it like day light in here.

The dwarves walk us to one of the closest condos to the fire. The heat feels like the summer sun.

The dwarf at the front calls out to those dwelling behind the hide. "Permission to enter with outside visitors?"

"Proceed." Answers a rough voice.

The dwarf in front holds the hide to the side and we are motioned to go inside. It is a few degrees cooler inside; enough to be noticeable yet still comfortable. The room is lit up with light bulbs; to my surprise.

There are two dwarves in the room with us. Both have crowns adorning their heads. They're dressed in modern clothes, and clean despite James' warnings. The whole room is in clean and modern order. Nothing like what James had me expecting.

Although the others hadn't come in with us, from their cautious behaviour before, I would bet they are all standing outside just in case there is any trouble.

"James, Ashlynn, rumours reach even these depths of the mountain. If there is a semblance of truth, you know we won't help you. We will not be involved in the puerile tirade of bratty beings." This dwarf seems to be a bit older than the others I have met. A couple wisps of grey are strewn in his long hair and beard. The creases around his eyes give a look of experience and the wisdom that comes from it.

His partner beside him looks almost the same, but her eyes are different as they look softer and more feminine. Her hair has a few braids throughout; held together in golden clasps.

"Sir, Ma'am, sadly the rumours are true, possibly even more so than you are aware. At this point, Seth and Aalayah have successfully taken over the world. They have destroyed many lives and land in the process and I fear he will not stop until he has destroyed more than can ever be repaired. The mountains won't deter him. To this, I ask for your help."

"Careful James, it's against the ancient laws to attack a race that remains neutral in the war and I would like to make sure it keeps that way." The dwarf interrupts James and states his position clearly.

"And if he won't respect ancient laws?" James pauses as the couple cross meaningful looks. "Let me put it a different way. We would like to propose a business venture. We require raw materials that only you can produce and we are willing to pay." James walks up to the two and places the bags down. He pulls out a folded paper from his pocket and places it on the folded corner edge of one of the bags. Once he lays it out, he backs back up to us.

The King reads the note while the Queen looks inside the bags. The King shows the Queen the note. She looks to him and nods once in an affirmative. The King looks back to us. "We accept. Your materials will be delivered through the trees by nightfall. I assume this is acceptable."

"Perfectly, thank you." James bows his head.

"We must do business again, but for now I will ask you to leave. We have a lot of work to do in little time. You will be escorted out." The door opens. James walks out into the small crowd.

Ashlynn guides me after him, and I see that many of the dwarves have left. There are only about ten remaining. Knowing part of the way I start walking without their guidance towards the huge doors.

Rayleen's weight becomes an issue as the strength in my arms starts to give out. I set the little girl down. In doing so, I can't help but notice that Rayleen is the same height as of some of these full-grown dwarf escorts.

Knowing of the dark road ahead, I grab Rayleen's hand to make sure she doesn't separate from us.

The large wooden doors look medieval with elaborate detail and metal adornments. There are five dwarves on each side of the door. One on each side heaves on a rope to cause the doors to open.

A deep thundering noise echoes loudly and I cannot determine the direction it came from. In a sudden panic, Dwarves are running in every direction; many coming out of the carved homes, disappearing down tunnels.

A shout above the crowd stops and reroutes the dwarves' panicked run. "Collapse in tunnel twenty-three! Collapse in tunnel twenty-three!"

All the dwarves run in the direction we came from. They go past the bonfire and around a corner; all except one.

He stands behind James. "I will take you through the tunnels.

Quickly now, I must return to help.”

“You may go help your companions, I know the way out,” James says.

“No!” The dwarf’s sudden word is blurted out just as fast as his expression turns to panic. He quickly rights himself. “Part of the collapse affected this tunnel. We have to go another way. Hurry, hurry.” He waves his hands in a motion meant to shoo us and makes us move.

James turns to us and nods his head. He starts walking. The dwarf quickly runs in front of us to lead the way. Almost immediately I can tell we are taking a different path; a little down the road we turn right. The light shines far down the tunnel. In the corner of my eye, I see the light reflected in something; when I look fully it’s gone.

The light quickly fades. After a couple of moments, I can’t see anything but darkness. Only the soft footsteps tell me where I’m going. Unlike the other tunnel, this one doesn’t have a single torch. Something up ahead makes a strange rubbing noise. A small light appears and slowly grows bigger, emitting a glow around James’ torso and head.

Rayleen lets go of my hand to go see what James is doing. He hands her the light and she slows down in her fascination. An orb, the size of a baseball, fits in the cup her small hands form.

Blue fire swirls in a sphere. James rubs his hands together and a spark of light ignites and cultivates. Almost to full fruition, James brings it up and breathes out deeply. A bubble forms around the flame and the orb is complete.

These two orbs produce enough light to help us see more than the torches did; even despite their size.

The walk back takes longer than the walk there. The longer we walk the more suspect of the dwarf I am. Something doesn’t seem right. It shouldn’t take this long, not even if it is a detour. And, he was a bit too quick to help us while everyone else was running to help in the collapsed tunnels.

Not too much longer and I can see the road ahead is blocked. The tunnel had caved in here as well.

The dwarf walks us straight to the rock slide. On the left-hand side, there is a hole big enough to crawl through. He walks through it easily. James lowers to his hands and knees; crawling after him.

Rayleen walks through and takes the last of the light.

Ashlynn's voice carries to my ear, "You go next."

Putting my hands out in front of me I feel for the hole. I cannot find it so I kneel down. Still trying to find it I alternate crawling and reaching a hand out in front of me. My shoulder crashes into the sharp, cold wall. I let out a breath and a small grunt. Adjusting my position, I crawl through the hole cautious not to bump into the wall again.

Coming out the other side, James helps me stand. Their orbs have gone out, but there is a dull light filling the cave. The dwarf lifts a hide and natural sunlight floods the room.

"Out you go." The dwarf says.

"Thank you," James says to the dwarf before leaving. We each follow his cue and say the same to the dwarf before parting.

The sun, though very bright, is welcome after so much darkness. Having to let my eyes adjust before continuing, I close them for five seconds. The light is bearable once I open them again.

I have no idea where we are, but James seems to know exactly where to go.

"James, what was the king talking about: ancient laws?" The question blurts out as it comes to my mind.

"The ancient laws are just that; they are laws that were made by the very first Council before the treaty with the humans. One of the ancient laws is that in times of war a race can declare they are neutral. If they help either side in their act of war it is considered revoking your impartiality and it becomes fairground to attack the race. So, trading for weapons and armour would be an act of war but giving us the materials isn't; as it is our choice to do with the materials as we choose. They cannot be responsible for what we decide to make from raw materials." James states as if reading from a textbook.

He's not technically wrong, but he isn't technically right either. The dwarf king knows what we will use it for, so it could still be considered picking a side.

It's not too long before James walks us into a tree, quicker yet, that we walk back out outside his house.

Everyone else comes back over the next few hours. A few look a bit battered, but nothing anyone would need medical attention for.

From what I overhear as we walk through the house, the others had found another large group of beings. They seem to be led by a human woman; though many of the beings were of supernatural background. Unlike us, they have already established a large base within the mall. However, they had not been thinking about rebellion, rather survival. They will help us if they are ever needed.

Gio has been walking around and talking with people while we eat lunch; getting their preferences for weaponry and their skill level. He writes some things down on paper attached to a clipboard. The group seems to split mostly between those that are human and those who are supernatural. None of the humans have done more than street fight while the supernaturals have been trained in at least one form of combat.

"Shake my hand." Gio contradicts what he says by not holding out a hand. I make the first move and hold out my right hand. The cyclopes quickly latches onto my hand. "Grip as hard as you can." I squeeze a lot harder. "More." My arm starts shaking when I do as he says. "Resist my movements." He moves his arm up and down. With all the strength in my arm, I cannot slow his movements in any way.

When he loosens his grip, I do the same. Without even one more look, Gio walks away. From the direction he takes I can assume he is going into the basement to make the weapons.

"Anyone who does not know how to fight properly is to come to the basement after lunch for a little boot camp." Kelly appears long enough to make her announcement, then leaves fast enough that if I had blinked I'm sure I would have missed her movement.

I had finished my lunch a few minutes ago so I slide back my chair and get up. Rayleen has only finished a couple of bites of her food as she seems too interested in talking and colouring with Miles. She doesn't need boot camp anyway.

I slip away with only a glance from the elf. Walking with a couple of others ready to go downstairs, unsure of exactly what we are going to be doing. Though, I am certain both during and after there will be a lot of pain.

Downstairs everyone sits in the middle of the room. Anything that was in the room prior is now against the walls. Kelly stands at everyone's attention with her hands crossed over her chest.

We wait a couple of minutes for everyone to arrive, and to be settled down. People talk quietly about what they want to learn and what they think we're going to be taught. Some are scared of Kelly calling it boot camp.

"Quiet. Everyone stand up and partner with someone. You will need to find a spot in this room. I understand we do not have much room to do this but try to space out enough that you do not get in anyone's way." We start doing as she says.

I look at the girl next to me, catching her gaze. She nods and I do the same; silently agreeing to partner up.

Kelly continues, "I'm not going to lie and say this will be easy. This will be like the gym class from Hell. But, it will also help you to possibly survive if you are being attacked. I will also drill into your minds the strengths and weaknesses of each of the more populated supernatural beings.

Start running on the spot. Put your hands out in front of you about waist height. Your knees have to touch your hands each time they come up."

Her voice doesn't skip a beat while switching between ordering us what to do and instructing. "Speaking from the majority, you can kill most supernaturals by cutting off their head or shoving something through their heart. However, if you count on this and this is your one-act show, you're not going to survive very long. The more you know about the type of supernatural the better."

Physical exertion is already starting to drain me; with hours left I get the idea that this really would be the gym class from Hell.

"Stop running and face your partner. I want you to fight; punch, kick, scratch, bite, I don't care. Just do what feels natural. The only guideline is that you can't do anything lethal or maim anyone. I don't care about proper etiquette or techniques. Go."

Schoolyard fights come back to me as a sucker punch collides with my head. It knocks me back a couple of steps and my cheek pounds. I launch myself at the girl, striking her back; beginning hours of fighting.

Chapter 23

Shawn hovers over me. He had shaken me awake. I can hear crashing and cheering in the distance. It sends chills through my bones.

He goes to the next person to wake them up. Gary is helping.

I go to the side of the boat. I really can't see that much. It's dark. Climbing the step, I creep over the plank. There isn't anyone around me, but I can see a bunch of lights from down the hall.

They must be breaking the windows to the stores. Probably stealing whatever they want. I guess they got tired of hanging out in the pool. Everyone is probably drunk out of their mind.

I don't think we want to be here; out in the open like this. If they decide to come and get Shawn, we have no escape off this boat. Well, except into the water, but I don't want to know what might be in that water. I heard that people who decide to jump in there tend to develop rashes from the contact. That was before any filtration system would have stopped when the power went out.

"We need to get out of here." I can hear Gary say to the group. I spring into action, grabbing my packed bags.

"We need a place. Where do we go?" I ask.

He thinks for a moment. "A theatre. There isn't anything they would want there. We hunker down in one with an exit to the outside. We put someone by the escalators to warn us if they are coming our way."

It sounds good to me.

I don't wait for everyone else to grab their things, but they aren't far behind me. Trying to be as quiet as possible, I go towards and up the two sets of escalators. There isn't anyone in the area. I don't think anyone saw us moving either.

That doesn't mean it's going to be a quiet night. Maybe we should just leave the mall and find somewhere else to stay.

I wait for everyone else in the lobby. Gary seems to know exactly where we need to go. He takes us to the first theatre on the right of the left hallway.

There is an exit door in this one.

I set down my things near the door. It's cooler in here than back over by the boat. I don't want to be in here. I feel antsy. I can't just wait here. Walking to Gary I tell him, "I'll take first watch."

He nods and hands me his flashlight. "Turn it off when you get to the stairs. Run back here at the first sight of trouble."

"I will." Shining the light a few feet in front of me, I quickly get out of the theatre.

Before too long, I plunk myself down on the escalator. I can hear everyone in the distance. They don't seem to get closer to us, and I don't think they have gotten far enough to realize that we are gone.

Maybe they don't plan to.

Curious, I creep down step by step. I still don't see anyone. Maybe they are all down on the first floor. The more popular fashion stores are down there. I keep looking to the escalators, watching for anyone coming up them.

I lean on the railing. The whole area is open, but I don't think anyone would see me without shining a light up here. I watch the lights in the distance and wait.

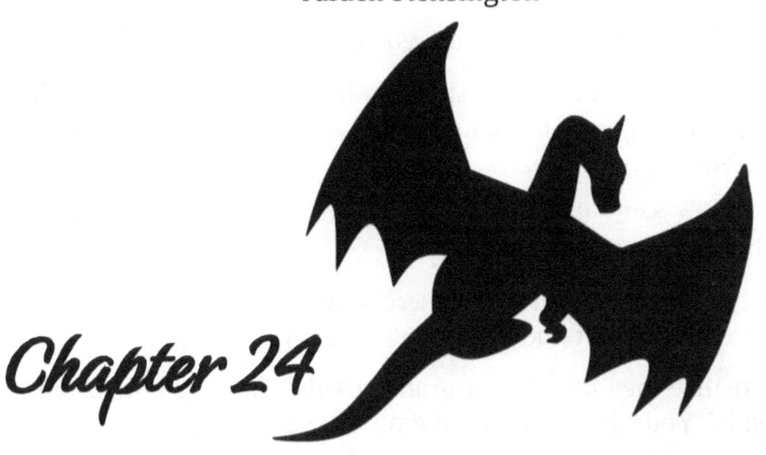

Chapter 24

The forest is covered in a light layer of snow. Missy follows me, but always at quite a distance either ahead, or behind, or to the side. I went off in a slightly different direction than the rest. Slowly we drifted apart, but anyone could trace my tracks if they wanted to. They could be following me to see where I'm going.

Someone catches my eye coming towards me. I remember this. It's from a nightmare about a year ago. The man continues walking, spots me, and rushes towards me.

I slip behind a tree. I don't hear any footsteps. Did he see me? Was I too late? I wait a couple of moments then get up the courage to look around the tree.

"What do we do with her?" I scream the moment I hear the booming male voice behind me. Though there was something familiar with it. I recognize him when I turn around.

"John!" John, he dated my sister. I met him this past summer. He lives in the area and there's something about him being family friends. I put my hand to my heart, and glare at him. Now I know why Missy didn't think anything wrong enough to rescue me. "You gave me a heart attack."

Once recognition hits him, he smirks a wicked smile. I can see he hasn't changed at all. His long dirty blonde hair frames his face and rests on his shoulders.

"You can put the knife away. I know her. She's good." He says looking behind me. I look behind me to see the male from the dream putting his knife down from where he would have cut my throat in another second. "What the hell are you doing here?"

"The Apocalypse Plan; to grandma's house we go. It was a joke at the time, but I figured if I thought of it then maybe others had too." John stiffens at my words.

"So, you're with them." The other voice is dead straight about hiding his anger out in the open.

"Sort of, not really. I just got there a couple of days ago." I try to explain to him. I don't know why he's so angry.

"You realize they killed your grandparents! They've killed some of our friends! You can't stay with them!" He says.

"I didn't think I really had a choice. I was sure they'd kill me too if I tried to leave immediately, they took my car keys, and, I mean they've got those two people locked up."

John cuts me off. "Who?"

"I don't know? I don't know their names. There was a girl and a guy." I stop when John pulls his phone out of his pocket. He searches for a little bit before he puts the screen in front of my face. "Those are them."

"And, they're alive?" He asks hopeful.

"They were when I saw them two days ago, but I had to bandage up the girl because Paul had stabbed her to show me she was a werewolf. That they were both werewolves."

"We need to go now!" The other guy urges John. He grabs my arm and yanks me hard in the direction I saw him coming from earlier. It hurts.

John intercepts him and grabs the wrist attached to the hand holding my arm. "Let her go."

"She stabbed them. I'm taking her to the pack. We'll get information out of her, and we attack them today." He isn't budging.

"I didn't stab her! When I arrived Paul took me into a room with two prisoners, said they killed my grandparents, and are werewolves, and then HE stabbed her to show me." I defend myself. A growl escapes his throat. It's too real to be human. Is he a werewolf too? Are they both werewolves? Did the family know?

"Those people killed your grandparents, not our friends," John says.

"I figured, so I asked your friends as much. But the other guys had guns, so I wasn't going to argue with them to their faces. Now, let my arm go, and I will help you break your friends out." He hesitates but reluctantly lets my arm go. John, in turn, lets him go. "Facing the house they have them in the left bedroom, in the right bedroom they have their lookout and a lot of guns. There are a few people out, and about right now hunting and gathering. When I don't go back they are going to be suspicious, and could change up their routine."

"You're not going back there." The other one gets riled up again.

"No, no. Let's go now. The three of us can storm the house, while a bunch of people are shooting at us with the hundred guns they have. I'm sure at least one of us will make it to the house before we're all dead." I hope the sarcasm helps him realize that isn't going to work. "We need more people, and you should attack at night."

"I'm not letting you go back there. You'll warn them we're coming, and they'll be ready with their guns." His eyes rage.

"Then you should let them know you've kidnapped me, or tell them you've killed me, or something because they'll get suspicious if I don't return, and will probably change their routines. Actually, they might just change it anyway." I try to reason. I don't know who I'd be safer with. The answer rings in my head, John. Not this guy or the others.

John finally chimes in. "We'll take her to the pack. She can stay at the house while we go rescue-"

"I can help." I interrupt him.

"No, you can't. If your sister finds out I put you in danger, she'll kill me."

"Fair enough." I don't think she would care that much about me, but I don't really want to get myself into an unnecessary fight. "I guess, we go to your house?"

"Yep, come on. It's this way." John says. He waits for me to follow, and I make sure Missy follows me. We don't go all that far considering this is considered farm country. The walk is quiet but edgy. I can feel the other guy's eyes burning the back of my head with his hatred and distrust.

As opposed to my grandparent's house, this house is bustling with people everywhere. I get looks and stares from everyone we pass in mild interest. We go inside the house and find a very warm living room. John takes me to the eldest man in the room.

John bows slightly, more of just a deep nod of his head, in respect. "Jaiden, I would like to introduce you to Ken. He is the Alpha of this pack. Grandpa, I would like to introduce you to Jaiden. She is a grandchild of the Boiko's. She says she will tell us information to help get revenge on the people who killed her grandparents. She saw Kayla and Tommy, alive."

Ken looks through me. I smile bigger and make sure my voice has a little bit higher than normal. I bow my head as John had done, then continue with the honouraries of an introduction. "Hello Ken, it's an honour to meet with you."

"I don't trust her. She's been living with those people. It could be a trap, and she stabbed Kayla." He's becoming a nuisance.

I talk to him but recount everything for the sake of all the others in this room; especially for Ken's sake. I need Ken to trust me. "We've been through this. I went to my grandparent's house hoping to find them. Instead, I got a gun pointed at my head and found Paul and his group in their house. I was then told that werewolves are real, and the prisoners killed my grandparents. Paul took me upstairs and stabbed Kayla to prove to me that werewolves are real. I convinced Paul to let me do first aid on her, and I haven't had a chance to go back, and check on them since."

Ken clears his throat. "We're all werewolves. Does this bother you?"

"No. I'm human. Does that bother you?" I raise my eyebrow for effect, and to dare him to say yes. The corners of his mouth twitch, and rise as he snickers. Apparently, I made the right response. I smile bigger. It doesn't bother me at all what they are. The only thing that matters is if they are good or bad, and if they mean me harm.

"What information do you have for us?" Ken asks me.

I round up the information in my head. What would be important? "When they realize I'm gone, they are immediately going to be on guard; ready for an attack, or ransom, or a trade.

Actually, they might just think I ran away.

They mostly stick to windows for lookouts. Some people go outside sometimes, but nothing that you should have to worry about. They have a lot of handguns and shotguns, but don't have huge amounts of ammo. You could try to get them to waste their bullets. I didn't see any handheld weapons.

They have a huge blind spot on the right-hand side; the garage blocks a lot of the view, and they have to jump out onto the roof to even see that way. The other garage on the left is right up against the woods.

Kayla and Tommy are in the upstairs bedroom to the left. They leave them unguarded, so if you were able to get there unnoticed you could possibly grab them unnoticed.

Bring water and something quick for food; like a granola bar. They are going to need energy. Their wounds might be able to wait until they get here, but I would recommend you bring something that could do as a quick twenty-second douse in solution, and throw on a bandage."

He mulls everything over in his head. "We take a decoy of you in for a trade. We will use that as a distraction to release Kayla and Tommy, and take over the armoury. The rest of us will attack then.

We leave in twenty minutes. Sammy should be about as short as she is. John take Jaiden to Sammy's room." As soon as the command is out John bows his head, and moves to gather me. I take his lead and bow my head before letting him lead me away. I still hear some things while we leave. "Mark, go find Sammy, catch her up, and tell her to go to her room.

Everyone will prepare to leave in twenty minutes. We will bring the van to transport Kayla and Tommy." John takes me outside, and I hear no more once the door shuts. He takes me out to the back of the house, and to a different house about fifty meters away.

We enter. This house is filled with more bedroom space than anything else. John finally brings me to a room on the other side of the house. He shuffles us inside a very girly room. I'm suddenly getting the feeling that Sammy is a kid. It bruises my ego a bit that the only person here that is my size is a kid. I know I'm short but it still hurts a bit.

John suddenly envelopes me in a hug. I feel awkward about it, but I close my arms around him. He lets go but holds me by my biceps. "Switch clothes with Sammy, and send her back out to the other house. You need to stay here. Got it?" I nod. "I have to go now." He briefly hugs me again and then exits.

Only a couple of moments after a young girl comes in. I assume she is Sammy, and introduce myself. "Hi, I'm Jaiden." I extend my hand out to shake hers. She takes it and does a quick grip before letting go.

"Sammy. You're really wearing that? They look like men's clothes." She says in what I deem a bratty tweenager tone.

"I had a choice. I could be fashionable or warm, but not both." I'm not going to tell her these are my real clothes, in extra layers.

"Whatever." She moves past me to grab some clothes out of the drawers. She lays some black yoga pants, and racerback sports tank tops down on her bed. She goes to the closet and pulls out a hoodie. On a normal day, I wouldn't be caught dead in any of these clothes. These pants aren't jeans and are form-fitting for one. Two, all these clothes combined cost as much as my entire wardrobe. "You can keep these. I have plenty of clothes, and I don't like these colours anyway."

I say. "Thank you." Colours? What colours? The entire outfit is black, with a couple trims of white on the sweater.

"What are you waiting for? Strip." She says expectantly. Sammy rolls her eyes and removes her shirt.

I turn away from her and start removing my layers. This is awkward. It's like the locker room with all the skinny girls changing out in the open, but all the others, like me or larger, get awkward and try to change by hiding in any way we can. All the judgment I know she is thinking about me warms my cheeks with embarrassment. I pray that all the words I had written a week, and a half ago are faded enough that they aren't noticeable. I'm not that lucky. It's noticeable, though a bit faded but thankfully Sammy isn't looking.

I get Sammy's clothes on in a hurry. They fit despite my worry they wouldn't. I feel uncomfortable in these, and I don't think they are going to keep me warm enough. There is snow on the ground. It's late enough in the year that it should stay, and it's been increasingly getting cooler, and cooler out.

Sammy finishes dressing up in my clothes. I don't know how this is going to work unless they are going to cover her head. I hope she doesn't get hurt in all of this. I hope none of them get hurt. "Thank you for doing this."

"If you want to thank me, then you'll come with us, human." The disdain in her voice is palatable. She obviously hates me now.

"Okay. I will." I tell her. If she's surprised, she doesn't show it.

"Follow me." She guides me out of the house, and back to the other house. There is a van near the garage that she takes me to, and tells me to get in before she runs off. Missy quickly finds me. I pat her head, and scratch behind her ears.

I get inside using the side door and shut it behind Missy. The van has no seats in the back. I would describe it as a white creeper van with the windows painted over if it wasn't for the company logo on the back doors. Missy settles down and lays down on the ground

I wait about five minutes before someone finally opens up the driver's door. "Hello." She says to me.

"Hi, I'm Jaiden, and this is Missy. Sammy said to wait in here to help you guys." I say sheepishly.

"Karen. That would explain why you are wearing her clothes."

Two other people come into the van. One enters in the passenger door, and another comes in through the sliding door. "This is Jaiden. She's helping us out."

"Nice to meetcha," He says. "I'm Tom, and this is Sara." He shuffles a bag to his lap and reaches to the back to shake my hand. I shake his hand and reach my hand out to greet Sara.

Sara evades my hand and goes in for a hug. Her one hand cups my cheek while her wet tongue swipes from my jawbone to my cheekbone. Her tongue stops as she barely lifts my glasses. "Sara!" Tom scolds her with only her name.

I have a moment of shock and panic. The germaphobe in me shudders in disgust that I now have her spit all over half of my face. My father's training of me to keep my composure under pressure still holds, however, and I am even able to stop myself from the knee-jerk reaction to wipe my face after she breaks away.

There is a thick silence in the air. The other two are just as shocked as I am, if not more so. I say the fourth thing that comes to mind. "Well, aren't you glad I don't wear makeup."

Apparently, that was the right thing to say, and do because Sara smiles big, and chuckles before enveloping me in a hug. "Nice to meet you." She says. She wipes her spit off with her sleeve.

Karen starts the van and tells us to "buckle up, sit down, and hold the sides. This isn't going to be a long ride, but I don't need any of you getting knocked out."

That's the last thing I need right now is to get knocked out, so I sit down and grab a hold of some metal bars on the wall.

Although, I might just be thankful for that embarrassment if it keeps me alive. Karen drives off. I can't see too much in the van, but I do see trees.

We drive for only a couple of minutes when Karen stops. "I think this might be close enough. We'll have to walk the rest of the way. Everyone, out the passenger door. We don't need more noise than necessary. Jaiden I hope you're good at charades."

"Is this the right time to tell you I've never played charades?" I wish I was joking.

"Great." She says, grumbling under her breath.

Tom opens his door as quietly as he can. He slips out, and then Karen. I look at Sara to see if she's budging to go next. "Go on. I've got your back." She whispers. "Missy, you stay here."

I mouth 'thanks,' climb up to the front, and go out. I recognize this place. We're on the road just outside the woods at the back of the house. The turn is just up a little way.

Sara jumps out next. She leaves the door open. I listen for any noise to let me know we were caught, but I don't hear anything. Then again, my hearing is probably useless compared to theirs. I wonder if it hurts their ears if I talk too loud? On the other hand, they would have to be used to loud people, though I guess it's now a good thing I am a naturally soft speaker.

Karen motions us forward, and into the woods. I cringe at all the noises I make on the leaves and snow. Is it just my imagination or am

I making the loudest noises here? I barely notice everyone else's footsteps.

I start seeing the shape of the house through the trees. If we continue, anyone looking out the back will be able to see us. I quicken my steps and get in front of Karen. I point to the window and veer us to the right. Going a rounded route we make it to the garage on the left of the house; when you look at it from the driveway.

Tom looks around the sides of the garage then comes back to us. He holds a thumb up. The others move to the side closest to the house. I follow them. Karen runs out and jumps up. She easily grabs onto the edge with her hands, pulls up, and rests for half a second with the roof digging into her hip bones. She pulls her legs up and flawlessly got up onto the something twelve-foot roof. She crouches down.

I can't do that.

Tom goes next. He checks to make sure the way is clear before he jumps smoothly hoisting up onto the roof. He hands Karen his bag, turns around, and lies down. He dangles an arm down, I assume for me to grab. There's no way I can reach that, even with jumping as high as I can, the tips of my fingers don't come close to hitting his hand.

I turn to Sara, and point at her, then to me, then intertwine my fingers to show her a boosting motion with my hands. She scrunches her eyebrows at me. I jump in spot to show her that I can't jump high at all.

I know she gets it when she smiles like an idiot and tries to contain it. She walks over to the house and gets ready to boost me up. I follow and put my foot in her hand. Very wobbly we manage to get me up in the air. I still need to go higher, so I brace my hands against the wall, and she lifts me higher. I finally grasp Tom's hand, and he pulls me up with no problem at all.

I crouch down near Karen. Sara jumps up as easily as Karen had.

I briefly wonder where everyone else is. Are we to stay here, ready in place, for their distraction? Tom moves to the window and answers my question. Apparently, we won't be waiting.

Karen growls. Tom looks at her and glares before he goes back to what he was doing. I'm guessing there was a different plan in place.

Tom tries to figure out the window. I know it's a sliding window with a simple lock system, one of those metal notch latches. It should easily come free with a little rocking. I crawl up to the window, and rock it back, and forth.

It makes a bit of noise but opens on the third rock. I open it fully. There is a slight hole in the screen that I make bigger with my finger. I hook the finger in and push the screen with my other hand. It pops free. I grab the screen and pull my finger out. I put the screen to the side, and go in through the open window.

Kayla stares at me as I come closer. I look her and Tommy over. They look horrible. I grab at Kayla's bound wrists and work them loose. Tom attends to Tommy. Kayla's wrists are raw and have dried blood all around them. When I lodge the rope free, her wounds bleed.

I look for Karen, but she's nowhere to be found. Tom pushes a bottle of peroxide into my hands. At some point, he must have grabbed the bag back from Karen. When did he do that?

I grab the bag and spot some gauze and tape. I grab a water bottle. I open that and give it to her to drink, but her hands shake too much to take the bottle. I hold the bottle up to her lips, and let her drink. I grab the medical supplies I need with the other hand. We can't do a proper job at this here, but I can help a little.

I give her enough time to gulp down the entire bottle. Opening up the bottle of peroxide I hold my finger up to my lips, and then pour the liquid over both wrists. She hisses in pain. I know that has to hurt, but I don't waste time and wrap the gauze around her wrists. I rip it and tape it. Moving onto the next thing, I unbound her ankles. She doesn't let me see them while she goes to Tom and Tommy's side.

I'm left for a moment wondering what I should do. We'll need help to get these two down, and back into the woods. I go closer to the window and look to see if anyone is in view. When I don't see anyone I poke my head out the window. Karen and Sara aren't here.

The door inside the room opens. I nearly jump out of my skin and turn around. He sees me first. There's a look of confusion, and surprise etched on his face. "I thought you-" He finishes opening the door enough that he now sees the werewolves.

Tom moves fast to grab him inside the room and knocks him out with a hit to his head. He slowly lowers the lifeless body to the ground. There is a thud on the ground anyway. The male had a gun in his hand; it fell as the muscles gave away at the last moment.

Did he come from downstairs or the next room over? I didn't hear any footsteps or a door click. Tom seems like he can handle himself, so I walk over and grab the gun off the floor.

From my new position, I can see the next room's door is open. Paul likes to keep two people in there, so there might be another person. I run over it through my head what I'll do. I will walk right into the room with the gun in my hand behind my back. If someone is in there I can maybe fake it.

Tom grabs Tommy and carries him out to the window. Karen helps him get out, then they all go to the left. I offer my hand to Kayla to help her to the window, but she rejects it and walks there with just a bit of a limp. Sara helps her get out. I go out the window next. Tommy, Tom, and Karen are already off the roof. I see the back of Karen going into the woods. We are almost clear. Three people are already good; as far as I'm concerned.

Kayla sits down on the edge of the roof before she hops down. I hear her draw in a hissing breath.

There is a commotion downstairs. I look at the open door, but there isn't anyone there. I look further and see someone walking out on the roof. In a jerk reaction, I reach my hand out to pull Sara into the room, but she moves faster and is out of reach before I get near her. She creeps up to the girl and puts her hand over her mouth, and her other arm around her waist. Sara lifts her and pulls her into the next room. I go over there. Sara struggles to contain the woman. Both settle when I get into the room.

I don't know what to do. "Are you going to knock her out?" Sara hits the girl on the head, but she doesn't pass out. She does it again. "We'll gag her, and tie her up." I go into the next room over and grab a gag and rope. I go back into the other room and tie the gag around the girl's mouth first. Sara turns her around and gives me access to her hands. I wrap the rope around her wrists and knot it. I don't know if it will keep, but it will slow her down.

The commotion has moved outside. I see why. People are coming out of the forest. They don't look like humans. They look like dogs, wolves that are standing on two feet. They transition to four legs. We need to warn them to go back into the forest. I jump out through the window, and onto the roof. I go forward enough that they have no choice but to see me. I wave my arms to catch their attention and then wave them to go back into the forest.

A shot bangs out. I don't know where it came from, but I fall down flat on my stomach. Nothing hurts so I don't think I was shot.

People rush out of the house. Shots keep firing. The werewolves half scatter into the shelter of the trees, and half charge the people with the guns.

They're going to get shot. I get on my knees and crawl closer to the front edge. I still have enough space for a bit of a shield. I aim with the gun. I don't want to kill the person, just maim them. I aim the guide at the person's legs, push the safety, and pull the trigger. The gun kicks my arms up. The gun and both my hands punch my forehead. Ah, the pain! I think I broke my head. I let go of the gun with one hand a lightly press the spot I hit. I don't feel a huge indent. I think I might be okay. I'm really happy I didn't hit my glasses. I don't even think I hurt anyone.

Nothing else seemed to change.

The werewolves are racing to the house, rather than picking off the shooters. I don't think they are trying to kill them. I get into a kneeling position, and decide to shoot the gun again; cover them so to speak. I aim at the ground near one of them this time. I shoot, ready for the kickback this time. The kickback just jars my hand, and shoulders this time; that's better.

A werewolf jumps beside me. He's wearing John's clothing, so I assume it's him. I smile sweetly, and say "hi."

He growls at me back. A shot through the roof beside me disrupts our conversation. I let out a little scream. It's not safe here. I get up and run back through the window. A werewolf has replaced Sara. She growls at John, and he back at her. John goes to the door and looks behind him at me. I look at Sara, and she just cocked her head at me. I assume they want me to follow after John. I do so, and Sara follows after me. John leads us downstairs.

There is a commotion down here full of growls and howls. I nearly dropped to my knees when I hear a gunshot. I try stopping, but I get a nudge from behind. Sara makes me continue. John leads us to the left, and right out the open back door. We nearly get off the deck when I hear another gunshot. This one is close. John jumps back, lunging in my direction. I feel a pull from behind as a human hand grabs my shoulder. Sara, now back in her human form, tells me, "Back in the house!"

I run back inside. This time following Sara as she takes us first into the kitchen, and then double backing into the hallway to the other doors. "Shit! They're everywhere." She says that as she looks out of the window in the door.

"Upstairs," I say. I don't have much of a plan, but it's better than staying down here. I turn around and pass by John. Making my way upstairs I go to the right into the gun room. I grab a couple of bullets. I know this. I pop the bullet chamber open, and put bullets in the empty slots. Closing it I put that gun down. I grab another gun and make sure there are bullets in there. I put this gun in my hoodie pocket. Then turning to John, and Sara I find them both looking like humans.

"How fast can you run?" Sara asks me.

"Not very fast. In gym class, I was always in the back half of the class." I admit. I'm not great in required athletic situations.

"I don't suppose you could jump right off the roof either?" She says.

I don't know whether she's actually asking me the question, or if she's being rhetorical. "Not without breaking bones. I might be able to if I hang down by my arms first." I might be fine jumping from that height. People do it all the time, then again those people practice doing that type of thing.

"Right. You'll probably be shot first." She says.

John and Sara turn their heads towards the door. John walks a couple of steps over and sticks his head out the door.

"The house is on fire. We need to get out of here." He says with urgency written on his face. He closes the door.

I'm guessing we aren't getting out that way. Who set the fire? Did one of the wolves set the fire to burn down the shelter of these people? Did someone from Paul's group start the house on fire to flush out the werewolves?

"You think?" I tease. He glares at me. "Can you help me off the roof? We can send Sara out first, and cover for her, then make our run for it. The van is on the road at the back of the house."

"Yeah, Sara head out. We'll be right behind you." John instructs. "You were supposed to stay at the house."

"Yeah. I know." Should I blame Sammy? Probably not.

"Out." He grumbles.

I go out the window, making sure I look around for any people wanting to shoot at me. Sara isn't on the roof anymore. I guess she didn't wait for us. I keep as low as I can while I go to the same edge we had come up earlier. I look over the edge, and to each side. I don't see anyone with their attention on me.

Guns sound off. I jump and launch myself back to lie against the shingles. Twisting around, I look for John. He looks fine, as far as I can tell. But wood chips fall where the bullets are going into the wall. He waves me off. I guess I can do this by myself.

I slink back to the edge. I make the mistake of looking over the edge. It's a far way down. One deep breath in. One deep breath out.

Looking side to side, I still don't find anyone paying attention to me. For a moment I wonder logistically how this will work. I decide to back down. I still need to do this as fast as I can, but as safe as possible.

I have enough forethought to toss my guns to the ground over by the garage. Turning around onto my hands, and knees, I crawl backwards to the edge. When I hit the edge with my knees I ease myself down to my stomach; dropping one leg down the side, and sliding the other down.

I feel stuck. I don't want to do this. Maybe I should have taken my chance with jumping down.

Inch by inch I slide myself back. The edge of the roof bites into my stomach then ribs. Giving up, I change tactics. I prop myself up with my hands on the edge. Weary of my chin, I launch out and fall with my hands still attached.

The jolt to my hands is too much. I fall the rest of the way to the ground, landing on my feet then my butt.

I don't have the time or safety to dwell on swore stinging so I make a break for the garage. I grab the one gun, but I don't see the other.

Peeking around the wall I see a group of people that are shooting at John. Aiming at the group, I fire off two shots. One person goes down, and the others crouch or scatter. Two more shots fire without being able to tell if I hit anyone fatally.

A thud alerts me to John's descent to the ground. He's gone all werewolf again. He growls at me then takes off, passing me, into the woods. I take after him, but he quickly runs out of my sight. I have the general idea where the van is so I head that way.

There is a mound. I get a bit closer. Bodies have been tossed into a pile. I recognize these faces, most of them anyway. These are all the family I met this summer. The grandparents, some aunts and uncles, Dominique's mom, and my biological dad. There is a little clench in my chest but it doesn't last long. I feel bad for them, and their death, but I also hadn't known them for long. There are bullet holes in a few of their heads,

I don't see Dominique. Maybe she is alive, and I'll find her in Banff with a troll. Werewolves are real, maybe other monsters are too.

I shake my head. I carry on to the van. When I break the tree line, I see John enter the van. Running faster than before, I muster up a sprint to make it to the van faster. It's my symbol of freedom.

Almost there. I reach the passenger side. Missy hops out to greet me, but she goes another way.

BANG!

I scream. Paul stands at the tail end of the van with his gun aimed at Missy. Her fall to the ground tells me she's been shot. She makes no noise and stops moving immediately.

"I should have killed you." He aims the gun at me and pulls the trigger. I jump at the click, but I don't hear a bang or feel pain. Raising my gun quickly, I shoot him twice. Both hit his chest. I pull the trigger again but this time I hear the click from my gun. He crumples to the ground. I've seen enough shows to know to disarm him. Walking up to his body I pull the gun out of his hand, put in my other pocket, and hurry back to the van.

I get in, leaving the door open behind me. "Are we waiting for anyone?" I ask.

Karen, Sara, Tom, Tommy, Kayla, and John are all accounted for. There are two people I don't recognize. They all just stare at me. I can feel my face getting hot. I know my face resembles a tomato, but I push beyond the embarrassment to raise my eyebrows to reiterate my question. Still, no one answers for a few long seconds.

John finally speaks up in an order. "Shut the door. Anyone not here already has probably found their own way back. Let's get back."

The statuesque people jump to action; close the sliding door, sit in the vehicle, put on seat belts, and get settled. I find my own spot on the floor against the wall.

It's an awkward, quiet ride back to the werewolves' den. There is too much staring in my direction for my comfort.

We arrive back at Ken's house. Karen stops the van, and we usher out. I'm the first one out of the back. "Ken would like to speak with us. Kayla and Tommy go get yourselves fixed up." I think the first direction applies to me too so I follow after John to the first house. No one says a word, and the rest of the van, except for Kayla and Tommy, follow John too.

We arrive in a bustling living room. I recognize a few from earlier, and a couple from the raid. I take cues from others in our group and bow my head to Ken when we approach.

The rest start for the outskirts of the inner circle, and I move to follow them but am stopped. "Jaiden," Ken calls my name. I bow my head again then look at him. "Why did you help with rescuing Kayla and Tommy? John had told you to stay here."

Because Sammy told me to and made it seem like you all would hate me if I didn't. Somehow, that doesn't seem like the response I should give. It's the most honest answer that I could give, but whoever cares about a hundred percent honesty. I settle on a saying. "The needs of the many outweigh the needs of the few. I was of use to the group and could help, so I did."

"Even though it put you in danger? You would have been okay with sacrificing your life to save one of our own?"

"Yes."

"You saved many of my pack. Thank you. You are welcome to stay." He bows his head to me. Getting up, he motions for me to come closer. I do. He raises a necklace over his head and places it around my own. The necklace drops to hang around my neck with a hard pendant bouncing slightly off my chest.

I bow my head to him again, and say, "Thank you."

"Could someone take Jaiden, and show her the showers?" Ken asks. He looks towards the group I came with for volunteers. It figures he would assume I would be the most comfortable with one of them.

Sara steps forward. "I'll take her."

Sara bows her head to Ken then takes my hand and leads me outside. We trek for some distance until we come to a shower house. It seems strange to see a shower house on a residential land rather than a campground, but with all these people here it would have been hard to coordinate between a couple of house showers, and toilets. We get inside, and I see immediately that the house is cut in half.

"Make sure you come in that side. You wouldn't want to accidentally wander into the men's side." I nod. That would be problematic.

Looking around I see remnants of construction. "Did you remodel recently?"

"Yes and no. This is new. Ken saw a revolution coming, and thought the bozos might actually attack, so he got us to prepare." She explains, but it brings up more questions than answers.

"How did he see the war coming?" I ask her the first of many questions that come to mind; that one seems the most prudent.

She turns around to look at me in horror. "I'm sorry. We have a whole network that's different than the humans. Like a different hidden section of the Internet, and governments and news. Anyone that had access to it, half a brain, and wasn't in denial could see that the revolution was coming.

It started with some of the older generations; from the time of the World Wars. They've always been unhappy with the treaty, and decided to gather up some of the youngest generations to come out of the closet; so to speak.

But they weren't just happy with that, they wanted to take over. They want to control humans, and enslave them."

"I think I'm going to need more than that. Like, pretend I don't know absolutely anything and need a full recap."

She chuckles. "I don't think there's time for that."

"Maybe later, then?" I'd prefer to quench my knowledge now, but I suppose it has to wait.

"Yes, of course." She turns to her left. "The sinks are this way, and the bathrooms are down there too." Backtracking before I can see down to the left, she goes to the right. There are many stalls down this way that have showers, and half walls for a little bit of privacy. "And, these are the showers." She walks down to the end where there are some cabinets. She opens and closes drawers as she identifies the objects in them. "Shampoo, conditioner, body wash, sea salt scrubs, hand soap, cleansers, and lotions.

Hand towels, towels, tampons, pads, toilet paper, and basically everything you could need." She turns around to face me. "You stink, so you should get your shower started.

Choose any stall. Check to see what's in there first, before you grab a new shampoo or something. I'll grab you some more clothes.

See you soon."

"Thank you, bye," I say as she walks by and leaves. I go to the cabinet and grab myself a towel. I can't justify grabbing a second one for my hair. I go to the nearest stall and drape the towel on the edge near the opening acting as a doorway. This stall has an assortment of bottles in it so I don't grab anything new. I go to the bathroom before I go back to the showers. Stripping down to nothing, I put my clothing aside.

The stall just barely covers my chest, and I'm short. I can't see how this was even necessary for modesty's sake. They should have raised the stall up by a foot at least.

Turning the knob, I know better than to stand in the way, all the way to the left where I see an 'H' declaring that to be the hot side. Expecting the water to come, but I didn't expect it to start getting warm in a matter of only a couple seconds. I adjust the temperature so it is warm, and step under the stream.

It's been a while since I've been able to have a proper shower. Savouring the heat, I quickly get through shampooing my hair twice, conditioning my hair, and washing my body so that I can take a moment to just stand in the warm water. I didn't realize how chilled to the bone I had been.

The door to the shower house opens, so I take that as my cue to turn the shower off. At the last moment, I remember my words inked on my body. I step to the side, so I am hidden mostly by the stall. In hindsight, perhaps, I should have spent more time scrubbing the most visible of my words. Sara comes closer. "I have your change of clothes. You still stink. Wash up again."

"I-"

Sara cuts me off and puts clothing down on the countertop. "One round isn't good enough to get the smell of blood, and sweat off you. You need to be a little more thorough when you're around any supernatural beings with an increased sense of smell."

She busies herself removing her clothes. I avert my eyes.

I turn the shower back on. I guess I'm not clean enough. I won't argue about having to spend more time in the shower, but I could say something about Sara's approach. Well, maybe. I'd rather her be blunt and honest about these things so I can correct it than to have myself in the center of a faux pas.

Sara picks the stall next to me to have her own shower. I make sure to scrub every square inch of my body. Other women trickle into the showers. I don't pay them any mind, but they seem curious about me. I try to face the shower as much as possible.

I finish up soon enough, but I hesitate to get out. Sara isn't done yet, and I don't know where I should go after this.

While trying not to draw attention to my markings, I look down for the status of those markings. They are more faded than earlier, but some are noticeable. Especially if these people have any increased vision. However, no one has mentioned anything.

I count my blessings and get out of the shower. Quickly, I wrap the towel around me, go out, and grab the clothes Sara brought me. I place them against my chest. Hightailing it out of there, and to a bathroom stall.

I let out a sigh. I look at the clothes Sara brought me. She brought matching pink underwear and bra, jeans, a brightly patterned spaghetti strap top, and a baby blue sweater. These have to be the brightest clothes I've worn in a while.

I throw out my 'no patterns' rule and put on the clothes.

I wrap my hair in the towel before exiting to the sinks, and mirrors. This has got to be the girliest I've seen myself in a long time. I can't say I look awful.

With all that weight gone, I look good in the girl clothes, and they actually aren't that uncomfortable.

Maybe, when everything normalizes, I'll start buying girl's clothes again. Thinking back, I started wearing boy's clothes back in grade six. It was the outlier cool thing to do; to be a tomboy. So, I stopped wearing girl's clothes because it was cool and a bit rebellious. That, and it didn't help that because of my size, and strength people said that I was more like a guy. It had become part of my identity. We mustn't upset people and their views of us.

I don't see any hair brushes here, and I don't want to go back through the shower room to ask Sara or check the cabinets. I settle for running my fingers through my hair. There are so many tangles and knots in my hair. My hair normally gets tangled so fast I don't know why I expected anything different after today's events.

"Oh here, let me help you. I can see the rat's nests from here." She comes out from the showers wrapped in a towel. If I had to guess, I would say she's maybe thirty.

She doesn't give me a chance to object. Her one hand is in my hair collecting, and moving while she brushes out the knots with her hairbrush. It's been forever since someone's brushed my hair.

"Your name was Jade, right? I'm Tammy." She asks.

"Jaiden, but some people call me Jade." It's been a while since people have called me Jade. My mom used to call me Jade. Jacob always said people should call me by Jaiden because it's an adult name. But, he's not around so he won't find out.

"Your hair is beautiful, so golden, and so soft." She fawns over my hair. It's my best feature. The feature people compliment me on the most.

"Thank you. It's natural; never been dyed." I try not to sound bitter with the last part. It's not my choice that my hair had never been dyed. It's never been a choice of mine to do what I want with my hair. At fleeting times, I have wanted to dye my hair. I have envied a classmate of mine that had a new hair colour every month. Jacob carted me to every hair salon in town and told them I was never allowed to have my dyed or cut short.

"Do you mind if I braid your hair?" Tammy asks. She pulls off a few ponytails from the brush handle.

"Sure. Go ahead." Tammy dives right into parting my hair, in half, down the middle. She French braids each side. I almost move when she finishes wrapping the last braid up, but she isn't finished. She takes both ponytails and ties them together loosely twice. She messes around a bit then ties a ponytail around it to make a bun.

"That looks great." She says.

"Thank you. I love it." The style looks sophisticated, though it is simple on concept. This style seems like it would last a while as is, then pull out to a lovely wavy look.

She excuses herself right before a cascade of women go in, and out of the shower house. Sara grabs me in the fuss and pulls me outside. She takes us out to a treed area I haven't been to yet. I can see the fire highlights before we get into the circular area with a large bonfire. Most of the habitants here are male. I would guess that's because all the women were probably in the women's bathroom.

Sara walks us over to a sitting area full of camping chairs. I smell food but I don't see any. I'm so hungry.

"That tiny human girl comes in like Rambo. I was scared for my life until John said she was with us, and then I was terrified."

"She saved your ass, and you know it," John says.

"And, you told her to stay home!"

I can't help but smile at the conversation. I'm flattered, though I don't get the reference. We interrupt the conversation when they notice us arrive and sit down in a couple of empty chairs.

"There you are. You ladies clean up nicely." Sara gives him the finger. I opt for ignoring him. Either way, he acts offended at our reactions.

"Here have one." John holds a beer out for me. I hadn't noticed him get up.

"Thank you, but I'm only fifteen." I decline his offer. I'm too young to drink beer. I've been allowed a glass of wine or champagne at special occasions since I turned thirteen, but beer is different.

"No, you aren't," Sara says.

"Seriously, I just turned fifteen on October thirty-first." I wish I had documentation with my birthdate on it. I would pull it out to show them I'm not lying. Why are people always so surprised?

"You're the oldest fifteen-year-old I have ever met. I started drinking when I was fourteen. Besides, it's only one beer. It might just get you tipsy; if it does anything at all." John says.

I reach out my hand and take the offered beer. "Thank you." I look to Sara. "So, how old did you think I was?"

"Twenty-five." Sara comments.

"Hm." I crack the top on the beer; the noise is satisfying to me. I don't hesitate to take a drink, but the bitter earthy taste is a surprise. I don't know how to feel about the taste, it's unlike anything else I've had before. When I take the second swig, I decide that it's not horrible, but not good either.

"When's food done? I'm starving!"

"Why don't you go check on it?"

"Maybe I will!" A man gets up and goes to the fire. I watch as he pulls down a door on the bonfire pit. He pulls food out and closes up the door again. That's neat. They built an oven into the bonfire pit. I look back to the group. Not interested in their conversations I register their conversation while sipping the beer, but I pay no mind to the people speaking it.

"So, we run to the house. Jaiden covering us with gunfire. I think the other guys were just as confused as we were."

"I think we were more confused either way, because we got into the house, and the two we went to rescue were already rescued."

"Someone forgot to tell us how to signal if we had them all clear before you made your move."

"No one thought everything would go so smoothly."

"We're you there? What about today went smoothly?"

"No one died."

"On our side."

"Are you okay?"

"I can't believe they set the house on fire."

"Dude, that was Tyler."

"What?"

"Jaiden, are you okay?"

At the sound of my name, I look at the source. John looks at me concerned. Why is he asking me if I'm okay? "Yeah, why?"

"You're looking off into space. You killed a few people today. Are you okay?" He looks genuinely concerned. I didn't register that I killed people today, well other than Paul.

I'm torn momentarily between pretending I have no idea what he's talking about to avoid the situation or telling him straight up that it doesn't bother me. I can talk my way logically through the situation enough that killing a couple of people doesn't bother me, and I can be nonchalant about it. "It was either I kill them or they were going to kill me or someone else. I did what needed to be done. Why?"

"You looked out of it," John says. He still looks concerned.

"Oh, I stare out into space all the time." I reason.

"What were you thinking about?" Sara asks. At this time I notice everyone in the group has their attention on me.

"Mostly about food. I would kill for cherry gelato right about now." I smile bigger to ease any tension or doubt from their minds. The topic is simple, light and easily relatable.

The conversation turns to food and the complaints about why the food isn't ready yet.

After ten minutes we are gathered into a line to plate up our food. There is a dark meat, I would guess it's beef, and many root vegetables. Supper is hot, delicious, and slightly smoky.

Darkness creeps and then takes over the sky. The crisp winter air chills me deep in my bones. I don't want to complain about how cold I am, but I wish I had gotten thicker clothes. My toes fare the worst of it, they're cold and tingly. At least I still have motor function in my fingers, as I've been tucking them into the sleeves, and grasping my hands together.

Somehow, I acquired two more beers. Maybe not somehow, John and Sara each handed me one more. On one hand, I feel warm from the alcohol, but I know the actual physical effects of it are thinning my blood, making it easier for me to get cold. One of the worst things you can do when trying to avoid hypothermia is to drink alcohol. While I'm not that far off, I'm sure it isn't helping anything.

When the alcohol flows, the inhibitions lower, and the conversation gets deeper in spirit.

"This isn't war. It's slaughter."

"This is the way it used to be."

"I doubt it was like this. If it was like this the humans would never have taken over."

"They reproduce like rabbits."

"We reproduce like rabbits too then."

"No, we reproduce like wolves."

"Demons would still rule the world if they never signed the treaty fifteen hundred years ago."

"Julien!"

"Oh sorry. Supernatural beings."

"That's not what I meant, you idiot. That treaty probably saved supernaturals from being wiped out."

"That's basically what happened anyway."

"That treaty allowed us to live beside each other peacefully, for the most part, for over a thousand years."

"That's in the past. We should be worried about the fallout that's taking place now."

"Nothing lasts forever. We've been fine so far. You heard their leaders. If we don't interfere with what they're doing, then they leave us alone. We keep to ourselves, and we'll be fine."

"We've already interfered with them by allowing Jaiden to stay. If Seth showed up right now and saw her here he would give us one chance to enslave her or kill her, or he'd kill us. That's how it is now." My ears metaphorically perk up. I didn't know how much I might be endangering them by being here.

There was that vision I had; all of my nightmares with dem-supernatural beings I have to assume are real now. I didn't see any of these people in my dreams. I obviously don't stay with them. Maybe I should just leave now, or rather in the morning.

"Shut up."

"No. She's a liability to us." I'll leave tomorrow morning. I'll go back to my house; the other people should be gone.

"She's pack."

"No, she's not."

There is no point in allowing them to continue the conversation on this note. They shouldn't fight with each other over me. It doesn't matter now anyway. "It's fine. I'll leave tomorrow morning. I need to find my family anyways." And, I wouldn't want to burden you all by my presence here.

"You don't have to leave. You can stay with us. Ignore him." Sara pleads.

"It's really fine. I appreciate everything that you all have done, but I do need to find my family. That was the whole reason why I had gone to my grandparents." Not to mention that you all could be killed for harbouring a human.

"No, you can stay here. It'll be safer for you, and I doubt anyone will come out here to spot check if we have a human with us. If they do, we'll smell them a mile away, and get you to safety before they get here." John steps in with his own pleading.

"Thank you, but I should go."

"The girl wants to leave, so let her leave. She's being reasonable." I never caught his name, but this one doesn't seem to like me, or at least he has a lower tolerance for this particular risk. I wouldn't take the risk if the situation was reversed.

Chapter 25

Everyone has taken their places around the room and at the table, when I get downstairs. I sit in the open spot beside Miles. Taking the cover off my plate I find the same breakfast as yesterday.

No one says much while we eat. Looking up and across the table, I catch Kelly's glare directed right at me. Redirecting my gaze back to my food, I try to think of what I could have done to get her angry at me this time. Thinking back to the last few moments, all I can gather is that I sat next to Miles. No matter how it happened I've gained the jealousy of a vampire girlfriend.

The only things I can think of is don't do anything else that might make her jealousy turn to rage and that in today's training she's going to kill me. I would swear by it.

Too soon breakfast is over and everyone in boot camp is called to the basement.

I kiss Rayleen goodbye before I follow everyone downstairs. Kelly already has people splitting off into the pairs and locations we were in yesterday.

"Run on the spot, knees hitting your hands." Kelly sounds like a drill sergeant while she calls out the commands.

Pain stabs through my calves with each hop. Any energy I may have gained from sleep and food is gone almost immediately. My legs quickly stop going as high and soon I can no longer reach my hands despite lowering them a lot.

Kelly looks disgusted as she looks at me. "Everyone gather into a circle and sit down. Alexa join me in the center.”

I bite my tongue to keep from saying every swear word I know.

Suddenly, I feel like the victim of a schoolyard fight. Everyone circling the two people going to fight, knowing full well which one is going to win and who is going to be beaten to a pulp. Knowing that no matter what happens not one person will come to save me.

Everyone gets settled. My heartbeat increases with each moment. Watching Kelly’s movements carefully, I try to figure out what she’s going to do. Her hand comes up and quickly swipes against my cheek, then goes back to her side.

Something feels like it’s running down my cheek. Without thinking I reach up to wipe my cheek of the irritant, but my hand comes back with a thin slice of red. A cut that wasn’t there a moment ago. Touching my cheek again my finger comes back wet with red.

Kelly takes in a deep breath. Her eyes turn darker; a trick of the lighting perhaps. Or, a vampire thing?

She gives no explanation to the questioning and horrified looks she receives. The obvious show of her power and speed frightens everyone in the room; terrifying me as she directs this and her rage at me.

“Let’s see what you learned yesterday.” Kelly slows her speed a bit. I have trouble dodging, but I do manage to miss a few swings.

Kelly slows her speed a little. I have some trouble dodging but manage a couple. I see an opening to swing a punch. She grabs my arm, twisting it around my back. Pushing me away from her, I stumble through a couple people and outside the circle.

Determined to not back down, I get back in the circle and throw a few more punches. Kelly backs up a couple of steps, so I try a roundhouse kick.

For just a moment none of my limbs are touching the ground. My back hits the floor and my breath escapes my lungs.

“Weapons.” Gio comes through the hole in the wall with two clanking bundles. He sets them both on the floor.

Breath regained, I stand up. Gio filters through the weapons and finds two. He walks to me and hands me a sword and dagger.

The sword has one straight edge and one serrated edge. The handle is wrapped in red leather and the guard is fashioned from the top to the bottom of the handle in a darker metal than the rest of the sword. The dagger has the same red leather on its handle. The blade is straight-edged.

"Thank you." I express my gratitude for the weapons, but Gio just turns his back to go get another weapon. Nothing more than watching some movies tells me how to hold either weapon. The sword in my right hand rests with the guard against my wrist. I hold the dagger in a stabbing style with my left.

Gio returns with a double-sided axe for Kelly. She takes it in hand, disgust written on her face. "Gio, what the hell is this?"

"It's an axe." He stares at her with one eye; raising his unibrow.

"I told you I wanted double swords. Why would you make me an axe?" I can hear her anger growing worse and worse as the moments go on.

"Your left arm control is nowhere near where it should be for double weapons. A two-handed axe is a versatile weapon for someone like you. With your strength, you can utilize it as a one-handed weapon." Gio states.

"Why would you ask what I wanted, if you were just going to make me something else?" Kelly practically growls out the sentence. Her fists clench.

"I'm told it's polite. This weapon suits you better." Gio ignores Kelly and starts to give out everyone's weapons. There are a couple more complaints about not getting what they asked for, but nothing as outspoken as Kelly's comments.

I take the time to get more familiar with the sword. The weight of it feels odd in my hand and strains the muscles in my arm. I cannot imagine having to battle for any period of time longer than a minute.

Swinging the larger blade in a couple of controlled movements I start feeling better about the possibility of wielding a weapon, yet I know nothing about how to. Beyond my concentration of making sure the blade does not hit anything, I can see Kelly trying to melt holes through my skull.

Everyone is trying the get a handle on their new weaponry. Gio made a vast number of different types of weapons; most of them I couldn't begin to place a name to.

Something large and heavy crashes to the floor. Glass shatters next before anyone moves. Kelly is gone before I can gather both my blades. I hold them in each hand.

All with the speed to do so are gone upstairs and out of sight before the first human reaches the bottom of the stairs. The mini stampede upstairs causes my own movements to be carried slightly faster as the crowd pulls me along.

Everyone breaks off at the top of the stairs, some go left and others right. To the left is the kitchen untouched compared to my right. The doorknob is buried in the wall and glass from the living room window is shattered all over the floor.

I see the open door and the fights happening outside; as the others see what's happening they immediately run to the action. The rest guard the living room window. I'm left at the top of the stairs with not a clue as to what I should be doing.

I'm not eager to fight unless I have to. Soft scraping upstairs warrants an excuse to go upstairs to investigate. I bet that Rayleen had run up there; I have to find her.

Thinking this is a good exemption to the rule of the use of the staircase beside me, I walk up the servant's stairs.

I hear the scraping again; slightly louder this time. Rounding the top of the stairs I pinpoint the direction of the sound. I see the closet door partially open; I open the door the rest of the way. Scanning it from top to bottom I spot a foot on the bottom shelf.

"Stay here, be quiet, and pull in your foot." Rayleen's foot disappears from my view. I shut the door and turn back around to go downstairs. A tiny thud hits the floor above my head.

Stepping down to the base of the stairs, I round the corner to the left. My intent to go into the living room is sidetracked at the crossroad center between going outside, into the living room, or back upstairs.

Looking outside I can see Taylor is slowly picking herself up from the grassy ground. My body feels as though it is encased by concrete; I'm frozen still.

Sandra walks from out of my view. She helps Taylor up the rest of the way by grabbing onto the back of her shirt.

Grabbing either side of her head Sandra says something into her left ear causing Taylor to twist her face in terror. Tears of blood flow freely from her right eye as a patch of red grows on her left shoulder.

Taylor's movement drops as she tries desperately to scream her pain to the world.

The crashes, bangs, and cracking stop at this moment. Someone shoves me into the door. My body freezes once again in this new spot. A couple more demons run past me. All the attacking demons are soon on the front lawn. As Sandra takes her hands off of Taylor, two things happen at once; Taylor collapses to the ground and the attacking demons take Sandra and retreat.

Stumbling back as people from our side rush out the door to tend to Taylor, I turn. My steps falter as I assess the damage to the house and to many of the people that live in it. A couple of bodies litter the living room; some I recognize and others I don't.

Furniture is turned over and smashed while walls have dents and holes in them. My hands release, and only once the two weapons I was holding reach the floor, do I actually remember I was holding them.

Purpose suddenly drives me as I remember the other thing I had forgotten; Rayleen is upstairs.

Gaining more confidence in my steps as I climb up the stairs I am almost at a steady speed by the time I reach the joint landing between the three staircases. The closet door is open and pumps the energy into my muscles to run the rest of the way up.

I throw the door the rest of the way open and start throwing the towels on the first shelf out as I hope that she was able to conceal herself better than the last time I saw her; though I know she couldn't be in there.

A towel hits the top of my head and sits there. Behind me, Rayleen stands amid scattered towels. Relief floods through me as she looks perfectly unharmed. I jump to hug her.

Not willing to let her go for the moment, I hoist her up onto my hip. Looking into her eyes I see a dead quality to them. She must have been terrified thinking that she may be next. Any progress we made in restoring her innocence from whatever happened at the airport was reversed.

We say nothing because I can't find anything to say.

I carry her downstairs to find out what we can do from here. The extent of the damage is overwhelming as James puts a quiet voice to his mental list. "Sixteen dead, eleven with varying degrees of injuries needing medical attention, irreparable damage to the veil, the house is in shambles; but necessary all of it."

"What do you mean necessary?" I ask as we reach the last stair.

He turns as he speaks and keeps his voice low so no one else hears. "It was a test; a preliminary attack. They attack us, bring down our numbers, weaken us, and show what they can do without even trying. They were testing to see if we were a real threat or not." He finishes this conversation by leaving.

We tidy the house after the attack. I feel like hours pass after setting Rayleen down.

Broom in hand, I squat down to scoop the pile of glass into the dustpan, and Rayleen empties the pan into the silver garbage can. Coming in for another round I ask her to keep pulling back the pan an inch, so we can pick up the smaller shards.

Satisfied, I look up and nod to her to signal she can dump the remaining glass in the garbage. As I stand up, I can feel the prickles in my legs from squatting for too long. Looking around for an idea of what we should do next I check things off in my head:

Miles and James are taking planks of wood from the walls and floor in the living room to board up the broken window.

Daniel is finishing up putting the door back into its proper place. It had been torn off the hinges. Gio fixed the broken hinge and has been making nails.

Ashlynn has a group bandaging up the wounded.

Rayleen and I have swept up the debris.

"What is this doing here?" Gio rounds the corner with my two blades held out. He marches to me in a huff.

"I um – I uh – uh" The rage in his voice and eye surprises me.

"I – um – uh – nothing. There should be no reason you ever dump your weapons. You are not worthy of them. I should have never given these to you. I should have safeguarded them myself. You're not a fighter or a survivor and you will never be one." The cyclops' rage causes his voice to raise with each sentence.

"Gio, that's enough!" Miles raises his voice over the cyclops as he walks into the room and catches the tail end of what Gio is saying. "Whatever she did, she's sorry and I'm sure she got the point to never do it again, but that does not give you the right to strike her down with words. Whatever your feelings are, you will keep them to yourself."

"Gio, enough," James says strongly. Gio shoves the weapons in my arms, drops the nails and stomps off in a huff; mumbling something under his breath.

Tears threaten to fall, swelling my vision as doubts fill my mind. Doubts of my capability to protect Rayleen and me. Doubts I can fight. Doubts of my position with this group. Nothing but doubts. My stomach is sickened with the words Gio said and the resulting feeling of inadequacy. Looking at Rayleen's straight face only furthers my thoughts.

Miles puts a hand on my shoulder but I shrug it off; not wanting the contact right now.

"Don't listen to Gio. He hates humans." Miles' explanation does nothing to affect how I am handling Gio's words. "How about you and Rayleen start setting up for supper. Set enough places for anyone who can come upstairs for dinner. Ashlynn should be able to tell you the number of the injured that are able."

I nod, not trusting my voice at the moment to not crack. I'm happy about the distraction.

Walking on my way to the kitchen I stop at the top of the stairs. Turning I find Rayleen following close behind me. "How about you go and ask Ashlynn how many we should expect for supper?" She says a quiet yes before hightailing it down the stairs.

Continuing to the kitchen, I open the cabinet. I grab enough bowls to fill the table and the same number of spoons. Rayleen meets me in the dining room once I have half the table set.

"Nine are coming for supper. Kelly is staying to watch everyone, but I'm supposed to ask James to get her something to drink." Rayleen tells me what I'm sure is exactly what Ashlynn advised her to.

"Thank you, why don't you go tell James that Kelly needs something to drink." I turn her around in the direction James is in.

"Okay." She runs off to go tell James.

I set the rest of the place settings by the time she comes back again; this time with everyone following, eager for food.

James stays behind in the kitchen getting the food together. Through the window I see each can opening, soup contents flying out, passing over the stove and floating into the dining area to land in each person's bowl.

Mine arrives and pours into my bowl piping hot. The scent of clam chowder reaches my nose. Taking up my spoon I take a bit out and start cooling it like many others are.

When James settles down to his own spot, he gets right to talking; a meeting over supper.

"Fifteen people. At lunch we had thirty-eight. What happened?" He gives us only a moment to think it over, but the question was rhetorical either way. "Darius organized a test attack. To do just this; bring down our numbers, weaken us and our defences. We have to work harder to regroup. One thing I know for sure is that we can't stay here."

James continues. "We need to gather up all the supplies to move them. We'll start this tomorrow morning. It shouldn't take too long if we all help. Chances are we will be attacked again within a few days if we don't leave quickly."

"Where are we supposed to go?" Daniel asks.

James thinks for a moment. "The mall." A few people in the room announce their liking to this idea.

"We should go a few at a time, maybe even use different routes to get there. So, we don't attract too much attention. They already know Kelly and me, so one of us goes with a few runners first and prepares them for our arrival." Miles suggests.

"I'll go first." Kelly stands in the doorway. "I can have two people ready to leave in a few hours. We'll prep them for everyone. You." She points to Nia. "And, you." She points to a male. "Be ready to leave at two." She turns around and walks back to the basement.

"I guess that's decided. We'll prep some bags for you to take to exchange for hospitality." James picks up his bowl and takes it with him into the kitchen. I hear a door open, rustling and a click of the door closing. James comes back moments later with reusable bags in hand. He assigns a bag to each of us, with what we should fill them with. Then, takes two and departs.

Finishing up my supper, I take my bowl in one hand and grab out two bags in the other. Leaving my bowl in the sink I double back to check on Rayleen's progress. She still has a way to go before she will be finished supper, so I go to the pantry. I stuff each bag with equal amounts of soup cans, pasta packages, and cans of fruit.

By the time I'm finished some others are starting to take their bags to fill them.

I go back to the table to find Rayleen two meters away from where I left her. Her bowl is mostly empty at the table. I gauge how much she ate, and figure that she ate enough.

She's smiling while Crystal walks over her lap trying to follow her hand; seeking the little girl's hand pushing for more pets. I don't want to ruin the moment, but I have to. It's good to see her smiling again.

I drop off the bags at the table. Kneeling beside her I put my hand out to start petting Crystal. She ignores my touch and continues to rub herself against Rayleen.

People drop off their bags at the table then go to their respective sleeping quarters.

The rooms quickly clear as almost everyone heads to bed from an exhausting day. A moment to stop and breathe tells me that this maybe isn't such a bad idea.

Rayleen looks as though she could fall asleep right where she's sitting.

Miles beats me to pick her up. When her head hits his shoulder and her eyes close, I know she's not going to make it upstairs. He was smooth so he doesn't disturb her.

I follow them to my bedroom. Going around him, I flip the covers back so he can settle her on the bed easier. Pulling the blanket over her, I check her for any signs of waking.

"Thank you," I whisper to him. A nagging thought on my mind slips into words without me realizing it. "What was up with Kelly this morning?"

"It was just a vampire thing. This morning, when I woke up, she was already in a mood. She's just been a little…"

I cut Miles off. "Bitchy?"

He can't hide his smile behind his disapproving eyebrow raise. "On edge lately."

"On edge? She tried to kill me." I point to my cheek.

"She'll get over it. You'll see." He leaves. Stopping briefly at the door frame to turn around, he tells me, "Have a good sleep."

Chapter 26

I don't know what time it was, but it was starting to get light when they noticed we weren't on the boat anymore. They didn't care though. I only heard a couple of jumbled comments before they just continued with what they were doing.

When they did get closer, I retreated to the top of the stairs. Waiting and watching from my perch; going unnoticed.

"Still nothing?" Gary whispers as he sits beside me.

"Yeah."

He stays quiet for a few minutes. "Where are they?"

I shake my head because I don't know exactly. "I think they kept to the first level. They got quiet about an hour ago. They probably went to sleep, or maybe they're on the other side of the mall."

"We need to make a decision. We could forage for items and build up supplies before it's all wasted, or try to stay hidden for as long as possible." Gary sounds like he's been thinking instead of sleeping. His voice is a bit raspy.

Maybe everyone stayed up talking instead of sleeping.

"Why can't we do both? If they are sleeping and keeping to the first floor, we could stay up here. There are a few places we could grab supplies that are near. We try to stay as quiet as possible. We don't need food right away. I know there is a blanket store near, there's the anything and everything store just a bit further down there. To the right there's an outdoorsy store, I know we can get some warmer clothes and jackets.

The hotel entrance is over there too. Maybe we should move there? Or we could look for guests that were staying there. They had to of had staff working at the time; guests staying at the hotel."

Gary cuts me off. "Right. I forgot the hotel was in the mall." I just look at him. How could he forget the hotel? He works here so shouldn't he pretty much know everything about the mall. "If there were people there, they would have come over by now."

"Maybe, but what if they thought it was safer in the hotel," I say.

"Weren't you supposed to search over that way?"

"Not that thoroughly." Searching the entire hotel would have been a risk, and would have taken hours. I think they just checked the lobby and locked the doors.

"The demons are regular people too. They may have done a quick once over for the mall, but they would have known there would be more people in the hotel. The mall hadn't opened yet, but all the guests at the hotel would have been sleeping or in the middle of breakfast. If we go there we might only find bodies.

It's almost been a week. Anyone that was there would have come out by now." Gary tries to reason and I can see his point but I still think it might be worth going and taking a look.

"They also might be thought it wasn't worth the effort to go room by room. I'll go. I'll take a couple of people and a few weapons and go over there. If we see any sign of trouble, we'll get out. If not, we might find a few people.

I don't think we could go very far anyways. Maybe the lobby? I don't know how much of the hotel is controlled by electronic locks or key locks. Or, if they have any security features for when the power goes out? If there aren't any keys for the stairs or if it's electronic locks that stay shut when the power goes off, then we won't be going anywhere." I seem to convince him.

"Okay, but be careful. And, take Shawn with you. He might be able to help if there are any problems." With the way he says problems, I know he means demons.

That settles it. I stand up and leave Gary at the stairs. I turn on the flashlight and go to the concession stand first. I take an arm full of the vitamin waters.

Gary left the doors to the theatre open. There is a light glowing on the wall. They had lit a fire while I was gone.

Everyone is awake. I put down the water and grab myself one. I nearly finish the entire bottle off in one shot. I must have been thirsty. No one grabs any of the waters, but it looks like they might have already had breakfast.

"I'm going to the hotel to see if there is anyone there; see if we can get to the rooms, or the kitchen or anything. Shawn, would you like to come with me? Anyone else?" I finish off the water and look for any volunteers.

Of course, Peter decides to come with us. No one else volunteers though.

We grab a couple of weapons and they get a flashlight each. In silence, we leave the theatre and go out to where Gary is still sitting.

"Be careful. Come back in about an hour, or we're going to come after you." He warns.

"Of course. Don't worry about us. We'll be fine." Shawn reassures Gary.

I slowly walk down the stairs; trying not to make much noise as we walk. I feel like telling Peter and Shawn to be quieter while they walk. They are making so much noise, but I'm sure it's just how it sounds to me.

I listen while we walk. I don't hear anything except the noises we are making.

Leading the other two to the side stairs, we quietly go down them. It's not much further before we get into the hotel lobby. There are no signs of anyone from the mall. That's good.

We unlock the doors to the hotel and try to quietly open and close them. The hard click makes a loud noise that echoes.

The lobby is empty and untouched. Frozen in time from a week ago. The only sign that anyone was in the lobby during the attack is a dark blotch on the counter with spots seeping to paper and keyboard. Someone must've spilt their coffee and never got the chance to clean it up.

I look at the door to the stairs and the nearby elevators. My flashlight shines off the golden doors. I wonder if the stair doors would've unlocked in the power outage. It seems like a fire hazard if they don't have that safety mechanism.

Knock. Knock.

I jump and turn around. Grabbing the dagger and readying it to attack. But the noise just came from Shawn. He knocked on the door behind the counter; probably a staff room.

I bite back a scolding. We've tried hard to be quiet and he decides to knock on a door.

"Is there anyone in there? We're survivors from the mall." Shawn calls out loud and clear. Peter stands behind him, tense and ready for anything.

I wonder if he heard something, or if he just knocked because the door was locked. I get in closer to them. I think I hear something shifting around in there. It might be better for them to hear different voices. "It's alright. We're here to help. We have food and water. There aren't any threats in the mall. We locked all the doors."

"We trapped a few of them up in the hotel." A muffled female voice comes through the door. I hear an angry mumble from a male back there.

The door unlocks with a scrape. An older man comes out first. He looks over the three of us. "Who's in charge?"

"She is," Peter answers without hesitation. He points at me.

I guess I'm in charge. I try not to look surprised.

"Hi. I'm Nikki." I introduce myself with a strong handshake.

"Eric." He says.

"That's Peter and Shawn." I point to each of them. "We're about forty people in total. There hasn't been anything attacking us since the war began." I start explaining.

A lady pushes the man out of the way. "You called it a war?"

"Some demons started a war to try to take over."

"How do you know it's a war though?" She pushes for further explanation.

I take in a deep breath and let it out slowly. "Because not all the demons are evil. Some of them are victims of this attack just like we are. One of my best friends is a demon and his family was killed for not agreeing to be a part of it. He's helping us."

"You're friends with one of them." She says.

Shawn waves once. "Elf."

The lady grabs a pack out of her pocket. She pulls out a cloth from it and wipes a spot under her sleeve. Underneath a lot of makeup is very blue skin. She must be a demon as well. The man beside her looks shocked. He's probably human. "I'm Alex." She turns to Shawn. "Lucky bastard. You don't have to do anything to hide from the humans."

"Don't be so blue. At least you don't have to hide anymore." She smacks Shawn on the chest but smiles as she walks past him. I don't think we'll have anything to worry about from these people.

"Nikki was it? Are all the humans here so open-minded?" She holds her hand out to shake mine. I return her handshake as business-like as I can.

I shake my head when I let go of her hand. "Not everyone. I think it might be a bit from shock over it all. And, some are too focused on partying to care about anything. They'll come around eventually. But, you won't have any trouble from anyone up in the theatre."

"Okay. Thank you. This is it. We rescued everyone we could. There was a fire. It- well, you know. So this is it." Alex explains. She turns around to face the door. "Come on, let's get out of here." She turns back to me and puts her hand out; motioning for us to start walking.

I take her cue but walk a little in front of her. I look back to peek at the people filing out of the room.

We go up the way we came. We can possibly hide the group for a little bit longer. I don't know what anyone's reaction might be to more new additions.

Gary sees us coming. I don't think he was expecting us back so soon and with so many people. I take a look back when we go up the stairs. There were quite a few people stuffed in that room. I can't count them with the quick look, but there has to be at least twenty.

"That was fast," Gary says.

Chapter 27

I take a sip of the brown liquid in a short glass. The whiskey is strong and heats the back of my throat. I fleetingly wonder if perhaps I have Scottish or Irish heritage. Not that I will ever know.

"You're in our spot."

Three men stand in front of me. Panic sets in. I look down and set to get up from my seat. "I'm sorry. I'll move."

They laugh at me. "No, no. You don't have to move. We'll join you." The one with really black eyes says. I can't tell if the black is a large pupil, or if his whole eye is black.

They sit down in the empty chairs around the round tabletop. I just about jump up and run away, but I settle for downing the rest of my drink. Jerry comes over to the table. He shakes hands with one of the men. "Don't scare the poor girl; she's very flighty and too young for any of you. You should be thanking her. She's been doing runs in your absence." I want to thank Jerry for coming to my rescue, but I don't know how I should feel about him calling me flighty.

"In that case, get her a double of whatever she was drinking, on us. We'll have three rum and cokes, and do you have someone in the kitchen?"

"Not unless one of you wants to start cooking."

A popping noise reverberates to the right. The noise catches the attention of everyone in the bar. It gets louder and louder. Glass crashes. Someone yells, "go out the back."

Jerry pulls me off the barstool and drags me out to the back. He stops, and I run into him. Someone yells, "it's locked. Into the cellar."

There is a lurch of the crowd around me back in the opposite direction. I am lured to the side room behind the bar. I grab onto the door jam and step to the side; slipping tight against the wall.

I get a bad feeling about the cellar. Nothing good could come from trapping yourself down in a place with only one exit. I no longer hear the gunshots, so I decide to take my chances elsewhere. If I could get to the stairs, and go upstairs, I should be able to escape using the roof.

I push through clamouring bodies, and head to the front of the bar. There are bodies littering the floor. Bullet holes are peppered on the wall. I hear shouting outside. I take this chance to run.

The popping starts up again. A dime-sized hot poke hits my stomach. I look down, but I don't see anything. I walk forward a couple of steps. Ow. Ow. I hold my stomach. The pain is too much to stand, yet it hurts to fall to the ground.

I clench my stomach, and my hand gets wet.

After this round of shots stop, I hear the shouts of men. "Run!" "The cellar's flooding!" "They're dying!"

Gunfire.

Black.

Gunfire.

"Jaiden!"

Black.

Lucas.

Black.

I hate dreams like that. Waking up in a sweat, and with my heart racing. The uncertainty of what the dream means or doesn't mean was erased with my knowledge of supernaturals. I must assume every dream and nightmare can come true until I know more about what's the new rules are to our new reality.

The room is still dark, and the bed is warm but surprisingly empty.

Sara had let me sleep in her room last night with her, John, and another woman. We had all cuddled on her bed. It kept us warm all night, but I had to awkwardly hold myself still all night. I finally stretch out on the bed, now that I realize no one is there.

Though it was short-lived, I think I will miss this. I don't generate my own heat very quickly, so the heat was welcome last night. I'm sure that's why I fell asleep so easily despite being in a bed essentially full of strangers. Or, maybe it was the exhaustion.

My hand goes into the opening of my sweater, and to the necklace, the pack Alpha gave me yesterday. I turn it back to center in my chest.

There isn't any use of dawdling. I know I'm going to have to leave today, and I would prefer to do it while people may still be asleep. Well, hopefully, some people will be asleep. The three people I slept with somehow managed to all wake, and sneak out without waking me. I don't want to face everyone.

I have to find a bathroom. I don't know if there is one here, nor if it will be vacant. Making up my mind I decide to go to the bathhouse from yesterday. When my feet touch the floor I regret taking off my shoes. It's freezing, well compared to the warmth of the bed. Quickly, I bound over to my shoes and put them on. There isn't anything else to remember so I leave the room. It isn't very far from the door to the outside.

The cold air drifts into my lungs. I hug myself to hold onto the ounce of heat I have remaining. Fresh snow blankets everything. This isn't good. Will I be able to last a Canadian winter?

No. Probably not.

South. I should go south. I should go to Banff. But, there was snow in Banff. If I go south will I meet up with Dominique? Could that have just been a dream? Should I just do what's best for my survival, and forget about Dominique? Should I just forget about that and let things happen as they were supposed to happen?

Those questions I can answer later. Step one is to get out of here, and back to dad's house. I can figure out some more things when I get there.

It takes a longer time to get to the bathhouse from the back house. I breathe a sigh of relief when I enter and hear no sign of anyone else there. This means that I don't have to worry about any of my smells. I'm caught halfway between being self-conscious about the way I smell, and not caring because there are some things that I can't do anything about. It's a different relationship when you know they can smell and hear everything you could keep to yourself in a crowd of humans.

I take advantage of the working plumbing, and hot shower while I can. I almost regret having to leave just for this reason alone, but I could endanger them by being here. I don't want to create a rift between people because of my presence. They are a pack, they are a family, and I am sure they will understand my reasoning behind leaving.

My body works on autopilot as I walk to the main house. I go over what might happen, and what I might say. I decide to stick with being straightforward, and telling them I'll leave to find my family.

I get into the house by the front door. There are a bunch of people in the living room that I don't recognize, but the one I do recognize is the Alpha.

"Good morning, Jaiden. Follow me." Alpha Ken gets up from his chair. He comes over to me, and leads me out the door I had just come in from. "I've been told you will be leaving us today. It's a very selfless thing you are doing. I know you are leaving us because of the danger you may pose. I wish to thank you."

I wasn't expecting this to go this way. I stumble out, "You're welcome." I feel like it's lacking or not the right thing to say.

"Perhaps later, when the war isn't so fresh, you can come back to stay. You will be welcomed as part of the pack." Ken continues. "I was very close with your grandparents; it's the least I could do to honour their memory as well."

John pulls up in a black car. He parks a few meters away and gets out. He walks over to me and hands me the keys before he hugs me. "If you ever find your sister, please tell her I said hi." He steps back to stand beside his grandfather. "The car is yours. We put a few things in there to help you out."

"Thank you. You didn't have to do this." Inside I jump with joy over their generosity, but I remember my upbringing to be humble.

Be appreciative but tell them it wasn't necessary.

Ken puts his hands on my upper arms. "You're pack. I'm not going to leave you to certain death." He hugs me. "You should get going. The scouts ensured me that it is safe in the area for now."

"Thank you, again, for everything. I will, hopefully, see you again sometime soon." I tell them. We've already done the hugs, so I raise my hand in a short wave. I go into the car. The inside is warm. I start the car up and set it into reverse. I wave once more at the duo before looking behind me and backing up the car.

I do not doubt where I have to go first. I need to go back to my house.

The drive is uneventful. There is a surreal beauty in the snow-covered ruins of the buildings I pass. Everything everywhere is peaceful. I don't know if the peacefulness is localized to the country and backroads I take to get home, or if the battle has moved on from the small town.

As I approach the neighbourhood my house is in, I slow the vehicle down. I turn down the last road and creep at my house. There aren't any vehicles out front. I decide to take the chance as far as parking across the street.

I get out of the car and lock it. I stare at my house. There isn't any movement there. I secretly hope that my father isn't there.

He'd be pissed if I return, because of my being gone. I strum up some tears before going into the house. I prepare for some crying to counteract his initial angered reaction. But, it all seems that it was for nothing when I call out his title, and there is no response.

Good. I blink away the tears in my eyes. I cautiously move through the house. No one is here. The house looks untouched, save for the lack of food. I don't think those people stayed long after I left. They didn't take anything I care to look for.

Cautiously, I go down to the basement. The first thing I check is to see if my room is disturbed and if my bag is still in its place. My chest fills with joy when I see my bag still in my closet. Something that goes right for me is a bonus.

The rest of the house is clear, so I decide to go outside and grab a few perishable items from the car. I may never know if I'll need to run away again, so I pack everything else into the trunk to make sure no one sees my supplies.

In the end, I take two of the bundles of food into the house with me. It will be enough to last me for a few days.

I lock all doors behind me.

Settling myself on the couch in the living room I listen to the silence, and I look outside at the stillness. I am back where I was just a couple of short days ago. I now know the extent of this war. There isn't anywhere that will be completely safe. The humans are hunted, the demons are hunting, good supernaturals won't risk helping the humans, and winter is coming. In part, I am thankful for the late winter, and yet I know that just means that the winter is going last longer into the spring. I wish for a chinook to help everyone in the north to survive; those not smart enough to go south. The question is now, am I smart enough to go south?

The timeline, the actions that were supposed to have happened thus far to ensure my visions to take place, have they taken place as they were supposed to?

I believe so, yes. Those people that came to this house would have come to this house while I was here. I would have run away, logically to get away fast enough I would have gone to Lucas' house, and stolen his car.

Oh no. His car is still at grandmas. There isn't anything I can do about it now.

I would have had to go somewhere. Where would I have gone, I didn't have anywhere to go. I may have drawn the same conclusion and went to grandma's hence all that happening, and I would return here with nowhere else to go. I should still be on the right timeline for my dreams.

But, this all still draws to the same question. What do I do now?

I think I may stay for now.

Chapter 28

"... survivors... come... safety.. army.. are any survivors... to safety. This is the army. Martial law has been declared. If any survivors are remaining, come outside and we will bring you to safety. This is the army. Martial law has been declared. If any survivors are remaining, come outside and we will bring you to safety."

These few sentences are repeated over and over. They slowly get louder and louder; both as I wake up more and the closer they get. Jumping out of bed, and to the window, I immediately spot several tanks rolling down the street.

There are a couple of people already on the lawn from this house. I take Rayleen, who is sitting up in the bed looking at me, by the hand and lead her downstairs. Miles joins us on the stairs.

James looks distraught by the tanks but goes out with the rest of us anyway. He pushes his way to the front of the group. The tank stops and a man comes out of the top. The loud recording goes silent.

A man jumps out of the back of one of the trucks and comes over to us. "I am First Lieutenant Harold and you will file yourselves into the truck three tanks behind. We will be escorting you to the high school where you will be safe from further harm. Are there any more people in the house?"

"Yes, there are a few injured in the basement." One of the triplet girls says quickly.

Harold motions to some of the others with him. They start jumping out of the truck and going towards the house. "Continue to the truck.

We will retrieve your injured."

James looks helpless as he watches people go into the house. "And what if we refuse?"

"We have the right to use force; if necessary lethal force. Please continue to the truck now." The look Harold gives James says not to cause any trouble.

It takes Nia taking the first few steps to the truck for the rest of us to budge. Troops run past us and into the house, and others place themselves around our group. We are escorted to the back of the truck and into the bed.

There are benches against three of the sides for us to sit on. From our small number, there is plenty of room when we all sit; even with the three soldiers standing guard.

I make sure to keep Rayleen between myself and Miles the whole time. Out of everyone here I know he would keep Rayleen safe if anything happens.

I take count of who is here; Rayleen, Miles, James, Daniel, the triplets, Amy, Taylor and a boy; I don't remember his name. I quickly deduce another group must have left in the night as planned and Ashlynn must have led it.

In the fuss of things, I had also forgotten Crystal. Surely, she would have followed all of us outside but yet I didn't see her. I'll wait to mention this to anyone until Rayleen is out of earshot. I don't want her to throw any sort of fit right now.

The loudspeaker message starts up again as soon as we start moving. Two tanks stay with the house while the rest of us move on. Our group is split further once we reach an intersection out of the residential area. Our truck is escorted by one tank to the west and the rest go east.

Nothing is recognizable and for the first time, I start wondering where James lived. This is how I decide I will pass my time. Obviously, we are not on the east side of town as I know it like the back of my hand. But I don't think we are too far away from there either or else why would Daniel have been so far away from home. I can believe that he skipped school to go somewhere nearby. This narrows the field down quite a bit.

I see a sign stating the west end's mall is northwest of here. We must be on the south west side of Edmonton. I'll have to ask Daniel how he ended up in the strip mall. I don't see a reason for him leaving Leduc to go to the strip mall; especially with Amy and Matt.

We drive past a lot of wreckage and carnage; however, it seems tame from what I witnessed the night Kelly took me to the airport. There is less live action. There are plenty of bodies dead and dismembered, rubble from buildings and crumbled unrecognizable objects, glass shattered everywhere, ash, smoke and flames in variable places.

I know we are at our destination when we start passing increasing amounts of militants and military vehicles. We slow to a crawl while a barrier is pulled out of the way. The tank starts up just to stop again once inside the barrier. The army men in the back hop out and pull the door to the truck bed down.

I jump down first and turn around for Rayleen, but Miles already has her. He keeps her in his arms while we are ushered in a line through the doors of the bi-level school. Right inside is another group waiting in line for some sort of processing. We are instructed to get behind them.

They have running electricity. It's a relief from the last few days. Maybe they have generators somewhere. Maybe they even have running water. I can hope at least.

They are patting everyone down, then ask a few questions, give them a small cloth-wrapped item and give instructions to where they need to go after that.

Something that becomes quickly obvious is the way they are separating people. Supernaturals are to go upstairs, and humans are to go straight down the hall. I keep my eyes on Miles; frightened that he might have to go upstairs along with the rest of the supernaturals in my group.

Which, I remember, would also include Rayleen.

The closer to the officials we get, the faster my heart rate rises. Something must have alerted Miles to this as he turns around. Both he and Rayleen take me into their arms. This act and probably a little help from Miles' powers, helps to calm me down. It doesn't last long because we are asked by an official to continue forward.

Soon enough, they are finished with the first group and have started with ours. James goes first and sets precedence for the rest of the group. He says he is human and has no powers.

The space clears up for the two officials on either side after the triplets and Amy gets through.

"Name?" The one on the left asks me.

"Alexa Brenner," I say my name. I think that the official said something else to me, but I couldn't care less.

"Names?" Paying attention to the official's words behind me, I wait for their answer. I look back to Rayleen.

"Miles McMillan and Rayleen Brenner." Miles answers for both of them.

The officials look at each other. "Miss, are you related?" The one questioning me asks.

"Yes," I say quietly. "Yes." Just a bit louder and this time I look at him.

"Please see that official. We like to process families together so you can be placed in the same room." He looks away. "Next."

I don't want to take any chance that he might change his mind so I quickly place myself beside Miles.

"Alexa Brenner was it?" I nod to him, "What are you?"

"Human," I tell him.

He writes something on his board and then talks to Rayleen. "And you? What are you, Miss?"

"I'm a girl," Rayleen says as a matter of fact. A couple of us have a quick chuckle at this. I stop when the officer looks at us with his serious face.

Turning to Rayleen I ask her the question again. "Sweetheart, the man is asking you if you are a human or a demon?"

"What's a demon?" She looks at me.

Rayleen's answer shocks me. After all this, I just assumed she knew. "Well, umm…"

Miles steps in. "Rayleen do you remember when we were at the airport and there was a monster that scared you?"

"Yeah, he went – grrrrrrrrrr." She scrunches her face up, snarls her lips, and throws her hands up and forward in a clawing motion.

I catch what Miles is trying to do, so I try to word things in a way that will get us the right answer out of her. "He was a demon. So, the man wants to know if you are one of those or if you're a human like me and Miles."

Rayleen looks at the man and tells him. "I'm a human."

The man seems lost in his own world for a moment while he looks at Rayleen. He switches the conversation back to Miles and me. "Uh. Do you have or any family member from your knowledge have any special abilities or powers?"

"No," Miles answers before I get a chance to say anything.

"Do you or any member of your family have any health issues we should know about?" The officer asks.

"No," Miles says.

The officer looks at me. "Are you currently pregnant or could be pregnant?"

"No," I answer him.

"Do you have any weapons in your possession?" He asks.

"No." Miles and I answer together. I want to slap myself. That came out a bit too fast for my liking.

"Please step over here, raise your arms, and spread your legs." I follow his instructions first. A woman officer gives me a quick pat-down. When it's Miles' turn he passes Rayleen to me. They seem to be satisfied enough that they don't pat Rayleen down. Miles is handed three packs, two for us and one for Rayleen, and a piece of paper then we are advised to follow the hallway and go to room 146.

I walk away, almost forgetting Miles, as relief and joy block out my senses. We walk as directed straight down the hall, around the corner, and down another hall. The numbers on the doors continue going up and up until we finally reach 146.

There are two more officers in front of the room. Another door is side by side with this one; room 147.

"Papers please." One of them asks.

Miles hands him the paper he received. The officer shows the other one the paper. He nods to the other one and opens the door. We are allowed through into the room.

The door is closed behind us. If I assume correctly the door should be set to lock automatically from the inside, as are most school doors set this way.

"What colour are you?" A blonde-haired man asks. He jumps off some piled desks in the corner of the room.

"Excuse me?" Miles asks.

"Your colour. The pouch they gave you contains a scarf for you." The man holds up his wrist with a yellow scarf. "What colour are you?"

Miles opens up the first pouch: the pouch assigned to Rayleen. He pushes around a couple of other items before he finally pulls out a white scarf.

"That would be for the kid, right? White means purity, innocence. The colour they assign to people, usually kids, which pose zero threat to them and everyone else here." He must have seen the puzzled looks on at least one of our faces. "Do I need to explain everything? Yes, of course I do. You've just arrived. You're disorientated from being sorted and I suppose they haven't bothered to explain anything." I shake my head in an automatic response to his question.

He lets out a sigh. "They sorted you depending on your race, mannerisms, and by their interaction with you. You receive a pack with some instructions, a couple of other items and a scarf. This scarf is one of eight colours or camouflage. Each colour has a meaning, they say it's random, but nothing is ever random here; everything has a purpose.

Camouflage is the only one they give a name to; honorary army members. Normal people can be upgraded. In exchange, you get special treatment, extra supplies for you and your family; if you have any left." He doesn't skip a beat during sentences and spouts it off in a spiel he had practice stating. "What colour are you?" The man sizes me up. His gaze creeps up and down me.

Miles opens the last two packs. "Blue, we're both blue."

"Hmm. Really? Blue matches your sweetheart there, but not you. I definitely would have made you orange or black." He turns to go back to the spot in the corner.

"What would those mean?" The words blurt out of my mouth as I think it.

He turns back to face us. "Everything, nothing, who knows? Figure it out yourself. Colours have different meanings to them. You just have to figure out how it fits in here." He turns quickly. The interaction was confusing. He seemed like he was going to be the welcome wagon but quickly lost interest.

He walks past James; shoving him slightly with his shoulder and goes back into the corner.

James already has his orange scarf on his wrist. Orange is usually a cautionary colour. James was our leader, which I could see them thinking is potentially dangerous to them. If he were to disagree with something and can get people to follow him easily it could threaten their operation here; that could be what orange means.

I start keeping a mental list in my head:

Camouflage = Army worker

White = Innocent, child-like, non-threat

Orange = leader, potential threat/danger

Blue = me and Miles

The rest of the room is filled with the people that came from James' place, two strangers, and the guy we were just speaking with.

"I'm Cary. This is Justin and you've already met Tony. We're supposed to explain things, not scare you to pieces and spout conspiracy theories. If you'll all gather in front of us we have a couple of things to explain." They wait a moment. Only a couple moves, but most everyone is happy to stay right where they are.

Tony stays in the corner of the room while Cary starts explaining. "As Tony was so kind to point out, we get scarves acting like wrist band admissions. It tells everyone that a guard processed you. You belong here. It has nothing to do with them sorting you by personality; that's just absurd. They just hand out bags and people get them at random.   The only scarf that does mean anything is the camouflage scarf for the army members and you can only receive one if you are chosen to join the army.

This is a primary sorting room. All new tenants get placed in one of these rooms so the proper arrangements can be made in the rooms for your stay here. In each room, you will be assigned an area. Don't go into or take anything from anyone else's area or you can be punished. Keep your space clean and organized."

Cary takes a break, while Justin continues the explanation. "If you will all open your packs now, you will find folded paper; take it out, please. There are two sheets.

One is a map and the other is a schedule. You will get to know these very well. You will be living your immediate future by these two pieces of paper; one to help you navigate these halls and the second to help you to be a contributing citizen here. You need to follow your schedule. It will help you adapt to living here.

If you have any special skills we ask that you inform one of the officials during your counselling time. This can mean anything that could be of any value; hand sewing, cooking, medicine, first aid, child care.

I suggest that you use the next ten minutes to start studying your maps and schedules. It will come in handy." The three of them walk to the door. They knock twice quickly and two slower knocks before the door opens and they all leave. The door is shut promptly behind them.

I look to the others who either have a confused or a complacent look on their faces. Others are looking to see how they need to react; unsure of the information they've heard. I don't know how I should feel about this yet.

The security of the place is a nice break over the risk at James' place. However, the mix of school, military, and segregation don't mix well with me. Too much control has never turned out well for any involved in the past.

I start to look over my schedule when a couple of officials come into the room and advise us they will be escorting us to our first activity.

Four people escort us, armed and I assume loaded, to the first aide room.

Taylor is being checked out by someone when we get there, sitting on a make-shift operations table. Her reactions seem to be getting tested. She looks a lot better than when I saw her last. Her one eye is covered.

A couple of officials see to us, asking a hundred questions, checking blood pressure, reaction time, and listening to our heart rates. As it does in doctor's offices, the time slows to a crawl and we can't get out of there fast enough. Before long, a few of our group are handed papers with instructions to give them to someone in the cafeteria.

When we leave Taylor is added to our group. She tags along at the end, between two officers at the back. The two officers in the front lead us to the cafeteria. We line up behind some others. Looking over the glass I see the flicker of a fire. Though there seems to be enough electricity for a few lights here and there; it doesn't seem like there is enough for the extra things like the grill.

They have one large pot brewing over the flame. The line moves fast as they ladle the soups into cups and bowls. Those who hand over their sheets of paper from the doctors are handed pills, vitamins by the looks of the bottles, with their soup. I get my soup in a cup and follow where Rayleen and Miles left to a table at the edge of the room. We get no utensils so everyone is sipping the soup straight out of their cup.

The taste is more palatable than I thought it would be. Within the one pot, they must have placed many different types of canned soups together, but they kept similar tasting soups together at least.

We have just enough time to gulp everything down before they are already telling us we have five minutes to finish up, wash our dishes, and line up to go to the gymnasium.

They have two tubs of water set out to wash our dishes in. One is full of filth of the remnants of our food and the other is for the second cleaning. Though it is not as bad, it is still quite dirty. My stomach turns at the thought that our dishes are easily plagued with the little particles of days-old food.

I wash Rayleen's dish for her as she cannot reach the tubs from her height.

We are rounded up and led to the gymnasium. Another group is filing out of the gym doors and they are escorted by officials too. By the look of their stained scarves, they have been here a while. I have a feeling that no matter the amount of time we spend here our escorts will always be with us.

Inside the gym, we are given basic directions of what we can participate in for each station. The gym must have been glorious for the teens who attended this school. There is a weight and machine mezzanine on one side. All the different types of sports equipment possible are being used by all the people in the room. Each station is for a different sport. Blue mats are set out in the one corner of the mezzanine.

James leads Miles upstairs to the weights; not wanting my sense of security to leave me I follow them up there. We go straight for the mats.

The rest of our group have the same idea as they follow us up here. Soon as James starts settling on the mat six officials come running up the stairs and one meets them at the top. They come over to us.

"There are too many people at this station. We must ask that a maximum of four of you remain here and the rest of you move on to other stations." His words and the readiness of the others warn of what may happen if we do not comply. Slowly a couple of people disperse.

James puts a hand on Taylor to ensure she stays here, as Miles does not budge from his spot I stay as well. Rayleen by default is to stay as well. The rest of the group seems to understand the importance that they leave. Two of the officials herd some people downstairs. The one that was up here originally finds his spot against the entrance to the stairs once more. The others remain here staring at us.

"We said four people maximum." One of the officers states.

James speaks for us. "There is enough room for five of us, surely it should not be a problem for one extra person to be here.

Please, we mean no harm. She just came from the doctors and is still healing. She should not exert herself lest she injures herself further. The child must stay with her parents and I fear that she is too young to play the sports downstairs with the other people.

And, I have a bad back. If I do much more than stretching I'm afraid I would be heading to the infirmary myself. Surely you can find that we are not acting out of rebellious nature but we are just not suitable to do much more than just a couple stations you have set out and must go at our own pace." He tries to reason with them.

The one officer mulls it over in his head and then gives the nod to the others to allow it. He seems almost reluctant to let us win this one, but he leaves us as well.

As the last to go down the stairs he has a bit of a discussion with the official posted up here. Looking over to us I know he is telling the man to watch us.

James notices this as well. He speaks a level just above a whisper. "Seems as though we've upset them."

"We need to lay low going forward," Miles says while staring straight at James.

James laughs loudly. What Miles said didn't seem that funny to me. "I suppose so. We wouldn't want to have them separate us." James turns his attention to Rayleen. "My dear do you know how to play Ring Around the Rosie?" Rayleen smiles largely and nods her head exaggeratedly. "How about you show me as I have forgotten how to play it?"

"Okay," Rayleen spins around in a circle by herself. "Ring around the rosie. Pocket full of posies. Ashes, ashes we all fall down." On the last word, she falls to the ground. After a second, she sits up and looks for approval from James.

"That was lovely, but as far as I had remembered the game you were supposed to play with a bunch of people." She tilts her head slightly to the side and scrunches her face in confusion.

I realize that she has not played much with other children her age and it's not like any of the adults around her have played such things with her. Something so simple as Ring Around The Rosie she's had to adapt to playing it by herself and completely forgotten the game is supposed to be a group activity. Like a ton of bricks, James' distraction for the guards hits me with guilt.

Miles probably came to the same realization moments before I did. He is already on his way to Rayleen to show her the proper way to play the game. I join them after they play one round. Helping Rayleen up from the ground, I don't release her hand and wait for Miles to take my other one. We all play, singing the words and spinning in a circle; Rayleen giggling the whole time.

We play more and more rounds of the game. I get increasingly dizzy until I fall on the ground and my world spins. When I don't get up Rayleen comes over to inspect what happened.

Miles asks me, "You alright?"

"I will be once my world stops spinning," I say.

For a moment I get mad at everyone from my embarrassment at them all laughing at me but I can't help but smile. It has been a long time since any of us has been able to more or less let loose and feel some joy; without any reserve. It's been so long that any of us has been able to feel the pure happiness that playing with a child can bring. It seems to be helping Rayleen as well.

Before any of this happened, it had been so long since I had even played with Rayleen like this.

Rayleen comes over to stand near me. My head has stopped spinning so I decide to continue with the childishness. Pulling Rayleen off her feet and gently tackling her to the ground I start tickling the little girl. She starts shrieking and laughing; as does everyone else.

Miles pulls me off Rayleen and puts me down right next to her. "Get her." Being so little she doesn't understand exactly how to tickle but I still laugh at her attempts. The game turns into a sort of tag with the occasional attempt at tickling again.

Miles and Rayleen have everlasting energy. Soon, I fall on the mats exhausted. Now an easy target the two both head for me. I put my arms and legs up in defence. "Wait. Pause. Stop. Time out. I'm exhausted."

Miles starts up the tag game with Rayleen again. The guard is plenty distracted and off his guard with us by now.

James calls me over. He whispers. "Keep up the family façade with Miles. They'll keep you together because of it. They'll likely separate all of us. Everyone needs to find out everything they can, and find a way to pass along information. Something doesn't seem right about this place. I don't think they're the real military. If it's as I fear, we need to get escape as soon as possible."

"This place doesn't seem that bad. Don't you think you might be overthinking this?" Taylor puts in her thoughts about the place. She is trusting of the people here already.

James frowns. "I'd rather err on the side of caution. From my experience everything is rarely so black and white; especially when humans are involved in excessive control."

A whistle blows. I get up and go to the railing.

"Please get in line. It is time for the next thing on your schedule." I don't see the person talking but I assume that it is one of the officers.

I follow everyone. Collecting Rayleen's hand in my own, I try to make more of an attempt at noticing everything that happens around me. However, nothing jumps out at me. Everything is so ordinary, as far as ordinary can be in this situation. The officers don't say anything to each other or us. People in the halls don't talk to each other either. The places we have been are for our basic needs; health, food, and exercise. It all seems good.

The next room we are brought to is filled with mats from the gym. The person inside tells us to come in and sit down in a large circle. The girl has a camouflage scarf around her wrist.

"Welcome to counselling. My name is Kate. You are new here so how about we all get to know each other a little more. We'll go around the circle and introduce ourselves. Tell us a little about yourself; whatever you feel comfortable sharing and after we'll play a little game.

I'll start everything off. I was born and raised in Edmonton. Went to University and attained a Diploma in Psychology and worked at my own firm counselling people for twenty-three years. I was at the school the day the demons attacked giving a speech to the psychology class here. Luckily, the military showed up soon after and saved us all. They set up base here and I have been helping people cope with their experiences." She looks at the person to her left, passing on the spotlight.

Each person shares their story. Kate had set the stage for what each person should share; where they were born and raised, what they did before the war, where they were the day the war started, and how they ended up here.

My turn soon comes and I get completely nervous that I might say the wrong thing or worse Rayleen might say the wrong thing. "I'm Alexa Brenner and this is Rayleen Brenner." I look beside me to Rayleen. Miles looks at me and I gain a bit of confidence as he reassures me with a small smile. His look tells me that I am doing the right thing by introducing Rayleen myself. "We moved around a lot until we settled here. We were on our way to school on the day of the attack. We were able to find safety at James' house and when the tanks came, we were brought here."

Miles takes up the cue immediately so Rayleen won't have a chance to talk. "I'm Miles McMillan. I was born in Scotland but soon after was brought here. So, no accent, sorry. I was on my way to Rayleen's school on the day of the attack. We went to James' and then we were brought here."

James takes up his turn and everyone else continues until we get back to Kate.

"Brilliant. So, I gather most of you know each other already. I must say that you are the largest group we've had come in since we started up here. It warms my heart to know that they may be many more groups such as your own. Now we will be starting the exercise. It's a laughing exercise. The rules of it are pretty simple; just laugh. Everyone join in at once. I will start." I am thoroughly convinced the woman has gone insane, as the loudest, most annoying laugh I ever heard, comes out of the tiny woman.

Rayleen is the first person to start giggling, then full out laughing. Increasingly, everyone starts laughing at each other. Not until Taylor starts laughing do I start. She snorts every couple of laughs and for some reason, I find this hilarious. Everyone in this room has completely gone insane with the laughter that fills it.

A few minutes of this pass. The officials break the laughter when they come into the room.

Kate collects herself. "This was a very good session. We will continue this tomorrow. Please everyone come to class ready to speak about the one thing that you love the most in the world. A memory works, a hobby, a person, anything. Now off you go."

We don't go too far this time. Down the hall, just three classrooms away, we are brought to a room filled with desks all in a row, and a pile of clothes and buckets in the front.

"Please sit down. Each person to one desk." Quickly we file into the classroom and find a desk. I sit Rayleen beside me. James and Miles take spots directly behind us. "I'm Barry. We've nicknamed this class the Greater Good Class. We will teach each other skills and come up with ideas to benefit our little community. We will also make things to help this place out. You might also go out as a cleaning team.

We pretty much do almost anything in this time slot. As you are all new we'll start this off easily enough. We'll just be doing laundry today. Unfortunately for all of us, there are no washing machines anymore. This means it will all be done by hand and hung to dry. Everyone come up and grab one article of the laundry, one bar of soap and a pail of water."

Barry instructs us how to properly clean the clothes, and we spend a long while cleaning the pile of laundry as guards watch us.

We are taken back to the cafeteria for supper. Variety is obviously going to be a luxury in this place as it is the same soup mixture as lunch. It tastes a bit different this time: a bit spicier.

Throughout the day, everyone has increasingly become quieter and quieter; I don't know whether they have nothing to say to each other or if each person is quiet from the almost forced silence that fills these halls and rooms.

Not soon enough, supper is finished and we are off to community hall; back inside the gym. Everything is cleaned up from earlier and a small crowd of people are lining up in rows facing the mezzanine. A free for all seating is allowed. Our group, of course, all sits together.

The quiet of the last couple of hours must have gotten to me. I'm relieved that there seems to be at least one point in our day that we will all be able to talk to each other in a more or less private situation; at least without any officials nearby.

One man dressed in uniform and medals come into view at the top of the mezzanine and everyone falls silent.

"Welcome to Community Hall. We have survived another day and what a day it was. We accomplished something that brings great hope to our community. We rescued a large group of people distraught from an attack they had endured from those beasts." People look around to find us, the newcomers, and roar into cheers. The man at the front puts his hands up and quickly hushes the crowd again. "What's more is the demons have retreated. We are winning this war. We are defeating the filth who dares to think they are better than us. Humans are proving to be the most supreme beings to have ever existed." The crowd cheers again.

Our group is the only one to remain in silence. All illusion crashes to the ground. We need to escape immediately.

"They thought they could come in and take our land, take our homes, take our families and take our world. They do this for no reason. Because, they felt like it. They have proven they do not deserve to survive as a species from their actions. By the end of this, not one will survive. Their race needs to be exterminated before they infect the whole world."

Is this the type of speech we can expect every day at this community gathering? The man is inspiring hope within people, using their anger at losing all they have known to brainwash them into exterminating every supernatural being in this world.

I tune out everything else he says while looking at each person's face. How they are completely hanging on this man's every word. Everyone's eyes are lit up in their excitement. They believe every word he says. Everyone is so completely far gone at this point that it would be useless to even try to tell everyone the truth. I feel that all it would accomplish is what has happened in all of history; I would be killed for my so-called treason.

I look at the faces of the people from my schedule today. Some seem to be almost buying into what he is saying. Others from James' are disgusted. Rayleen's face almost matches those of the people cheering. She doesn't know anything. She is just a child. She doesn't fully understand what this guy is meaning.

A final standing ovation from the crowd is my last straw. I don't want to subject her to this propaganda anymore. I don't want to show her that all these people are happy with what that man was saying. There is nothing to cheer for when you are speaking about killing people because of their race.

I quickly grab Rayleen and take her to the nearest set of guards. "Excuse me. We need to go to the washroom. She won't be able to hold it much longer."

They look at each other. "We don't need an accident on our hands. Alright, I'll take you and escort you to your rooms after."

"Thank you so much." We don't go far. There are washrooms right outside the gym. I take Rayleen inside and both of us go to the washroom. I turn the handle on the toilet and it works.

I lift her on the counter to wash her hands in the bucket of water while whispering. "Sweetheart, I need you to do something for me and don't listen to anything anyone here says. They're lying. You need to listen to me, Miles, and James. That man is trying to convince people to kill some of our friends because of the way they were born. It's not right. Okay? Do you understand?" Her lips turn into a pout. "I'm not mad at you. I am mad at these people. Okay?"

She nods her head. I lift her into a hug and don't let her down again. I get her to dry her hands on the towel.

We leave the bathroom and get escorted to a room. I know we've been brought to the right one when we see Miles in there. The door shuts behind us and Miles sweeps us both into a big hug.

"We had thought something happened to you. Been relocated or something. That's usually what happens when someone disappears." Tony says. I guess he's in our room. There's no one else I know that's here.

Something doesn't quite sound right about the word relocated, so I ask. "What do you mean relocated?"

Tony comes closer. "Supposedly, there are places like this all over. Sometimes people are asked to relocate by the officers and are escorted to the new location. Never seen again. I'm glad you weren't disappeared. You should have seen your man, he was frantic with worry."

Two other children start to whimper when the lights suddenly go out. "Lights out. Time for bed." A call comes from the darkness.

Miles takes my hand and guides us to our quarters. Two larger blankets for the three of us on the cold floor. We put one under us and one above. Placing Rayleen in between for the most warmth. She quickly falls asleep but the same eludes me.

My mind won't shut up. My body is restless. Minutes. Hours. I can't tell how much time passes before my eyes finally start to feel heavy.

Chapter 29

The smoke exits my lungs in a long breath out. My own breath, even without the smoke, is visible in the cold air. A few people have the same terrible addiction as I do.

I should've listened to mom and dad, and never started. Not that they were the best influences on that. All smokers will tell you not to smoke, in between their puffs.

It started as a social thing at the bar with flavoured smokes; a dumb drunk socialization community moment. I thought I could control it.

We each take in our cigarettes in silence. We'll run out once the smoke shop does, then we'll quit. Can't smoke, if there's nothing to smoke.

Calm is settling in. This is the new normal.

It won't last very long; it can't. We're going to run out of food and water, or someone bad is going to find us. At this point, I would stop complaining about how crappy work is to get back what we used to have. But, this is fine with me for now.

Matt doesn't seem like he wants to do anything more than party, still. There isn't anything to fear from him as long as we don't get in his way.

No one has seen Brad since he walked away from us on the boat. I miss him. I hope he figures things out soon.

We head back inside after our break, though I prefer the outside. The darkness of this place gets to me. I wish that we could go back to the boat or the pool. The skylights there let enough light in that we wouldn't need fire or flashlights during the day.

We might still need the fire for heat though. I hope it ends up being a warmer winter. I don't know if we'll survive a minus thirty winter.

"Nikki!" Eric says in a panic behind me. I turn around to see him halfway in between bolting and attacking two people making their way inside. We must have left those doors unlocked. I rush up to Eric and put a hand on his shoulder. We don't have any weapons bigger than a knife on us and they look unarmed.

They make it through the second set of doors. Eric tenses under my hand. The pair doesn't do anything. They look human, but I can't be sure anymore. The lady with bleach blonde hair and black streaks looks fierce and angry. Her male friend looks happy and a bit more friendly. He looks like he might be a ginger but there isn't enough light in here to tell for sure.

"Leave us alone!" Eric warns them. My hand leaves his shoulder so I can smack him on the back of his head. I don't know why, but it seems like the most appropriate thing to do with the audience. Almost like a swift kick under the table to shut up your friend who is spilling too much information to your parents.

"I'm Nikki. Who are you?" I ask them. I take a couple of steps forward and put myself between Eric and the couple.

"I'm Miles and this is Kelly. Nice to meet you. We're looking for survivors to join us. A wizard friend of ours has a house. There's heat, electricity, food and plenty of room. We've got a group of about forty people already and are looking for any survivors that would like to come and stay with us." He seems genuine, but I can't be sure. It sounds like there is a catch.

"Hell no! Why should we trust you? You could just be trying to lure us out to kill us." Eric yells behind me. A couple of people agree with him.

If I don't do something soon they might force the two to leave or worse. They're probably demons themselves. We might not stand a chance in a fight. Especially, if they have backup. "He's right. There's no reason to trust you. But, there's no reason not to trust you. What happens if we go with you? What's the price?"

"You might die. We're going to make an army to fight against the rebellion. But, if you stay here you might die anyway. You'll die of hunger or you'll freeze to death. Or, maybe someone else finds you and kills you." Kelly says through Miles' glare.

"You're probably right." I turn around. Gary and the rest of the group have drawn into a crowd behind us. Gary walks to join beside me. He continues, "We put it to a vote. But, we'll need to include the rest of us."

It doesn't take a genius to know what their response will be. No one's going to agree to fight and die. Gary and I take lead and guide everyone through the lobby and down the stairs. I'm not sure exactly where he thinks he's going. He might already know where everyone is. He has been on the lookout for a while.

Matt's people notice us as we walk through the halls. Some broke off into different stores and it looks like they slept there through the night. They are dressed in all fashions of brand new clothing.

With all the people possibly scattered through the entire mall, I have no idea how we are going to be able to find Tyler and everyone else all that quickly.

Maybe we should split off into groups. Or, maybe one of the others can tell me where he went off to. We see a group looking out at us from a clothing store. I don't know their names but I remember their faces. "Do you know where Tyler is?" I ask them. They look unsure; like they shouldn't tell us.

I'm about to move on when finally one of the guys speaks to us. "Probably in Sears, but you don't want to go in there. He might not be decent."

"Thanks. Could you meet us in the water park and ask everyone else you can find too?" I say before going towards Sears. The upstairs entrance goes into the store right at the bedding department. I stop to talk with Gary at the 'Y' in the road. "Do you want to get everyone to the water park? We'll need as many people as we can find. I'll see if I can find Tyler."

"We could split up; half and half. You take downstairs and I'll take upstairs. We do a quick walk-through and meet back at the waterpark." Gary says.

His idea sounds better than mine. "Yeah, let's do that." I raise my voice and take it back to the rest of the group. "We're splitting up. Half go with Gary upstairs and half with me to search down here. Everyone we find, we need to ask to meet at the waterpark."

They're adults and can split themselves up, and Kelly and Miles can decide what they want to do. In no time at all, it feels like, my group makes it to the end of the mall. We really could see some of the destruction that Tyler's group did. Lots of stores had their windows broken so the people could get inside and take what they wanted. We didn't find too many people. But, most of the higher fashion stores are upstairs. That's where I would have gone.

I peer into Sears, but I don't see anything. The windows aren't broken here, so I decide to leave Sears to Gary.

"Let's go back," I say to my group.

People we found are slowly making their way to the waterpark. They aren't in as much of a hurry as we are. Many of them are noticeably hungover, so that might have something to do with it.

We go into the park through the main level beach entrance. The air inside is colder than the last time I was here. It's colder than the other side of the door.

A few people wait for us in the lounge chairs on the beach by the kiddie pool. As I get closer I spot Brad. He glares at us on our walk over. His look softens when he sees Stephanie, then he looks away. If he wants to be angry at us and pout that's fine with me.

It takes about ten minutes for Gary to return with Tyler and a couple of girls trailing slightly behind him. Tyler looks at our new additions with disgust, more so with the obvious demons.

Tension thickens the mood. We can't wait too much longer or a fight is bound to break out. There is no telling what an angry mob will do. I start. "I'd like you all to meet Kelly and Miles. They come from another group and are rescuing people to bring back to their base. A wizard's house that has electricity and food and heat. They want to eventually fight back against the demons that caused this war. We have a choice. We can either stay here or we can go with them."

"We're staying." Someone shouts before I can get through my speech.

I try not to roll my eyes at the interruption. "I figured we'd put it to a vote. We-"

"It's simple. We're staying here." Tyler interrupts me. "They're monsters and they will eat us the moment we get to this wizard's house."

"How do we know we won't die here tomorrow? Someone could come here and kill us all." Gary tries to reason.

"Then, we kill them." He points to Miles and Kelly. I move between them and Tyler.

Heated rage books over. "Would you get over yourself? You're acting like a child. Demons exist. So, what? Stop being a racist bastard and start judging them by their individual actions. And stop partying. Obviously, this is going to last a while. Grow up and start helping us survive.

These two are offering shelter, food, electricity, and more. They will exchange it for us helping fight against the ones who caused all this.

Or, we could stay here. Maybe we survive and maybe we don't. We certainly won't if no one puts in any effort. So we're going to have a vote. Raise your hands if you want to stay here."

A couple of hands shoot up immediately; including Tyler's. I wait a couple of seconds. Other people raise their hands after looking around at the others. It becomes a clear majority without having to ask the other half to this vote.

"I guess we're staying here." I walk away. I pause to address our visitors. "I'll escort you out."

They follow me out the side doors into the mall area. I lead them back to the theatre entrance. This can't be the end of it. I already regret the decision. I should have forced people to go. Not that that would work with most of them.

We stop inside the outer exit doors. "It looks like we're staying, but if you ever need any help, a place to stay, please don't hesitate to ask us."

"Thank you," Miles says.

"Could I get the address? Just in case I can change their minds."

"16 Walnut Street. You're welcome any time. See you soon." He grabs onto Kelly's hand and pulls her away. I can tell she has something to say, but he's trying to make it so she doesn't. I think this turned out as best as it could have.

"Bye." I wave to their backs. But stop, when it catches up that they aren't looking. I lock the doors behind them. Turning around, I lean against the door and let out a large breath.

I hope this wasn't a huge mistake. It already feels like it was.

I itch to call them back. Tell them that I'll go with them, but Brad. He voted to stay.

Chapter 30

I get out of the car and walk into the Canadian Tire. The place is busy. I go to the flyers, and search for what I need, and want. I don't know what I need and want.

I decide to walk counter-clockwise around the store.

Christmas decorations, children's toys, yard supplies, light bulbs, storage, tools, hockey, camping supplies. Along my way, I slowly register the population lowering to nothing, and the light dimming to almost nothing.

I jump when something falls behind me. I can't see what it is when I look back. I pick up my pace to leave the store. The hairs on the back of my neck are standing on end. There are things in here with me.

I can see the exit. It's bright outside. Something else falls behind me. I look back, this time catching a glint of red-eye. It was a mistake to come in here. They're here.

I pick up the pace, now running. I look back when shelves crash behind me. White creatures with red eyes, vampires I think, perch on shelves everywhere. They come out from aisles. They chase after me with a roar.

If only I can get outside.

I barely pass between the two of them. I hit the door, and it gives away. Now the second door. I can smell smoke. The deceptive light was not from sunlight, it was from a fire burning away the city. I look back, a hoard of vampires burst through the doors.

I'm scared. I can't escape. I'm grabbed. I close my eyes.

But, nothing happens. I wake up from my dream. I'm happy it was just a nightmare.

I have to pee. Opening my eyes, annoyed at myself, and my bodily functions, I scowl and get out of the warm covers. I stumble to the bathroom. I close the door behind me and turn on the light.

A black-cloaked figure ignites fear in me. He growls a whispered "REAPER" at me as he reaches for me.

I hit the door behind me, and crouch in fear. He reaches for me.

Just as his hand is inches from my face I wake up. I look around my room for any danger. Once I realize I'm safe, I relax. That had to of just been a nightmare, right?

Paranoia, despite inconsistencies in the dream compared to reality, makes me avoid the bathroom in the dream. Instead, I go upstairs to use the toilet up there.

I settle upstairs and eat some of the dried fruit and jerky the pack provided.

It's peaceful in my neighbourhood.

I think I might prefer this solitude. I know it won't last, but it is so peaceful, and freeing to be alone.

I know exactly how to spend my time here. I don't have to bend to anyone else's ideas. It's like a vacation where no one knows who you are, you know you'll never see these people again, so you can act any way you like.

I think I'll eat then, perhaps, read a book all the rest of the day, and, not one of the encyclopedia books either. No, a fiction book with no intention of learning a skill or history.

I'll read a book for fun, and lose myself in the plot for entertainment. Kendra always had books, she loved that sort of thing. Jacob never was able to rid her of that 'ridiculous waste of money, time, and space' hobby.

Chapter 31

The next two days go by much as the first one did. Immediately, we had been filed into a routine and were told to look forward to the comfort and security of this. In a way, it was comforting to know that I wouldn't have to worry about being attacked and the security of knowing that everything will be taken care of for me.

However, Community Hall and the constant presence of the, possibly fake, military always remind me that this is all a lie.

Two more people were found after our group. They have adapted pretty quickly into society. The two men had their families killed in front of them. Devastated, they cling to everything they are told; they're out for revenge.

Everyone had been separated and despite what I thought, there is no way to communicate at the Community Hall. There are too many people here watching us; silently forcing us apart.

Tony is no longer here. He disappeared after the first day. Rumour is that he and five others were relocated. Relocation is likely synonymous with killed.

Miles and I take our spots at the top of the mezzanine for the fitness slot, playing with Rayleen up here. We have badminton rackets and two birdies. The guards have let us be up here since the first day. Courtesy of James' reasoning I suppose; as Rayleen could get hurt if she tries to play around with the adults downstairs.

After a brief lesson to Rayleen, we play by taking turns hitting it high in the air for her to hit back. Rayleen misses the birdie at first, however gets the hang of it eventually and finally hits one back.

Our gameplay is stopped by an officer grabbing the birdie out of the air. "Miles McMillan." Dread fills my stomach. It's the man who leads the Community Hall.

"Yes." Miles answers.

The man says, "We have a proposition for you. We would like to offer you a camouflage scarf and the benefits and responsibilities that come with it. Normally, we would find your significant other a job as well, however considering you have the child we thought it would be best to allow a flexible situation. You would be moved to better quarters. You work for eight hours of your day and can spend the rest of it with your family."

"What would my family be doing while I'm at work?" Miles loops his arm around me.

"Activities that would benefit the community. They can visit the library, gym; with an escort. Or, stay in your trailer." He explains.

"How do I sign up?" Miles responds without hesitating.

The man brings out two camouflage scarves and hands one to Miles and one to me. "Replace your scarves with these. The child doesn't need one because she's too young." Miles takes off his scarf before tying the new one on.

"Now you're an honourary member of the army." The man shakes Miles' hand and then mine. I can't help but think it's all a little anticlimactic and odd. "Do you need to return to your current quarters for anything particular?"

"No," Miles says. "We don't have anything personal there."

"Great, then Officer Gren will escort you to your new quarters. I will meet you there shortly to pick you up for your first day's work." The man walks away and takes a few others away with him. Officer Gren, who looks my age, nods then turns around.

It's not long until we are led outside the school building through the front doors. We go right. Turning around the corner we find a bunch of trailers. Officer Gren takes us to the furthest trailer away. He opens the door with a key and turns to the side. He hands Miles the key.

"Enjoy." He walks off.

Now that we are on the other side of this society, we have gained back some of our freedom.

Miles walks in first and holds the door open behind for us. Inside is a kitchenette, dining room, bedroom, and washroom. Curious, I try the taps; we have running water. Hurrying about, I open the fridge and find it full. Electricity works too. There is a television in the corner and some DVDs on the side of it. The cabinets are loaded with things to do; board games, books, magazines, and puzzles.

Rayleen starts exploring with me. We don't get a chance to open every drawer in the place when the door opens.

The colonel nods to us. "Miles, if you don't mind coming with me and we'll start. Only four hours today though; just so you can get settled in."

"How about you two go back and play at the mezzanine? I'll meet you there at the end of my shift." His look tells me that there will be no arguments about his decision. Is he trying to warn us about something? He appears unnerved.

"Sure, come on Rayleen, let's go play some more." I hold out my hand and wait for her to grab it. We go out ahead of Miles. Two guards wait outside.

They split off as one follows behind us, and the other goes with Miles and the colonel.

I pick up the pace enough that Rayleen has to slightly jog to keep up. When we get back to the gym and see James and Taylor at the mats it is a huge relief. However, they seem concerned about my sudden appearance.

The guard is kind enough to stay at the entrance. He starts up a conversation with another guard. Maybe they'll keep each other distracted.

"So, they put you on the same schedule?" I ask them to break the silence.

"Where's Miles? What are you doing here?" James whispers. He looks worried.

"We got promoted today." I show my scarf. "Miles is a guard now. And, we get a bit of freedom and privileges."

"Congratulations." James smiles. Taylor echoes.

"Thank you." I sit down and pull Rayleen down in front of me. Taking strands of her hair and finger combing through it. Getting her hair done is one of the only things she will sit still for.

"How long does he work for?" Taylor asks me.

"Eight hours every day. Except, he's only doing four hours today. We don't really know much. It was kind of sudden. I'm sure I'll be able to tell you more tomorrow." Rayleen moves around. Letting my hands move with the chunks of hair I hold on to, I let her resettle.

"They've got trailers on the side of the building for officers to stay in." I nod towards the wall to let them know which side of the building. "We have our own. I think everyone gets their own."

"Really? And, you're here instead of your trailer?" Taylor says.

I notice Taylor isn't wearing her bandage; not sure why it took me this long to figure it out. She seems fine. Nothing looks out of place. Her eye looks fine. I mentally shake when I realize it's been too long of a stare. "Miles said it would be a good idea to come back here and play some more until he comes to pick us up."

"In four hours." James' smile falters for a split second. He's as suspicious at the request as I was. "Have you had your supper yet? You should join us."

"Not yet. We'll join you." And, then after is the Community Hall. And, then what? Go back to the mezzanine for an hour?

Rayleen's hair is untangled, but I still run my fingers through it. Grabbing a mass of it I start a French braid with full intentions of taking it out and redoing it time after time.

"It's getting colder out there. It'll probably snow again soon." I let them know what is going on out there. You can't really see the outside much in here. Most windows have been blocked and boarded up. The rest were blacked out with paint.

"It's good. To have a solid roof over our head. The snow is going to stick around. And, when it does, people will be stuck where they're at until spring." James watches over our heads at the guards.

I get what he's saying. We need to leave soon or we might be stuck for three or four months. Brainwashing and disappearing people aside, would this be such a bad place to get stuck? We seem to have everything needed to last a long while. We have the military protecting us.

Out there, we're grasping at straws. Hoping that things work out. Necessities are a question. Each has a disappearing timeline.

James, myself, we all have a target on our backs.

"It's also just a couple of weeks until Santa Claus comes." Taylor stares right at Rayleen as she says this in a sickly-sweet voice.

"Santa Claus isn't real," Rayleen says very bluntly. "You shouldn't lie."

Taylor exaggerates her surprise. "What? Santa Claus isn't real? Of course, he's real. He brings me presents every year and once he even left footprints on our floors."

Before she continues to try to convince the five-year-old that Santa Claus is real, I intervene. "Taylor it's okay. You don't need to try anymore. She knows that Santa Claus isn't real. Our last foster parents ruined that for her; and everything else; Easter Bunny; Tooth Fairy."

"What?" She grimaces. "Does she at least do Halloween?"

I shake my head. "If I take her out, yeah. A lot of foster families don't do extras for the kids who aren't theirs."

"Don't they give the foster parents money for that?" Taylor asks.

Taking in a deep breath I prepare to erase disillusions about it. "Not for that. Most money is just a general amount they get once a month for general expenses. Some foster kids get extra budgets, but I didn't qualify. Rayleen got a soccer ball for her extra exercise expense; that stayed at that house after we left."

Taylor's face scrunches up a bit. "Are you sure? I thought..."

James cuts Taylor off. "Well, I supposed it's futile at this point. It's a completely new world out there. There's no sense in dwelling on the injustice of the past. This revolution could have been good for a few things, had it been executed properly."

The hair in my hand gets harder to control as I near to finishing.

"Here, I have a ponytail for you. You look adorable with a French braid." My decision to undo her hair and start over is overruled in the couple of seconds it took for Taylor to say a few words and pass me a ponytail. I twist the ponytail secure in her hair. Rayleen sits long enough to wait for me to finish and get up to admire the work in the mirror.

Instead of asking me to play something with her or sit in front of me again, she twirls behind me. Little hands go into my hair. "I can do your hair now."

"Sure." Her hand hits a snag and pulls my hair. My neck strains as I try to hold my head in place. I cringe. "Remember, be gentle."

We indulge ourselves in regular chit-chat until the whistle is blown for the switch over to supper.

My personal bodyguard helps keep people away in the halls. But, the further he gets, the more bold people get. First people seem to pity me, then they are curious, and finally there's jealousy; after one guy pipes up about the promotion.

James and Taylor feel the heat from everyone's gazes and go for a silent supper. I assume this is how a person might feel if they are being read their rights. I have the right to remain silent. Anything I say or do, can and will be used against me when these people see fit to it. I finish quickly and clean off both dishes. I can't get out of here fast enough when we are told to go to Community Hall.

This time, Rayleen and I can sit with James and Taylor. I search around the gym, but I don't see Miles. He's working, but the colonel will be here so maybe Miles will be too.

The whole gym is still whispering when General starts his speech of the night. "Tonight, we celebrate!" To my horror Miles is standing in a full military uniform atop the mezzanine. He stands on the left of General with another official to his left. There are another two of the right of General. The three of them I recognize just from seeing them around. "As we grow as a community, we grow in power; it all gets us one step closer to taking back our world. It is the individuals who work together that give us this power. We would like to congratulate the four newest individuals contributing to our cause." He claps his hands and all but four follow suit enthusiastically. "We extend our congratulations to the hope of our world. Would the family of Miles McMillan please stand up?"

Rayleen stands up right on cue, but I take a moment to realize that means me. There is something ominous about the attention that General is placing on us. Using us for his message.

"They are the inspiration for our cause. We have all lost family and friends to these demons, but new families will be made. A new family has been made here in this school. Our community is one big family. We work together, learn together, and eat together. We are all contributing ourselves to a common goal. Together we stand stronger. Together we will gain back our world." The booming cheers make him stop his speech.

Slowly, at first, I hear the word 'Humans' being yelled out from a couple of places. Like a wave, it spreads over the crowd until almost everyone is yelling it in synchronization. Some salute the General. For the first time, I see an overjoyed look in his features. His smile falls into a smirk soon after.

The assembly soon breaks off when we are told to have an early night. "It'll be a long day tomorrow, so we will need our strength. Tonight, all will return to our rooms early and each will have a surprise waiting for them there. Good night." General walks to the back of the mezzanine with the rest of the officials up their following closely behind him.

The majority of people wave and say their congratulations as they pass by. Some decide a glare is more appropriate.

I just stand where I am, holding Rayleen in place. We wait until most have cleared the room. Patting her back gives her the signal that it's okay to go now.

We walk towards the stairs to the mezzanine. Footsteps pound in a hurried run. The sound comes straight for us so I turn around.

Officer Gren stops quickly a few meters away. "Sorry, you can't go up there right now. I'm escorting you to your trailer now."

"Why? Can't we just hang out until Miles is done?" I ask.

"McMillan wasn't aware of protocol and has been advised that I would be taking you back." Officer Gren says. It's weird to hear him refer to Miles by his last name.

"Okay." Keeping my voice down I just agree. There really is nothing much I can do to disagree with him.

Officer Gren leads us through the deafly quiet halls. He stops abruptly just when we were about to turn a corner. I put a hand on his back to stop myself from fully crashing into him.

The angle lets me just barely see around the corner. Two men hold a chained beast between them that appears to be sniffing under a doorway as a dog would. I don't get to have a really good look at it before I rebound back.

"Sorry. Sorry, I forgot they were cleaning the halls tonight. We shouldn't disturb them. Let's go back this way." He pushes us in the other direction.

"Of course. No worries." I say cheerfully. My heart pounds in my chest. I could have written off the beast as a large dog. Explain it away as a drug dog type search. But, his lie about the hall getting cleaned when it clearly wasn't, immediately sends up red flags.

We take a long way to get out of the building and come out closer to where our trailer is than if we exited through the front doors.

Officer Gren drops us off at the door of our trailer but doesn't stick around to see us inside. Too eager, I assume, to get back to his actual duties for the night.

Chapter 32

I don't like it.

A pit has settled into my stomach and hasn't dislodged.

The larger group decided they didn't want to stay in the theatre. They moved down to the second floor. Claimed the Europa and mini-golf areas first, then branched out a bit further.

I've lost track of where everyone went.

Shouts and screams. Grunts and smacks.

It starts up fast and loud. I can't pinpoint where it's coming from. It seems to come from everywhere with the echoing halls.

At first I thought, a demon must have gotten in and started picking us off. I rush down the immobile escalator and towards Europa.

I find an almost worst scene.

One of the people that left with Tyler, is beating someone to death with something gleaming in my flashlight. I tackle him off the person. I hear the thud of his head hitting the floor. His entire body goes limp. I prepare myself for him to swing at me, but he doesn't. He reeks of alcohol. Lifting my flashlight, I find him unconscious. That's good.

We didn't fly too far away from the person. I shine the light onto them next. Immediate tears flood my eyes and run down my cheeks. A person's face isn't shaped like that. It's not natural. The dark blood pools around her blue head. It's Alex. I don't have to check her pulse to know that she's dead. No one could survive an injury like that.

A sob forces itself out of my throat.

I have to find his weapon. A quick scan of the floor with my light and I find a meat hammer. I don't want it anywhere near me, but I also don't want anyone else to use it. I grab the handle, it's a bit wet. I toss it into the water around the ship. No one will be grabbing it out of there.

I need to stop this.

Running to the next closest noise downstairs, I find a group of five people in a dog pile brawl. I can only think to yell, "Stop this! Stop fighting!" Grabbing onto someone's shoulders, I yank them off the top of the pile. I let go of them and do the same to the next person. After two are off the pile the others break themselves up.

"WHAT THE HELL IS WRONG WITH YOU? STOP FIGHTING EACH OTHER! WHY ARE YOU ATTACKING US?" I scream.

My answer is a fist coming towards my head. I easily grab his wrist and use his momentum against him to wrap his arm up the middle of his back. While he's still off balance I kick at the back of his leg so his knee buckles. From there it's easy to push him to his stomach and situate me on him to make sure he can't get up.

"Answer me. Why are you attacking us?" My voice is firm and calm. It warns of more if he doesn't listen.

"Bitch! No one said you could fight. Let me go!" He demands.

I hitch his arm up another inch. I know he's in pain without him even having to make a noise. "Answer my question!"

"Matt! OW! Tyler planned it! He said you were going to kill us all! We're just teaching you a lesson not to mess with us!" I get off of him. He can get up on his own.

"That's bullshit! He's going to get us all killed! His lesson has already gotten Alex killed. Who knows who else?" Are you kidding me?

"No one was supposed to die. I swear!" The one says.

"Then why would some of you have weapons? Alex's head was bashed in by a hammer." These guys are idiots, but I don't think they knew exactly what they were being a part of.

"I swear we didn't know. We were just fist fighting I swear. No one was supposed to get anything but bruises. We need to stop this. It's stupid." Maybe he's starting to sober up. I think he's starting to see how stupid this all is.

"Then help us stop this. Find Tyler and get him to call this off." I let my body relax a little bit.

"He was going to the theatre. That's where he thought you would be." Well, that's discomforting. He was going to take care of me and seek me out personally.

"Okay, come with me. We're going to find him and go talk with him. I'll need help." All five respond with some sort of agreeance.

I turn back. We aren't that far from the theatre. I must have just missed him.

I pick up our pace. I'm nearly jogging to get back to the stairs. There he is. A couple of people are with him. Tyler has a baseball bat and the rest are armed too. Some lesson this was.

I stop out of range of his swing. "Stop this! What were you thinking?"

"You're a pain in my ass!" He lifts his bat but doesn't swing.

Oh yes, because that's a reason to attack us. "What's the logic here, Tyler? Let's kill off a bunch of people because they are ruining your fun. What are you going to do? Order everyone to have fun or else they'll be killed? Just like Alex was just murdered. Once the alcohol runs out everyone will go after you. Stop all of this. Call everyone off!"

He doesn't want to listen anymore. I duck to avoid the bat swung at my head. He swings again. I move backwards to avoid a hit at chest level. He lunges forward and swings again. He does this a few times. I avoid the bat each time. At this rate, I think he'll tire out and I won't have to do much.

The alcohol helps me out. He trips on his own feet. The bat flies out of his hands and passes by me. I get between him and the bat.

He stands quickly and lurches for his weapon. I block him. He punches me in the stomach. It winds me, but I can't do nothing.

Uppercut, cross punch, cross punch, side kick. The mixed martial arts from my childhood comes back to me. At this point, I wish I had kept up with it.

He steps back and looks dazed. My hand stings a bit because I am still gripping the flashlight, but I bet his face hurts a lot more from it. I get into a fighting stance encase he attacks again. I look over his shoulder. The people with him and my group of five have started fighting.

In the small distraction, I am almost too late to notice that Tyler is attacking. I can't dodge this one. He knocks me to the ground. The flashlight flies out of my hand. When he goes to attack me on the ground I kick at him with both my legs. Tyler falls to the ground. I don't waste any time getting up.

Something comes at us fast in the corner of my eye. The shadow attacks Tyler. At least, this person is on our side.

I use this to grab the flashlight. Shining the light on the figure and Tyler, I see Brad punching Tyler multiple times. At least he's not too mad at us to not come to my rescue.

"Hold him still!" I tell Brad. I don't want Brad to hurt him too much. I need to stop this. "I want to make a deal." Brad finally gets Tyler into a hold. Tyler seems to calm down after he figures out that he can't move Brad; that he can't get free. "I want to make a deal. I leave your group alone and you leave my group alone. We can split the mall in half. You stay on your side and we will stay on ours. We get this half. Bourbon Street is the middle ground. You have five minutes to stop this and get to the other side of the mall. If you don't, you won't live to regret it. Brad, let him go."

I clench my hand into a fist and prepare for him to attack. He stumbles away from Brad and turns to the group standing near the stairs. They must have stopped fighting while we were busy.

"Retreat," Tyler says quietly; defeated. He finds his voice again and says, "I said retreat."

Only one person moves. I guess this means everyone else is staying. Tyler and his friend walk towards the stairs to get to the ground floor.

Brad gives the next orders. "Go find any groups fighting and tell them we have a truce. Anyone that side's with Tyler goes to the other side of the mall and those siding with Nikki go to the food court." He looks at me. "We should follow Tyler to make sure he leaves."

"Okay." No one moves an inch after Brad tells them what they need to do. They might not trust him. "You heard him. Get going." They quickly split off into two groups and start running towards any noises.

"They listen to you." He remarks before he goes after Tyler. I follow after. I don't feel the need to say anything to his comment.

As soon as Tyler reaches the bottom steps I can hear him start yelling. "RETREAT! RETREAT!" The other guy starts shouting with Tyler. They walk and yell the one word over and over. I'm not sure if it's an echo, but I swear I can hear other people shouting it too.

There isn't enough light from the flashlight to see if anyone else is moving. I keep the light trained on Tyler. Brad and I follow him towards Bourbon Street. It's not until we get to that point that we finally start seeing other people walking that way.

I stop Brad when we get to Bourbon Street. We need to respect the deal, even if this is just the start of it and no one knows yet.

Brad and I supervise the people retreating. They collect around Tyler. Too many of them have blood on them. Half of it looks like it belongs to them and other patches probably came from other people. I hope no one else died.

"Make your choice now! Choose a side, because if you cross Bourbon Street after this we will shoot first and ask questions later. You're either with me or you're with her." Tyler shouts. I don't agree with it, but I don't think that anything I could say would help. He's still drunk and is probably exaggerating. Would he kill people if they cross Bourbon Street?

Everyone that comes down the hall sides with Tyler. I can tell there aren't as many who sided with him at the pool. He probably pushed some people away with this attack.

Eventually, he walks away. Brad and I stay for a minute before we head back. "Where have you been?"

"Chapters. I'm sorry. I was-"

I interrupt him with a hug. I don't need an apology after he helped me out earlier. "Don't apologize. We're good. You just needed some time to figure things out."

We part and start walking back.

I try to not focus on the floor. There's a lot of blood on the ground in some places. I don't see any bodies, so it's a good sign. We are going to have a lot to clean up when we get more light out.

The food court is filled with light, but you can only see it once you get almost all the way inside. Everyone brought their lights with them.

People are crying and moaning in pain. When we finally get close enough to see everyone, I can see exactly how much damage was done. We were completely unprepared and they were organized. They had weapons. Almost everyone has bruises. Some have gashes. There's a lot of blood and discoloured skin.

It's a horrid sight.

I try to help anyone I can. Take stock of who is there and who is missing as I go. Tim and his parents have no physical injuries. A bit of relief goes through me. Gary only has a bit of bruising around his one eye. Kayanna and Steph are helping some people from the hotel. Shawn is talking with a small group of Gary's people. Brad is with some others.

When we come up with five missing, I tell myself that it's possible they went with Tyler, or are still hiding from what happened. I'd like to fool myself into believing that until I know for certain.

We can't let this happen again.

Chapter 33

He holds up both hands, "I am very sorry. I hadn't seen you until it was too late to stop. We have medical supplies. Let us fix you up." He turns his head back to the truck briefly to say his orders. "Taylor open up the first aid kit." He turns back to me. "Let's get you onto the truck bed." A girl runs to the cab, while Miles puts down the tailgate.

"I'm fine, really. Thank you." I say sweetly. I know they will help anyway, but I must still be humble.

"Please humour me? I feel awful." He says.

"Okay." I agree. I stumble over to the truck and jump up on the edge of the tailgate.

"Once again, I am very sorry." He apologizes again.

"It's okay; at least you didn't actually hit me. It really could have been a lot worse than it was. I'm fine but thank you. No worries." I lift my right leg on the tailgate. Miles sets to work examining my leg, and working to bandage it.

"Since we did just almost kill you, is it too much to ask your names?" A woman with pale skin, piercing blue eyes, and black hair non so tactfully requests.

"I'm Callista, but you can call me Calli." Calli introduces herself. I hiss as Miles cleans the rubble out of my leg with an alcohol swab. He places his hand over the wound. My knee itches. When he pulls his hand away I am amazed that it has disappeared.

"I'm Lucas." Lucas introduces himself.

"Hi, I'm Jaiden." I introduce myself. I look at Miles and say. "Thank you."

"I'm James. This is Miles, Taylor, Leah, Kelly, Daniel, Alexa, Brad, Shawn, and Stephanie." He motions to each person. It comes in a whirlwind, and I don't think I will remember all their names. I've never been very good at remembering names. It may be a blessing that I know some of these people already.

"James, it's an honour to meet you." Calli shakes James' hand. I'm about to dismiss it as a friendly greeting, but Calli turns around and explains why she is honoured to meet him. "This is James Ellesworn. He is the Magic Folk Representative of the Council. So, his position would be like our Prime Minister."

"I didn't know you were so important." Daniel blurts out. On one hand, this affirms the modesty of James as a person that people in his own group didn't know his status, on the other hand, it might attest to secrets within the group. Or, I could be looking for trouble where there isn't any.

"That title doesn't hold as much value as it did a month ago." James realistically states.

"Oh, I doubt that. You can't blame the humans for not knowing our hierarchy, but you've assumed a leadership role even with their ignorance." Calli says.

"I suppose that is true." He says.

"So can't you just order your people to stop the war?" Brad says. I catch the glare Shawn sends his way, though he seems oblivious.

"It's not as simple as that. First, we need to find people who are willing to stop the war. Then, we need to convince the rest to stop fighting, or they die trying. We could die trying to stop the war. It'll likely take years to stop the war." James does his best to simplify his response. I'm sure there is a lot more to it than this, but at the very basics, I suppose he is correct. Wars tend to last a while, especially if there is still someone to fight on either side.

"So, do you have a plan?" Calli asks him.

"In a way, yes. We do need all the people we can find to help us. Would you like to join us? I must warn you though; we are going to go up against the rebellion. If you join us you will probably die."

James asks.

"Stop telling people that." Kelly admonishes James.

"I don't want people to be disillusioned. If they are going to join us they need to be aware there is risk involved." I do prefer James' tactic. I wouldn't want to think I'll be safe in a bubble when they are going to ship me to the front lines.

"Where are you headed now?" Lucas asks.

"South. They took two of our people on a dragon south of here." James explains just enough, and yet it makes me curious as to what the actual plan is. Are we going on a rescue mission for two people? Why are they so important?

Calli turns to look at Lucas and me. "We are heading south either way. We should join them. If nothing more it's extra protection if we're attacked."

"No offence, but we don't know these people. How do we know they are doing the right thing?" Lucas objects to joining them. I understand the want to distrust, but Calli trusts James. Safety in numbers.

"I say we do it. If Calli trusts James, then we should too."

He stares at James for a couple of moments and says. "Okay."

"Alright then. Welcome. Everyone get back in the truck, and we'll get going." James says.

"We've got motorcycles. Jaiden and I will go grab them."

I wake up gently to a soft light.

Okay, so I guess I find Lucas at some point. There were a couple of other faces I recognized. I go to school with a few of them. I wonder what happened with Darius and Shale, because I never thought that group could ever be separated from their almost blind loyalty.

After the fiasco of grandma's house, I think I will just let things happen as they might happen.

I stretch then get up. After all my relaxing yesterday I already feel antsy. I need to do something productive. By no means do I rush to get through my mental list of things to do, but I do keep busy all day. There is always something else to do.

Most of the jobs I take on have one of two purposes; direct for my survival or preparing for leaving.

In the evening, when the sun goes down near four in the afternoon, I finally remember to take a break to eat.

I don't have much for food, but I have no problem making what I have last for days. I have enough water to last me a long while. I have heard that the average person can last approximately a month with only water. I am not in an immediate hurry to scour for food.

The dark puts a damper on my work. There is only so much you can do by flashlight, less when you are trying to conserve the light. My solar power only works so long. The energy saved up is vastly different than what could save up in the summer.

I now know this may last for years, so I need to think longer term. Maybe set up shop somewhere, and plant seeds. Food is going to become scarce.

I doubt currency still relies on metal, paper or plastic. A trade and barter system is more likely. Things like food and water will be more and more valuable as the grocery store non-perishables run out.

I can always trade my excess for other necessary items.

We'll see how things turn out. Maybe they'll turn out better than the worst things that come to mind.

I find people, while I would work for my keep, we might have an alternative survival lifestyle.

Chapter 34

Eggs and bacon reach into my dreamland and pull me out. The smell of breakfast wakes me up.

I slide open the door separating me and the bedroom from the rest of the trailer.

Rayleen sits at the table already digging into her food. Miles is filling two more plates.

"Good morning, Sunshine," I say to Rayleen.

Miles chimes into my greeting. "Sunshine? Alright, I'll take it."

"I was actually talking about this Sunshine." Taking my seat next to Rayleen, I watch her scarf down her food. "How was your sleep?"

She answers me with food still in her mouth. "Good."

Miles places the two plates of food down on the table. He goes back to the fridge and gets us all glasses of orange juice before he finally sits down. We eat a little slower than Rayleen had. She's just finishing the last of her scrambled eggs.

"How was work last night?" I ask Miles.

Miles' face falls and he puts down his fork. "Enlightening." There are too many connotations possible; I assume however that it means something horrible happened or was discovered.

Something tells me he won't continue the thought with little ears listening. I try to distract Rayleen, so I can hear more. "Rayleen, how about you put on a movie? You fell asleep while we were watching last night. How about putting that back on?"

I stand to let her out and turn on the DVD player and TV. Once she's settled, I set the remote next to her.

Getting back to my seat, I question Miles in a more hushed tone. "What happened?"

He shakes his head. "We'll get a chance to get everyone together today and make an exit plan. No one is actually allowed to leave, so we'll have to sneak out. I start work at noon, so we should get everyone gathered soon."

Looking at the clock on the stove for the time; it is 10:13. "That doesn't leave much time." We have less than two hours to get everyone together and things sorted out.

"Get ready, and I'll clean up." Miles grabs the plates, then goes over to the sink.

I go to the bedroom and change quickly. Getting ready doesn't take too long; however, it takes a few minutes to comb out all the knots in my hair. Going to bed last night with my hair still wet from my shower was not the brightest idea.

Rayleen turns off her movie to change and gets done before me.

We exit the trailer. A thin, bright white blanket of snow fell on everything while we slept. The air is not too cold yet, but we'll need warmer clothes soon.

As we enter the school, we stomp our feet to get any excess snow off them. Still, we trail wet footprints behind us.

Our first stop is atop the mezzanine. James and Taylor frequent the space, so it's the obvious choice. We enter into a group meeting in progress. James is talking with many of the people we arrived with.

We all take seats on the mat facing into the center of the circle. No one takes center stage.

"If someone says tulips, it means we've got a visitor, and you need to say your favourite flower." James sets the guidelines to be cautionary and make sure everyone is on the same page.

James stares expectantly at Miles. "We have to leave. We'll have to do it in the middle of the night."

"What if we want to stay?" Amy asks.

"Then stay, but you leave now and don't interfere." James gives fair chance for anyone to leave.

After her comment, Amy sits and shakes her head.

"Why would you want to stay? The brainwashing not creepy enough for you?" Daniel tries to make his point.

Amy brings her hands up in silent defence.

"Did anyone else hear the screams last night? A few people disappeared last night, relocated supposedly. But, I heard screams and suddenly this morning that room is locked." One of the triplets says.

My heart stops. "I saw something last night. Gren was escorting Rayleen and me to our trailer and he stopped and turned around. He had us take a different route suddenly.

I only saw it for a moment. It looked like an old movie monster werewolf. It was sniffing at the doorways and there were two officials with it; holding its leash."

"Exactly my point. The people supposedly supposed to be protecting us are feeding us to demons. That's fucked up. You sure we can't just leave right now?" Daniel starts to stand up, but Taylors grabs onto his arm and pulls him back down.

For a group that hates demons, it makes no sense to feed the demons. Why wouldn't they just kill them and get it over with?

"I'm sure they'd make us disappear too; if we tried," Taylor says in a huff.

"Get back here!" The male shout echoes through the gym.

Everyone gets up and runs to the glass railing to see the commotion. The guy, I assume did the yelling, tackles another man to the ground. Grabbing the back of his head and smashes his face into the ground. Two men from the sidelines get into the mix and start a brawl when they pull the man off the other one.

Miles heads to the stairs, but before he makes it out into view two other officials have made it to the group and have broken it up with a flash of their guns.

Miles helps them take the men away. He probably won't be returning until after his shift now.

The people below us look shaken from the events. Eventually, we turn back to go to the mats as they go back to doing what they were before.

Everyone looks to each other and finally to James for his guidance. "We leave at midnight. Leave your rooms and go out the closest entrance. We'll meet across the street from the entrance we arrived at. If you aren't there we will leave you behind. If you get lost, meet us at the mall."

"Are we allowed to bring people with us?" Amy asks James.

"No. Most here will sell you out in a heartbeat. We're not taking that chance." James hangs a silent warning over his words.

He wouldn't want to risk anything happening to the group because one person screwed something up.

"Tulips. How about we all go for lunch now? I'm so hungry." Taylor says popping up from her spot on the mat.

I look to the side and see a few people are starting to migrate up here. At least someone was paying attention.

We go down to the cafeteria and get our food. Moving tables and chairs together, so we can all eat together.

Only half of us are served and sitting down when a boisterous group comes in. They had to of come from the art room. Some of them have paint in their arms.

They look like they're going to make a mess.

I seek out a guard. The male I find is scrunching his eyebrows at the crew. He leans forward but decides to stay where he's at.

"Attention Everyone! Attention! Attention! When you arrived here you were all given coloured scarves; as were we.

The military has been grouping us based on several different factors by giving us different coloured scarves. We've decided that this shouldn't be privileged information. Everyone should know who you are." One of the teenage boys declares.

"We have the actual list from an informant military member. The actual list of colours and their meanings." The boy pulls out and unfolds a piece of paper from his pocket.

A woman grabs the sheet from his hand and starts reading it to herself. "This can't be real." She says after only a moment.

"It is. It's even got General's signature on it." He points on the sheet. "You're blue. A regular old, common person. Average. Congratulations. Who else is blue?"

No one puts up their hand. Most just look around the room waiting for the first person to do so.

He continues. "Average. The common person with a common mentality. No threat. Do we have any White scarves in this room? I see one for certain."

James pulls Rayleen closer to him.

"Innocent. Child or child-like. Any purple scarves?" Again no one raises their hands. "Purple people are Royalty. They are very important people and must be saved above all others in case of an emergency. Green?"

Two people raise their hands. One looks beaten up; newly arrived here and came straight from the infirmary. The other looks normal.

"Infirm. Sick, wounded, or pregnant. People who visit the medical station often or have any health problems. Yellows?" No one holds their hand up. "Didn't think so. Yellow is Insane. They are classified as mentally wounded people."

"Orange?" James hides his wrist, but two others put up their hands. "Whoo! You are labelled as a potential threat to all of us. Or, a potential to do great things for the community. They're kind of wishy-washy on this one, aren't they?"

"That leaves two colours and four people. Please stand up so everyone can see you. Red scarves hands up." Three out of the four left are red. They stand up on pressured looks. "Congratulations. You are Danger. You are the people most likely to fly off the handle and murder us all. The officials have been ordered to shoot you on the spot if you cause trouble."

"And that leaves you, Black. Come here." The girl looks terrified. She gets pushed to the front. "Scum. You are a suspected demon. They have reason to believe, but not enough proof that you are a demon faking being a human. Without the evidence the military allowed you to live with us humans."

He spits at her; hitting her leg. "You are the scum of the earth. The reason we're all here and our loved ones are dead."

If I could see her face I'm sure there would be tears rolling down her cheek. The humiliation this is to her must be unbearable. Whether she is a supernatural being or not this is not how she should be treated.

A bowl flies through the air and hits her back. Soup splatters everywhere; her hair, her arms and her clothes. The glass breaks on the impact.

James can't take any more. "Stop, this is enough. What if she's human and this is all a mistake. It said a potential demon, not for certain a demon; or else she'd have been detained by now!"

"Whatever. It's not our problem. Do with the information what you will; we've got information to spread." They leave.

James grabs the girl's hand and pulls her out of the room. I gather Rayleen and follow after him.

A cup of soup flies past my head and into the glass display case. The glass shatters and falls to the floor. Lifting Rayleen we run from the room.

I look behind me to make sure no one is following us with any more projectiles.

James leads her to the women's washroom. "Get yourself cleaned up. Alexa, go with her. I'll stay here and make sure no one goes inside." He holds the door open long enough for us to go through.

We get inside the washroom and I let Rayleen down at the entrance. The girl stops and stares at her image in the mirror.

"What's your name?" I ask quietly.

Automatically she states in a soft voice, "Leah."

I take a good look at the girl. Her blue eyes stand out against her white skin and black hair.

"I'm Alexa. Are you going to be okay?" She doesn't answer. "So, what are you?" The question bursts her control. Her eyes darken to black and she's in front of me in a split second. "You're a vampire."

"Yeah. And, I'm hungry." Her voice strengthens in sharp contrast to how she was speaking earlier. A sweet act, versus the danger she can be.

I involuntary sigh. "Are you going to eat me? Or are you going to let me tell you about us escaping tonight?"

She backs up about an inch and stops her threatening act. "You've got my attention. Go."

"You should get yourself cleaned up while I tell you."

"If I do, you could try to escape and tell everyone." Leah closes the inch of space she gave me.

I raise my eyebrow. "I'm not going to tell your secret. If I did I'd have to tell everyone that Miles is an elf, and James is the head of all magic folk out, and the triplets are… well I'm not actually sure what they are. Rayleen here has some magic blood in her too. So, I'd have to tell on all my friends and my family here, if I tell on you."

"James Ellesworn? I thought he looked familiar. Okay, I believe you. Now tell me about how I'm getting away from this place." Leah pulls off her sweater. The cloth of her tank top underneath doesn't look like it was touched by any soup.

"We're leaving tonight. Middle of the night. What room are you in?" I ask her.

"Same as the triplets." It didn't answer my question about the room number but it works just as well.

"That's good, then just leave when they do. We're meeting across the street, then going to mall. You're welcome to join that too." I say.

Leah turns away and goes into the bathroom stall. She comes back out with a roll of toilet paper. Getting it damp, she starts wiping off some of the soup. She gives up on dabbing delicately.

"Sounds like a plan." Leah pulls out a small bottle of lotion from her pants pocket. She applies it to the areas of skin that she had to wipe clean.

"Can I have some?" Rayleen asks Leah. I had almost forgotten she was there.

"Sorry, sweetie. This isn't regular lotion. It's specially made for vampires so we can go out in sun without spontaneously combusting." She turns around to put some more on before turning back to Rayleen. "Umm. Bursting into flames."

"Is that how you do it?" As soon as I ask the question I remember the conversation Shale and I had, but it is too late to take back the words.

"Yeah, you'd be amazed at the amount of product out there for the different supernaturals to help them blend in with humans or just outright counteract their weaknesses. The beauty of technological advances." Leah finishes up with her lotion and puts it back in her pocket.

"I think I've seen a few things before. I dated a vampire for a bit." I tell her.

Leah appears intrigued. "Not anymore? What happened?"

Thinking about it for a moment, I try to think of a way to say it nicely. "The revolution. He leads this region and is now dating an ancient priestess and threw me down in a basement to be eaten by the hobgoblins they kept there."

I can't help but sound scorned.

"Oh? Good choice in dumping him. He sounds like a loser." Leah goes to the mirror again. She looks herself over before her eyes jump to me. "Wait, you wouldn't be talking about Darius, would you? Really? You were the human pet? Hm. Well, it's nice to meet you." Her spirits have lifted a lot since the lunchroom.

She spins abruptly. "Can I have some of your blood? I just need a little to get rid of my eyes and I'm kind of holding in a blood rage right now; feeling weak. I don't think I can wait till nighttime before I would-" She looks at Rayleen and changes the words she was going to say. "freak out." I just look at her. I don't know quite how to respond to the request. It's not like anyone has ever asked me that before. "No way. Darius never drank from you?"

The way she can read me is a bit spooky. "Can vampires read minds?"

She chuckles at my question. "No, we can't. Don't worry your mind is safe from me. Your face gives you off. It's okay, like I said I just need a little. If I go out looking like this they'll catch me for sure."

"How do we do this? My neck?" I feel like hitting myself from how dumb that sounded.

"No." Leah rolls her eyes. "Have you ever tried to bite someone's neck? It's not that easy and you're probably going to kill the person that way. There are too many veins, arteries and points in the neck that if you hit them, the person's a goner. Besides that biting a neck is unnecessarily messy.

So, unless we're actually trying to kill the person we don't bite necks. Hold out your arm please." I do as she says.

She takes her nail and cuts a small line on my arm; barely stings. Her mouth covers the cut and I feel slight sucking. Before long she's done and steps away. Her eyes are now a darker shade of her blue, but it is a far cry from the pure black.

"Thanks." Leah leads the way out of the washroom. I feel the need to inform James that Leah is coming with us tonight. Knowing that I can't just say it encase someone overhears I work out a way to say it on our walk back to the lunchroom. "Leah's going to hang out with us now. Did you know she's in the same room as the triplets?"

James catches on quickly. I get a raised eyebrow, probably because not too long ago he was telling us not to tell anyone. "I did not know this. It'll be nice to get to know you, Leah."

"Same. You know I thought I recognized you before but I didn't connect it until Alexa said your name. We haven't met before, but I've gone to a few conferences you've spoken at over the years." Leah speaks naturally in the code. She's had to practice.

James joins in with the same ease. Suddenly, I have a feeling that he is okay with me telling Leah. "Did you enjoy them?"

"I've always found them a bit stuffy. The last one was nuts." Leah swirls her finger by her head. "I watched it online. I bet it was crazy in person. I think you left at a good time. The mood shifted fast."

"Yes, it was quite crazy." James agrees with her. He moves a table closer to the one the rest are sitting at.

We just sit down at the make-shift large table when the room goes quiet. I turn around to where the gazes of everyone else are directed.

I feel it in my gut, we shouldn't have come back.

Six male teens stand in a group behind us; two reds, one orange, and three blues.

"You're not welcome here." The orange states. He must be the ring leader and the rest of the men must be his backup.

"We're not bothering you. We're just sitting and eating our lunch. Same as the rest of you. Please do not make this into a scene. She looks like a human, acts like a human; she must be a human." James says. "No one wants a witch hunt."

Growling and screams echo down the hall and interrupt everyone's attention.

The beast from last night leaps onto a girl it had been chasing. Effectively knocking her to the ground before it takes a bite out of her.

It stops and sniffs the air for another target. Immediately, it goes after one of the people in blue that is still sitting in their seat on the other side of the lunchroom.

Two people are dead in a matter of seconds. People spring into action after the shock subsides.

I get out of my chair, and panic for the half-second I've lost Rayleen. But, she is already safe in James' arms.

It sniffs the air again.

This time it focuses on me. It walks for a few steps before lunging to me. Leah's powerful grip yanks me out of the way.

The creature yelps.

Miles stands where the creature should have been while it lays a few feet away. It gets back on four paws and goes after its new target. Miles knocks it to the side again reminding me a little of a matador and a bull. He moves unnaturally fast.

Blood starts falling on the path the creature runs. Miles appears unharmed, so it must be the beast's own blood. They play their little game a couple more rounds.

On the next passing, the creature gargles and shakes when he hits the ground. It then lies still. Dead.

Miles looks at me apologetically, then behind him. He raises his hands. A bunch of the officials have guns pointed at him.

"Keep your hands in the air! No fast movements! You are under arrest for treason!" Officer Gren shouts every word.

Two of them break off from the group and point their guns at Rayleen and me.

"They had no idea about what I am. I lied to them. Rayleen is not my child. She's human. Please don't hurt them. They had no idea." Miles pleads.

Leah places herself in front of me as a shield and James does the same for Rayleen.

"What the hell are you all doing? He saved us all. That thing would have eaten us and you're going to thank him by killing him." Leah's voice has gotten deeper, stronger; almost darker.

Rayleen screams. Orange has a hold of her and is trying to pull her from James. Leah runs and grabs a hold of the guy's arm and simultaneously I hear a snap. He lets go of Rayleen and falls. The bang of the gun is joined by his scream. Leah looks from the official to the bullet hole in her arm.

"Ow! You shot me. There is a child a foot away from me and you shot me!" Her hand reaches out in a blur. Leah grabs the gun away and shoots all of the officials before they have a chance to react. "We're leaving now."

James secures Rayleen in his arms. I want to grab her, but she's probably safer with him.

Leah grabs a knife off the belt of an officer and leads us out of the building. She creates a fair distance between us to clear the way. Any officials that try to stop us are cut down with a signature cut to their neck.

There is no resistance once we get outside. There are officers, but they don't try anything to stop us.

One truck fits all of us. They left the keys in it. We load into the back while Rayleen, James, and Leah get the cab. I notice we are missing the boy I never learned the name of and the triplets. I look back to the doors, but they don't appear. We'll have to leave them behind.

Once all settled Miles knocks on the roof of the cab and James starts driving.

Chapter 35

I feel like I should be walking around with a clipboard and writing all of this down.

We have people on guard on both the upper and lower levels. They are trying to get some sort of barrier up. We've got people moving all food and drinks to the food court. People are deciding on the new home because we decided it was safer to have us together. We're starting a fight training thing every day. We've got people working on first aid kits, weapons and survival.

Everything is starting to piece together. People's wounds are healing and more people can help out today.

"Nikki! Kelly's here!" I can hear Gary shout, but I can't see him. I walk towards where his voice came from. Why is she back so soon? "Up here." Oh. He must have seen me looking around for him. I still don't see him though.

I go up to the second level. He's waiting up at the top of the stairs for me. He doesn't look too worried.

I turn the corner and see Kelly with two people. Miles isn't with her. They look beat up. "This is Nia and Ethan. We need refuge, please. The house was attacked. We'll all need somewhere to go."

"Of course." What else can I say? We already told them we would help. They need somewhere to go, but they might change their mind after they find out what happened with Tyler's group. "Is this everyone?"

"No. We lost about half in the attack. Everyone else will be here over the next day. Why is there blood everywhere? Were you attacked?" I guess there isn't any hiding it from her.

"The group split off permanently. Tyler's group attacked us. We've split the mall in half. Stay on this side of Bourbon Street and you'll be fine." It's sort of what happened. I don't want to give her too many details. They might leave. We could use them. They have bags. I didn't notice them until now. Each person is carrying a bag. "What's in the bags?" I try to change the subject.

"They're for you. We packed a bunch of supplies into each bag as an offering." Nia says.

"Thank you. Let's go put them downstairs in the food court." I lead the way. We go to the food court. A pile is already growing with food. "You can put the bags here. We will grab things when we need them." They do as I say. There is an awkward moment as we just look at each other. What to do next? I was on my way to check on the first aid station under the stage. "I have some work to do. If you want to come with me you can, or you can do your own thing. Just stay on this side of Bourbon Street."

"I'll come with you," Kelly says.

Nia and Ethan look at each other. Nia speaks up. "We'll find something else to do."

It's settled. "We'll see you later then." I look at Kelly. "Let's go."

Kelly and I walk towards the stage. Gary follows behind us until we go past the stairs to upstairs. He goes up them.

We continue to the stage and go down the celebrity entrance/exit stairs. I open the door and enter the room. Shawn and Steph are working on prepping the room for any emergencies. The first aid kits have been raided from every store we have access to. Flashlights light up the room.

"Shawn and Stephanie, you remember Kelly?" I introduce them. I don't remember which introductions have been done yet. "The wizard's house was attacked so they're all headed over here." I feel like a little explanation is needed.

"Hi, nice to see you again." Shawn stands up from his spot. He walks over to Kelly and shakes her hand. Steph catches Kelly's eye and waves at her.

"What were you able to find?" I ask Shawn.

He looks behind him at the boxed kits. "Not much. Most of the kits have some bandaids, gauze and maybe some alcohol wet wipes. We don't have much for large wounds and barely anything for sterilization and cleansing. Especially, after bandaging everyone up, so-" He trails off and looks at Steph for help.

"What did you do?" I look at both Shawn and Steph.

"Sent Kayanna to the dollar store to go get some things," Steph says a bit guilty.

I fume. "What? When did she leave? Is it too late to catch her? Are you guys stupid? If they catch her they'll kill her." We need to hurry, find her and get her back on our side.

"We're not too stupid." Shawn grinds a stupid grin. He's joking about it.

"Exactly, what happened here?" Kelly asks me.

We ignore her as Shawn continues. "She went through the back ways. There's a very small chance anyone would see her, let alone catch her. There is no point in going after her because we would be more likely to get ourselves caught in the process. We'll just wait for her to get back and that will be the last time anyone crosses into their territory."

"Great, now that's settled. What exactly happened here?" Kelly makes sure she has my attention by pushing a bit on my shoulder.

I take in a deep breath to calm myself down. This isn't really settled, but there isn't much point in going after her. She knows the backs and we don't. "Matt hates demons and just wants to party it up until the world ends. He gathered his group together and attacked us last night. I guess he decided it was his way or no way. A couple of people died. We called a truce and divided the mall in half. No one crosses over Bourbon Street or they risk Tyler's group killing them."

"Alright." She pauses for a moment. "I guess it's better than nothing. Everyone's on their way already. Then, we'll have strength in numbers."

I wait anxiously. Busying myself, I organize the already organized items in the room. Kelly watches bored. No one knows what to say to each other, so we don't say anything.

As soon as I hear a squeaky cart heading towards us, I run up the stairs. Kayanna looks scared when she sees me come out of the rabbit hole.

"No one saw me or heard me I swear." She says a bit fast.

"You're back safe. That's what matters. And, you're not going back there again. That was dangerous and stupid." I scold her.

She bows her head. "I know, but I got a bunch of good stuff."

I walk closer to the cart. She piled a lot of boxes onto the cart. There are crates of drinks and baskets full of items stacked on top of each other.

I grab one of the baskets on top and take it down the stairs.

With all of us helping it doesn't take long to empty the trolley. I can admit she did get a lot of crucial items. The trip may have been worth the risk and it might be worth the risk in the future.

The room is smaller now.

The three of them have a lot more to do, so I leave them to it. Kelly follows me up top. I start heading towards Chapters.

"How dangerous would it be for the rest of our group to come through one of the doors on the other side of the mall?" Kelly asks. I stop and turn to her.

I didn't think of that. "Potentially deadly. Tyler might kill first, ask questions later. They have close-range weapons. I don't think they have guns. Humans. But, if you have anyone faster or stronger. Or, better weapons."

"Right. I'll monitor things from the outside. Try to intercept." Kelly says. It's not a bad idea.

"Do you want any company?" I ask.

She scowls a little. "Not unless they can keep up."

I take that as a no. "I will see you in a bit then." I wave goodbye but she doesn't see it. She runs fast. It only takes a couple of seconds for her to get out of my sight.

I walk into Chapters. Brad is playing cards in the back with a couple of people. I go into the staff room and close the door. Opening up my purse, I pull out my notebook and a pen. I sit down at the table.

I grab the flashlight off the table and shine it over my yellow notebook. Flipping through the pages I get to the last entry and look at the next blank page.

What do I write about? How do I describe what I'm feeling?

How do I put into words the chaos that is my life now? How do I say that people are dying, buildings are burning and nothing will ever be the same?

My family is lost to me. I can only hope they are out there.

My eyes well up with tears. They fall down my cheeks; streaming down my chin and falling to my lap. I let go.

I want everything back to normal. I want my mom and dad to wake me up after this nightmare and make it better with a pie for breakfast.

God forbid, I actually want to go to my crappy-ass job.

They say you never know what you have until it's gone, but you also would do anything to get it back. I had an awesome life before all of this; great friends, amazing parents, an okay job for now and a future. Now people are killing each other over nothing, it's going to be a struggle for food and shelter and I'm probably going to be dead soon. I'm never going to see my family ever again.

The trail of thought is making my breakdown worse. I don't have any tissues. I shine the flashlight around the room and I don't see anything I can use. I wipe my nose on the inside of my sleeve.

I need to think positively. I can't think like this. It's not going to help anything.

There is no proof that my family is dead. They are out there somewhere and I will find them when this war ends. The war will end. Things might be tough at some points along the road, but I will get through them. I will live through this; I will survive.

I wipe the tears away from my face.

I don't know how much time has passed, but I should get out of here. I leave my notebook on the table, take a deep breath and leave the room.

Brad is still playing cards, so I decide to join them. Quickly, I pick up that they are playing poker. Great! I'm awesome at poker.

I get in on the next round. It doesn't take long before I'm cleaning up.

Kelly scares me when she comes in. I was so focused on the game that I didn't hear her or the other people with her.

I get up and introduce myself. "Hi, I'm Nikki."

"Nice to meet you. I'm Ashlynn." I shake the lady's hand. She goes into the light and I freeze; she is incredibly beautiful. I stare for a moment. I've never seen anyone like her. I wonder what kind of demon she is. She's very tall, even at my taller height, she is taller than me. Her eyes swirl in brown and green.

She points to the people still in the shadows. "This is Spencer and Gio. Thank you for taking us in." Ashlynn holds up a bag of goods. I see that the other two have bags in each hand.

I try not to stare, and quickly look back to Ashlynn. The one man has only eye in the middle. What kinds of supernaturals are they bringing with them? How many are real?

Chapter 36

Someone's in my room.

I can almost feel them leaning over me.

How did they get so close without me waking up?

I resist screaming and jumping. Maybe they'll leave me alone if they don't know I've woken up; probably not.

Where is my knife?

My heart races when the person leans closer to me. Hot metallic breath warms my face. The person breathes in my face three times.

Wet lips touch mine.

My eyes fly open. I panic and throw my hands out against the woman's chest. She screams from shock as she falls back, and to the floor.

I quickly find the knife and jump out of my blankets. "Stay where you are!" I muster up the sternest tone I can. I grab the flashlight and shine it at her.

I know her. I've seen her in a couple of dreams. Calli, I think I remember is her name. My gut twists from the iron taste drifting in from my lips.

What do I do? She seemed like a friend in my dreams, but she was just, I don't know exactly what she was doing. She was kissing me. Why was she kissing me?

My head feels light. I think I'm going to pass out, but I hold my stance until the faint feeling passes.

"What were you doing?" My voice squeaks at the beginning.

Get it together.

"What are you?" She slowly draws her sleeve across her chin.

What a strange question to ask. "Human. Why did you kiss me?"

"You can't be completely human." She taps her head. "I started the process; you shouldn't have broken the paralysis."

Not completely human. Could she be talking about my visions? Am I not human? "What were you doing to me?"

"Kissing you."

"Calli." I shouldn't have said her name; I know as soon as I say it. She hasn't told me yet. Not missing a beat I continue my questioning. "Why were you kissing me?"

"You're a prophet. Well, shit that could have been dangerous for both of us. How strong are your visions? What kind are you?" She jumps up from her spot on the floor. She no longer looks frightened. Should I take her actions to mean I shouldn't be concerned about her? "Here touch me." She offers up her hand.

"I'm not-"

She cuts me off. "It's the only explanation that makes sense. You already know me. Only my friends call me Calli." She moves slowly towards my dresser before she hops up to sit on it. "So, it's rude that I don't know your name."

"Jaiden." I put the knife down to my side, but keep ready. "So, you want to explain to me why you kissed me, and why whatever it was you were doing didn't work?"

She points to her bottom lip. "You have some blood there." I push down a gag. The iron taste leaching into my mouth is unsettling. I think the danger is over so I set the flashlight down facing up, and wipe my mouth.

She shrugs her shoulders. "I don't know how much you know. I'm having this conversation for the first time."

"So am I."

"Well, I'm Callista, Calli to my friends. I'm a succubus, and I was trying to eat some of your soul. My breath should have kept you sleeping, so I could loosen up your soul and take some for food. I was only going to take a couple of years off your life and leave the rest for you, but someone decided to have a mental power that could have killed us both if you hadn't woken up."

"So, because I have visions, that would have killed us?" There isn't much point in trying to fool her anymore.

Calli pauses to scrutinize. "Don't they teach you anything anymore? What family do you belong to?"

"I don't know what the last name was. My mom didn't seem psychic, and she died when I was a kid; never mentioned anything, and, I've only met my birth dad a few times.

He asked if I kept a dream journal once, so maybe that's what he was getting at. But, I never thought to ask what his last name was. I've kind of had to figure this dream vision thing out on my own.

I just kept having dreams that would then end up happening. But, sometimes they also don't happen.

You're the second person I've ever told about it. My dad threatened to send me to a mental institution before I rescinded, told him I was joking and asked him as a social experiment." I lay it all out. Maybe she can make sense of it all. She seems to know much more than I do. And, if we end up friends, then you're supposed to share these sorts of things.

She hops off the dresser. "Ouch, I'm sorry. Can I hug you? Is that weird?" I'm hesitant to let her hug me because, I don't do hugs, and, I've just met her.

She could still try to kill me; you never know what can happen when you change things. My hesitation is exactly the moment she needs to hug me whether I agree to it or not. I close my arms around her and awkwardly pat her back. She lets go after what seems like an awkwardly, inappropriate long time.

"You didn't answer my question." I set her back on track.

"Yes." She pauses. "What was the question again?"

"Why would it have killed us?"

"Right, well I attach to your third eye, and suck your soul out. But, because you're a prophet, especially a dreamer, your head works differently. You have natural defences that stop anyone from getting into your head, into your dreams, and into your soul. If I had attached myself to your third eye, your defences would have seen it as an attack and would have fiercely defended you. It could mean instant death for me. Might've killed you as well, sometimes the defences work too well. So, where are we supposed to go from here?"

That explains a little. I guess it's helpful to know that people can't get into my head. It's a little disheartening to know that an attempt means I could die too.

Does that mean she could just kiss someone and steal their soul whenever she wants? Would they even know their soul is being stolen?

"I don't know. At some point, we meet up with a group led by James Ellesworn, but I don't know how far away that is." I stop myself from revealing anything else. "It might be better if you forget that. If we try to do it when we aren't supposed to then it won't happen, and other things may not happen as I've seen them. Uh, so, yeah, maybe, just, do what we would have done normally. Without any knowledge of what should happen."

"Loot your house for some essentials, and go onto the next place. Once done we would go back to Safeway for the night. Got it." I unveil my bag to her. She chuckles a little. "So, if you didn't see this happen, how do you know if it didn't happen exactly the way it is now?"

She has a good point. "I don't know. I have no idea how this works, but I do know that a few things in my life have gone differently just because I knew something is supposed to happen. Whether I consciously decided to change events or not." I gather a few extra belongings. "It could be something like a test. I see a vision about me marking a multiple-choice science test, so I know what questions are going to be on the test and the answers. So, without even studying, I get a better mark on the test than what I did originally."

"Cheater!" She accuses rightly. We go up the stairs.

"I can't help it. I don't choose what I have visions of." It's a sad excuse of reality, but it's the only thing I've got. "I have a car full of things. I can follow you to Safeway."

"Sure. I just have to get a couple of things from next door and we can be on our way." I don't think anything of it until she goes towards Lucas' place.

Things click together. "Is Lucas at Safeway?"

"Yes. Oh my god! Did you just see something?" She's too excited, and it's weird.

"Not now. My visions only happen in my dreams. That dream I said where we meet up with a group, Lucas was there too. It was you, me, and him meeting up with a group on the road." We walk into Lucas' house. "His watch display is in his room. This way." I lead the way to his bedroom. It doesn't take me long to find the display in the dark. I grab the top watch. "Did he say which one he wanted?"

"Top shelf. He said stuff, but mostly I caught that it was his most expensive one. So you're a dreamer, eh? That's kind of rare." She says.

"Yeah? I didn't know that. Um, yeah, when he talks about his watch stuff it all sounds like gibberish to me too." I completely get it. We walk out of the room. "Did he say he wanted anything else?"

"Nope, just the watch, and a thing from the black car."

"That's not going to happen." She turns around and looks at me for further answers. "I stole that one a few days ago, and it didn't make it back home."

"Did you crash it?" She smiles big.

"No. It's nearly out of gas and near Alberta Beach."

She walks us both out the front door. My car is in the driveway, while hers is in front of Lucas' house.

"I'll follow you." I press the lock button to make the lights flash. We walk to our cars.

I unlock the doors and throw the bag into the back seat. I get in and back up. Calli waits for me to right my car, before driving away.

Safeway is on the edge of town. It's in the same parking lot as the Canadian Tire in my dreams. I shudder at the memory. Hopefully, it was just a dream, either way, I'm not going in there.

I rebel against the law and park in the handicapped parking spot. I get out. "Should I bring my bag in? I mean, I don't think we'll be staying here very long. We'll need supplies, and I'd rather not lose everything here."

"You think something happens here? Like a fight or something?"

"I don't know what happens. I mean, I know we meet up with that group when there is snow on the ground, but the road is still pretty clean. But, I didn't recognize anything around us, so I think we were in a different town, and, we're with that group in Banff too, but there was snow everywhere at that point."

"I'll bring in what I found. You bring Lucas' watch and leave everything else in here. I'll take the keys." I toss over the keys. I leave the car and wait for Calli to catch up on my side of the car. She leads me to the front doors. We immediately get inside. That's a security issue. I try to open up the second set of doors, but it's locked. Well, I guess that works well enough.

Calli knocks on the door five times. I back away to, sort of, hide behind her a little. Harry, a friend that graduated last year, comes to the door. I guess I don't have to worry about it being someone I don't know.

"Jaiden!" He says after he unlocks and opens the door.

"Harry!" I echo his tone.

"Sweetie, I go by Carrie now." He, I guess, she says. The cross-dressing had been a semi-normal thing for Harry. I had known Harry as this flamboyant gay guy that was in grade twelve when I was in grade ten. We took a CALM class together, and he was in my group for one of the projects. He graduated last year, and we had lost touch. I don't know if this transgender change happened before the end of the world, or after, but either way good for her.

"Carrie!" I repeat in the same tone.

She passes Calli and gives me a big hug. "Sweetheart, I was so worried about you. Where have you been?"

"Carrie, let's get inside." Calli interrupts. We pass through the inner doors.

I see we have attracted a small crowd.

"Who's she?" A stern voice says.

"This is my girlfriend, Jaiden. You don't have to worry about her. She's harmless, and the smartest person I have ever met." She puts her arm in mine and pulls me to the other side of the store. "How have you been? Where have you been hiding? Did you have any trouble?"

I look behind me. Calli is talking with a few people at the door; Lucas is there now. I trust Carrie, but I didn't want to break away from Calli. I hope both of them will find me later.

The key being, Carrie wasn't with us in my visions. I haven't seen her at all. This means, that she isn't a large part of my future. Whatever that ends up meaning.

Calli and Lucas have been in multiple dreams, spanning some timeline points throughout winter. My focus needs to be on them. I need to stay with them. I need to make sure that happens.

If it doesn't, it's likely I'd be working off of an unknown timeline.

"I've been good. Reading mostly. It's been, what two weeks since the attack? I've spent most of that in my house. I tried to go to my grandma's house, but that didn't work so well."

"And, your father?" The word father is said with disgust.

"I haven't seen him since before the attack."

"Good." She smiles and shakes her head. She never did like my dad. Due to his homophobia and an impromptu visit to work on homework, she saw the side of him that he doesn't normally show the public.

Mentally, I gasp. What would he think of her now? Would I get another conversation about making sure I don't let her turn me gay? But now it'll be, make sure she doesn't turn me trans.

Doesn't matter now, does it? He's probably dead.

"Have you been here the whole time?" I ask.

"Yes, most of us have been. Anyone that was in the store shopping at the time just shut the doors, turned the lights off, and stayed here. We've ventured out a few times, but it seemed safer this way." She leads me to the other entrance, and into the employee-only stairs.

We go up, and into the staff breakroom. There are a few more people here. "Hey, I want you all to meet my girl, Jaiden."

"Hi." I give a short wave. I don't want to do the awkward introductions, but I guess it's necessary.

"Said."

"Fatima."

"Jackson."

"Alice."

"Jose."

"And this is my boyfriend, Marc." Carrie introduces him. I shake his hand because he put his own out.

"Hi," I say a bit meekly.

"Hey. So, how long have you known Carrie?" He tries to make conversation with me.

Marc motions to the couch he had just been sitting on. Carrie and he settle cuddled together. I sit on the other side of the couch, to give them their space.

"A year, about. We met in CALM class last year. We were in a group together to do a project on life after high school." I explain.

"Is life what you imagined it would be after high school?" He questions further.

"Actually, I'm still in high school. But, no this was not part of the project." I say.

"That project was awful." Carrie scowls.

"How so?" Marc asks.

I answer. "It was like, you graduate high school so now what? So, we were given a package of tasks that we had to complete. It was broken down into the first year, and up to five years.

So like the first year, you had to buy a car, go off to college, and move out of your parent's house, and, for some dumb reason go on a vacation when you were already in so much debt from all that, and you had to go somewhere out of the country, and, we had to find real-life examples of things, and saying we already own this or my parents are giving it to me, or garage sale item or I'll do without was not an option.

So, like we had to find a car online, and grab the pricing details from that. Find an apartment for rent, and clip the article for that. Get the pricing for the courses you would take in school. Pick out the dining table you want. On and on.

So basically, despite the project trying to be realistic it ended up being a project about how much debt can you accumulate. I ended up forty thousand in debt in my first year, and three hundred thousand in debt by year five. I was one of the cheapest ones too. There were a few people who hit a million dollars."

"At least it was giving perspective to some people." He says.

I can see his point. "No, because if high school students need that much perspective, they have bigger problems."

"Jaiden, where is my car?" Lucas booms into the room, and heads straight for me.

"Hey, Lucas. How are you?" I evade his question. "I have your watch." I hand him the watch. He immediately puts it on his wrist.

"Where's my car?" He asks again.

"I had to take it. People broke into the house, so I had to escape, and took it to my grandma's house. There were people there, and they took the keys. The neighbours gave me a different car to take home, cause I'm pretty sure yours caught on fire or had a few bullet holes or something. But, it was pretty much out of gas anyway. I don't know how I would have gotten it back here."

He looks angry? Stunned? Shocked? I can't read him. "Say that again."

"I took it a few days ago. People broke into my house, so I had to get away. I took it to my grandma's house, but when I got there there were a bunch of strangers there. They took the keys because they didn't trust me. I helped the neighbours attack the house to free some hostages. There were bullets exchanged, and someone set the house on fire. The neighbours gave me a different car to take home." I have everyone's attention now. They stare.

"Are you okay?" He finally says.

"Yes. I'm fine." I smile to let him know I'm okay. My explanation takes the wind out of his sails. He sits down in a huff.

Chapter 37

A couple of houses away, it becomes obvious that the house is not in the condition we left it in. My stomach sinks with dread. We should have gone straight to the mall as we had planned. James, instead, decided we needed this detour.

I'd tell him it's not too late to turn around, but he's inside the cab. And, I don't think he'd listen to me anyway.

All of the remaining windows have been broken and the door is left wide open. Spray painted on the front of the house is a written warning; 'Humans Will Rise Again, Death To All Demons'.

We stop right out in front of the house and unload ourselves. No one speaks. I assume this is out of respect for James, as we enter his trashed house. Everything is thrown out of place and some things are torn apart or smashed.

All the supplies we had in the dining room are gone, probably taken by the military.

The upstairs isn't completely trashed. There are rocks and glass in the places they had landed when the windows were broken and snow has landed inside the house. Otherwise, it doesn't look like they had done anything up here.

I hear a horrified, "Oh my god!" It comes from the basement.

Miles and I hurry down. Four bodies lay in one giant pool of blood in the middle of the room. The people that had been injured were killed by multiple gunshots; a gruesome overkilling.

Before Rayleen can make it down the stairs enough to see anything,

I cover her eyes. "Back upstairs, now."

Something explodes upstairs, and part of the ceiling collapses at the far end of the room. Books from the dining room library, on fire, fall from the floor above.

James opens the tunnel up to the tree. I hear someone yell, "RUN," but I am already moving. Another explosion and the air rushes past me. I'm thrown onto the ground in the tunnel as it closes up behind me. I catch myself on my knees and elbows. Rayleen cradled under the cage my body makes.

Soft light creates a dim glow. James has a fireball in his hand to help us see.

Miles picks himself off the ground next to me. I look back. The entrance to the tunnel is covered.

Miles helps me off the ground. Together we're able to pull Rayleen and me up without detaching her. My hands are bleeding and have rocks lodged in my cuts, but there's no time to fix it. He leads me to the tree roots.

The nymph looks frightened this time, and her movements are rushed. Not two seconds after she picks us up, Miles and I run through the wall and come out into the familiar forest. Everyone has gotten through without a scratch except for me.

"What the hell just happened? Who the fuck attacked us?" Amy yells out for some sort of answer.

"Language," James reminds her of Rayleen's presence.

"After everything, we've gone through and you're worried about the kid hearing swear words. Really, James? Prioritize. Your house just got blown up and we almost went with it." Amy shouts.

"So, you just answered your first question and as for the second question, it's obvious who blew up the house." Daniel states.

Amy doesn't hesitate with an answer. "Demons?"

"Yes, because instead of getting a lunch out of us they're going to make explosives and toss them into the house while they stand by watching the fireworks." Daniel's sarcasm just looks like it angers Amy.

"The military? They came after us." Taylor puts together the pieces of the puzzle; a little faster than Amy does.

Amy looks like she is about to say something, but Leah beats her to it. "Not to put a damper on your conversation or anything but can we continue this elsewhere, specifically out of the sun? I'm starting to get a little hot here."

"Of course. How much sunscreen do you have left?" James looks a bit worried.

Leah pulls out her sunscreen and checks the level in the tube. "Maybe a couple of days' worth. But, I didn't put too much on in the bathroom because the plan had been to leave in the middle of the night. No sun then."

"It's not much further then we'll be inside the mountain. Think you can make it without lighting up?" James starts us walking towards the cabin. She nods.

I put Rayleen down so she can walk on her own, and so I can pick the stones out on my hands. A burning sting is left behind by each pebble.

We make it to the house and go down the door in the floor. Leah goes first by jumping down. Miles jumps down with Rayleen, but the rest of us use the ladder.

Our welcome is non-existent. No dwarves come to even acknowledge our existence. Something must have happened. By this point last time we already had a fully armed crew threatening and escorting us further inside the mountain.

"You know, maybe, I should have stayed in the house. The dwarves will not like that you brought a vampire with you. It breaks our treaty." Leah sounds like she might be a bit nervous.

"Times are different. As long as you behave, I don't think it's going to matter." James leads us through the tunnels. He lights up a glowing ball in his hand so we can see better. I just follow the light.

We walk for a while, down the winding tunnels without another word.

Leah pushes open the doors enough for one person to filter through. The yelling starts as soon as she steps through. The sleeping city awakes with shouts of "Intruders!"

We all slip through the doors. They all rush around us like last time, their weapons pointed at us. King Zircon comes over to us.

"Lower your weapons. James, your presence here last time brought on an attack. We delivered your materials as requested. Why are you back now?" King Zircon's tone hints at the trouble we have caused and probably will cause by having us here.

I look around at the dwarves surrounding us. Some do appear to have been moderately injured and most have bandages on them.

"I'm sorry you were attacked, but it was a coincidence. I hope that with that you see that you can't be neutral in this. They will attack for no reason. And, now humans are hunting us too. We need to take action to stop this rebellion. We will be attacking the same side as the ones who attacked you." James tries to convince the King to join us; to help us fully.

King Zircon thinks it over for only a moment before he nods to James. "We will help you kill them like they killed our queen."

"Thank you and we are sorry for your loss." James looks around him at all the dwarves.

"You all look worn. Your clan will be taken care of while we speak privately. The members of our last meeting will accompany us, yes?" The dwarf King doesn't wait for an answer. He turns around and starts walking back to his home. I assume two things: that Rayleen and I should follow after him and that he doesn't trust the others in his home.

Rayleen, James and I follow King Zircon through his doorway. A stench of perfume wafts through his place. On a stone table lays the queen's corpse. Her body is decorated for a funeral; dried flowers circle the body. Precious stones are placed on top of her, crystals, and diamonds of all different colours and sizes; pinks, yellows, clear, metallic, rainbow, purples, browns and greens. The perfume seems to be coming from burning oils placed in the dried flowers. There is a picture in her arms of a small child.

"One of the differences between our cultures is how we handle our deceased. While humans tend to get rid of the body immediately, dwarves hold onto the body for days after. It is a sign of respect and love to the person who used to inhabit the body. It is also a chance for family and friends to say goodbye after they get over their initial shock. When royalty passes on the whole clan comes to pay their respects." King Zircon explains. I don't know what to say so I just nod. It seems disturbing to me. I wouldn't want my dead loved one's body anywhere near me.

King Zircon goes to his throne while James sits down on the floor in front of him. It creeps me out that we will be having our conversation here, while the queen's dead body is just a few feet away.

The King waits for the rest of us to get settled and comfortable before he stands and goes to the table beside the queen. He pours liquid into small stone cups and hands us adults each one before he sits down with his own. He raises his cup and moves it slightly forward, towards us in a motion of cheers. James follows him, so I do the same. We each take a gulp of the liquid. Intense heat and burning hit my throat. I cough through the itch; as I had not been expecting that strong of an alcohol to be in the cup. The liquid tastes like nail polish remover; a hint of an earthy herbal aftertaste makes it somewhat bearable.

Concerned and amused people look at me. I clear my throat. "I'm okay. I wasn't expecting that." King Zircon is the first to start laughing, and then everyone else follows. King Zircon also stops the laughter. "I apologize you're still new to things. I should have warned you. It's a traditional drink for funeral respects.

Anyway, I suppose we should get down to business. James, what is it you need from us? Do you have any plans?"

"Of course." James sounds confident. "How far are you and your clan willing to go at this point? We don't want to make you do anything you are not willing or prepared for."

"They have already infiltrated our home, killed our Queen and many other members of our clan. We are willing to do anything you need." The King's anger is not only in his voice but also in his white knuckles from gripping his cup hard.

James puts his cup on the ground and clears his throat. "We'll need weapons, armour, and fighters. We plan on attacking Darius' farm. We need to kill the leaders in our region. If we can show that there is a chance that they can lose this battle and that there will be consequences of being on their side, they will lose support. The more people we can get on our side rather than theirs, the better chance we have. We'll regain land one bit at a time. We'll have allies all over come together for this battle. We win and word will spread. Ten days from now, we will attack at sunset. Hopefully, we can be ready in time."

King Zircon raises his eyebrow. "What size of an army can we gather in ten days?"

"We'll gather enough. We have the twelve amongst us, your clan, allies at the mall, and I'll get the word out to old friends. Any help we can get will help us win." He pauses for King Zircon to think about the number of people we could gather for our side. "What is the size of your armoury right now?"

He brings his hand up to his chin to scratch through his beard. "Enough to fully equip the clan and then some. The rest of the armour will have to be altered because of size, but that will take no time. About fifty others could be clothed. We'll have enough weapons for about three hundred."

"We'll gather everything and go to the mall tomorrow. We'll inform everyone there. We'll take everything through the tree. I'll take a few back tonight to ensure the danger is gone and see what is left of my house that I can gather." A gong sounds five times; interrupting James. I look to King Zircon to see his reaction. Immediately, I suspect danger, however, there is no concern on his expression.

"Dinner is ready. I believe we have finished here anyway. We shall go to the hall. Tonight we feast, rest and relax. Tomorrow is a big day. Get lots of rest tonight. You all look like you could use it." King Zircon stands up and goes over to the queen's body. He kisses her lips and leaves.

James gets up and follows after him. I help Rayleen up from her seat and we hurry out to catch up. The King walks fast for the length of his legs. We have to almost jog to catch up. We go through one of the other set of large doors to a grand hall. A stone table and benches are carved from the rock. They are simple but effective long stretches of rectangular stone; two shorter slabs on either side of one larger one in the middle. The one table and two benches in the room are set out like one large dining room table for one very large family.

King Zircon sits down at the head of the table at the far end. When I get there myself, I see that the two benches are connected on this side.

The food is already on the table. Wild meat is carved but still in the shape of its original forms; likely attached to the animals' bones to keep it that way. Various berries are laid out. Bread loaves and bowls of butter are placed directly on the table. Everything here smells fresh and homemade.

The seating and table are slightly uncomfortable as they were not made for people of our size. My knees press against the tables' side and others taller than me are sitting slightly sideways to fit.

Finally, I notice a few things are missing; plates and cutlery. There is no room on the table for them. Down at the other end, two people are handing them out from carts. When each person gets theirs they just place it on their laps. So, when the cart comes around I do the same. The cutlery is different. One is a knife with a sharp edge, but the other thing is just like a metal rod with a sharp point at the end.

When everyone has a plate, people start grabbing things off the table. They are using the rod and knife to grab most things and hand-picking the berries. I copy them. It's a bit awkward but I fill my plate. The dowel is used as a fork would be.

Stabbing the piece of pig I had claimed, I start eating. Everything tastes fresh and clean. The room is filled with boisterous laughter, chatter and excitement. I can barely hear myself think, so I have no idea how anyone is having any conversations and actually hearing what the other person is saying.

The supper is never-ending. Long after people have cleared their plates they continue to talk and pick at the food in front of them. Seats are exchanged every once in a while, so people can talk with others. Finally, after what seems like three hours people start leaving. Some of our group leaves with different dwarves.

"Alexa, " King Zircon says my name and I immediately turn my attention to him, "and the little girl will stay at my house as well."

James finishes something in his mouth. "Thank you for your hospitality King Zircon. To keep the four of us in your house for the night is more than we could have expected."

"Nonsense, you are my guest and allies. It'll be nice having a child around once more." King Zircon takes a drink from his cup. "We go there now. Everyone is settling down or going to work."

"If you don't mind, I will head back to my house now. It should take no more than two hours." James stands up.

"Very well. Please, take a clan member with you. We don't want you getting lost." The King motions over to someone behind me. "Agate, would you mind going with James to collect some items from his house?"

"Of course." Agate and James leave through the giant doors.

The small King gets up from his seat. "Come."

King Zircon leads us back to his place. We go through the doorway at the far end of the meeting room. There are three bedrooms, one bathroom and a living room.

Rayleen and I are set into a baby's room. James in the other one.

The makeshift bed is just a bunch of fur blankets on the floor. We are instructed to lie on top of all but one. The one pelt is sufficient to keep us warm. The King bids us good night.

Rayleen falls asleep as soon as she lies down. Wide awake, I roll over to face Rayleen. The darkness of the room makes it so that I can't see her though she is only a foot away. I close my eyes as they are useless to me anyway.

Chapter 38

Where are they?

Hours, then days pass and no one else shows up. As each day passes, Kelly gets antsier and antsier. She's probably worried about her boyfriend.

What happened to the rest of their group? Something had to of happened after Ashlynn and her group left. Were they dead? They could have been attacked again.

Ashlynn left after one day had passed. She had business to deal with and said she would check on the house. No one returned in the hours after that, so Kelly went. She returned with a baby griffin and said they weren't there. Her eyes were haunted. I wonder if she told the whole story?

I finish applying the mascara to my right eyelashes in the dim light.

Days seem to get longer without anything to really do. We've done as much as we really can to prepare for just about every scenario.

There's only so much work to get done in a day. And, very little in ways of entertainment.

I wouldn't trust any of the water for swimming anymore. There are only so many times you can play poker and mini-golf. Most entertaining things we have won't work without power or a lot of light.

I've taken to a long drawn-out process to get myself looking fantastic to waste even more time.

After a sponge bath in melted snow, I dress into a brand new outfit. Today, I picked out a white leather jacket, purple decorative tank top, white jeans and purple flats.

Hair is set up in a bun, and make-up is now done complimentary to my outfit.

I have enough clothing, jewelry and make-up to choose from that I can do this over and over again. It's like getting to play dress-up with an unlimited closet and make-up. The little kid in me is ecstatic. I just wish all the fancy dress stores weren't on Tyler's side.

Looking over myself, one last time, I'm satisfied with how this look turned out.

There isn't any point in putting the makeup away completely, but I do tidy up what I used.

I walk away from the makeup store.

I think I'll grab some supper next.

We've calculated up the food we have and how many people there should be. We'll need to make runs to gather more food or we won't last through the winter.

Water will be fine during the winter because we can boil the snow. However, water will become the main issue during summer.

I hope this won't last that long.

By then someone, maybe the military, has to have something under control. Maybe there will be a truce or safe zone we can get to.

But I've resigned to spending the winter here. Without rescue, no one is going to be able to do anything when there is four feet of snow everywhere.

"There you are. I've been looking for you. Gio has your sword ready." Gary catches me once I get near the food court. He has a short sword attached to his hip. I hope Gio's swords are as good as he's been boasting.

"Thank you. I'll head over there now." I tell him.

Rushing off towards the theatre, I realize I am excited to get my sword, however, I have no idea what the rush is. It's not like he's going anywhere, or that we are on any sort of timely schedule.

I slow my pace down a bit, but it still doesn't take too long to get there.

When he sees me, he immediately grabs the sword and presents it to me. I draw the sword from his hand and step back. It feels heavy in my hand; the longer hilt lets me get my other hand on there. The weight is more manageable now. I draw the sword up and swing it around in well-practiced movements.

"Good, good. Put it in this and you may go." He says very to the point. Gio doesn't seem to be a very talkative guy. He hands me a stitched belt and loop.

"Thank you for the sword. It feels amazing." I compliment the craftsmanship.

"You're welcome, now go," I swear I can see a slight smile before he turns around.

I slide the sword into the loop. It will prevent me from cutting myself. I don't put the sword on because it will be a bit too heavy to carry around all the time.

I decide to put it down at the first aid center. It would probably be most useful there.

Two sets of stairs later, down the hall and down one last set of stairs; I place the sword near the entrance and go back up the stairs.

A sign, the Shooting Centre, catches my attention. Why didn't I think about it sooner? Why hasn't anyone? Oh wait, I think someone did mention it back on our very first day.

It's not too well known in the mall but there is a gun range. It might be hard to get into any of the gun and ammo lockers, but it would be worth the effort. The guns would be useful against any person or thing that tries to get us.

It might not be good to mention it to too many people though. We don't want Tyler to catch wind that we have guns. It is hard enough to defend ourselves without adding guns to the mix. That would only change, if we were the only ones to have guns.

Perhaps opening up the gun lockers isn't the best idea until we are going to attack someone else. That's the plan then, we will only grab the guns if they are 100% needed.

What should I do next? Right, I was on my way to eat.

Chapter 39

"Come with me." I feel an instant pit in my stomach like I'm in trouble. What did I do? Did they find my car stash?

"Excuse me," I say to Carrie, Marc, and anyone else who was listening in.

An apology readies at my lips. If I can figure out what I did wrong, then I can be more specific.

I get up from my spot at the table and follow after the manager of the store.

I wonder if he has more nefarious ideas. My gut says there's something wrong with this guy. That I shouldn't be alone with him. But, I don't have much bargaining position power here. And I don't know how much wrong is with him.

I create plans of escape while watching his movements carefully. If he turns and gets too close, I can push him down the stairs. If he tries to take me to a dark corner, I will run away before he can get close enough to grab me.

He leads me downstairs and along the front of the store to the entrance. Just outside of the door waits Calli, Lucas, and three others I met yesterday. I try to remember their names, but I can't even conjure up a sound for any syllable in their names. I've always sucked at remembering names.

"Hospital didn't check in this morning. I've tried all morning and not one peep. I want you to go check it out." He says as he lets me out.

Calli takes my keys out of her pocket. "I have room for three." I think she's suggesting I can go with her. I nod once hoping that was right.

Calli leads the way to my car. Lucas joins us as our third. We take off, leaving the other three behind, as soon as we get settled in. I sit in the back.

I sigh in relief at seeing my bag is still where I left it.

It's a short ride to the hospital. We leave the vehicle when we arrive. The air is chilly enough for a thin layer of snow to stick around.

I need warmer clothes soon. I'll likely bundle up with layers, like an over bundled child that can't move in their snowsuit. On second thought, while it would keep me warm, I doubt it's very safe. I need better winter gear.

"So, you had a group at the hospital?" I say. I am curious as to what happened after the attack. There wasn't much explained to me; not that I asked.

Lucas explains. "We have radio contact with a few groups in Leduc. There's another group at the old main street mall and the rec centre. We're supposed to check in every day, and if someone fails to check-in then another group sends someone to go check on them."

I make an 'ah' sound of acknowledgment. It's good to know that all of society hasn't completely crumbled. I would have, however, preferred to have stumbled upon the mall group. There would have been more diverse goods to choose from: clothes to wear, entertainment, crafts, boots, first aid items, camping gear, bikes. Not that a food store with a pharmacy isn't good too, but there are more diverse items at the mall.

The other people take overly long to get here seeing as they were supposedly right behind us.

Just as I'm about to get back into the car and out of the cold, they finally show up.

They drive up the emergency entrance route. We half walk, half jog up the hill to catch up to them. Why didn't we park up here?

They are opening the sliding glass door up when we get to the top.

What kind of people are here, I wonder? It's a hospital so I assume doctors, nurses, and patients. Maybe some of the police officers, and firefighters from next door fled here.

Did anyone check on the Elementary School across the street? All those small children and half of them might not be able to find their way home. They certainly wouldn't have just let them loose as the high school did.

Hopefully, all the parents would have rushed straight to the school, and been able to rescue their kids immediately.

The door slides open, and we go inside. They have a swinging door in here that we can open.

"None of the lights are on." Someone whispers. Are they meaning flashlights, or did the hospital have its own generator?

I don't like the eerie darkness. I feel like something is going to leap out and grab me.

A flash of memory comes to mind. A dream I had about a year ago. *A door opens behind me. Flashlight in hand, running down a hall, around a corner, and down into a double-doored room. I close the doors behind me and drop a filing cabinet in front of it. A couple bodies ram the doors but it doesn't budge. They can't get in.*

I feel instantly flighty. That could happen. I wrote it off as a nightmare, but it could happen now. I suppose the scene could have played in a hospital. Note to self, run out the entrance at the first hint of something gone wrong, and get Lucas and Calli to follow me out. Sorry other people, but frankly you aren't that important to my future. I've never seen any of you in any of my dreams.

Flashlights turn on. I missed grabbing one.

I see the deep red-hued brown first on the floor, then outlines of dead bodies. Well, that's it then. They're dead. Too bad. Let's go.

But, no. The others keep walking forward. A couple checks out the bodies, then Fatima pulls a radio out from the side of one of the bodies. She fiddles with it then talks. "Connor, you there?"

"Yes, are they gone?" A muffled voice calls over the radio.

"We've found a couple dead. We are going to search the hospital for survivors." She tells him.

I think that's a horrible idea.

Even without the vision nagging at me, I have enough common sense to know this can't end well. Whatever attacked them could still be here. There are likely no survivors.

"Be safe. Radio back in one hour if you haven't finished by then." He says.

"Got it." She puts the radio on her belt and then orders us. "Pair off, we each pick a hall and go down it. You-" She points to me, "are with me."

Why? Why do I have to be with selfless people?

I could just get this over with, and tell them I'm psychic, and we're all going to die if we split up, and search the hospital.

"Shouldn't we stick together? All of us, I mean. If the thing or things that killed them are still here, we'll be easy pickings with just two people." I interject.

"No, it'll be faster this way." She disagrees with me.

I just about give in when looks exchange between her, and one of the other guys, but when she gets to the next guy he doesn't take it. "She might be right. We should all search together."

"Are you kidding me?" She makes an exasperated noise. "Whatever. We'll stay together then. We're going this way."

Maybe this will help?

We barely leave the lobby when I heard a faint door opening. I bolt back the way we came.

Four shadowed people are coming in from the outside. "Look Danielle, lunch."

Back, running, the way I came. I run right into Fatima. "Run," I say while I pass around her. "Run!" I yell to the others.

Pushing Lucas and Calli into moving forward, I hold on to make sure they stay with me. There is enough light down at the end to see that it is a dead-end. There are screams from back where we came.

I see the door for the stairs. Taking this chance of escape, I veer to the door. I open it, letting go of both Lucas and Calli in the process.

I immediately go downstairs; we can make it to the parking garage. Lucas has other ideas. He grabs my arm to pull me to the other door. "The parking garage is downstairs."

"We can loop around up here!" He insists.

Calli finishes whatever argument could happen. "They can hear you." She grabs us and jerks us both towards downstairs. I'm happy she took my side, though I am not sure if it was because she knows I have visions or because now those people heard us, and might cut off our exit.

Calli leads us downstairs, and through the door. I hear the door open to the upstairs as Lucas passes through this door. We hurry up and run down the hall.

Between the three of us, we only have one flashlight. I try to focus and get as much information from the small spot of light, but Calli mainly keeps it on the ground.

The door behind us opens. Whether I like it or not the vision is happening, but this time I have Calli and Lucas with me.

"Do you know where you're going?" I ask.

"No." She responds.

"Go right!" I yell. It was almost too late. The corner is upon us. I end up in the lead, from the harsher turn Calli had to make. I run us right into the same room I had gone into before.

Just as everyone gets inside, I pry the filing cabinet away from the wall and drop it. Without any warning from me, I nearly drop it on Lucas.

The filing cabinet does its job and keeps the predators out. It soon goes quiet. They stop banging on the doors.

I'm content to stay here and wait them out, but I'm not the person who needs to be convinced not to go out prematurely.

I watch the light spot as Calli scans the room. We are in a file room, most likely holding patients' records. There is only one way in, and one way out.

Well, somehow I had escaped this room.

"So, now what?" Calli asks directing the question at me.

"I don't know." I try to subtly tell her to be quiet. Drawing my finger up to my lips, then pointing to the door and finally at my ear. She gets the message.

Now we wait.

And wait.

And wait.

Every once in a while we hear a noise outside the doors. It restarts an invisible count down.

And wait.

Chapter 40

I feel like I only blinked my eyes and suddenly Miles is telling me that I need to wake up. "James is back. The tree nymph died, so we can't travel that way anymore. There's a new plan. Rayleen's staying here while we go to a city near here to get some vehicles."

It is a lot to process in the couple of seconds I've been awake.

I wonder what time it is. Then again, as I feel like I just closed my eyes, I don't think I want to know.

We leave the bedroom and go to the meeting room. I seem to be the last one getting the message. King Zircon, Agate, James, Amy, Leah, and Daniel are already here.

"Rise and shine, Princess. Okay, she's here now. Let's get going." Leah starts walking for the door.

"Impatient much? Don't you remember how much you needed sleep when you were human?" Daniel sounds irritated. They probably just woke him up as well.

Leah sprints across the room to right in front of him. "Oh, shut up. I still need sleep." She sneers quietly.

"Enough. You're acting like children." James goes from lecturing them to focusing on me. "We're going to a city a half-hour walk away from here to obtain some vehicles to transport everyone and everything back to the mall. You know how to drive, correct?"

"Yes." I just about tell him that I don't have my license, however, I figure he wouldn't care about that.

"Good. I believe we are ready to leave now." James tells Agate and King Zircon. Leah is already on her way out the door.

Agate nods his head. "Right then, follow me." We leave through the one last door we have not been through yet. Torch in hand, Agate leads us through many winding tunnels. We walk past some of the tunnels that had been caved in during the attack.

Moonlight beams through holes in the ceiling. It's not long before we reach the end of the tunnels and are going through the forest. There is a highway, in the middle, then more forest.

It is one tree after another; they all look the same to me. After a while, I now understand how people lose their way in a forest.

Just up ahead I start to see a clearing behind the trees, then buildings further away. Reaching the edge of the forest, there is a large clearing with a city right in the middle of it.

Even from the distance, we are from the city, something seems odd about it. There is no smoke in the night sky, no buildings are burning or collapsing. The light coming from the city is from regular light bulbs.

Agate stays at the forest edge.

Closer and closer more details are being clear. People are walking around going about their business. The whole situation is strange especially when I think about the city we came from.

"Vampires and humans. The people walking around, they're both. I see some other supernaturals too." Leah informs us.

"Be careful. We don't know what we are walking into." James warns.

When we finally reach the city boundary the whole town notices. Everyone, within eyesight and further, rushes to greet us.

"Welcome to our fine city. I'm assuming by the members of your party that you have no problem with inter-races co-mingling; you'll fit in just fine here. Also, assuming from the looks of you, you all came from a city at war. You'll be happy to know that there's no war going on here." A very excited man shakes James' hand. He moves on to Daniel, intent on shaking everyone's hands.

"So, no one from the rebellion is here?" James asks.

"I'm personally part of the rebellion, but we decided to take a different approach. We announced everything at a town meeting, everyone accepted it and the rest is history. We now live together in peace. Look at me, just babbling on. You all must be exhausted and hungry, James. Come, come we'll get you everything you need." He tries to grab onto Leah's hand, but Leah avoids it. My ears ring for a moment.

"We weren't planning on staying," Leah informs him.

James walks in front of Leah. "We hadn't planned on it because we thought this city would be at war too, but I believe we just might reconsider now." He looks back at Leah to tell her silently to not say another word. I think he wants to check everything out.

"We'll take you to our leaders now." He turns himself a bit and waits for someone to start following him.

"We're not aliens, but we do come in peace." Daniel laughs at his joke. When no one else joins in, his laughter dies. "Because in movies aliens say we come in peace, take me to your leader; get it?" He pauses for a moment waiting for a response that doesn't come. "Well, I thought it was funny."

James walks beside the man and we follow after them. The crowd splits, while some people closer to the outer edge go back to whatever they were doing before, others watch us as we walk past. I feel like I'm royalty with everyone eager to get a view but also like a prisoner taking my last march to the gallows.

The man looks back now and then. He stops the group suddenly. He walks over to Daniel who's looking through a store window a few stores back. "We best hurry. The sun will be coming up in under an hour and we don't want the beauty over there to get fried."

"I have SunShield with me," Leah tells the man.

"Where? In your pocket?" Leah pulls out her small tube from her pants pocket. "That would, maybe last you a day. Make sure you pick up some more on your supplies run." He starts walking back in the direction we were headed.

We're taken a couple more blocks away to an old brick building. Gold lettering on the wall announced this is the City Hall.

We are led down a hall, up some stairs, down another hall with a bunch of doorways, and another hall, until we are told to go into a meeting room. He shuts the door behind us as soon as we get inside. We sit at the large table in large, comfy leather chairs.

A man walks in as soon as we're settled. He's dressed in a silk robe and black pants. He looks like he should also have a pipe in hand. "Welcome! It's so good to see that there are still people alive out there. This is very exciting. What is it like out there? We haven't had anyone from the outside make it here yet. No communications are working. From what I've been told of the rebellion's plans though it must be terrifying out there."

I realize that is why everyone rushed to us. Why everyone was so excited to see us; it makes me feel a bit sick. I tell him with anger in my voice. "Is that why everyone is so excited we're here? Because they want to know what it is like out there? It's war. What do you think it's like? There's death everywhere. Everyone we once knew is dead or going to be."

He sits down. The smile turns to a frown. "I'm sorry; I didn't mean to offend you."

Another man walks into the room. He is neatly presented, unlike the other man. He dresses in a tuxedo, tie, dress shoes, and his hair is slicked back. "Welcome. I'm Kris, the supernatural representative. I'll personally see to the arrangements for the supernaturals of your group. Owen will arrange everything for the humans. James, it is nice to see you're still alive. Perhaps you would lend us some of your experience?"

"I would be delighted," James answers back politely.

"James and miss vampire, if you would follow me we have a lot of arrangements to make."

"Leah. And Miles is an elf." Leah says.

"Of course. Follow me." Kris doesn't wait for either of them to get up. He walks right out of the room; leaving the door open.

The three of them hurry to follow Kris.

"The rest of you are all human, correct? No special abilities?" Owen breaks the silence.

Now, all that's left is Amy, Daniel, and myself. We shake our heads.

"Alright, let's get down to business then." Owen walks over to the cabinet in the corner and pulls out a piece of paper, then sits down with his copy. "Alright, so you get weekly rations. You can go into any store, grab what you need, sign out at the cashier and walk out.

We don't work off a monetary system; we work off a trading system. You trade work and items for other things.

You need to work twenty hours a week to cover your weekly rations. The hours are transferable. For example, for a couple living together one of the partners may work forty hours a week while the other stays at the house.

If you need to buy anything else you, trade for it at the market in town square for it or you can work more hours.

The living quarters have their sector power shut off from sundown to sun up. You might want to work extra hours to get matches and candles if you want any light through the night.

And." He looks at the sheet of paper. "We can find you permanent jobs or temporary; whichever you'd prefer. Temporary jobs are handed out just inside the entrance here. If you'd like a permanent job, just talk with me about it when I check in with you next week.

We'll get you a week's worth of rations and a place to start with. You can have a week to adjust and settle in before we meet up again and discuss jobs. Any questions?"

It seems like a simple enough system. I shake my head. No one else has any questions; none that they are willing to voice if they do. I itch to mention we hadn't come to stay.

"Good. Let's go to the apartment now." Owen leads us out of the building. He talks to Daniel about something to do with their trade system, but I couldn't care less, my mind is scattered.

We aren't supposed to be staying here long anyway. I need to get back to Rayleen and we have the battle to think of and what about all the people at the mall. Yet, it may be a good idea to stay here despite all that. If I went back and got Rayleen then she and I could stay here. We could live in peace.

Rayleen shouldn't be out in the middle of war anyway. It could work here. We wouldn't have to worry about anything. I could work to support us and she could go to school. Do they have school? They must have something in place if they are trying to remake society.

We finally get to an apartment complex. It is an older building. The stucco is falling off in places, but otherwise, it seems well maintained. We go up the elevator to the fourth floor.

"I assume you all would like to stick together. This apartment has three bedrooms." He hands Daniel a set of keys. "There are only two of them, but we can get another cut later today." He stops outside the door of suite 412. "Go on in."

Daniel opens the door. We all go inside. None of us bother to take our shoes off.

Owen plays guide and shows us around the place; the kitchen, living room, three bedrooms, and two bathrooms. They are furnished completely with squares of lightened paint on the walls where pictures had once been.

Drawings made by a child are still on the fridge.

One bedroom is furnished with a bunk bed and dinosaurs and there are toys still on the ground. Another bedroom has a single bed and a pink princess theme. Then the master bedroom has a queen-size bed and two dressers. The closet is open and still has clothes in it.

When we are done the tour, Amy is finally the first one to say something about the obvious. "Are you sure you grabbed the right keys? It looks like people already live here."

"People leave here for different reasons, and when they do, they leave what they can't carry. We have a team that comes in afterwards and takes out the personal items like pictures of the person and perishable food items, leaving the rest for anyone looking for alternative housing.

Let's move on the sun is rising and we can get to the stores before the morning rush comes in." We leave the apartment building immediately.

Only a block away we go into a store. We each take baskets and are taken down each aisle until our baskets are full and we have all the items Owen suggests.

We go to the cashier who goes through our baskets and puts the items in a burlap bag for each of us. We sign a paper with our names.

Retracing our steps back to the apartment to unpack all our items, ends with us placing food in the refrigerator and leaving again. This time we are taken on a tour of the city.

People are out and about. They look happy enough. Everyone looks to be on their way to work or the market.

The market is full of tables and tents. People are trying to trade off items in the street. There are many hand-crafted items, baked goods, tools, jewelry, and furniture. There are some other things like a litter of kittens for trade and some solar panels.

People are getting in discussions about what is worth the trade or not. As we go past them I hear one man rejecting the offer of a trade of a wool blanket for a small metal wagon.

We go to a park next, then a high school that has been turned into a trades school. If we want to learn something we apply and log work hours at the school instead.

Owen takes us all over the main parts of the city. We are explained the ins and outs of how things work around here. My feet are sore by the time we end up at the jailhouse. This is the first building on the tour that we do not go inside.

Owen seems to want to stay clear of the building. He just waves it off, "The officers are very busy people and we wouldn't want to disturb them. Anyway, there is nothing interesting in there you'd want to see.

Let's go to get something to eat at the community kitchen. We're very close to it and I'm sure you're hungry." A block away is an old fast food restaurant.

"They don't have much on their old menu anymore. Things started running out a few days ago. Without shipments coming in, of course, we knew this was going to happen. They don't have a menu anymore it's more like they will just list the ingredients they have that day and you let them know what you want. Don't get anything too complicated though because they might not know how to make it." He steps up to the counter. "I'll have a sandwich please; anything will do."

I look at their ingredient list; bread, rabbit, potatoes, water, juice, butter, moose, lettuce and cherries. Various other items have been crossed off the list already today.

Daniel and Amy order sandwiches so I decide to do the same when I get to the counter. We each get our sandwiches on a plate and go sit down.

There are quite a few people here; no one seems to be saying much.

We eat in silence. My sandwich is quite plain; butter, a leaf of lettuce and mystery meat stuck between two pieces of dry bread. I need water to wash the sandwich down, but it feels too awkward to go up and ask for some so I just force it down without.

We leave the place. The sun is high in the sky so it must be sometime around noon.

Owen takes us back to City Hall.

"Are you able to find your way back to your apartment?" Owen asks.

"I think so," Daniel responds for us. I hope he does because I don't know if I could.

"Wonderful. I have other duties to handle today. Once again, welcome. We're excited to have you join us. If you have any questions, don't hesitate to ask. My door is always open."

Owen shakes each of our hands.

"I was wondering if you knew where James, Leah, and Miles went. We've been with them so long, I'd hate to lose track of them now." Amy asks.

"Of course. I can ask around and find out which location they were moved to, and let you know next week."

"Would it be too much trouble for that to happen now? I had a couple of things to talk to James about." Amy pushes.

"No trouble. Come with me." Owen tells Amy.

"I'll meet you at home later." Amy leaves with Owen.

"Wonder that she needs to talk about?" Daniel mumbles.

"Don't know." I shrug.

"Well, let's get back and hope we don't get lost." Daniel leads us successfully back to the apartment.

He opens the door for me to go inside our apartment. Daniel shouts through the apartment. "Hunny, we're home."

No one answers back. I take off my shoes at the door and put them on the rack while Daniel goes into the kitchen.

I follow to get some water but find Daniel cracking open the lid on a bottle of whiskey. He takes a swig straight from the bottle, then holds it out for me.

"You could have used a glass you alcoholic." I bug him.

He tips the bottle towards me so I take it. "It's not like you have any diseases that I don't have. You don't have any diseases right?"

I take a swig from the bottle. My eyes tear slightly from the burn in the back of my throat. "No diseases that I know of. But, we should use glasses anyway."

I put the bottle down and start a search through the cupboard for glasses. I find a bunch of mismatched glasses in one of the cupboards and take three of them out.

Daniel has the bottle in hand again. He probably took another gulp while I wasn't looking. I take the bottle from him and pour the whiskey into the glasses; halfway full.

Only after I pour it do I think that there might be something to mix it in. I check the fridge but don't find anything good.

Opening the cupboard the alcohol should be in I still don't find anything for mix, but I do find a lot more alcohol. Daniel reaches above my head and grabs a bottle in each hand. He sets the on the counter and goes for more. I get out of his way.

"Awesome stash. We're going to have fun with this." He says.

I take my glass and go into the living room. Exploring the room, I find some things of the old owners. The clean-up crew must not have gone through the drawers.

I find a couple of pictures of the family. A mom, dad, a girl about five years old and a son probably four years old. Both the children look like their father but the girl has the mother's eyes.

"What are you doing? It's probably best not to look at those. You might get attached. The family's probably dead by now." He grabs the picture from me and shoves it back in the drawer.

"Thank you, Mister Optimism." I walk away from him and continue around the room.

"Just realistic is all. What do they have for fun around here? Wait, does that TV work?" He turns on the TV by the button on the side. It turns on but there is nothing but static. He clicks the button on the game console and the lights go on to tell us it is running. "Entertainment at the touch of a button." Daniel clicks some buttons on the remote and finds the game channel. "You play anything?"

Slightly embarrassed that I haven't played a single video game in my life I just tell him, "No."

"Alright then, so something easy. No shooters, or RPGs; that will just take too long. Ah, a racing game. Simple, fun, and you'll catch on real quick." I have no idea what he just said. He clicks a button to make the controller work and hands it to me. "We'll do a practice run so you can start getting the controls and how it works then we'll make a drinking game out of it." He comes over with his controller in hand. He points to each thing as he says what it does. "That joystick makes the car move left or right. This button makes you go forwards and this one makes you drive backwards. If you press this button you use the items you collect."

Daniel sits on the couch. I sit on the other end and put my glass on the coffee table in front of us. We go through the menu and pick our characters; I pick the one I landed on to start with.

Next, we choose our vehicles. I flip through them. They each have their own scoring for different things like speed and acceleration. Assuming Daniel knows more about that than I do, I pick the same car that he does for his character.

He picks the course and the race starts. I press the button he told me to. 3, 2, 1 and the car spins out.

"If you press the button before you're supposed to, you spin out. Sorry, forgot to mention that." Now Daniel decides to tell me this.

I look at his screen; he's in second place. My vehicle has started to move forward, so I try concentrating on my screen now. I'm in last place. Moving the joystick left and right, the vehicle on the screen does the same. I get the feel for this controller. It's not long before I start passing some of the characters.

I don't use any of the items for the first two races. Daniel slides into first place and I am catching up. At the start of round three, I am in fourth place. I release the red turtle shell I had collected. Now in third place. Around the next corner, I should be able to pass into second place. Over the edge, I go. The screen blackens and I am back on the road. Now in eighth place, I have to try to catch up again. I only pass two more people by the time I pass the finish line.

"You're catching on. Let's play for shots now. One shot for each lap you lose and one shot if you win the whole race." Daniel gets up quickly and goes into the kitchen

"Sounds fair enough," I say.

Daniel comes back with six bottles of different kinds of alcohol. "So that we don't have to go into the kitchen each time." He explains. "You ready to lose?"

"Oh, I'm not going to lose." I fully intend on winning the next race. Getting ready I hover my finger over the button to make the car move.

Daniel fakes laughs. "We'll see about that."

The next race starts. I hit the button at the right time this time. Concentrating on driving around the route well, without hitting anything that makes me go out of control rewards me with third place at the end of the race. Unfortunately, that means three shots for me as Daniel was in first the entire way. One shot of whiskey, one of vodka, and a shot of Raspberry Sourpuss later and I'm ready for the next race.

The next two races are much of the same things; with me closing the gap and I end up with three shots while he gets one. The gap between us on the couch gets smaller and smaller as races go on.

We start the sixth race. Right off the start, I battle Daniel for first. We trade a couple of times in the first and second rounds. He's at one shot and I'm at one shot. In the third round, he gets hit by a blue turtle shell and falls off the edge of the road from the impact. We end the race with me in first and him in seventh.

I stand up reaching my hands above my head. Victory, finally after so many games lost and so many shots. "Haha, I win." My head spins from getting up too fast, and the alcohol probably didn't help either.

Flopping back down to the couch I try to stabilize the world. Daniel is right there handing me my glass. "Drink up winner." I hold my breath and down the two shots in one set of gulps. "That was nothing but luck. Think you could manage to beat me again?"

"Of course." I'm confident that I can beat him again.

He says. "Prove it."

"Set up another race and I will." He scrolls through a couple of screens and the next race starts up.

Another race down and I won all the rounds this time. I choose Sourpuss this time. "Washroom break," I say half on my way to the bathroom already.

I go to the washroom and wash my hands in the sink. My cheeks are red already. My body sways when I try to stand straight. My head is fuzzy. I'm sure I'm forgetting something but right now I don't care. I'm warm. This shirt is too hot. I walk to the master bedroom; the woman must have had something I could wear. I go into the drawers of the one dresser and it's filled with men's clothes.

The other one has women's clothes in it. I find a plain tank top with embroidery on the front low-cut collar. I put the shirt on. It's a bit loose. In another drawer, I find some sleeping shorts. I put that on the bed in favour of a ponytail I found on top of the dresser. I pull my hair up into a ponytail.

I take my pants off and put the shorts on. Turning around I jump. My heart races as I find Daniel standing in the doorway.

"How long were you standing there?" For some reason, I can't be mad at him, though I know I should be. Oh well.

"Not long enough. I was worried. You were taking a long time." Now I definitely can't be mad at him. But, I don't have to show him that.

I push past him. "Yeah, right. Did you make my shot?" I get back to the couch and sit down. The liquid in my cup looks more like it should be three. Daniel sits right next to me, while I gulp the liquid down.

I pick up my controller. More shots and more races. More shots and more races. My head spins. The light outside gets darker.

I get up and go into the bathroom. My head is spinning and my stomach doesn't like it. I kneel over the toilet. My stomach doesn't like the movement. Everything in my stomach comes up and out. Once my stomach is empty I feel a lot better.

Flushing the toilet gets rid of the evidence. There is a cup on the counter. I rinse my mouth out with water and get the gross taste out of my mouth.

I head back out to games and Daniel like nothing happened. I'm enjoying myself and throwing up will not ruin it. It only leaves more room to drink.

Daniel hands me another shot when I sit down. I gulp it down. Another race. More shots. Race then shots.

The scores of the races have gone down. Daniel and I are lucky if we get in the top five. "We suck." My mouth doesn't work as it should and the s sounds slurred.

"Yeah. How about we battle now?" The power turns off. I look outside. Half the city has gone black. The sun has set. "Or not."

Daniel's lips find mine. A feeling grows in me that I have missed since the last time Darius had kissed me. He pulls away slightly. "Sorry, I've wanted to do that for a while."

I pull him back to me and kiss him.

I push my tongue into his mouth.

My back hits the couch cushion. He lies on top of me.

Our hands wander up each other's shirts.

His shirt's off.

Daniel stops. "Don't hate me. I have to pee." He gets up and goes to the washroom.

I get up and notice my shirt disappeared at some point.

I walk to the master bedroom, using the wall for support.

I hit the bed. I push the covers aside and lay down on my side. Close eyes. My vision is shaking.

There's a kiss on my neck.

Chapter 41

Just as everyone quietens down for a moment, I hear people coming this way. I look over to the darkness and wait for shadows. Eventually, they hit the light.

"Look who I found wandering around. Nikki I'd like you to meet James." Kelly introduces one of the people. This must be the wizard. I stand up and walk over to him to shake his hand.

While shaking his hand I politely say. "Nice to finally meet you."

James lets go of my hand. "It's a pleasure. Thank you for the hospitality and for agreeing to help us. This is King Zircon" He says back to me while motioning to the dwarf king. I shake his hand too.

"It's no problem. I know we can't continue living like this. We might as well strike them down before they can make another move. Make yourselves comfortable. Do you need anything? Water? Food?" I ask.

"No thank you. We ate on our way here. We brought some supplies with us. Water, dried fruit and jerky are among these. We have some weapons as well." James explains.

"So what's the plan exactly?" I ask James.

"So far, retaliate in a couple of weeks." He says.

Surely, he's going to say something else. No? Okay, he's got nothing. Who is this guy again? "Great, but I think we're going to need a few more details worked out."

"Yes, we will work that all out later. First, I'd like to get a better sense of everything." James asks.

Shawn and Brad move to either side of my back. I feel like I suddenly picked up two bodyguards. "How about I give you a tour?" I lead the way. It's a very quick tour. They don't need to go down the hallways and I assume people know what the mall looked like before the war.

I try to explain a bit of what goes on. Mostly they just need to know where the food and drinks are. Other supplies can be scavenged from stores. First aid down under the stage. Washrooms are in the food court. You can sleep wherever you want, but a lot of people have chosen the theatre. Entertainment is all around. You can even mini-golf by candlelight or play some of the arcade games. Don't go into the waterpark or boat water because they are toxic by now. Don't cross Bourbon Street.

I leave them when we get to the food court. They don't need to be babysat and James isn't forthcoming with his plan. I take Brad and Shawn back to Chapters with me.

We get settled in and start playing cards with other people at the table.

Gary mentions we need to meet with their leaders soon; James and King Zircon. At the moment though we can just stay and do our own thing, so I don't worry about the meeting too much. In a moment it's practically forgotten as we deal out cards for War.

Not too long later I hear something faint that drops my heart into my stomach. "NO! ALEXA HELP ME!"

I'm out of my chair and running out of Chapters before I can even think. That little girl is crying and screaming for help. Is Tyler attacking? Is a demon attacking?

I use her voice to help me find her.

I can see someone carrying a small struggling body out from the golf course. They disappear behind the corner in the food court. She's still screaming. As I round the corner I can see them again. She tries to run away he grabs her and throws her into a seat.

Why is no one doing anything? I push by a girl and go straight for the male. I punch him in the face; hard. He falls to the ground. I scoop the little girl into my arms while I kneel and hug her. Trying to comfort her. "Shhh now, it's going to be okay. I've got you." I look back at the man who is now getting up from the ground. I don't hide the anger in my voice. "What do you think you are doing?"

"I was punishing her. Putting her in a time out. What do you think I was doing?" He looks like he is going to attack me.

"What did she do that was so bad? You were hurting her and she's terrified." I get up off the ground and angle the little girl away from him. I'll use my body as a shield if I need to.

"She threw a tantrum and swore at me." Are you kidding me?

"That's all? That does not give you any reason to do this. She's a child. You could easily have broken something if you didn't already. God, it sounded like you were murdering her. You went too far." I have to walk away before he pisses me off anymore.

I walk past the girl's guardian. I raise my eyebrow at her. Why didn't she do anything about that worthless piece of shit?

I take the little girl back to Chapters. She starts sobbing on the way there. Everyone who hadn't followed me out there looks at me when I get back, but I don't feel like answering any questions before I comfort this little girl.

Someone asks, "Rayleen, are you okay?" She doesn't answer, probably because she didn't hear them. I don't answer the question either.

The woman, whoever she is, walks in and sits next to us. I try to watch my words; I don't need to be swearing in front of Rayleen. "You need to control him or next time something really bad could happen. She's a kid. She's going to throw tantrums every once in a while. I'd be frustrated too. When was the last time she played with an actual kid or did some silly kid thing?" I have an idea. She needs something to distract her. I'm sure Tim would like to play with another child. "How about we go find Tim?" I stand up and put the little girl on the ground.

"Who's Tim?" She asks me.

"Tim is a seven-year-old boy. He should be in the music store with his parents." I answer. We go to the store and walk up the escalator.

Tim greets us at the top. "Hi, Nikki!"

"Hi, Tim. I've got someone I'd like you to meet." I move Rayleen in front of me. "Tim this is Rayleen. Rayleen this is Tim. Would you like to play?"

"Yes." Tim reaches out and touches her arm. "Tag, you're it!" He runs away. It takes a moment for Rayleen to realize what happened before she takes after him.

I watch them for a moment before I talk with the girl. "I don't know if you want to stay here or go off somewhere, but I have to go meet with James and King Zircon to talk about the battle coming up."

"I'll stay here for a bit." She says.

"Alright, I'll see you later then." I walk down the stairs. We don't really have a meeting set up but I can't be around her any longer. I'll probably say something I'd regret.

I go back to Chapters. I get looks when I go back in there. I ignore them and just sit.

"Are you okay? Do we have to keep him away from you?" Brad jokes.

I glare back at him; abuse isn't a laughing matter. "Let's just play."

Chapter 42

I look over at the two sleeping bodies. I woke up, what feels like, hours ago. I don't have anything to distinguish time.

I shift to my other side. The paper under me crinkles.

"Jaiden, are you awake?" Calli whispers.

"Yes," I whisper back.

"Morning," Lucas whispers.

"Oh, hey," Calli says awkwardly. There is a long pause before she finally says. "Do you think it's clear?"

"Probably, I haven't heard anything in a long time," I say in a normal volume. I doubt anything waited out there for probably twelve or eighteen hours.

I'm hungry.

Calli turns on her flashlight and aims it at the door.

Two stacked file cabinets block the door. Lucas helps me flip the second one back around the original spot. He takes the one side and just pulls it away from the one door.

We have enough room to get out the one side. Lucas takes the flashlight and leads the way.

I go next, with Calli following behind me.

Nothing so far.

Lucas turns right, down the hall we had been travelling down first.

We go to the end. There is a door with glass in it. He opens it. The fresh, cold air hits me like I stepped into a barrier.

I should have ignored the dream. If I had, maybe, we could have been free yesterday. Or, maybe dead.

There is light on the two open sides. We skirt the outside edge. Lucas turns off the flashlight.

We walk to the car. Calmly I go into the open car and buckle up. Calli gets into the driver's seat, and Lucas is in the passenger's seat.

Calli starts up the car and drives out of the parking lot. She turns left to go up the driveway. "I'm going to grab the walkie-talkie."

"Do we really need the walkie-talkie? We can just drive back, and tell them what happened." Lucas says.

"We don't have that many. We need all the ones we have." She stops the car right outside the doors. "I'll be right back."

Calli opens the door and gets out. She goes into the hospital.

Lucas gets out of the car and follows after her. I have no want to follow both of them. I watch the doors for any sign of trouble or their return.

They return without a fuss. By my guess, the looks on their faces mean they found what remained of Fatima; if not, all three of the other now missing people from our mission yesterday.

They get back in the car, and Calli drives. Neither says anything the whole trip back.

They exit the vehicle into the Safeway parking lot and walk to the doors. I trail behind them.

We get through the first doors to be greeted by two people; Connor, and one of the men that were with us at the hospital.

"You're not welcome here anymore. I'm going to ask you to leave once, or you'll regret it." Connor says in his stern tone.

"What the hell are you talking about?" Lucas gets angry.

"Lucas, let's just go. It's not worth it." Calli puts her hand on his arm, but he shrugs it off.

"Listen to the girl, and leave." Connor takes a step forward.

"Lucas, do you have anything important left here." He doesn't respond to me. "Lucas!"

"No." He responds quietly.

"Then let's go. We don't need a fight, and it's not worth staying here. Between the supernatural beings, and the humans, someone is bound to try to raid this place sooner or later. It's not safe here." I explain to him. He backs down, and storms out of the room.

"Are you threatening us?" Connor has taken my words and their meaning, wrong.

"You have nothing to fear from us. We're leaving." Calli pushes herself between Connor, and me.

I leave there, and Calli follows me out to the car.

"What the fuck are we going to do now!?!" Why is he so angry?

"It's okay. We'll be okay. Jaiden's got it all figured out." Calli tries to calm him down.

"I don't really have it all figured out. But, I would guess that we should go south. It'll be warmer the further south we go. We should survive the winter. I have some food, and water in the car that should last a few days." I say. "Let's just go. We'll drive south, and figure it out where ever you end up."

"We can't just drive without somewhere to go," Lucas says. His tone is a little lower and softer, so I think he might be calming down.

"I have a friend that owns a hotel, and bar in Red Deer. We're close enough that he'd give us a room to stay in. But," She looks at me momentarily, then talks to Lucas. "You would have to pretend you're a supernatural being of some sort. It's a demon bar and hotel."

"No." Lucas looks appalled. He shakes his head and takes in a deep breath. On his exhale he looks at Calli. "Are you a demon?"

"Succubi." She proudly exclaims.

He looks at me. "You too?"

I go to say no, I'm human but Calli talks in my stead. "She's physic. She has visions of the future."

I don't know how I should feel about her outing me. Betrayed? Relieved? I've gone from no one knowing about my visions to two people in just a manner of a couple of days.

I guess it's okay for Lucas to know, as long as he's okay with it.

"So you have sex with people and suck out their souls, and you know everything that's going to happen before it happens." He says bluntly and naively.

"I don't see everything." I defend quietly.

"I don't have sex with all of them. I don't have to have sex with people to eat their souls." Calli defends herself louder.

"You both can have each other. I'm going to ask Connor if I can stay." Lucas gets out and heads towards the doors.

He can't go.

He is crucial to the future timeline.

I get out too. "I know it's a lot to take in, but you've known me for a long time. Have I ever done anything to hurt you?" He stops and turns around. The least I get from this, he's willing to listen. "I don't know everything, but I do know that I've seen you in visions travelling with Calli and I.

At some point, you become okay with how we were born. I can't help that I was born with the ability to sometimes have visions of the future.

No one knew about it until Calli." I throw a hint of shade at her; perhaps she will take the hint that I'm none too happy about her spilling the beans to Lucas. "Calli would be human if she didn't have to eat souls sometimes to live. We're both 'human' if you mean human as a state of mind.

I mean what I said. Logically and sociologically speaking, society crumbles, and after three days people's survival of the fittest instincts kick in. If you are starving to death where is the logical place to get preserved food? You can get a can here and there at people's houses or you can try for a big haul at the grocery store.

If you are the wrong type of person this can mean by all means necessary.

Connor could be one 'no' away from a bullet in the brain. You stay here, and you risk the same."

"Oh, just come with us. We promise not to bite; hard." Calli gets back in the driver's seat. She starts up the car.

I look at Lucas. He seems like he still mulling it over. "You know Connor isn't going to let you back in. Something obviously happened, and he's not going to even try to listen to us.

I'm still me, and you've known me for years. You liked Calli before you knew, something like that shouldn't change anything."

Calli honks the horn twice. I go into the car. I take the back seat.

"Is he coming?" She asks.

"I don't know." I check my bag. I go into a pocket with a water bottle. I drink half and hand it over to Calli to finish it. Fishing through the pocket for a granola bar.

The door opens, and Lucas gets in. "What's for lunch?"

I hand him the granola bar. "There's more in the trunk. Can you open the trunk, Calli, please?"

I hear the click of the trunk, and get out. I open the trunk up and grab the bags inside. I'll sort it out in the car. I close the trunk.

Loading it all into the seat beside mine, I then settle into my seat, close the door, and buckle up. "We're good to go, if you want."

I hand out food while Calli drives out of the parking lot. She drives south down the main street. We munch on our food.

Main Street leads us straight out of town, and onto the main highway. The highway lets us pass right by towns without having to go through them.

Looking out the window I notice we are slowing down. We roll to a stop right outside the driveway to a house. I look at the back of Calli's head for an answer.

"We're running out of gas. We need to see if there's gas or a vehicle we can syphon from." She says.

There isn't anything left in the trunk. I package up any food that escaped the bags.

Calli and Lucas leave the car. I follow them to down the long driveway. Ever cautious, I scan the windows of the house. There is no sign of movement. It doesn't mean much, but at least no one has noticed our arrival.

Lucas goes to the garage man door. He kicks at the door. Did he try the doorknob? He keeps kicking at the door, but it doesn't budge.

I turn on a notion. The garage door at my house didn't lock anymore It was an old door, and you just had to pull up on the door to get inside. I go around to the door. There is a handle. I yank up once, twice, three times, and it flies up. I let go of the handle and lift it up the rest of the way by the bottom.

I turn to go get Calli and Lucas when I hear a bang and crash behind me. I turn back around and look inside the garage. Lucas is on the ground, and the door is open. He helps himself up.

He looks at me. I wave. "Hi. The big door was open."

"I see that." He huffs. I look around the garage. The first thing I notice is the huge vacant space in the middle. The rest of the garage is down to barebones; except for tools, two covered bikes, and some farming paraphernalia. "I don't see a jerry can."

"They probably took it with them when they left." Calli states.

Lucas removes the cover on one of the bikes to reveal a red motorcycle. He fiddles around with it for a couple of moments. Then, he does the same to a black motorcycle. The roar of the engine wasn't what I expected. He moves the black one to the middle. He starts up the red motorcycle and drives it beside the other. He turns them both off.

"Do either of you know how to drive a motorcycle?" He asks us.

Is he serious?

"No," I say. An afterthought, more of a piece of memory, comes to the surface. Lucas had stated, he and I would go grab the motorcycles.

Are these the motorcycles?

"No way in hell! I'm not driving one of those things. We get the gas out, and we go by car." Calli freaks out at the prospect.

"Look around. There isn't anything to get the gas out of these tanks, and into the car. The gas in both of these will last us to Red Deer. We need to take the motorcycles. Jaiden, do you think you could drive the other motorcycle?" Lucas seems to want to ride the motorcycles.

I don't know how practical motorcycles are in a snowy world where we're trying to hide from everything.

Although, that might be the trick to convincing Calli's friend that we're all supernatural beings. They wouldn't need to hide.

"Yeah, I think so," I say.

I never thought I would.

Calli looks at me defeated. "Are we supposed to take the motorcycles?"

This is still weird to me. I spent so long guarding this secret, and now the information seems like it's up for grabs for everyone. I'm not so sure that's a good thing. "I think so. Lucas wore a motorcycle jacket and told a man that he and I had to get the motorcycles. I never saw the bikes, so I'm not sure if these are them or not."

Lucas points his finger at me. "That is good enough for me. No more arguments, we take the bikes. Ladies, go get the bags from the car, and meet me back here."

I wait for Calli to reach me before I make my way to the car. "Hey, do you think we could downplay my visions when we get to your friend's place? Like, don't tell anyone else that I have visions. Don't ask me questions about the future in front of people."

"Why?"

"I just think that the fewer people that know the better." I'm not ready for the whole world to know.

She scrunches her face and huffs. "Okay. We'll just tell him you're a-ah empath."

"Like, someone who feels the emotions of other people," I say.

"Close enough. Most people who have visions tend to be empaths anyway. You shouldn't have any issues."

We get to the car. I open my door. We'll only be able to bring two bags. I shove everything I can into two bags before handing Calli one. Grabbing the strap for my bag I pull it behind me on the way out my door.

After situating the bag on my back I look back to the garage.

Where did Lucas go?

He comes out of the rear house exit when we near the garage.

"Hey Lucas, the prophet doesn't want anyone to know she sees the future, so she's just an empath; if anyone asks." Ouch. Calli's rough tone sounds like she's angry.

She can't be mad that I asked her to stop telling people about my visions.

Lucas looks at her for a moment. "Yeah, sure." He's wearing a black jacket, holding another jacket, and two helmets. "They only had two helmets. Put this on." He hands the helmet to me and holds on to the other one.

"So, I don't get one." Yes, she's definitely angry.

"No, you'll be on the back of my bike. I'll shield you from a lot of the wind and bugs. The drivers should have the helmets." Lucas reasons.

"Do I get a jacket at least?" She sneers.

He doesn't say anything. He just hands her a jacket. Apparently he had two extras.

I remove my glasses, and hand them to Lucas; I hope they fit in the helmet. I squeeze the helmet onto my head. It's a mix of wiggling and manipulating the helmet, and my face. My earrings almost get ripped from my ears, but I put my fingers upon one side, and free the earring from the cloth. I tilt the helmet that way and repeat on the same side.

It's a process.

I finally get the helmet on my head, and I grab the glasses back from Lucas. They won't go in straight, but I tilt the glasses to get in one arm at a time. It works. I feel the pressure on the back of my ears. I'm already looking forward to the relief of taking the helmet off.

Lucas hands me the other jacket. I just about fall over from the weight of it. I wasn't expecting something so heavy. It seems big.

I take off my backpack.

I slip my arms in and zip it up. It is a bit big, but just a little roomy. I don't think it'll affect me detrimentally. It just lets me have extra layers beneath for warmth. With this time of year it could be above zero one day, and the next we have six feet of snow. You just never know what you'll wake up with.

Grabbing my backpack off the ground, I put it on my back. The straps take a bit more effort to put into place over the armour. I feel a hundred pounds heavier.

Lucas motions to put my visor up. I try to find the edge, but I can't. Lucas reaches over and pulls it up easily. "There are tabs on both sides. We'll get you going, then I'll pull ahead, and lead the way."

"Okay." I take a deep breath in, and out. I can do this. I've done this or rather will do this.

We walk over to the bikes. He stops at the black one. "This one's shorter; you'll probably need all the help you can get with that. Hop on."

Okay. I go to the side it is leaning on, and throw my leg over. My right leg is about a foot off the ground. I scoot as close to the seat as I can and lift up to the very tips of my toes. Teeter tottering the bike, I bounce from my left foot toes to my right.

He puts the key in the ignition and turns it. I expect the bike to start up, but it doesn't.

"Kick up the kickstand." I do as he says on my next bounce to the right. "This is your kill switch. Has to be on to turn the bike on, and off to turn the bike off. Clutch. Break. Throttle. Gear shift is on your left foot; down for one, and up for the rest. Right foot is back break." He points to each one. I try to pay attention to it all.

"Hold in the clutch, hold in the break, and press this button to start it up." I hold in both clutch and brake. He presses the button for me. The bike starts up, and I don't go anywhere; so far so good. "Hold in the clutch when you want to switch gears. Go down to gear one now." I do it.

"It'll be in gear when you let go of the clutch. Slowly let out the break, and you'll go forward. When you want to stop you pull on the breaks, but not too fast. You'll need to be in gear one to go again. If you slow down from one-twenty to forty, you'll want to shift down. It's the same process as shifting up. Just pull the clutch in while you switch the gears.

Do you need me to go over it again?"

"I think I have it. I just have to let out the clutch, and the brake to go forward now." I do just that. The bike lurches forward. I grab the brake fast in a panic. My heart pounds. I let it out slower this time. This time the bike rolls forward slowly. "I'm just going to keep going," I shout through the helmet, and hope he hears behind me.

I give the throttle a little roll. This isn't too bad. I turn the motorcycle like a bike to turn the corner onto the highway. It turns wide. I set the speed at fifteen.

They are taking forever. There is nothing on the road in front of me, I shoulder check. They aren't behind me. I turn back around. Where are they, and why are they taking so long?

Should I turn the bike around? Do I have enough room on the road to do that? What if the bike falls?

A bike with two riders zooms past me. Apparently, I need to go faster. Okay. I roll the throttle. The engine whines a little. I probably need to shift. I pull in the clutch, pull up the shifter, and then let out the clutch. Back, and forth I shift and roll the throttle. I catch up with Lucas pretty quickly. He speeds up, and I do the same.

Wind whirls by the helmet making a whooshing noise in my ears. My hands are cold from the air temperature, and the wind from the speed. I'm getting stiff, and sore. Why did we take the bikes again? There was heat in the car. I could move, and stretch out in the car. I'm not one mistake away from dying.

Lucas turns on his right signal light. I guess we are taking the exit from the highway here. We turn off the highway and go left over the bridge.

I hadn't been paying attention. Where are we?

We drive some ways straight from there. From the name of a café, I figure out we are in Red Deer. I'm guessing we either need gas, or Calli's friend is here.

We cross over a river and then take a few turns. Lucas stops efficiently. I shift down. I break comfortably, overshooting Lucas, and stopping some distance away. Turning around feels like a drawn-out walk of shame. I have to place my one foot on the ground to make sure I don't tip over; shuffling it as the turn requires.

A short rev pulls me ahead, and closer to Lucas and Calli. I drive to the space in front of them before stopping. I hit the switch that I remember Lucas said was the kill switch. The bike turns off.

I lift my other leg over. Oh yeah, the kickstand needs to be down. I put it down, and slowly lean the bike to sit on it. I don't want to take my hands away from bracing the bike. I'm almost certain the kickstand is going to snap up, and the bike will fall. Lifting my hands just one centimetre away from the bike I'm ready if it does fall, but it doesn't.

I look at Calli and Lucas. He's breathing into his hands to warm them up. She's combing her fingers through her tangled hair.

I hope mine stayed inside the jacket; it knots enough without help from the wind.

My numb fingers undo the strap under my chin. Lifting the visor by a tab, and then removing my glasses. I put my glasses on the seat, so I can remove the helmet easier. Just as I had issues with my earrings when I put the helmet on, I have issues with them sticking on the way out. Detaching them I get the helmet off. I don't know where to put the helmet, so I carry it. I put my glasses back on.

Lucas goes over to my bike, turns the key, and removes it. He hands me the key.

Calli says. "Let's go."

She leads us into an old building, brick-walled, and large wooden doors. They have power here. The entrance leads to a lobby, to the side is a bustling bar, and stairs go up, and down on the other side.

We walk into the bar. Calli sits us down at a table; the closest one she found to the lobby.

"Stay here." She says

Calli walks up to the bar. She waits until the bartender notices her. They talk while he keeps busy making drinks. He looks over at our table, so I wave.

He puts his hand up in a motion to reciprocate. He turns his attention back to Calli.

Eventually, he goes to attend to someone else. Calli comes back with three beers.

She sits down and passes the drinks around. "He said he'll help us; one room and food. We will have to work for it by working for him. Mostly, he needs people to do deliveries."

Chapter 43

"Whoa! Hello! I see you both are doing well. But you both need to get dressed and I'll see you in the living room. We need to go to the town square." Leah stands in the doorway with a smirk on her face.

My head hurts from joking up. She walks away. My head hits the pillow. I try moving but there is an arm around my waist. I jump out of the bed though not too gracefully.

I can assume we did more than just cuddling last night by feeling and lacking clothes. I try to remember what happened in the missing gaps of time in my memory while I find undergarments, yoga pants and a halter top in the drawers. While I'm putting my clothes on, Daniel starts to get out of bed.

Still pulling down my shirt, I almost run from the room and disappear from his view into the bathroom.

The first thing I do is turn the taps on full blast. Grabbing the toothbrush I run it under the water, put toothpaste on it and stick it in my mouth. Scrubbing and scrubbing the nasty carpet feeling from every surface in my mouth, I spit the foam from my mouth. I then repeat the process another two times before I am satisfied.

My headache blares. Looking in the medicine cabinet I find Tylenol. Taking four pills from the bottle I throw them into my mouth. Cupping my hands quickly I gather enough water in them to wash down the pills. Swallowing takes a bit of effort but I accomplish it with only a bad taste in my mouth.

There is a face cloth next to the sink. I wash any skin showing from my clothes. Pulling out my ponytail, I brush my hair next while I let my skin air dry. My hair is slippery with the oil in it, so I pull it back into a ponytail.

In the same drawer is make-up. Excitement fills me. There is everything I could ever need in here. It takes a few minutes of careful and practiced movements before I put the finishing touches on my face; beautiful. Finishing up in the bathroom, I take one more final look in the mirror.

Leaving the room I meet Leah and Daniel in the living room.

Daniel looks upset. He turns to me. Pulling me in for a hug he says, "Amy's dead. Demons killed her last night. They're calling a town meeting. Everyone has to be there."

"We have to leave now if we don't want to be late. Someone took a little too long getting ready in the bathroom." Leah deserts us to go to the front door.

I break our hug and dash away after her. Slipping on my shoes is easy enough. I catch up to her quickly. Daniel rushes to catch up with us. He almost misses the elevator.

The outside is a terrifying clash against the day before. Posters with sayings or pictures on them. There is one of a boot about to squash a human. On a white wall, someone wrote in red 'Learn your place.' Others have Missing or Dead written on them with pictures of people.

I take a double look at something on the power lines. I don't believe my eyes at first; an arm is hanging on there like a pair of shoes would.

Leah takes us to the city hall. A bit of a stage has been set up for the leaders to stand up on. They are already there and Owen is trying to tame the crowd. We get settled in standing behind everyone. We have just enough of a view above everyone's heads to see the upper portions of the two leader's bodies.

The human leader is trying hard to get the crowd to calm down, but it isn't working. You can tell he is trying to yell as loud as he can but one voice isn't enough to overpower the growing crowd. I can't hear a word he is saying. Kris stands there saying nothing but looks disgusted at Owen's attempts.

A lady runs out and hands Kris a megaphone to amplify his voice. There is a screech as he turns it on and it gets feedback. Once under control, he says one word that creeps a shiver up my spine and hushes the crowd. "Silence!"

He hands the megaphone over to Owen who continues with what he went there to say, "A tragedy happened last night. A young girl was murdered most horribly and whoever committed this crime had no respect for her body and placed parts of her all over the city.

Allegedly, this looks to be a demon or a group of demons who no longer believe in our ways. They have decided that they no longer want to live together in peace with humans. We will not tolerate that here. The people who did this will be caught and justice will be served.

The racist words and pictures will be removed from every surface. Anyone supporting any rebellion will be caught and persecuted for any crimes they have committed. If they have not committed any crimes, they will be asked to leave."

Owen hands the megaphone back to Kris. "Things will temporarily change around here until such a time that the criminals are caught. You will be seeing more police patrolling the streets. We expect full cooperation will be given to any police officer who stops you.

There is now a stricter curfew for everyone. On days of work, you must be at the job by eight and you must leave by five. The first time you go back to work you will be given a pass stating you are working as a particular job. If you work temp jobs you will be given a permanent job.

If you are not at work you should be in your homes. If you need to leave your house for whatever reason you need to come to city hall and report the reason. You will receive a pass good for an amount of time and with a condition to sign in at the particular place.

The market will now be moved to the gymnasium at the high school. These restrictions and tracking is being put in place to ensure your safety and will only be temporary. Please bear with it.

Now off to your permanent jobs. Everyone without a placement needs to stay behind and you will be assigned one." He steps off the stage and goes inside the building behind him.

Owen stays behind. He gets off the stage and helps some others place papers on the stage. Many people leave.

The crowd clears out enough that I can see Miles and James in the line-up.

I ask them. "Did you see Amy last night? Before-"

"No, we didn't. Why?" Miles says in a whisper.

"She left with Owen to find out where James was, and to go see him," I respond. James shakes his head.

So, Amy didn't even make it to see them. Whatever happened must have been done soon after she left.

"Don't you think we should be focused on our job placement right now? We will see each other later." James turns around and ignores us. By now I've gotten used to his sudden change of subject; his way of saying that we shouldn't talk about the subject any longer. Act a certain way.

Most have left the area now. There is a lineup with the rest of everyone lining up for their jobs. The line-up goes quickly until there are only ten people left including Miles, Daniel, Leah and I. James is the last one to get a placement off to the fields for harvesting.

Owen looks at us. "I am very sorry to do this. You are on clean-up duty. Painting over the graffiti, and picking up debris here in the square. If you find a body part, call over an officer and they will remove it for you. Again, I am very sorry but it needs to be done there's nothing else left. The paint, paint supplies and garbage bags are just inside the doors. Here are your passes." He hands the passes to Miles, turns around and leaves.

Miles hands the passes out to each person. We each take a bit of the supply and start with the city hall area. Each can of paint is pure white and looks out of place on the building, but it is still better than the previous sayings and pictures.

No one talks. The larger cleaning group splits in half; half painting and the other half picking up garbage. A couple of times officers get pulled over for a yell of 'I found something'. One male was, ever so kind to say 'I found an ear,' loud enough for all to hear him.

I don't dare to look while they take each part away. Concentrating on painting over everything makes the time go faster and keeps my thoughts from turning into who might be next to find a body part and hoping that it won't be me.

Goosebumps rise on my skin from the cool air and a slight layer of sweat covers me. My fingers are cold and prickle where I grasp the paintbrush, but I don't dare to stop. The three officers left in the area are a little unsettling.

Leah finds another body part and one more officer leaves with it. Hours pass of the same things. One more part is found and we are only left with one officer now.

The sun is high in the sky. The air is significantly warmer than in the morning. The area is cleaner now. It looks a lot better. White spots of wet paint are everywhere. Windows are covered in cardboard from where they had been broken. There is no more glass on the grounds. No more posters.

I set about to cover the paint cans when we hear some shouting.

The officer goes to look at the commotion, but turns and runs into City Hall.

The shouts get closer. "Please don't do this! I'm innocent! I didn't do anything! Please!" The shouts of this sort continue on. It sounds like a man begging for his life.

I turn the corner. There are a few people that have someone surrounded. He is tied to a lamp post with a bunch of people holding him to make sure he doesn't go anywhere. Someone throws a bucket of clear liquid on the frightened male. He struggles more now. Someone throws a towel over his head while some more people restrain him even more. A woman rubs the towel against the skin of his face and pulls the towel away.

Immediately, he is dowsed with more water.

Steam rises from his skin. Red boils grow on his cheeks. The crowd goes wild. Throwing more water on him. Someone beats him with a bat, another grabs something silver; it looks like a pipe and each takes their own turn. They stop throwing water and a few seconds later his cheek catches on fire. It spreads quickly.

Everyone lets go of the male. The male's entire body is on fire. A mangled wail comes out of his throat for only a second. His body slumps and falls to the ground after the rope burns. All his flesh is gone. The fire turns his bones to ashes. There is nothing left in minutes.

I barely register Leah grabbing my shoulder. "We're leaving."

Miles and Leah ran slowly enough for Daniel and me to sprint after them. The speed is exhausting but doesn't last too long.

I hear our names being called. Looking slightly to the right, James is hanging out the driver's door of a large moving truck.

The back door is open so we all run into the back. Daniel closes the door while James puts the vehicle in gear.

"Hold on," James warns a second before he slams on the accelerator. Fortunately, I had the second to grab to the side railing and brace myself. Some boxes fall off of a stack in the corner. One box collides with Leah's leg.

The whole room echoes in a thundering crackle from just the movement of the truck. It gets louder if we go over any size of a bump.

Daniel goes up to the cab to sit next to James. I sit on the ground to catch my bearings and settle down for the trip to the other side of the mountain. My breath and heart eventually calm down.

James finally slows the truck down and the clanking metal sound stops. Leah pulls open the back door. Miles leaves out the back and goes around the corner out of sight.

We're stopped on a highway. With a 4x4 truck, perhaps, we could have gotten closer to the mountain entrance. However, the moving truck would never make it that far.

I step down from the truck bed, turning around. I look at the mountain. Having no idea where the house would be doesn't much help me in figuring out how much of a hike we have to do there and back today.

Dread prickles through me as I think about how much stuff will also need to be dragged down the mountain; possibly more than one trip will need to be made.

I turn back around to face Leah in the back of the truck. She has gone to the cab and is talking with Daniel and James.

Something moves in the corner of my eye. A body collides into my side. Without meaning to, I simultaneously jump and scream.

A mess of red hair floats into my vision. I feel foolish for my reaction. Rayleen and just about everyone else laugh at it.

Seemingly out of nowhere about a hundred dwarves come carrying crates large and small. I get out of the way still attached to Rayleen, to let them load everything into the truck.

Rayleen lets go of my waist. Seeing as neither of us will be much of use, I lead us around to the passenger side of the cab.

I wonder if Agate made this happen, or if James did. Someone notified the dwarves that we would be here.

Daniel opens up the door and lets himself out. He leans towards me for a kiss, but I hesitate. I don't know what last night was. Whether it meant nothing at all, if it was just a drunken booty call, or if it was the start of something more. I do know one thing; I miss that feeling that someone loves me. He goes the rest of the way in and kisses me with just a peck of the lips.

Looking away from Daniel I see Rayleen smiling back at me.

"Up you go, darling. We'll be leaving as soon as we're all packed up." He picks Rayleen up and places her on the seat. She crawls closer to James. He holds open his hand to help me in as well. I shake my head and climb in.

Loosening the middle belt I can buckle up both Rayleen and myself. Daniel slides in beside us and shuts the door. Leah now sits on a crate.

The dwarves are quickly packing up. They are leaving space at the top; where some have already started to sit or lay down. Every bit of space is being used by the time the large door is shut; either the space is filled with a person or a crate. Everything back there is tightly crammed in.

Looking around James to the outside, many dwarves are going back up the mountain. They also have a few crates they are hauling back with them. The plan had been to have more than just one truck, so they probably had brought enough stuff and people to completely fill four larger trucks. Instead, they had probably stuffed half of everything in the one moving truck.

James warns everyone before stepping on the gas this time. "Everyone stable? Watch out for falling crates."

The truck slowly and steadily climbs in speed. Most of this highway is straight with a small curve every once in a while. The mountains slowly disappear behind us, but there are trees for miles around. I don't think I've ever travelled such a distance before seeing at least some sign of a city. There are only trees, fields and lakes as far as my eyes can see in all the kilometres we travel.

Looking out the window, I am mesmerized by everything going past me. Wondering where it ends. It takes a while but I finally see signs of civilization. A green sign on the side of the road states 'Edson 10 KM'. Searching in the distance for the city keeps me busy for the next couple of minutes to pass. At the speed we're going ten kilometres doesn't take long. It is finally within the last kilometre that I finally see some of the city.

James slows down once we get into the city. I look out for all the signs that this city is anything like ours or the one we just had come from this morning.

No people looking out from windows, no signs of destruction, and no signs of life. Vehicles, mainly trucks, are parked everywhere, but none are moving. Some do seem out of place and abandoned, but other than that there are no disturbances.

Chapter 44

I innocently sat down with Gary for breakfast and was then joined by King Zircon and James. Quickly, what then started off as a small meeting of four people, has turned into a large gathering of practically everyone on our side of the mall.

We've run through plans of every kind; too many people have their own ideas about what should happen. Every idea comes with its own battle. Someone thinks we should sneak attack, another thinks we should just run down the driveway. We should wait until spring, or we should attack in two weeks. We should build a bigger army, or we could defeat them with the numbers we have now. The guns at the shooting range.

Back and forth. Back and forth.

We have settled on one thing so far; we need to train. We are going to start training after breakfast every day. I'm in charge of one of the boot camps.

"We need to have the surprise aspect and we need to do it before they attack us again. We need to attack them immediately." A dwarf says.

"Two weeks. We can have everyone ready in two weeks." King Zircon echoes the previous remark.

"We should wait until spring or summer. We can train all winter so we're sure we can win." One girl says.

"Why? Half of us could be dead or starving by the end of winter. " Another girl says.

"Sooner may be better, than later. We could be ready in two weeks, if we push and train hard. We can't wait around for them to figure out where we are or risk an attack. It won't be any good to wait until spring if many don't survive the winter, or if we weaken from the lack of protein in our food. We attack in two weeks at dawn." James settles that issue. He seems to have one of the final words on the matter.

King Zircon got what he wanted. Gary and I agree with a nod. I can't speak for Gary, but I am just letting James and King Zircon take the reins on this. It is their battle. They know more about what is going on than I do.

"We should attack at night. Surprise them while they are sleeping." Brad pipes up.

"Dawn is better. Many of the stronger supernaturals are nocturnal. Attacking at dawn would be like attacking right before you go to bed in the evening. The ones up during the day may still be asleep." Miles explains.

"We'll take the trucks and drive right on down the driveway. Everyone jumps out and attacks. Simple, but it'll work." King Zircon looks between the three of us at the table as he says this.

"We should sneak attack them. It's surrounded by forest. We spread out and attack from all around them." Another voice says from out of our circle.

The meeting takes forever, but we finally end it when every possible detail has been talked to death.

People are so excited that they have decided to start the first boot camp right after.

We split off into groups. Because of my history, I get to teach a hand to hand combat to one of the groups. I almost wish that I didn't know anything or that other people didn't know I can fight, so I could take a lesson from someone else. It would be nice to go over sword skills or learn the basics of fighting a demon. Instead, I am to lead a gym-style course.

Everyone is eager to learn. The group gathers quickly and awaits me to start teaching them. The problem is that I have no idea how to do this. I haven't taken a class in years.

I know it's important to warm up and stretch before workouts, so I should start there. It might help me get some time to figure out what I should teach the group.

"We're going to warm up first. Ah, we'll do a few laps around this area. Follow me." I start a good easy pace around the immediate area. People are quick to follow me. I don't know how long I should do this for, so I just run.

Maybe I should just start with basic moves and then move on to sparing. Yeah, that seems like the simplest way to do this.

There are a few stragglers. I stop before we lap those people. The group as a whole has gotten winded from the run. It was a good warm-up for me, but I guess the others here aren't quite at the same fitness level as I am.

"Gather around, but make sure you have enough room to stretch out without hitting the person next to you." I start stretching my muscles. I expect that everyone will just copy me, and they do. They are making this easy enough. I would probably be slaughtered if this was a high school gym class.

I work through all the muscles from my neck to my calves.

"Alright, everyone needs to space out more. We're going to go over some basic moves, you'll practice them. Then we'll break off and you all can spar with a partner." I start with stances. "Fighting is personal and everyone can pick a different fighting stance and fighting style. You just need to make sure you are balanced. You pick something where you are braced and ready to defend against an attack without falling over, or you can quickly attack. You will want to lower your center of gravity otherwise you will be easy to push over."

We move on from there. I show them all the punching and kicking moves I can remember.

Some people catch on really fast, and others struggle. I don't know if we will be ready in two weeks.

A couple of people look like they've trained to fight their entire life, then there is everyone else that looks like they've never fought a day in their life.

I send people to break off into partners. They can spar. I can show them moves, but it is something entirely different to practice something and put it to use in a match. Even more different to use it in an actual fight.

Chapter 45

I feel like someone is watching me. I lower the book I'm reading. There are twins, one girl and one boy, standing at the foot of the bed. Where did they come from?

"Hello," I say sweetly.

"Hello." They say in sync.

The one on the left asks me, "Can you play with us?"

"Sure."

They reach out together and grab my feet. "Tag, you're it."

They run out of the room. I give chase after the both of them. We run down the wooden stairs. I take note to not knock down the picture frames. They split off, so I chase after the one going down to the basement. It's even darker down here. I lose sight of the boy. I hear a door close. I pick the closest door to me and open it.

Twin voices chime behind me. "We aren't allowed in there."

They disappear in front of my eyes. For a moment, I think maybe they just backed up into the darkness, but I know what I saw. They faded in spot.

I hear a scream upstairs. I need to check it out. I run back up the stairs. Shouts and screams come from all directions. I need to run. I need to get Lucas and Calli and leave. "LUCAS! CALLI!" I yell.

If they answer, I can't hear it. Maybe, they already made it outside. I know I don't want to be here. My flight instinct is too strong to ignore. The closest exit is out the back, so I run down the hall. A male runs towards me, but just as he's about to pass, he is pulled up against the ceiling. I hear a sick crack. I look up; there is the twisted face of the girl twin smiling at me. My heart skips a beat. I bolt before I realize I'm moving. I exit the house through the kitchen.

There isn't anyone out back here, so I run to the front. I'm out of breath when I get there. No one else has made it out of the house. Do I go back in? I couldn't. They need to come out of the house. It's a haunting, and the haunters can't leave the house; if they follow movie lore.

There is a metallic taste in the back of my mouth, and I feel a bit of faint sickness.

That was slightly frightening.

I need to work out more. Although, even if I went back in what could I do to help? Either way, I need to work out more. It's dumb of me to think that I don't need a lot of cardio now. If I can't run a minute sprint without passing out, I'm not going to last very long.

I slowly drag the covers over me, until I'm free. I get up and go to my bag. I remove a change of clothing, and hygienic items, and go fix myself up in the bathroom down the hall.

Returning to the room, I deposit everything back into the bag. I grab some dried fruit from the main compartment of another bag. It's a small breakfast, but it works. This bag is dwindling of its food. I stuff it inside my larger bag.

I go back out to the hall. Should I leave a note? No, I don't think I will be going very far, and I can just get Jerry to tell them a message if I go anywhere.

I walk down the hall, and down the stairs. There is a little bit of noise coming from the bar area; a slight thud then glass chiming against one another.

Jerry is working away, so early too. Or, perhaps, is it late for him? He may not have gone to sleep yet if the bar kept open until the early morning.

He notices me. "Good morning. You're up early." He asks as he walks past me to the back door. He comes back with another box of alcohol.

"Good morning. I couldn't sleep." I pause. "I was thinking about going for a run, but would you like some help."

"Yes, please." I follow him out back. There is a U-Haul trailer full of varying boxes; some drinks, and food for the bar, and some seem like supplies for the hotel. "Carry the boxes inside. We'll take the food, and drink to the cellar, and anything else goes behind the counter in the lobby."

Simple enough. I grab the closest box to me. It's heavy, and, according to the label, contains Fekete Vér. The clinking inside lets me know it is encased in glass. Is it French? The accent aigu leads me to believe that this may be true, but it could very well be another language, and I don't recognize either of the words. Not that I should be giving so much credit to my French classes. Perhaps, I will try this drink later.

I take the box inside. Unpacking the truck takes about a half-hour. We don't say much more than a couple of task-related questions, and answers.

"That's it. Thank you for your help." Jerry thanks me.

"You're welcome," I say. I stand there awkwardly. Should I go? Stay, and make conversation or unpack the items we brought in?

"Calli said you would all work for your room, correct?" He interjects my thoughts.

"Yes." I stop myself from tacking on that I don't know what I can do but I learn fast. It's not an interview. I don't have to convince him to hire me.

"A few of my delivery boys are on an errand, and I need someone to replace them. You'd deliver the order directly to the person named on the paper. Think you could manage that?"

"I think so."

"Good." He walks past me to the lobby desk. He grabs a key off the wall and comes back to me. He hands me a key with a built-in key fob. "The truck is out back. The addresses and box numbers are on the order sheet on the passenger seat. You need to make sure you get a signature from the name of the person on the sheet. If they have any issues you can tell them to talk to me."

"Perfect. Sounds good." I say. "I will see you later. Bye."

I go out the back door. There are a couple of pickup trucks parked in a line against the back of the building. I look at the face of the key fob and click the lock button. The rear lights flash on the second truck in line. Walking up to the truck I feel small. It has to have some sort of lift on it. Unlocking the truck, I open up the driver's door. I am happy with the stretch in my pants, the emergency handlebar, and the foot railing. Without the combination of all three I may not have made it up, and into the seat.

I close the door behind me. It's freezing in here. I put the key in the ignition, and turn the engine on. I crank the knob to High to blast the heat.

I pick up the clipboard in the next seat. The page is full of names. This is going to take all day. Glancing down the addresses, I don't have any luck, they are all different. I don't know where we are exactly, and I don't know where I need to be for any of these. I'll just drive out of here, and out of view, and then I can find a street sign, and figure out where I am. It might work.

I reach down to the side of the seat groping for a button to move the seat forward, but I don't find anything. It must have a lever under the seat. Sure enough, I find a horizontal metal piece that pulls up. I pull on the steering wheel and dig in with my heels to move the seat all the way forward. I test my reach.

I still have a ways to go. I pull the lever again, but the seat doesn't go forward anymore. Big trucks just aren't made for short girls. I scooch forward, until I reach the pedals, and can floor them. Subsequently, this means I am half the way up the seat. I forgo the seat belt because it's going to be uncomfortable in my position.

I start the truck and drive out of the parking lot. I go to the right and drive down a couple of blocks. When I know I'm in the clear, I stop the truck, and orientate myself. I have a penchant for getting lost, and I hope I can navigate well enough to make it through the list, or at least back to the hotel.

It's going to be a long day.

Chapter 46

The movement comes to a stop. My brain wakes me from this initial change in my surroundings.

Everything is slow and foggy as the sleep slowly drains away.

Sleeping sitting up was not the best idea. As I get out of the truck I can feel the toll on my body. My muscles and joints are stiff.

Rayleen doesn't seem to be affected by her nap against my side. James opens the back of the truck. Dwarves climb out and gather to unload the crates.

Rayleen and I get out of the way and follow James up the long stairs and through the two sets of doors into the theatre portion of the mall.

There is not a sound to be heard. The only light comes from the little glow of the natural light behind us.

"Hello?" Daniel calls out loudly.

"Shut up." Leah's words sound harsher than they should.

"Why?" Daniel says a bit quieter. "We came here because we have allies here. It's not like they're going to kill us."

"They might not be here. Who knows who's actually here? Unless you've spoken with people here while you were off hooking up in the mountains." Leah makes an unfair pass at the previous night.

"She's right you know. You're just lucky you came through these doors." Kelly stands at the end of the hallway; her voice slightly echoing from her silhouette. "What happened out there? You're working with the dwarves now? At least you had the good sense to add another vampire."

"Be nice Kelly." Miles tries to stop Kelly.

She looks at him and turns serious. "No, seriously, what happened out there? You were supposed to be here a few days ago. And, where're the others?"

"We were taken to a school by the military and were tossed into a dictatorship lead by a military leader bent on killing every being that is not pure human. Some of us were able to escape and went back to James' house where we found the bodies of everyone left in the basement and then we were almost blown up with the house.

We transported to the mountains with the portal closing behind us as the nymph was killed and went to see the dwarves. They agreed to help us because they had been attacked too.

We needed vehicles to get back so we went to a town that seemed to work fine with everyone living together until someone decided to kill Amy. We got a bunch of supplies and came here." Miles sums up the past few days.

"Okay. Let's go let the others know you're alive." Kelly leads us out of the theatre and down to the main floor.

People are walking around on this side; bags in hand. Some are wearing clothes with tags still on them. Some others are gathered in the different stores. They look like they have staked claims in the stores as to their own living quarters.

Kelly tells the dwarves to put the crates down in the stage area.

We go past everyone to the book store. Candles are burning to help light the far back.

A few people are gathered here. They pulled some chairs from other areas but this children's section had more than enough sitting space for everyone.

"Look who I found wandering around. Nikki, I'd like you to meet James." Kelly introduces the most important of us.

An indigenous woman stands up from the table she's sitting at. She comes over to shake James' hand. "Nice to finally meet you."

"It's a pleasure. Thank you for the hospitality and for agreeing to help us. This is King Zircon." James states his pleasantries and introduces the dwarf king.

They shake hands.

"It's no problem. I know we can't continue living like this. We might as well strike them down before they can make another move. Make yourselves comfortable. Do you need anything? Water? Food?" Nikki asks.

"No, thank you. We ate on our way here. We brought some supplies with us. Water, dried fruit and jerky are among these. We have some weapons as well." James explains.

"So, what's the plan exactly?" Nikki asks us.

"So far, retaliate in a couple of weeks," James tells her.

I expect him to say more but he doesn't. I wonder if he doesn't have more than that, or if he's holding back the information. I would expect the latter, knowing James.

There is an awkward silence before she figures this out as well. "Great, but I think we're going to need a few more details worked out."

"Yes, we will work that all out later. First, I'd like to get a better sense of everything." James asks.

Two men get up from the couch and walk over to Nikki. "How about I give you a quick tour?" I follow her as they walk to the store entrance.

Our whole group follows except for King Zircon. He says something in a murmur of going to see his clan.

Kelly tags along too. She makes a point of walking opposite to the side Miles is walking on.

I don't watch her further but can swear I feel her glaring at me. Why is she so mad at us? You'd think she'd want to stick by her boyfriend.

Nikki takes us around. Everything is more or less centralized to this one area of the mall. It has the most natural light, so candles or flashlights aren't needed in the main area during the day.

Candles and flashlights light up the darkest areas.

Food and washrooms are found in the food court. Living quarters is where ever you want; most have either picked the book store or the theatre.

Ashlynn left a couple of days ago for some business and was going to drop by the house to check on us.

"There are places you can find entertainment here. If you don't mind playing by candlelight you can go to the mini-golf course. There are a few games in the arcade that work without power. You don't get any of the electronics but you can keep score yourself.

Don't go into any of the water that is sitting. The water's too toxic now.

Don't go past Bourbon Street. There's another group on that side that doesn't take kindly to strangers. Some of us are still healing from the last fight we had with them." Nikki explains.

The last point concerns me. Did we walk into another dangerous living situation?

People can be volatile, no matter what they are.

The tour only takes about five minutes but we see each section in this part of the mall and get a bit of information on how things work around here.

Nikki and her bodyguards go back to the bookstore. Most of us need to go to the washrooms so we go to the back of the food court. I go quickly, but Rayleen takes her time.

"It smells in here." She complains.

"I know. You just- the faster you finish the faster we can get out of here." I tell her. To my surprise, she doesn't complain more. I'd usually expect her to complain about it longer than it would take her to just pee and go.

We wash with hand sanitizer then return with people trickling back.

I try to focus on my surroundings rather than the awkward silence until Leah breaks it. "So, what can you tell us about this place; about Nikki?"

Kelly thinks for a couple of seconds. She looks around to see who could hear her. There are a few other people in here. "Nikki seems competent enough. I don't know if she'll be any good at strategy when it really counts or if she just got lucky.

She took some sort of martial arts when she was younger, so she sort of knows something about fighting.

Overall, people seem to listen to her and that's what counts. It helps though that quite a few people knew her from before and I think she was a cheerleader or something; she just seems like the type, if you know what I mean.

As for this place; they haven't suffered too much here. I don't know what they'll actually do when faced with a battle. We should take over the other people; they're being dumb. And, they've got most of the food supplies over there. "

The dwarves come into the food court with some of the crates; the ones that probably contain the food.

King Zircon comes over when he sees James standing with us. "The cyclopes says he wants to see anyone who does not have a weapon to their name. He's up in the theatre lounge. "

"Leah, do you want to go to the theatre and Gio will make you a weapon," James asks Leah. I guess she would be the only one of us that didn't get a weapon at James' house.

"Sure thing." Leah runs away.

"Where's the crate with our weapons in it?" Daniel asks.

"Theatre. We left them with Gio." King Zircon tells him.

I had forgotten about my sword and dagger. I'm scared of what Gio might do if he finds out I had forgotten them again.

People walk off in different directions. I don't know who I should follow or what I am supposed to be doing.

Rayleen starts to drag Daniel off somewhere. I decide to catch up with them.

"We're going to play mini-golf," Rayleen says joyfully. She grabs for my hand to hold and I let her. That sounds like a better idea.

We go out the other side of the food court to the little but for the golf course workers.

Daniel lets go of Rayleen's hands and jumps the counter. He puts three putters on the counter and shoves some golf balls in his pockets.

He jumps the counter back to our side.

I look at the gate and discover an easy latch. He could have easily gotten in and out without having to jump anything.

While Daniel grabs the three golf balls out of his pocket, I hand out the putters.

I look out to the mini-golf course while we enter through the gate. A few others are playing. Candles are lit along the whole course, just barely enough to slightly light the way. The hole is not visible from where you start, but you just aim towards the other side of the area and hope you get somewhere near it.

We let Rayleen go first, second, and third. Though her first two shots bounced off something and came right back to her, the third shot finally makes it to the other side.

I go next. Learning from Rayleen's mistakes, I shoot where she had last gone and make it. I don't wait for Daniel to putt before I make my way along the candles to find the two balls. Rayleen's ball made it closer to the hole than mine did. Daniel's ball goes past me and bounces back off the side.

Rayleen and I get the ball into the hole on the next turn, but Daniel putts too strong and bounces over. It takes him a couple more tries before the ball finally goes in.

We move on to the next hole in silence. There is something about the darkness that seems to hush everyone. I cannot hear a word coming from anyone on the course.

Rayleen quickly gets tired of the game. Daniel and I finish each hole with ease, but Rayleen keeps missing the hole. Her anger rising, she keeps missing the hole because she putts too hard.

"Rayleen, you're swinging too hard." Daniel tries to help her out.

Daniel's words are the last straw for the little girl. The golf club is thrown to the ground. It bounces and nearly hits Daniel. Rayleen crosses her arms and glares at Daniel. "I don't want to play anymore. This is stupid."

"That's no way to act and don't say the word stupid; it's a bad word." He scolds her.

"You're stupid!" She glares at him. Shocked at what she just said

I'm speechless and frozen.

Daniel booms his voice. "You do not call people stupid! Apologize! Now!"

"No!" Rayleen screams at him. She stands her ground.

Daniel grabs Rayleen by her arm. "You're going in a time-out!"

"No! Alexa, help me!" Rayleen starts crying and screaming in terror. She reaches out to me while struggling to get away from Daniel. He yanks her up and carries her out of the course. She is a mess of kicking, screaming and hitting.

I stand frozen. Never have I seen her throw something in anger. Never, has she thrown a tantrum like she is now.

When I get over the initial shock I run after them. Daniel takes her to the food court and sets her roughly on a chair. "That's enough. Stop right now and stay here. You're on a time out." His voice booms.

The moment he lets go she is out of the chair. He was ready for it and grabs her. He pushes her back on the chair. Rayleen wails. People are coming running from all directions.

I don't know what to do. I freeze. Not understanding why either of them is acting like this.

Nikki pushes past me and punches Daniel. Taken by surprise, he falls to the ground. Nikki grabs Rayleen and holds her in her arms. "Shhh now, it's going to be okay. I've got you." Her voice changes from soft, comforting, and motherly to furious. "What do you think you are doing?"

"I was punishing her. Putting her in a time out. What do you think I was doing?" Daniel looks like he is about to start a fistfight with Nikki.

"What did she do that was so bad? You were hurting her and she's terrified." Nikki stands up with Rayleen in her arms. She turns her body as a sort of shield for the little girl.

"She threw a tantrum and swore at me." Suddenly Daniel sounds like a child himself.

"That's all? What, are you five years old? That does not give you any right to do this. She's a child. You could easily have broken something if you didn't already. God, it sounded like you were murdering her. You went too far." Nikki turns around to walk away, but not before looking at me with her eyebrow raised.

Daniel gets up from the ground. The people that have gathered stare him down; daring him to do the wrong thing that would allow them to beat him. He looks at me to do something. He must realize that I am not going to because he quickly looks devastated.

I can't look at him any longer. Feeling like I am the traitor in this whole situation hurts me, but by everyone's reactions, I think it's best to go to Rayleen.

I follow the sobs back to the book store. When I arrive Nikki has Rayleen still in her arms. She sits on Nikki's lap with her head buried into her shoulder. I sit down beside them on the couch.

"You need to control him or next time something really bad could happen." I feel like I should say something to her; anything. But, I still can't talk. Nikki continues. "She's a kid. She's going to throw tantrums every once in a while. I'd be frustrated too. When was the last time she played with an actual kid or did some silly kid thing? How about we go find Tim?" She stands up and puts Rayleen on the ground.

"Who's Tim?" I ask while standing up.

"Tim is a seven-year-old boy. He should be in the music store with his parents." She explains.

The music store is just a couple of stores over from us. We go inside and walk up the escalator. The little boy must have heard us coming because he meets us at the top. "Hi, Nikki!"

"Hi, Tim. I've got someone I'd like you to meet." She places Rayleen more in front of her than before. "Tim this is Rayleen. Rayleen this is Tim. Would you like to play together?"

"Yes." He leans towards Rayleen. He reaches out and touches her arm. "Tag you're it!" He shouts quickly before dashing away. It takes a moment for Rayleen to realize what happened before she takes after him.

Nikki breaks the silence. "I don't know if you want to stay here or go off somewhere, but I have to go meet with James and King Zircon to talk about the battle coming up."

"I'll stay here for a bit," I tell her.

"Alright, I'll see you later then." Nikki hurries down the stairs.

Looking back to Tim and Rayleen, I see Rayleen is hugging something. At first glance, it looks like it might be a dog. When she lets go of it I finally see all of her; it's Crystal the little griffin. I guess, I now know what happened to her.

Two older people are around the two. I assume they must be Tim's parents. I wave at them and they wave back.

Deciding that Rayleen will be okay here, I go back down the escalator to find food without another word. Rayleen might get upset if I leave, but I know she wouldn't let me go if I talk to her about it. It's better this way. Two responsible adults to look over her while I sort myself out.

My stomach suddenly growls from hunger.

The food court is alive with people. Everyone has come to eat some of the new food. It might be the first time in a while they've had anything different so I can understand.

I scan the crowd. There are the people that came directly from James' house right before the military came, the people I travelled here with and many I have never seen before.

I go to the back of the line-up for people still needing to get food. They have it set up cafeteria-style. I pick up a can of peaches. There is a can opener lying next to the cans that I use to open it.

Each person only seems to be grabbing one to two things so I leave the line up with my peaches. It's like the school cafeteria all over again. People have grouped together. The only visible separations I can make out have grouped people into those I recognize and those I don't.

I don't have to make my own choice of where to go. Taylor calls me to sit at the table with her.

Each table has a bottle of something. I immediately recognize the expensive vodka on ours. Cups are almost nonexistent so we just drink straight from the bottle.

I need this. I need to numb myself.

Chapter 47

A canned snack of pears was good enough to settle the hunger in my stomach. We're going to run out of food faster with all of these people here. Smaller raid finds aren't going to stretch far.

What to do? We've prepared as much as we can and I can't spend all day training. I ran out of smokes, so I can't even waste ten minutes going for a smoke break. Maybe, I'll go grab a book and read it. I have a few daylight hours left.

I walk to Chapters.

I hear faint counting, getting louder as I reach the store. Just inside Rayleen is counting. She notices me immediately.

"Five, six, seven. Nikki! Come play hide and seek with us!" Rayleen shouts out as loud as she was counting. When a kid asks to play a game of hide and seek and you have nothing else to do, you play hide and seek. "One." I run to find a spot to hide. I duck behind one of the bookshelves, then keep moving around slowly sneaking. I don't know how much time I have to hide. "Two, three, four, five, six, seven, eight, nine, ten, eleven, twelve, thirteen, fourteen, fifteen, sixteen, seventeen, eighteen, nineteen and twenty. Ready or not, here I come."

"Hi. Have you seen Nikki?" Rayleen asks someone just moments later.

"I have no idea where she is." I recognize that voice. It's Alexa; I think I heard Rayleen call her that.

"Can you help me look?" Rayleen asks her.

A different female voice answers. "Sure. We'll both help you and hopefully we find her soon. How about we look over here?"

I wait to be found. It takes a while before I finally hear footsteps coming towards me.

"Nikki, I found you," Rayleen says as she finally sees me as she comes around the corner.

"You did," I say. Alexa and Taylor follow quickly behind her.

"Alexa, you're it. Count to twenty." Rayleen runs off. I guess I'm off the hook for this turn. I run off to find another spot. I hear her start counting. I'll need to find a better spot now that adults are playing too. She gets to fifteen. I sit down on the floor behind a shelf in a dark corner.

"Not ready!" Rayleen yells after Alexa finishes counting.

She recounts. "One, two, three, four, five, six, seven, eight, nine, ten, eleven, twelve, thirteen, fourteen, fifteen, sixteen, seventeen, eighteen, nineteen and twenty. Ready or not, here I come."

Rayleen doesn't yell again, so I guess Alexa is going to start looking now. I don't hear her. She's either really quiet or she isn't anywhere near me. I look around the corner to see if I can spot her. Wrong timing, she sees me but doesn't say anything. Maybe she didn't see me. Is it too dark here?

I hear a, "Boo!", and a scream right after.

"You didn't scare me," Rayleen says.

"Oh, course not but I did find you. Do you want to help me look for Taylor and Nikki?" Alexa asks. Well, she already knows where I am.

"Okay. I think she went in here." I hear a door open. Are they going into the Staff Room?

"Hey, you aren't supposed to tell her where I am," Taylor says.

"What are you reading?" Rayleen asks.

No. My heart quickens. The only thing in there is my poetry book. I rush to go make sure she isn't reading it. That's personal.

"A poetry book. It's really good." Taylor shows Rayleen the book.

"Excuse me. You're not supposed to be reading that." I push past

Alexa and grab the book away from Taylor.

"Well, sorry, it was just here. I didn't know it was yours." Taylor says.

That's no excuse. You're in a book store and you decide to read a journal-type book with handwriting in it? No consideration. "You shouldn't be reading any type of book that's in someone's writing. It's a violation of privacy. It's like a diary. You wouldn't like it if I read your diary with all your personal thoughts would you?"

"How about we play another round of hide and go seek?" Alexa tries to switch the subject.

"I'm done," I say before I leave.

The theatre? No, too many people. The water park? No, too cold. All the stores are occupied or closed.

Where can I go where I will be alone?

I get an idea. Like many people do in the movies, if you want to be alone in a place with a lot of people you go into a bathroom stall.

I start off for the food court but I have a better idea for a first stop. I walk down towards the music store and down to a lesser-used hall of the mall. I go into the liquor store. We've raided the store of a lot of its booze so there isn't much left in here. Behind the counter, however, are a bunch of tiny bottles virtually untouched. Who wants a shot of liquor when they can have the two six instead?

I grab a plastic bag from the checkout and fill it with a few bottles of everything. I've got some booze, I've got my notebook. I grab a pen off the counter and I think I'm ready to go.

We have the food court bathroom lit up, so I go to those bathrooms. Someone is using a stall already. I can smell the stale urine and I don't want to think about what else, from the toilets. This may not have been the best choice.

I go into a stall anyways. I wait until the other people leave before letting out a big sigh. I leave the stall and settle down onto a sofa meant for breastfeeding moms. I get comfy. The first bottle I reach in and grab is a premade shot. Opening it, I 'Cheers' to the space in front of me and gulp the liquid down.

The empty plastic goes into a garbage can in reach.

Three Souls

There is enough light that I can see the words in my notebook. There is more than enough for me to write.

Is nothing safe anymore?

How dare she?

How dare she?

Does she think of herself as the Queen?

Society crumbles, but we don't have to.

It's not the best work I've done, but it helps me and that's all that matters. The dramatic tone helps me see a bit of ridiculousness to it.

I take another shot; this time it's a tequila shot.

There's nothing more that I can do right now than drink and write. There's nothing I can do to fix the situation; the whole situation.

Chapter 48

I tire of lying in a dark and quiet room. Thus are the woes of waiting on people to wake up. Lucas and Calli sleep hours longer than I do. I don't understand it. How productive can you be when you regularly sleep half the day away?

I decide I've had enough. I silently get up and do my morning routine. It ends with breakfast downstairs; a hard-boiled egg, and a thick slice of bread.

Jerry gives me the keys to a loaded up truck, and I head out. I figure out quickly it's the same one from yesterday. The seat is still set at the forward position. No one else is as short as I am.

There are only three places on the list today. I decide to do the second one on the list first. It only has one box number next to it.

I drive one direction until the street number matches the same on the address. Next, I do the same with the avenue. I stop in the middle of the intersection for the two. The house number is twenty-nine. I drive slowly down the houses. The neighbourhood is simply laid out, and I quickly find the house. I pull the truck over to the side and park. I need to grab number thirteen.

Opening the truck door lets a cold chill in the air. I slam the door shut as soon as my feet hit the ground.

I round the back of the truck and climb up on the back bumper. I look for the number thirteen written on the outside of a box or bag. It turns out to be a bag. It's rather small for a delivery. But, I guess some people are just as lazy in war as they are in peace.

I walk up to the front door and knock. I knock again after ten seconds have passed. The door opens as soon as I finish knocking.

"What?" The large man sounds angry. He glares down at me.

"I have the delivery from Jerry." I hold the bag out for him to take. He snatches the bag from my hand and shuts the door in my face. "I need a signature!" I yell through the door.

I just about bang on the door with my fist again when it opens up. He grabs my clipboard from me, quickly scribbles, shoves it back at me, and shuts the door again. I look at the paper and find a signature, surprisingly, in the right place.

I move on to the next delivery. It brings me to a large building. I roll to a stop near large doors. I look at the clipboard and see that I need three numbers; fourteen, fifteen, and sixteen.

I get out of the warm cab and shut the door. I jump at the start of a voice above me. She's so tall.

"Hello, little one." I turn around. A large woman, three times the size of me, stands in front of me. She's so tall.

"Hello, tall one. I have the delivery from Jerry's for a," I look down at the clipboard, "Mrs. Crane." She's so tall.

"Oh yes, that's me, of course. What's your name? Unless you want me to continue calling you little one." She holds out her large hand, so I hand her the clipboard. She takes it and signs it.

"My name's Jaiden. It's nice to meet you." I give her a bright smile. She hands the clipboard back to me. I climb up to the back of the truck. I spot the three large boxes that belong to her. They are at the front of the truck bed. They must have been loaded in there first. I point to them. "Your boxes are right there. I'll just have to move a couple of things to get them out of the back."

"Don't bother yourself. I'll get them." She bends over the side of the truck and easily grabs the three boxes one by one. She stacks them on the ground before lifting all three together. "Wait here. I have something for you."

"Okay," I tell her. I watch as she goes into the building. She has to bend over slightly to get inside. She only takes about a minute to return. She holds a fabric bundle in front of me.

"There's some sweets in there for you. I hope you like chocolate." She tells me.

I take the bundle from her. Excitement bubbles up, but I remember my manners. "Thank you, you didn't have to do this. Thank you, so much though. I love chocolate."

"They're homemade, so you'll have to tell me what you think."

I nod. "I definitely will."

"Yes, in about a week or so? You should get back in the truck. You look like you have lots more to deliver and you're shivering."

"Yes. Thank you again. It was nice meeting you. Bye." I wave.

"Bye." She goes back into the building while I go into the truck. I take a peek in the bundle and find a dinner plate sized cookie.

I look at the next address and figure out where I need to go. The next place leads to an apartment complex I remember from yesterday; the vampires. The rest of the load is for Chad.

I obviously can't carry everything to the building, so I just go by myself. The front door is unlocked, but the second door is locked. It's dark in the lobby, but I can't see anyone. I knock on the door.

Someone comes out from the next room over and opens the door. "Are you lost human?" Her distaste is palatable. I suddenly miss the friendly guy from yesterday.

"I have a delivery from Jerry. I need to drop off the items, and get a signature from Chad." My voice comes out more confident than I thought it would. I still imagine I creaked and waivered, but nothing that should have been noticeable.

"I'll sign it for you." She says. Her lips move slightly, and then I hear a high-pitched ringing.

"Jerry gave me strict instructions to get the signature from Chad himself." I don't know exactly how high I should hold that rule. Can I break it? I don't think I should. I don't want to get into trouble. It's Jerry's rule. I have to follow it.

She huffs. "Follow me." The other guy took the clip board, and returned it signed. But, I guess this might be okay too; maybe.

She doesn't hold the door open for me, so I have to rush to stop it from closing. I follow after her. Shortly down the hall, there is a group of people we pass. The girl points out the truck to them.

We climb upstairs to the fourth floor. She stops at the third door on the left. It opens up without her knocking. We are brought to Chad. He sits at the kitchen table with two other people.

"Ah, delivery girl." He beckons me to come closer to him. I hand him the clipboard for him to sign. I look around to pass the moment. There is a male making drinks on the counter, and he drops something into only one of the drinks.

Chad holds up the clipboard for me to retrieve it. I take it and watch the man bring the drinks over to the table. The spiked drink is given straight to Chad.

Chad goes to take a drink. My hand reaches out instinctually to grab the cup. Chad's fast movements were undetectable. My hand stings from being pushed to the table. "The drink. What did you put in it?" I look to the male.

He doesn't move. "It's blood."

"Yes, but after you poured the drink. I saw you drop something else into Chad's glass." He's swarmed by four people who hold him in place. Hands go into pockets, and one pulls something out. The woman brings it to Chad. It's a vial.

"Escort the delivery girl out of here." He tells her.

She takes my arm and leads me out. I hear the male screaming from the door until we get a little way down the stairs. The woman leads me out of the building, and to the now empty truck. She opens the door for me.

"Thank you," I say to her. She closes the door. I pull away and glance back. She watches me until out of view.

I get back to Jerry's and park the truck. I take the clipboard and food bundle with me. I settle everything with Jerry and eat a late lunch. I guess this is normal life now.

Chapter 49

My eyes open and the first thing I check is whether my stomach and head feel as awful as they did yesterday. They seem normal. Even after getting up, the signs of the hangover I should have do not show. Maybe it will appear later. Maybe I'm still drunk.

I must have slept late. I am the only one left in the theatre. Time isn't really important now. For however long I did sleep I probably needed it anyway.

I go to the bathroom in the theatre's washroom. With no candles lit or natural light in this washroom, I go in blind. I do what I need to do quickly and get out as fast as I can.

Getting back to the lighted areas, I go to the outside doors to look through the window.

Snow is everywhere; white as far as I can see. Nothing is moving out there. The sun is out, making the white sparkle.

Having enough of the sight outside, I go back to the lobby and start searching for people.

I make it down the set of escalator stairs to the theatre before I start hearing voices. They sound like they are coming from right below me. Taking another escalator downstairs, I see everyone immediately. They are scattered in front of the book store.

They are fighting one another; it reminds me of the training that we did at James' house. I can't help but think I missed a couple of things while I slept.

Taylor is with the closest group; sparing with someone I don't know.

As soon as I get close a punch is swung at my head. I duck in time to miss it. Taylor switches her partner to me at that moment's notice. Her leg hits my side and knocks me off balance. I catch myself before I crash to the ground.

"That would be a roundhouse kick. One of the things you missed. Where have you been anyway?" Taylor crouches into a fighting stance and waits for me to do the same.

"Sleeping," I say simply.

She throws two punches; one after the other. I land a punch on her arm.

"Okay sleepyhead, I guess I'll have to catch you up on everything."

"I guess so."

We continue our sparring match as she fills me in. "We had a meeting this morning. The leaders had gotten together last night and figured out a plan to attack the farm.

We're going to train a lot for the next two weeks. We'll travel there to aim for a dawn attack. Use the element of surprise. Just drive down the driveway and get out and attack.

There's a bunch of people that know different fighting styles, so we're supposed to figure out what suits us best and focus on that. Some supernatural lessons too. So we know weaknesses."

"Maybe I should have stayed in that city." I think aloud.

Taylor kicks me to the ground again. "What?"

"The city we had gone to get supplies and trucks. I had been thinking of taking Rayleen there and staying." Getting up from the ground, I continue to talk without starting up our fight again. "It seems dumb to train our asses off for two weeks to go fight a whole bunch of demons that will probably kill us anyway."

"If you really want you don't have to fight. You can stay here and wait for us to come back. But, I would recommend training with us. Might as well, right? Not like you have anything else to do for the next two weeks." She throws another punch.

It doesn't take long for me to tire of the fighting even with the small amount of time we've been doing this. The exercise could do me some good at least. "Fine, yeah, I guess you're right."

Taylor is a decent fighter. I try to remember what Kelly taught me at James' and I pay attention to what Taylor does; trying to copy a few things here and there. Try to beat her.

Taylor says, "We should take a break." There are a few others that have gone off. "Rayleen was playing in Chapters with Tim."

Taylor and I go to the entrance of the book store. Rayleen's voice yells out from the semi-darkness. "Ready or not. Here I come."

Nikki hides behind one of the bookshelves. It takes a bit until we see Rayleen. "Hi. Have you seen Nikki?"

"I have no idea where she is," Taylor says to her.

"Can you help me look?" Rayleen uses her puppy-dog eyes on us.

I am about to tell her no. The last time we played this game it didn't work out too well. However, Taylor speaks first. "Sure. We'll help you. How about we look over here?"

I follow Rayleen as Taylor leads her in a productive search.

"Nikki, I found you!" Rayleen taunts.

"You did!" Nikki sounds excited.

"Alexa you're it. Count to twenty." Rayleen runs off.

"I guess you're it. Count to twenty and no peeking." Taylor tells me before she runs off. I turn to Nikki and she's already gone.

I start counting out loud to twenty. "Ready or not here I come."

"Not ready!" Rayleen yells.

I shake my head and smile. Of course. "One, two, three, four, five, six, seven, eight, nine, ten, eleven, twelve, thirteen, fourteen, fifteen, sixteen, seventeen, eighteen, nineteen and twenty. Ready or not here I come."

Waiting a moment, I listen for Rayleen to yell out again, but she doesn't. That is my sign that I can start looking now. Walking slowly, I look down the aisles for any of the girls. I see Nikki hiding down an aisle. Our eyes meet, but I just keep going. I hear giggling for a moment. It sounds like Rayleen is in the very back. Slowing my pace, even more, I make it take a bit more time to get to the back.

She is hiding behind the couch. I creep up on her. "Boo!"

Rayleen screams quickly. "You didn't scare me."

"Oh, of course not, but I did find you. Do you want to help me look for Taylor and Nikki?" I ask.

"Okay." She gets up from the floor and sets off out of the children's section. "I think she went in here." I follow her to a door labelled Staff Only. I open the door. Taylor sits at the table with a flashlight in hand reading a book.

"Hey, you aren't supposed to tell her where I am." Taylor jokes.

Rayleen walks up to her. "What are you reading?"

"A poetry book. It's really good." Taylor shows Rayleen the book.

"Excuse me. You're not supposed to be reading that." Nikki shoves her way by me to go over and grab the book away from Taylor.

"Well sorry, it was just here. I didn't know it was yours." She tries to defend herself but it doesn't seem to help calm Nikki.

"You shouldn't be reading any type of book in someone's writing. It's a violation of privacy. It's like a diary. You wouldn't like it if I read your diary with all your personal thoughts would you?" She's furious.

I try to distract them from the fight that's sure to break out. "How about we play another round of Hide and go Seek?"

She glares at me. "I'm done." Nikki leaves.

I look at Taylor and shrug. "Let's play tag now. You're it." I grab Rayleen's hand and pull her into a run.

Chapter 50

I hold my notebook tight as I walk through the halls. After earlier, I'm not letting this thing out of my sight. I'm not as mad about her reading it anymore, but she did cross a line, and I want to make certain that never happens again.

The flashlight lights my way for my turn at guard duty. I had thought I heard a crash earlier. After not seeing any lights on, nor any other sounds, I'm not too sure anymore. There are so many people around everywhere, that it really could have been anything and anyone.

It's eerily quiet at night. There is no one at golf, no one in the food court and no one at the boat. Then another stark thought crosses my mind; what if Tyler's attacking us again? It's too quiet. Maybe he's killed everyone along the way.

I silently go onto the boat and to our weapon stash there. Lifting up the back of my shirt, I slide my notebook into my pants at my hip and lower the shirt over it. I put the flashlight into one hand and grab a broad sword with the other.

I shake my head. The darkness is getting to me. The paranoia crept up and is making me imagine things.

There is a noise again; this time a squeaking scuff of a shoe. There was only one. The sound echoes into the grand space, but I can tell it came from down the hall towards Bourbon Street.

I get off the boat; taking the sword with me for the just in case. Shining the flashlight further down the way, I jog along the glass railings until I get to the entrance for the hall towards Bourbon Street.

I see a person going down the hall. They run when the light lands on them. That's suspicious. I start running after them.

Whether it's someone from their side or ours, I don't know, but I need to catch them. I almost yell out to the person but I stop myself. Who knows who else could be down the hall?

I chase the person down the hall, past the Bourbon Street line and further down. They stop suddenly. Something must have happened. I hear more people. I stop too and hold the flashlight against my stomach to stop the light.

A thought hits me, where were our guards? People should have been guarding the Bourbon Street crossing. One set down here and the other set upstairs.

Matt has been having people guarding his side too. Shoot first, ask questions later attitudes. Don't dare try to talk to them attitudes.

Did I walk into a trap? I suddenly feel very stupid. I pivot to turn back. If I sprint as fast as I can, I should be faster than many of them.

Someone screams. I turn back towards the ice rink. Something big and shadowy chases someone. I run once again towards the person. They're in danger and maybe I can help. The person jumps the half wall and onto the ice. The large humanoid creature does this more easily than he had.

I recognize the male now. It's Spencer; he's on our side.

"Hey! This way!" I shout as I get to the half wall. Neither shows that they noticed me. About to shout out again, I'm shut out by an awful creak and shattering. I hear it before I see something falling onto the ice. I look up. A large shadow, of a dragon I think, is trying to get inside the building through the large skylight. "This way! SPENCER!"

He notices me and tries to run my way as well as he can on the ice. Ten feet away he loses his balance and wipes out on the ice. He tries to get up. The creature is going to catch him. I get one leg up on the half wall.

A large shard of glass slides through Spencer's head easily. His body gives out and he falls to the ice. He's dead.

I hop back down off the wall. More people are coming from either side of me. The dragon has opened up enough of the sky light to be able to come inside. There is more than one.

I need to get out of here. I'm grossly outnumbered.

I run back towards the boat. I need help.

I hear someone further up yelling, "THE MALL IS UNDER ATTACK! WAKE UP! RUN!"

They're coming in from everywhere. One stops me. She looks human, but I would bet she isn't. I thrust the sword to her. She grabs it and wrenches it out of my hands. I kick her in the stomach and run past her while she's distracted for a moment.

The hall behind me lights up and I can feel the heat. Is the dragon breathing fire?

"DRAGONS!" I yell as I reach the grand opening.

I run towards Chapters. I have to get to Steph, Brad and Shawn.

James appears to my side. "Get out of here!" He runs past me towards the demons.

"NIKKI!" Steph screams my name. I look towards the bridge. All three are running towards me.

We need to get out. "This way!" Brad shouts. "Get to the truck!"

"They're attacking from there," I say.

"They're coming from everywhere," Shawn says.

"Follow James!" He's a powerful wizard. He's likely our best chance of survival. And, if they're attacking from all exits, there won't be a safe route out. We can make one with him.

I sprint towards James. Steph, Brad and Shawn catch up to me quickly when I have to punch and kick a large dog-like demon. Brad stabs the dog with a dagger. It falls to the ground.

I see James when a dragon lights up the upper level. He's only a few meters away fighting his way through the demons. There are a few people with him. A few more are in the hall fighting against some of the demons.

I wish I still had my sword, or at least any weapon. Instead, I pull up all the hand-to-hand combat skills I know. Though, I mostly just push the demons away from me. Brad and Shawn are able to kill a couple of them with daggers.

We catch up to James. He briefly looks to me with a frown. He pivots our direction back towards the other end of the mall. The hoards try to follow us, but James blocks the way with a water wall he pulls out from the pond.

The path looks clear after we get upstairs. We make a break for the doors. James and I lead the way. We rush through the doors.

We come out beside the theatre stairs. There is a large moving truck right in front of the stairs. With more trucks lined up and running.

There are a few people here, getting into the different trucks. Yet, still, there is maybe a quarter of those we should have. I don't see Tim and his family.

I pause. Should I go back? See if I can find more people, lead them this way? I look to the doors, it would be too dangerous.

Air whooshes by me. Something lands behind me then I'm grabbed from behind. I scream and try to struggle but it's no use. My scream is stopped in my throat when I'm thrust away; my ribs aching from the pressure. We land roughly on the back of a dragon. A lady is in front of me and a man behind me; still holding on to me painfully tight.

The dragon spreads his wings and jumps up.

The woman shouts, "Hold on."

I grab onto her shoulders at first instinct. I don't think it would be enough as the dragon flies up and away. It takes me minutes to get my stomach out of my throat and realize I won't fall off.

Who are these people and why did they take me?

Chapter 51

After a long day of deliveries, a shower was just what I needed before supper. I'm happy that I didn't have to go back to Chad's today, but I'm sure that delivery will come up again soon.

When I get downstairs I find a busy bar. Jerry is running back, and forth across the bar helping people get their food and drinks. There's no one else around to help him out. People passive aggressively comment about how long they've been waiting. Shout about being next, and argue over one another.

I push my way to the front and behind the bar. I go to the opposite end of where Jerry is, and ask the first person I see, "What would you like?"

"Two beers." He puts a coin currency into my hand that I have never seen before. It has some weight to it and has a ten written on it. It's a golden in colour, and perhaps may be gold itself.

I go to Jerry and show him the coin. "A guy wants two beers."

He takes the coin and jumps to the till. "Hit two for amount. Beer. The amount owed shows here, and ten cash. Two change." The till shows the total up top, and the drawer opens. He gives me two coins. They are both gold and say one on them. Each beer is four dollars no tax or cents involved. I think I've got it. "Open everything with caps, they go in here." He waves his hand towards a garbage can under the counter. Jerry goes back to his job, and I grab two beer bottles.

I'm nowhere near as fast as Jerry is to open up the beer but I manage to open them both after working away at the cap in a couple of places. The metal bends, and the seal pops.

I take the man his change and beers. He runs away without another word.

The next person is already shouting their drink order. The orders come quickly in. Jerry quickly shows me new things as I get to them, but soon I get a handle on it all.

I quickly notice a segregation of customers. My orders consist of beer, vodka, rum, and whiskey. Meanwhile, I hear mostly blood or brew orders with Jerry along with food.

He hands out the Fekete Vér bottles in coordination with the blood types ordered out, and mugs full of something coming out of the spout of a metal barrel.

I won't be trying that anymore. I assume I should stay away from the brew as well. I don't think I want to know what that barrel contains.

The crowd dies down at the bar once everyone gets their drink, and settles around tables. Jerry disappears into the kitchen for food now and then.

I handle all the drinks when it becomes manageable to do so.

My stomach growls. I ignore it but apparently, Jerry has super hearing. He pours a half glass of whiskey and hands it to me. "Go sit. I'll make you something to eat."

"Thank you," I say. I scan the room, and there is one empty table. Jerry goes back into the kitchen so I go to the table.

I sit at the table, and I take a sip of the brown liquid in a short glass. The whiskey is strong and heats the back of my throat. I wonder if perhaps I have Scottish or Irish heritage. Wait.

"You're in our spot." I panic. I wasn't expecting this to happen today. Oh no. What do I do? How can I fix this?

Three familiar-faced men stand in front of me. I look down, and adjust, pretending to get up from my seat. I know they are going to decline and join me. "I'm sorry. I'll move."

They laugh at me. "No, no. You don't have to move. We'll join you." The white man with black eyes says.

They sit down in the empty chairs around the round tabletop.

I know now to stay here. Rescue is coming. The onslaught doesn't last long. Perhaps, I can save a few people this time around.

I down the rest of my drink. Jerry comes over to the table right on cue. He shakes hands with one of the men. "Don't scare the poor girl; she's very flighty and too young for any of you. You should be thanking her. She's been doing runs in your absence."

This time I take offence to him calling me flighty. I let it go, however, because he doesn't know that I've now heard him insult me twice. Once is questionable, but twice is an insult. Although, to him, this is the first time so I have to give him the benefit of the doubt.

"In that case, get her a double of whatever she was drinking, on us. We'll have three rum and cokes, and do you have someone in the kitchen?"

"Not unless one of you wants to start cooking." Jerry jokes back. I wonder what he was planning on getting me for food if he's declining these gentlemen. Unless, he's joking. Who was cooking things back there earlier? Or, was Jerry quickly throwing things together?

There isn't any time to eat anyway.

I ready myself for the attack. How do I fix this?

There's not enough time to think.

A popping noise reverberates to the right. The noise catches the attention of everyone in the bar. It gets louder and louder. Glass crashes. Someone yells "Go out the back!"

I yell, "Stay here! Get down! Rescue is coming!" No one listens to me. I should have known it wouldn't have been so easy.

Jerry pulls me off the barstool and drags me out to the back. He stops, and I run into him. Someone yells, "It's blocked. Into the cellar."

I've changed nothing. People are still running up front and getting shot. Next, they go to the cellar to drown. What do I do?

There is a lurch of the crowd around me back in the opposite direction. I am lured to the side room behind the bar.

I go in this time. People are climbing down a hole in the ground. It's my turn, maybe this I can change. I turn around and climb down.

There is no bottom. When I get eight feet down, I'm told "right here" by black eyes behind me.

There is a space as big as the entrance as far as I can see below. There is a large tunnel across the chasm. Black eyes holds out his hand to assist me. I take his hand and jump to cross.

"There's an exit; just follow the tunnel." I walk past him. It's a tunnel in the ground. I can't see too much, but there is a bit of artificial light down here. I walk further into the space. It goes down only a small way before turning a corner. It opens up to a bigger room with crates and bottles.

I look for danger; they said the cellar was flooding. I don't see where from. There doesn't look like there is anything that could be the source of it in here. There's a ladder to the side leading to the exit. Someone is trying to open it, but it's not budging. They argue about snow/ice freezing it shut, or possibly someone parked on it.

I can't stay in here. But, I might get shot out there. Flooding couldn't come from here. Maybe from the deeper hole. I walk back to where black eyes is. He's still helping people down. I walk behind him and look down.

I see it right before I feel it. Black liquid rising from the hole. "EVERYONE GET OUT! WE'RE GOING TO DROWN!" The people in the immediate area are the only ones who seem to hear me.

Most don't seem too concerned yet, but the person climbing down retreats. I run to the corner of the tunnel, and shout the same thing to the people who've made it there. "EVERYONE GET OUT! WE'RE GOING TO DROWN!"

There is a surge of water that almost upends me. People seem to get it now. There is a rush of people pushing past me. I nearly get trampled before I squish myself to the wall.

The water quickly rises up to my hips. I have to work to push passed the rushing water.

People are clamouring for the ladder. I can only describe it as fear-induced survival of the fittest with people pulling others off. I hear horrifying screams with hints of garbled screams. I can see someone ripping another off the ladder, so they can take their place.

The water is up to my chest. At this rate, no one is getting out of here alive. I'm not going to get out of here alive. I'm going to drown waiting for my turn.

My chest hurts. I can't get through to the ladder, let alone up it.

My shoulders get grabbed, and a large body closes in on my back. "Let's get you out of here." I recognize black eyes' voice.

I have no push compared to him. The water may be up to my neck but it's still only up to his lower chest.

Almost like a wedge, we split through the crowd, and reach the ladder. He rips people off shouting commands and obscenities at them to work together to get everyone up.

I swim off the edge, and into the hole. My foot gets grabbed. I go under with little breathe. Hands bring me back up.

Black eyes pulls me to the ladder. I catch myself and climb alongside another person. They get out first. Someone grabs onto me and pulls me backward. I wrap my arms around the ladder. Their hands disappear.

The water keeps getting higher.

Finally, I get myself out of the hole. I kneel down. Bracing myself I put my hand into the hole. I grasp at hands. I pull when I catch a hand.

Someone else comes to help. They grab at the hand in mine and pull. We get one woman out of the hole.

Going back for another, I hit the water. I search through nothingness until I hit a head. Black eyes emerges from the water. I help him out onto the side.

I say, "Thank you." I look back into the pit, expecting to put my hand back in, but I see the water receding instead.

"JAIDEN!" I hear Calli shouting.

"In here!" I shout back. Relief fills me up. I hold in a laugh. I almost drowned, but at least I didn't get shot.

"JAIDEN!" She yells again.

She might not be able to hear me. I stand up and go to the door. "Calli!" I see her so I go to her. I run to her and grab her arm.

"JAIDEN!" She screams at me as she throws her arms around me. Water squishes out of my clothes.

Other people rush by us. There is panic but in a rescue vibe. She leads me to the front. I hesitate when I remember being shot in this area.

Logically, I know it won't happen the same this time, but I can't help my body's reaction to freeze. It doesn't want to get shot.

There are other people here that weren't lucky enough to have my vision. People I couldn't save. People who could have been alive if I had prepared a bit more; if I could have been a bit more convincing.

I have to start assuming every dream could happen for real, no matter how strange, illogical, or implausible they seem.

Bodies are littered everywhere. Dark liquid pools around each body. Is that one tinged yellow?

My chest aches from the guilt. I should be dying here with these people. I could have warned them better.

My head feels light. I shake it a little. I feel cold.

"I'm going to pass out." I announce as I realize it. My body moves out of my control forward. Everything turns black.

Chapter 52

"Alexa. Alexa." A hand is on my arm shaking me awake. Opening my eyes I look at Rayleen. "I'm not feeling good. I have to go to the bathroom."

"It's just around the corner, take a candle with you." I close my eyes to try to go back to sleep.

"Can you take me? Please, I'm scared. I don't want to go alone." I can't say no to that.

"Okay." I get up. Crystal notices our movement and decides to follow us. "Let's go." She grabs my hand. On the way out, I grab one of the candles in the hall. I take her to the washroom. She doesn't take long at all before she's done. "Are you feeling any better?"

"No." She shakes her head and pouts.

"Do you need to go back to the toilet?" Rayleen only answers me by shaking her head. "Okay, then let's go back to bed and maybe you'll feel better in the morning."

"No, I don't want to. Can you read me a book?" Rayleen tries to delay having to go back to bed. I'm tired and I just want to go back to bed. I don't want to deal with this right now.

A good timing yawn from her helps me. "No, come on Sweetie, we should go back to bed. You're so tired, you're yawning."

"No, I want story time." Rayleen raises her voice and throws her fists to her sides.

"I'll read you a book in the morning. We don't want to disturb the people sleeping in the library. Now, let's go back to bed." I raise my voice to go over hers.

"I don't want to! NO!" She is almost at a full-blown temper tantrum now. Her screams must be waking people from how loud she's being. Crystal tries to back her up by growling at me.

"You don't act like this. What is wrong with you? We are going back to bed and that's final." I scream at her, trying to scold her.

"NO!" Rayleen screams as loud as I'm sure she can. She throws herself onto the ground.

"What is going on here?" I jump from Miles' voice suddenly behind me.

Rayleen runs past me and grabs onto Miles.

"I don't feel good. I don't want to go back to bed." Her small voice is back. Rayleen wavers like she's on the edge of crying.

He touches the top of her head. "You said you want story time right? How about you and Alexa go to the cafeteria and I'll get a book. Just one book and then it's back to bed. Okay?"

Rayleen nods her head. She doesn't let go of him until he picks her up and carries her out of the bathroom.

Crystal follows right after them.

We go downstairs to the cafeteria. I grab her a bottle of water on our way in. Miles sets her down on a tabletop.

"I'll be right back." He runs off.

I open the bottle and hand it to her. She drinks a bit and gives it back. I put the cap back on and set it on the table beside her.

We say nothing. I don't know what to say to her. Why is she acting like this?

It doesn't take long for Miles to come back. He doesn't have a book with him. "We have to go!" He looks panicked. "The mall is being attacked! We've got to go, now!"

Standing up, I turn around and pick Rayleen up. Even with the extra weight, I still can run a lot faster than she could.

We run out one side of the cafeteria and towards the doors to the outside.

Someone yells. "THE MALL IS UNDER ATTACK GET UP! EVERYONE WAKE UP! WE NEED TO ESCAPE!"

Miles tries for the next nearest exit point, but before we even get there people run past us. "Don't go that way!" A chilling scream comes from that hall.

We run towards where the rest had gone. Fire lights up the ceiling. I hear someone yell, "DRAGONS!"

I spot the first demon after it drops down from the upper floor. I have no idea what it is. It doesn't look human; with its horns, elongated head and long body. The blue skin almost looks black in the lack of light.

The demon grabs someone running by. Opening its mouth, which takes up half its face, it bites her head off. The crunch sickens me.

Miles charges the demon. It jumps out of the way onto the railing. There is a knife in the demon's chest. It growls at Miles when he charges the demon again. It grabs Miles in both of its arms. Kelly comes from above and with a sword, in hand, she cuts off the demon's arms. It falls back into the water as the arms fall away from Miles.

Kelly says something to Miles before he comes over to us. "Theatre exit. Make it to the trucks."

I nod though it's useless. He's already turned away and started running. Going after him down the hallway, we get quite a ways away. We make it to the doors and outside. Climbing the stairs to the upper floor.

The cold air hurts my lungs but I keep running until we get to the moving truck. There are multiple vehicles to choose from but this one has a cover over it. The other trucks are sticking people in the back with no protection.

I get Rayleen in first, then myself. Crystal jumps up beside us and snuggles into Rayleen.

People run over being led by James. Nikki stops her approach. I look at Crystal and her sudden screech.

A thud makes me look back outside. A dragon has landed right behind the truck with Sandra riding on top.

Nikki screams. Darius grabs her then jumps and lands on the back of the dragon with Nikki in his arms.

The dragon spreads its' wings. It jumps up, flaps its wings and is gone quickly.

James gets into the back with a few others and yells, "That's it, Miles, let's go. Everyone hold on!" He waits to close the door until after we start to move. I crouch to the cold floor and grab onto a railing. Rayleen is now on the ground but still clutched to my side.

"Why did he take her?" I ask quietly. Darius was here, a few meters away, and decided to take Nikki. Why her?

"Who is she?" James asks everyone. He was wondering the same thing. "Out of everyone here, what would Darius and Sandra want with Nikki?

No one offers up anything. They look around to each other for an answer, and shrug and shake their heads.

"Is she working with them?"

"No!" One of her male friends defends her. "I've known her most of our lives, there's no way she would be working with them."

James puts his hand up to concede and hush the friend. "We have to assume it's something important then. They attacked tonight, we have to assume specifically to take her. Why would they do that?"

"I don't know." He admits.

"We should attack the farm tonight," Kelly announces. "We don't have anything near the numbers we had. But, they won't be expecting us. We can guerrilla warfare from the forest."

"It's too soon." Miles objects.

"We have to assume she's important to something. What if this is our last chance before their plan becomes irreversible?" Kelly counters.

Kelly continues, "They're still attacking the mall. There won't be as many people at the farm."

"Miles, head to the farm," James orders. "She's right. This could be our best chance. Does anyone have paper and something to write with?"

"I think there's something in the glove box." Miles shouts over the noise of the thundering walls. James goes past everyone to join Miles up front.

"Open the crates. There should be a crate of weapons and armour somewhere." James shouts to the back.

Various people get up and open the crates, then hand things out. I stay with Rayleen and just let them work.

They hand out food and a weapon first. The armour will be handed out when people can change without falling over.

After everyone settles we sit in silence, until we pull into a long driveway surrounded by trees. I assume we're at the neighbouring farmhouse.

James comes to the back with papers clutched in his hands. "Once we stop no one speaks, just go into the house. Find a place to settle and wait for further instructions." He hands me a paper. "Some of you will get papers, others won't." He hands Rayleen a piece. "They have instructions for each of you."

James hands the last paper out just as the truck and the noise stops. Kelly pulls up the door. All the other trucks park shortly after us.

James jumps out the back and goes to the closest pick-up. I get up, pick up my blade and jump out. Seeing the height of some of the snow where we will need to walk, I grab Rayleen out of the back and carry her.

The snow chills my ankles and clings to my pants as high as my knee. Kelly goes in the front door so I follow her. I let Rayleen down once we hit the covered deck. I stomp my feet on the deck to shake off some of the snow. Crystal leaps onto the deck and shakes off a bunch of the snow.

The house is almost as cold as outside. I set down my weapons by the fireplace. I know Rayleen is cold so the first thing I do, is search for a closet or a bedroom with blankets.

To the right of the entrance is a hallway with three bedrooms and a bathroom. I pull all of the sheets off the beds and bring them into the living room to wrap around Rayleen. A couple of people get the same idea and pull more blankets and towels to wrap up in.

"Better?" I ask her. She nods back to me with a small smile.

I pull the pieces of paper out of my pocket. The first one says, 'Stay at the abandoned farmhouse.' Flipping open the second one I find an ominous, 'Come see me.' That can't be good.

I assume Rayleen's is the first and mine is the latter. I tell Rayleen, "I'll be right back. Stay here. Keep warm."

James is sitting at the kitchen table discussing something with Miles. I walk the few meters up to them.

"Have a seat," James says without looking at me. He moves a piece of paper and a pencil to me. He hushes his voice, "I need you to tell me everything you saw there. How many people? Draw me a map of the farm. A layout of the house."

My mind is filled with the different memories of the place all at once. I start drawing the house in the middle of the paper. Just a box with an 'L' shape of the outside to show the deck. "Umm. There are three floors. Ram and Sandra babysat us. Darius came in every once in a while. Shale too. But, no one else was in the house. I think they stayed elsewhere. Oh, there were hobgoblins in the basement."

"How many entrances?" James asks.

"Two. One on the main floor and the other is in the basement." I place darker lines on the square showing where the doors would be.

He points to the door on the right side of my drawing. "Is this door hidden by the deck?"

"Yes, it faces the forest and you can't see it from much of the road." I draw the road coming out from around the toy barn, in front of the house, winding around to the back of the farm. Next, I draw a couple of quick trees to show where the forest would be.

"Do you know where they would put Nikki?" James asks.

"They'd probably put her in the room beside Sandra's upstairs. Or, maybe the bedroom on the main floor?"

I set back to working on the map while James talks. I draw the toy barn, the open field near the house, the hill gets labelled, the slaughterhouses and the barn in the back.

"Good. We have to be as quick as possible. Since you know the house layout, you'll be in charge of rescuing her from the house. While we take care of them, you need to get Nikki out of there and back here." James notices my map. "What is this?" He points his finger over the area with the slaughterhouses and barn.

"Part of the farm too. Darius and Shale took Rayleen and me to the barn to see the griffins back there. I saw the slaughterhouse while we were there. Oh." I draw a pathway and a pond somewhere in the forest. "We went to this pond and saw a dragon too."

"Damn. I didn't know the area was so large." He thinks for a moment. "Is this all?"

I look at the map for a moment. "Yes."

"Okay. I'll be back in a moment." He takes my map with him. I turn in my seat. He doesn't go far. James says something to King Zircon. Nodding to James, he starts gathering the dwarves telling them to go outside and to prepare to leave in two minutes.

James comes back to the table. "Can I see the pencil?"

I hand it to him. James boxes out an area on the map and labels it 'Dwarves'. The area covers a third of the map; the areas in and around the toy barn, the field, and the pond.

He names the house 'Us'. James gets up and goes downstairs without another word. He returns a moment later with a herd of people following after him. They go out the front door while James comes back to the table.

He sections off most of the rest of the farm, excluding the slaughterhouses. This gets labelled 'K and D'. The large section is named 'Rest'. James looks up "Daniel, you're not going with them. Kelly come here." She jumps over the couch and stairway and lands in the kitchen beside Miles. "Take Daniel back here to the slaughterhouses. Free everyone, you find there. Kill anyone that tries to stop you."

Kelly looks at Daniel with a disgusted glare. "He'll just slow me down." James gives Kelly a hard stare to dissuade all complaints. I get a feeling that if he doesn't return it will probably be because of friendly fire. Daniel's face goes white and I think he just had the same thought. Kelly walks past him, grabbing his shirt and making him follow as she stomps out of here.

Almost everyone is gone now. Only Rayleen, two unknown people that came from the mall, Tim and his parents remain in the living room. From the lack of noise, I assume that everyone else has left; except us at the table.

"We'll be leaving in about five minutes. That will give them all the time the others need to get into place." James informs us.

"We're doing this right now!" The words explode from my mouth. I had thought that's was what was going on but hearing it still comes as a surprise. I wish I could take the words back as soon as everyone starts staring at me.

"Yes. Say your goodbyes, and get ready."

I get up immediately. Rayleen must have been listening because she is already on her way over to me. She latches onto my waist.

"Don't go away like mommy and daddy did!" Her eyes are puffy and tears stream down her cheeks.

My mind blanks. What do I say to her? I can't guarantee that I won't die. I can't guarantee that I will come back to her. My eyes blur towards the bottom.

Miles kneels beside us. "Rayleen, I promise that I will protect her and make sure she comes back. Okay?"

She lifts her head off of me enough to look at him. "Okay."

"Up." Her arms loosen briefly, while I pick her up, only to wrap around my neck. I take her back over to the couch. Miles and James grab their things quickly and go to the door while I tuck her into the blankets. I kiss her. "I'll be back in a few hours. Get some sleep."

"I love you. I'll miss you."

"I love you too. I won't be gone long." Kissing her on the top of her head, I can't look at her anymore without a searing pit in my chest. I turn around and I grab my weapons off the ground and go meet Miles and James outside. I close the door behind me.

"Are you okay?" Miles asks me.

I take a deep breath before answering. "Let's just go." On our walk, I try to scrub the goodbye from my memory. Focus on the upcoming battle, so I can return safe and sound. Focus on what's going on around me so I'm not caught off guard.

We don't say anything as we travel through the dark and quiet forest. I can't see too far in front of me but Miles and James seem to know exactly where they are going. I keep close to James to make sure I don't get lost.

My footsteps are loud against the silence and for a few meters I try to make them quieter, but it doesn't help. Finally, I see some lights in the distance.

James slows down the pace. He seems to be hiding behind trees at some points, so I fall into step right behind him. Miles takes his own path. A few meters from the tree line we stop and crouch behind some bushes. Miles grabs onto a nearby tree and scales up it.

We sit and wait. I don't know for how long. James busies himself by looking around us. I can't see Miles up in the tree.

We wait. My legs cramp up so I kneel down. The moment I do, I feel wetness seep into my pants. I have immediate regrets and get back up.

A boom sounds in the distance right before I see the orange glow of a flame. James takes off. It takes Miles grabbing my hand and pulling me up before I realize that is probably a sign that something's happening. When did he get down out of the tree?

We run across the short space between the tree line and the house. James doesn't wait for us to open the door and he heads into the basement. It doesn't take long for us to reach the entrance.

Miles stops me outside the door. "Stay." He goes inside. I can hear the tiny footsteps and whispers. I'm unsure if the shiver up my spine is from the cold or the chilling sound.

I am blinded for a moment. The basement light turns on. The hobgoblins screech from the light. I hide further behind the doorway. Miles pulls out his sword and slices some of the creatures in half. James stops one from running. It floats into the air and slams into a nail on the stairway. Others scurry away to hide.

Ram is halfway down the stairs by the time I notice anyone coming down them. There are two other sets of feet coming down them.

Somehow, I don't think I will be able to get by three people. There is another entrance though. Before any of them could realize I am here, I back away from the basement entrance. Turning around, I look for anyone that could be coming down the path. There are a few people there fighting but no one would be paying attention to me.

I hug against the deck wall to peek around the corner. Everyone is fighting.

Taking the chance I run; around the deck and up the stairs. The front door was left wide open in someone's rush. Avoiding the basement door, I go through the kitchen way.

I almost fall as I trip over something. Looking down it was a small leg.

It's not Rayleen's. She wasn't wearing jeans.

No, I stop. She is at the other house.

They killed some other child.

I take a deep breath. Back to my job. I go through the living room and up the stairs. I don't hesitate for a second to go straight to my room. Opening the door and rushing in all in the same movement to come face to face with Nikki thrusting a broken chair leg at me.

A little scream escapes. Nikki's reflexes help her to stop before she hits me. Noises float up from the basement battle. Someone sounds like they just about went through the floorboards. Time isn't something we can waste here.

I tell her, "Let's go." I run out ahead of her back down the path I came through. I'm a bit quicker this time. I feel like this is a home run from this point. Rushing out the door and around to the side of the building, I stop for a brief moment. Ram, Sandra, Miles and James are all still fighting.

I pull out the dagger I had placed through my belt loop and hand it to Nikki. Pointing towards the forest, she gets the idea that we need to go and starts running.

She's faster than me. She makes it into the tree line before seeing that I am falling behind. Nikki slows her speed only a little but enough for me to catch up.

In a blink, she is thrown to the ground and my neck is being gripped by a cold hand. I can't breathe through the pain and Darius' squeeze.

Tears roll down my cheeks. I can't get any air into my lungs.

Staring into his eyes, there is something different about him. His eyes have darkened. His skin looks ashen and sunken in; even in the lack of light.

Lips and teeth smack with mine. More pain. Liquid drips down my chin before his tongue laps it up.

Floating for a split second, before I hit the ground. I gulp for air.

Darius walks over to Nikki and picks her off the ground. I can only look at him for a moment before he disappears as fast as he appeared.

Still gasping in the air, I get up with the help of a tree. I pick up the dropped dagger. Steadying myself, I run back towards the farmhouse.

Swiping my hand across my chin and lips, I pull it away immediately wishing I hadn't; my lips sting and blood is now on the palm on my hand. I rub it on the stomach of my shirt.

Getting to the door frame I quickly stop myself. "Darius got Nikki," I yell to James and Miles.

Shit. Ram is in front of me. He pushes me to the side. I fall unbalanced and land on a pile of cut-up wood. Ram runs towards the front of the house. Sandra pushes Miles and James back in a whoosh of air, then runs after Ram.

Miles recovers first. He helps me stand up. My lips itch, but the blood flow stops.

He turns back through the doors. I make it there in time to see someone fly across and into the wall. Something cracks. I'm not sure whether it was from the wall or the person or even both. They don't move. I'm sure they're dead.

James looks at me. "Are you okay?"

"Yes," I say automatically though I am not sure at the moment. I must look awful. My neck has probably bruised and I have my own blood everywhere.

There is a loud roar from a crowd of people outside. I go to take a look. James and Miles follow behind me as a crowd of people run down the path. They go out in front of the house where the demons are fighting the dwarves. Some I recognize but there are many I don't.

They're closing the area of the battle. The extra people from the slaughterhouse must have decided to help us.

James and Miles rush to help. I stay here. It's a debate for me on whether I should go help or stay behind. We seem to be winning. More of them are being killed than us. Before I can change my mind, I run towards them.

I ready my dagger to stab someone when I get there. Just out of my view I see something rush towards me. I stop. A wolf humanoid creature blocks me from the rest of the battle. It snarls and growls at me. It stands up on its hind legs and walks towards me; slowing turning back into a person.

Frozen in my spot I tighten my grip on the dagger. Kelly's brief lesson rings in my head; aim for the heart and head. My eyes go to where its heart should be. I focus on that.

It lunges towards me.

My hand goes forward and hits something hard. I let go of the dagger lodged in its chest and move out of the way. It slumps down to all fours and growls. Keeling over to its side; it stops breathing.

I need my dagger back. It was dumb to have let go of it. I cautiously walk over to it. Watching for any signs of movement I grab the hilt of the dagger and pull.

I turn around. One of the blue demons at the mall has its mouth open ready to bite my head off. A blade slices quickly through the opened mouth. The sword pulls out and Miles pushes the body to the side to fall.

"Are you okay?" He asks.

"Yes." I hear flapping above. Looking up I see a dragon.

"We leave now!" Darius yells out to his group. The battle was won by us, but not completely. They still have Nikki.

My heart stops when I hear Rayleen scream. Sandra holds Rayleen on top of the dragon. They are at enough of an angle I can see Nikki on it too.

"RAYLEEN!" I scream. Sandra looks at me and laughs deeply. The dragon starts flying back in the direction of the abandoned house.

I run after them. There is no hope.

Miles passes me. I stop at the tree line. Miles has disappeared and the dragon is far off in my view.

James comes up behind me. "It's no use, Alexa. You won't be able to catch them. Come back and help. We have many injured that need to be moved into the house." I hear the words but half of them don't make sense in my mind. "Now."

He wraps his arm around my shoulder to guild me to the house. "Go into the washrooms and see if you can find any type of first aid supplies. Bring it into the living room."

"There's a dead body in there." The words come out in all one tone; escaping as I think them.

James turns around and orders people from his place on the deck. "Everyone who is injured please go around the side to the basement door. If you can, help those who are more injured than yourselves." He turns back around to me and ushers me into the house. "Go find the supplies, I will take care of the body."

I start in the bathroom just down the hall. Rifling through the cupboards, I find a large tin filled with a thrown together first aid kit. I grab that and the few towels that are hung up. The bathroom doesn't have much else. Backing out, I spot the soap and grab that as well.

The lights to the basement are still on. The stairs don't look like they were damaged at all from the fight but I still go down cautiously.

People are already starting to make the basement into a makeshift hospital. Some blankets are being laid on the concrete and some are laying on them. I am swarmed as soon as I reach the floor. The supplies are taken from my arms.

I go all the way upstairs to the second bathroom. There is nothing useful in this one except a few towels and soap. I look in the mirror. I look like I belong in a horror movie. Drying blood covers my chin and the front of my sweater. Taking the sweater off, I turn it around and use the back of the shirt to clean myself. I turn on the tap enough to wet the cloth and start rubbing the blood away.

It takes a bit of work to get most of it off, but it doesn't take long. I abandon the sweater on top of the bathroom garbage.

I grab the towels and the soap and return to the basement. Fewer people notice me this time. They are busy helping to bandage people up. James is delegating people different tasks; go boil water; we need to sterilize; rip the bedsheets up for more bandages; go to the other farmhouse for more first aid supplies.

People take the soap and towels. I just stand here. Watch the chaos around me. Miles has come back. He walks towards me. There's no Rayleen.

"How are you doing?" Miles asks as he reaches out the touch my arm.

"How do you think?" Knocking his hand away from me; I don't want his touch right now. I don't want him messing with me.

He gets upset. "I'm sorry. I couldn't catch up to them. They were going too fast. But I swear as soon as we are able, we'll go look for her."

Now, he makes me feel worse. I shouldn't have thrown his hands back like that. "I should have stayed with her."

Miles shakes his head. "Then, you might've been captured too."

I can't handle this conversation any longer. It's my fault. If I hadn't left Rayleen alone, we'd still be together.

I turn away from Miles and go back up the stairs. The upstairs bathroom calls my name. I close the door behind me.

I look through the drawers. I find a pair of scissors. The edge might be sharp enough. I set the toilet seat down. Putting the scissors down on the counter I undo the button on my pants and pull them down to my shins. I sit down on the cold toilet seat.

Griping the scissors in my left hand I look at them. They call to me.

I sob. Hot tears cool quickly. My heart races so hard my chest hurts. Apprehensive of what I'm about to do, I hesitate. I know I shouldn't do it, but confusingly it helps me cope.

I open the scissors up and run the blade against the skin of my thighs. Lighter at first, I make white lines on my skin. The blade isn't sharp enough that the small amount of pressure even would break my skin. I swipe the blade across harder and harder. Finally, a bead line of blood is drawn. My hands shake from the sight. Not in fear but pleasure. The blood releases my hurt; it makes me feel better. Scars from my previous sessions remind me how addicting this feeling is.

I tire of swiping once I get a few lines drawn. Closing up the scissors I put my hand in it to get a better grip. Pushing together a bit of skin, I open the scissors and snip a tiny circle of skin off.

And again.

And again.

And again.

Finally satisfied with my bloody art, I put the scissors down on the counter. I watch the blood for a bit. Tearing some toilet paper off the roll I set to cleaning up the mess. The bloody tissues go onto the counter. The second batch of toilet paper gets a quick douse of cold water. It soothes the burn when I touch it to the wounds.

Once the bleeding has pretty much stopped and all the blood is cleaned up, I stand up. I pull my pants up carefully.

I feel much the same now, but more in control. A numbness creeps in.

I wash the scissors in the sink and put them back in the drawer. The tissues go into the toilet and I flush them away.

The makeup I had used previously is still in here. I do up my whole face in the makeup routine I love: foundation, mascara, eyeliner, purple eye shadow, blush, and light red lipstick.

Ready to face the outside I unlock the door. One deep breath and I open the door. No one is on this level but I can hear some people have gone into the living room a floor down.

Not wanting to deal with anyone else I go the other way into my room.

Stepping over the broken chair, I go to the dresser to change into my own clothes. Nikki's notebook sits on top. I'll keep it with me. Make sure I can get it back to her.

I open up the drawers to the cabinet and my clothes are still there. I pull out a pyjama set and get dressed in fresh clothes. The shorts barely cover my new wounds but they do well enough. The tank top is cold, so I grab a sweater as well to go over top.

Exhaustion makes my head fuzzy. I pull the covers on the bed up and get in.

I hug the one pillow to myself and lay my head on the other.

Chapter 53

We start to descend. As soon as we reach the ground I have my chance. I swing and hit the woman controlling the dragon. My feet barely touch the ground when I realize this plan sucked.

There are too many people to catch me. How far would I get? We are in the middle of nowhere.

A man grabs my arm and yanks me towards the house. Looking around for an escape route is futile. I won't go like this. I won't make it easy for them to drag me around.

I try ripping my arm away from his grasp. When that doesn't work, I thrash my entire body back and forth. He's too strong. I still won't give up.

Each door, wall, or heavy object we pass gets grabbed. Nothing phases the man dragging me through the house. It feels like I'm not even trying. My fingers hook around the door frame but are quickly pulled loose. Even when we get to the stairs he pulls me up despite trying to grip the banister.

The strength he possesses is terrifying. I know that he could literally do anything, and I wouldn't be able to stop him.

He pulls my arm, then pushes me into the bedroom. I catch my balance on the dresser. Turning around quickly I leap towards the door, but not fast enough before it's shut in my face. I bang on the door. Twisting the handle I try to see if they forgot to lock it, but I don't have that kind of luck.

I settle down on the bed and think. Scanning the room I look for anything that I can use for a weapon.

The notebook in my pants is scratching up my hip. I pull it out of its place and set it on top of the dresser.

I need to do something. I double-check the room for weapon-type items. Going through the closet, dresser, under the bed, and everywhere else in here.

I don't find anything useful as is.

I'll have to ambush the next person who comes through the door and makes a run for it.

There is a chair in here. I walk to the door and place my ear against it. I listen for any noise. I don't hear anything but that doesn't mean there isn't anyone there.

I lay the chair down on the floor and kick at the leg. The wooden chair doesn't take long to break.

I grab the leg and ready myself into an attack position. I wait. And, wait.

There has to be something else I can do? Some other way I can escape? I start thinking about my choices, and the best options. We're on the second floor, which makes the window not an ideal place to escape from.

The door is locked, and looks like an old fashioned solid door, so I can't kick my way through.

The hinges! The hinges are on this side of the door. Dad used to pop those out with a screw driver and a hammer. I doubt I'll find either, but I might be able to find something to pop the pins out. Then, I can pull the door out.

I scour the room for a handful of objects that might work as replacement screwdriver and hammer, and put them to the test. The chair leg works well as a mallet, but the screwdriver replacement is harder to find.

The clothes hangers aren't strong enough. I try the inside metal of a belt clasp. Sticking it up through the bottom hole, I smash the mallet into it. The pin budges up an inch with work, but I can't work it out further.

A dull bang puts me on edge.

Screams come from a distance beyond the window. I don't know what's happening but something is. The screams are quickly over. I tense.

I look out the window, but I can't see anything in the light to dark contrast.

Am I next? I wait in silence while trying to figure out my next best option. Do I continue to try to break out? Do I prep for an attack? Am I being rescued?

Silence.

Waiting and waiting.

Someone's coming up the stairs. I leap off the bed and get back into the fighting stance. The door swings open and I lurch forward; swinging the chair leg.

It's Alexa. I stop my swing before it hits her. Something big is happening. It sounds like the battle is going on in the house.

Alexa says a quick, "Let's go," and runs downstairs.

I follow after her. Going down the stairs I spot the bodies. There is a body on the floor. I don't have time to stop.

Alexa is ahead of me by a few seconds. I pick up the pace and follow her to the side of the house. Alexa stops and hands me a dagger then points towards the trees. I nod and start running.

In the open, I'm faster than she is. I slow down a little because I have no idea where I am going.

The world blurs as I fly to the ground. I don't know what happened, but I crash to the ground. The dagger flies from my hand. I look up to a gasping noise and see a large man; the one who dragged me through the house.

I start picking myself off the ground when I am pulled from it. I'm tossed over a shoulder and ran back out of the forest. I hit my fists against his back trying to make some sort of fight but it is useless.

He jumps up onto a dragon and finally lets me go. The lady from earlier is holding onto Rayleen. I settle down behind the lady. We go up into the air.

The man yells. "We leave now!"

Rayleen screams. The lady puts a hand over her mouth to muffle her screams. She's struggling to get off the dragon. We're too high up; she's going to hurt herself.

"Rayleen, Hunny. It's Nikki. Rayleen, it's Nikki. I need you to calm down Sweetheart. I'm here with you. Everything is going to be okay. But, I need you to stop struggling because I don't want you to fall off." I talk in a calming voice; however, I know we are screwed.

My effort is wasted as soon as Alexa yells out Rayleen's name. In all her cruelty, the lady laughs at her. Rayleen starts crying again.

We fly up and away. I don't know where we are going now.

"Shut up or I'll throw you off." She growls to Rayleen.

"Pass her to me," I say. She might be calmer with me.

She lifts her up and over. She holds her over the edge. I can't help but get the feeling that the lady just might drop her.

Rayleen screams and begs in incoherent sounds. My heart breaks for her. She's terrified.

I reach as far as I can without losing my balance. The lady finally decides to keep passing Rayleen over to me. I swoop her up and get her straddling the dragon's back.

The little girl sobs into my chest. I let her be for now. She needs to work out her feelings, so long as our captors let her.

"Shut her up or I'll feed her to the dragon," Darius shouts in my ear.

The warning is enough to quieten Rayleen to small whimpers and shakes. I grip her tighter. Lending comfort as much as I receive it.

I peer off into the darkness. Where are we going now?

Chapter 54

My face hurts.

Something in my mouth feels odd. I move my tongue to swallow.

Is that my front tooth touching the roof of my mouth?

Sliding my tongue under the tooth, I push it back to where it should be. I hope I don't lose that tooth. I glide my tongue across the back of my top teeth, then over the bottom. This helps put the tooth in its exact place.

My face hurts.

I reach up to my face with both hands. My glasses are gone. The sides and top of my nose feel proper. I know I face planted, but I don't think a broke anything. Well, maybe my tooth and my glasses.

I open my eyes to see the lobby ceiling.

"Jaiden!" Lucas rushes to my side first. Others follow quickly after.

"Did you just leave me where I fell?" I ask rhetorically.

"We rolled you over. You were alive, and we didn't know when you might come to." Calli answers. "There's a lot going on."

Another thought comes to mind that it might have been unintentionally medically better for them to leave me. If I had broken my neck or something, they could have done further damage by moving me.

"How are my glasses?" I ask.

"They bent. We tried to bend them back into place as best we could." Lucas hands them to me.

I put them on, and they don't feel right. I twist the frame a little and adjust the nose pieces. I try them again, and I'll live with the results.

I sit up slowly, despite protests around me. There is a hand on my back helping me sit up, but I haven't the care to check to see who owns that hand.

Everything seems okay, and I don't feel dizzy at all so I stand up. I may still have a concussion, so I should stay up late tonight. Or, was it having to wake every couple of hours? Both?

The pub is mostly empty now. Some bodies have been removed, and able-bodied people have vacated the area. The few people remaining are helping with clean up.

"Jaiden. Jaiden, come sit. Drink this. Eat this." Jerry catches my view at the second mention of my name. I nod to him and take the proffered seat.

The four-legged seat keeps me grounded, and level. I drink the liquid. As far as I can tell it's just brown pop. He probably thought the sugar may be good for me. I may have passed out from low blood sugar compounded with a panic attack, so he may not be too far off in his thoughts. The granola bar will help too.

I try to pull away from a suddenly touchy wrist against my head, but it's to no avail. The hand belongs to Calli. She persistently holds her hand to my forehead.

"What are you doing?" I ask her.

"Checking for a fever." She says.

I relent. Would I even get a fever from a concussion? I don't think so. A concussion happens when your brain bounces off your skull. I didn't think there were many outward signs of a concussion.

Perhaps the best detection would be questioning and remembering things.

My name is Jaiden, and I'm fifteen years old. I have a narcissistic, misogynistic, chauvinistic, xenophobic father. Well, not my father. I have a Jacob. I have a man who provided basic necessities of life, but even that went downhill after my mom died, and he found himself a male heir to carry on the Kensington name.

My mom died when I was a kid, and I only met my birth dad this last summer. Well, can I really call him my dad? We aren't at the place and relationship where I feel like he'd be what a dad is supposed to be.

I'll come back to it.

I'm a high honours student in school; whatever that's supposed to mean once I get out into the real world.

2x2=4.

5% tax on a $28.00 is 8x5=40 20x5=100 so 140. $1.40.

A hand in front of my face catches my attention. "Yes," I ask.

"Oh good. I thought we lost you there. Are you okay? How do you feel?" Calli looks concerned over my not paying attention to her.

"Yes. I'm fine. I was just going over a few things in my head. One of the signs of a brain injury is lacking memory, so I was going over basic information and math. I didn't notice anything off, but I should stay up late just encase." I advise her.

She looks dumbfounded for a moment. "Well, it sounds like you have everything taken care of."

I sip my drink, and take in my surroundings; moreover, the people bustling about.

Should I have responded to Calli? It doesn't look like she was looking for one. She has moved to a seat at the same table.

I open the granola bar and take great care to make sure I don't bite or chew with the tooth that bent backwards.

I run my tongue along the tooth to make sure it stays in place. I'm too scared to test the tooth much more than that. I hope I won't lose it. There are no dentists around to fix it. I don't want to go years without a front tooth. I press my tongue down on it to keep trying to keep it in spot; if that'll do anything.

Time ticks by. Calli and Lucas go to bed when they get too exhausted to stay awake with me.

Jerry, black eyes, and a couple of others promise to babysit me. This means more pop, and pieces of conversation while they continue tidying.

Other than to go to the bathroom, I'm not allowed up from my seat. It's been debated about whether I should move to sit on the ground or not; five times.

They eventually give in hours later to take a break. Light chit-chat quickly gives way to talk about the events of what happened; theories at the least.

Jerry's theory involves a rival gang he's been in disputes with. He spins a classic tale of claims to a territory, and a cut of the money. Jerry resisted so this was a message to stop fighting it.

Black eyes, or rather Ziam, poses a rather important question. He asks will they attack again. Jerry doesn't think it will be soon but has plans to move operations to a secondary location.

There is a long silence.

"Tell us about yourself, Jaiden." Ziam finally breaks the silence, though I wish he hadn't.

"What do you want to know?" I take a drink.

"Where are you from? What did you do before the uprising?" Ziam's questions are extremely general. The answer spans over fifteen years. But, I don't want to reveal much.

"I'm from Leduc; born and raised. I umm, didn't do much before the uprising. I was an honour student in high school."

"How old are you?" Ziam interrupts me.

Momentarily, I think about playing the 'how old do you think I am' game, but I think better of it. "Fifteen."

Ziam leans back. "Well, now I feel like a creep." He shakes his head and huffs. "You're not old enough to drink alcohol. You're not old enough to drive. Jerry?"

Jerry shrugs. "She acts old for her age. Old laws don't apply."

"I've always been told I have an old soul." I offer up.

"Shouldn't you be with family?" Ziam asks.

"My mom passed away when I was a kid, and my dad didn't come back to the house for me. I waited a week, but he didn't show up.

My parent's cut off most of their family years ago, so there wasn't anyone else on those sides. I tried going to my grandma through my other dad's side, but they were killed by a group staying in their house."

"Go back. I think you need to explain a bit more." Jerry says. "Other dad?"

"Oh, umm. My mom slept with one guy and got pregnant, but she met an older man, slept with him, and told him he got her pregnant. So, I thought that I was his until after she died.

I don't know if he knows, or not. I never told him. We snuck around because we didn't know how he'd take it.

So, one of her old friends showed up to the funeral, and kept in touch afterwards. She eventually told me about the secret, and started tracking down my birth father.

So, I was introduced to that family last summer.

And, we were joking about an apocalypse and agreed to all go to Grandma's house if it ever happened. When I got tired of waiting for Jacob to get home, I went to Grandma's house, but when I got there I found a group of humans.

They said werewolves killed the people there, but then I found out the werewolves were the neighbours in the area, and family friends with my grandparents. The son of Alpha Ken, was dating my sister actually.

The humans had kidnapped a couple of the werewolves from the pack so we attacked, and when we were rescuing them, I found a bunch of dead bodies belonging to my family. Some had bullet holes, so I naturally can imagine what happened."

"God girl, you should write a book about your life, and then get it made into a soap opera," Wren says.

"You have no idea. I've been told that by a few people. My life was crazy even before all this happened.

But, enough about me, let's talk about you all." I try to switch the subject off of me. "Are you from Red Deer?"

Each responds affirmatively. An awkward silence follows. No one uses the opportunity to continue to talk about themselves. I can't think of a good follow up question.

"I'm beat. You're probably safe to get some sleep now. You seem fine." Jerry declares as he gets up from his seat.

"Sure, yeah." We all follow suit and head off to our respective rooms for the night.

Chapter 55

Dried blood clings to the fabric of my shorts. Patiently, I pull down the cloth trying to minimize the amount of scab I pull off.

It takes a while, but I eventually get the shorts to come off. There aren't too many scabs pulled off and they are not bleeding much, so I don't think I'll need to worry about it happening again.

I pull on a pair of black yoga pants and grab the notebook before going out of this room and to the bathroom.

My make-up smudged only slightly through the tears and during the night. I fix my face. Looking presentable, I decide to find anyone else.

By the looks of the sky, I cannot tell if it is early morning or early evening, but I would guess it to be the latter from how exhausted I had been last night.

Stepping out of the bathroom door, I notice a couple of people sleeping on the furniture. Curious, I check to see if anyone took Sandra's bed; four people are crammed onto the bed.

I go down the stairs quietly. A couple more are sleeping on the couches down here. Bandages are wrapped around different parts of each body. They both appear to be breathing, so that is one good sign.

Crashing metal makes me jump. That noise is followed by someone shushing.

James pokes his head out of the kitchen. He examines the two bodies sleeping on the couch then motions with his finger for me to come into the kitchen.

"Good evening. Are you feeling any better? You looked like a ghost last night." He puts his arm up to my forehead to get an idea of my temperature.

My mind blanks. I don't think I can form any sentences that wouldn't immediately be taken as a lie, so I just nod.

"Good." He tries to hand me a box of crackers. "What's that?" James motions to the book in my hand.

"Nikki's notebook. She left it behind."

"Can I see that?" He pulls the notebook from my hand and cracks it open.

"Nikki doesn't like people reading it." Letting him know, doesn't stop him.

He slowly frowns as he flips through the pages, then shakes his head. "She's a prophet. That's why they took her. We'll have to get her back."

"What do you mean?" I ask.

He shakes his head continuously and sighs deeply. "She has visions of the future. A Marshall right under my nose. No wonder she never introduced herself by her full name."

"It's a poetry book," I state. She said it was a poetry book.

James gives me a hard look. He tucks the book into an inside pocket of his jacket. "Would you mind helping us take food downstairs?" He finds a couple of cans and gives them to me. "Off you go."

I want to ask for the book back, but I don't think he would give it to me. Was she really a prophet? Are the poetry entries, actually visions of the future? It would explain why she was so pissed off at Taylor for reading it.

Carefully, I watch my step while going downstairs. Kelly is opening mason jars up and handing them to the people. I give her the items and she returns to me an opened jar of pineapple and a fork. "Eat." She points to an open spot against the stairs.

I sit down and start eating the pineapple. Looking around the room I notice there are a lot fewer people here than there should be.

"Kelly," I whisper. "Where is everyone?"

She comes over to me. "Dead. Or, at the other house."

I nod. She goes back to what she was doing.

James brings another batch of food and puts it in a pile. He grabs a jar of pickled carrots and joins me on the floor. "Rayleen is a bright girl. She'll stay alive long enough for us to get to her and they took her for a reason so they won't kill her.

A few of us will be heading out to look for her and Nikki. That's the main priority at this point. Then, we'll see about killing Sandra and Darius.

It will be a tough road ahead and I can understand if you would rather stay and try to settle down. It would certainly be safer."

I almost choke on a pineapple. Swallowing a few times I clear my throat. "No, I'm going with you. You can't expect me to just settle down when Rayleen was kidnapped by my ex and a psycho bitch."

"No, I guess I really can't. We'll be leaving as soon as we can get most back up on their feet. Should only be another day or so." James tries to reassure me by placing his hand on my shoulder for a moment.

I ask, "And then what?"

He thinks for a moment. "Try to catch leads on where they might be. It shouldn't be too hard, and we have a few guesses to where they might've been going; some bases we've heard about."

One problem could be Nikki's ability. If she can see the future then she will know we're coming. "But, what about Nikki? If she tells them. If they know we're coming, it'll be hopeless."

"Not if she doesn't tell them." He says.

"If they torture her?" I didn't say it would be willing.

"She still might not tell them we're coming." James shakes his head. "They won't hurt her much. It would be easier to convince her to give them the proper information. Could be one of the reasons they took Rayleen. The girl stays safe as long as she cooperates."

"But, she barely knows Rayleen." I know I said it a bit too loud the moment it came out of my mouth.

"Did you see the way she protected Rayleen from Daniel? She has a strong mind and the will to protect people. No matter who they are.

And, have you met Rayleen? She's got one of those personalities that just make people like her.

I'd bet that Nikki will give them just enough information to keep both of them alive and anything about a rescue she'll keep to herself. Rayleen will be okay." James places his hand on my shoulder briefly; trying to reassure me.

He gets up and goes over to someone lying on the ground. I assume he is finished with our conversation.

I get up. Bringing the pineapple with me, I quietly go upstairs. Up the other set of stairs, I go into the bedroom and close the door.

I set the tin down onto the dresser and crawl back into the bed.

Chapter 56

It becomes a quiet ride too quickly. I did however learn my captors are, for sure, Sandra and Darius. I don't know why they're so keen to keep me.

I wish I hadn't offered to help James. It obviously made me a target for something.

The chilled air freezes my skin. Looking over to Rayleen, I pull her in closer to me. Hopefully, we can both get a bit more heat.

My stomach jumps to my throat as the dragon swoops down. Lower and lower. My ears pop when I swallow. Right before we hit the ground the wings move in a way that catches the air underneath; softening the landing.

At the same time, Sandra grabs Rayleen from my arms and Darius pulls me off the dragon.

Rayleen cries out as she's placed on the ground. I struggle and break free from Darius' arms. Quickly scooping up the small girl to try to comfort her.

Sandra looks around us and mouths the word 'stop'. I turn around. Darius is right behind us and he looks pissed.

"Come," Sandra says. I hesitate for a moment, but with the girl in my arms and with the demons around, I doubt I could get far if I tried to escape; then who knows what they would end up doing to us.

I follow Sandra towards the jailhouse. Maybe we're here to pick someone up? Or maybe this is another base.

The building looks like it's in the shape of an L from here. We go through a set of doors and immediately I rethink that I should have tried running while I was still outside. There are masses of demons in here. Guarding the place against what, I'm not sure.

No one says a word as Sandra leads us through to another door in the room. I feel like I am taking a death walk; my stomach sinks and I am nauseous.

A couple of gates and doors in, and we are walking down a long concrete hallway towards another door. There isn't any escaping from this place now that I'm in here. The walls are closing in, the demons around me are getting closer.

The next door opens for us. A male with black hair makes Sandra stop with only an angry look. "Put them in a cell, then report to me immediately." His voice is deep and threatening. He promises the contrary will not be pleasant.

Sandra and Darius are probably going to get in trouble over the farm and losing the battle. Or maybe he is mad about Rayleen and me being here. Is that man the one in charge of them?

What do I do now?

Obviously, it would be suicide to try to escape right now. Not that I could. Jails are made to hold people in and prevent them from escaping.

We walk forward again when the guy steps off to the side. Coming into the room, I stop. These cells are packed full of people just staring out at us.

Pushed from the back, I almost fall forward. Okay, I get it, keep walking. Geez, you could have just said something.

At the very end of the line, there is a cell they take Rayleen and me to. I'm sure it is the only empty cell in the entire place. The door is open already. From the expectant look Sandra gives me, I know that I need to go inside. I take a deep breath and work myself up into walking into the room. The door screeches shut and is locked before I turn fully around.

No one says anything. They just walk away. Standing where I am; I just freeze in place.

Nothing. No feelings, no thoughts. Nothing.

The moment they leave the area, I can tell because the people in the other cells start coming to life. They make noise, talk to each other quietly, I hear clanking.

Walking closer to the front of the cell I try to get a better look at these people. I don't think they are criminals. None of them are dressed in jumpsuits. They are dressed in regular clothing; some of the women have smears of makeup on their faces. Everyone is dirty. They aren't demons, they look human.

Some of them looked starved, while others look completely healthy. I wonder if it's because some have been here longer than others, or if the healthy ones are the people who steal all the food from the others.

Looking at Rayleen I am happy that, for now at least, we have a cell to ourselves.

Someone comes into the cell block again. Everyone goes deathly quiet. I try to look over to see if I can see who it is, but they are too far away for what I can see. Their footsteps are heavy. The ground feels like it should be shaking, but I think that is just my legs.

I put Rayleen down and set her behind me.

A massive arm moves into view. It grabs on to some bars of a cell diagonally across from mine. All except the size of it would make me think that it was a normal human's arm. Maybe a giant, or something else; probably something else. I'm not sure. A giant would probably be bigger than that.

He moves to the side and I get a better view of him from the back. He's shirtless and I can see scars and fresh wounds all over his back. His back is bent slightly over as he struggles to not hit the ceiling.

Screaming starts. I cover Rayleen's ears and move my body to cover her view. People are being brought out of the cell. They only take about half the cell's people and take them off somewhere. The door shuts, but this time most stay quiet. There is crying coming from a couple of the cells, mostly from the cell across.

Picking Rayleen up, I can feel her shaking. I take her over to a bed and sit down. Cradling her in my lap, I try to comfort her.

The moment doesn't last long before we are interrupted. The door to our cell is opened. It startles me. Standing up, I put Rayleen behind me and shield her from the intruders.

"You, out." Sandra points to me. I look down at Rayleen. "Just you. The brat stays here." Darius grabs my arm and escorts me out of the cell. I can hear the wail Rayleen cries as I'm taken away.

They better not do anything to her.

Darius leads me out the way we came in; through the concrete hall. In the next room, we go through a different door and down a hall. He shoves me into an interrogation room.

Darius and Sandra come into the room. He closes the door behind himself. I can hear the click of the lock.

"Shall we?" I jump. The black-haired man from before is sitting in a chair in the corner. Standing up, tensing, I prepare to fight them off. I haven't got a chance at winning, but I need to try. "Have a seat."

Three against one. If I get a choice in this there is no way I am sitting down. "I'd rather stand."

"Don't be rude. I'll give you another chance. Have a seat." His dangerous tone from before is back. I guess I had hoped I wouldn't have been on the receiving end of that. I don't think I get a choice. Darius starts towards me. So, I sit down.

"I'm Seth. How are you today?" I just stare at him. I'm not going to answer that question. "Straight to the point, eh? I like that. Look either you help us or you die. It's as basic as that."

I think for a moment. I need to be careful here. Why would they need me to help them? It doesn't look like they need help and it's not like they have any humans working with them. "Help you do what?"

"Win this war. With your talents, we will know the enemies' moves before they make them, so we don't have any more setbacks like the farm." He leans forward in his seat. I'm not that good at strategy. Do they want me to be a spy? "You tell us the future; everything that's going to happen and we will spare your life. It's unfortunate that you lost your vision book, but I'm sure you remember everything anyway."

"I can't tell you the future. I'm not a psychic." A clap of skin on skin first sounds in my ear. In the next moment, my body is moved from the force, then I feel the pounding sting.

Sandra recovers from the slap quicker than I do. She grabs my shoulders. "Don't lie to us. We know who you are; Marshall. I saw your notebook. You still even follow the old practices." Sandra's eyes look wild. She lets go of my shoulders. Reaching into her pocket she grabs an army knife. She opens the blade and locks it into place.

Adrenaline flowing into my system, I see the knife and try to jump out of my seat. Strong arms hold me to my spot. When did Darius get behind me? I can't get away. Panicking, I start kicking. I knock Sandra away for a moment, but she just walks up beside me to avoid my legs.

Hot blood runs from a cut she makes on my chest. The blade must be sharp; I barely feel it as another shallow cut is drawn beside the first one.

"Sandra stop," Seth says firmly. He waits for a moment. Sandra comes in again to cut me. I think this time she's going for my cheek. "Sandra STOP!" He yells out. My eyes follow him as he jumps on the table and grabs the knife from her hand. She looks surprised at the interruption. "No more cutting. We don't want her dying of an infection."

Seth walks off the table. He knocks on the door twice and leaves the room once it's opened.

My cuts start throbbing in time with my head. I'm nauseous from: the cuts, my swelling cheek, from the thought of this continuing, that they might do something like this to Rayleen.

"Listen to me, Bitch." Her voice has changed. It's low and threatening and well compliments the wild look in her eyes. "My ass is on the line because of you. You've caused a lot of trouble and I'm going to get my payback for it. You will tell us everything we want to know or you're going to have a very slow and painful death. Darius stand her up."

His cold grip tightens more as he lifts me. The chair screeches against the floor as he moves it away. My toes barely touch the ground. I want to touch the ground.

Sandra uses her full weight behind her punch right to my stomach. Tears fall from my eyes. I can't breathe. Forever passes before I finally get a breath of air into my lungs. Kicking up at her I manage to kick her in the stomach.

It was a soft kick and didn't look to cause her any pain, but it is a small victory.

A blur of her fist just before she pounds it into my left cheek is only the first warning I receive not to do something like that again. Each hit to me just hazes in after the first ten. I don't even know where she is hitting me anymore. I can't breathe. I haven't been able to since that one swing I managed.

Everything hurts. I can't stop it, can't avoid it. She keeps swinging. She won't stop.

I wish it would stop.

My lungs force my mouth to open. I try to take a quick breath, but my throat itches violently.

Through my coughing and choking Sandra stops.

My body forces me to take quick breaths and just as quickly makes me cough until I have nothing left.

Darius lets go of me. Immediately I collapse. I can't hold myself up. Curling into a ball I wait for more pain; my entire body aches but still surprises me as my back shoots a sharp pain everywhere. Another coughing fit starts up damaging my already stripped throat.

"Weak."

Chapter 57

The moment Calli opens the door I'm awake and looking over to her. She closes the door behind her. "Get up. We have to leave. Take your bag."

I hear shouts. I'm up and grabbing my stuff. Calli wakes Lucas up more forcefully, and they both get their things. I throw on my jacket and bag. I head out the door but am stopped when Calli calls to me. "Not that way. Out the window." I open up the window and climb through easily. From there, I go down metal stairs.

Calli is above me. She points behind me. "Ogre!"

I turn around. Panic arises, and I drop my bag. The ogre swings his fist at me. I duck. He lines up to strike again, but Calli sticks him with a knife. It doesn't do much good. She lets go of it, and it falls to the ground. Certainly, it doesn't slow him down any as he aims the strike for Calli instead.

The ogre turns his back to me. Lucas picks up Calli's knife. He strikes the ogre from behind. This time I see the wound Lucas was able to inflict. He is stronger than both Calli, and I, so perhaps he can get through the thick skin easier.

Unfortunately, Lucas moves out of the way, and the ogre looks to me as the one who cut him when he looks behind him. He charges me. The only thing I can think to do in my panic is run.

I can't delude myself into thinking that I'll be able to outrun him for long, but there are places I could perhaps hide where he couldn't get to. I run into the street.

I see it in the corner of my eye. A truck! It's going to run me over. I use my momentum to dive to the ground, on the side of the road, and hopefully out of the way of the truck. I hear the truck slamming its breaks.

I expect an impact to my side, but it only comes from the ground. I jump up and look at the truck. If I had been there, I would have been hit.

The truck is full of people, in the cab, and the back. I recognize the faces. Well, I guess this is when we join up with James.

I don't have time for this. The ogre crosses in front of the truck. I duck a punch, tripping over a hill in the process. I turn it into a roll to get out of the way. I can feel my muscles, and abrasions protest loudly with sharp pains all over. I can't deal with them right now. I have to run.

Behind the truck, I go until I hear a thud behind me.

Lucas is there when I turn around. He is on the ogre's back with Calli's knife in the ogre's back. The ogre isn't moving at all, so I assume he is dead.

Calli is at my side before I realize it. She grasps onto me and helps me stand. It is only then do I realize my knees are pounding.

Lucas yells, "Jaiden!" He climbs off the ogre's back and runs to me. He hugs me, then pulls away to examine me.

To his side, I notice James Ellesworn, if I remember his last name correctly, coming towards us. Others are leaving the truck.

James holds up both hands, "I am very sorry. I hadn't seen you until it was too late to stop. We have medical supplies let us fix you up." He turns his head back to the truck briefly to say his orders. "Taylor open up the first aid kit." He turns back to me. "Let's get you onto the truck bed." A girl runs to the cab, while Miles puts down the tailgate.

"I'm fine, really. Thank you." I say sweetly. I know they will help anyway, but I must still be humble.

"Please humour me? I feel awful." James he says.

"Okay." I agree. I stumble over to the truck and jump up on the edge of the tailgate.

"Once again, I am very sorry." James apologizes again.

"It's okay; at least you didn't actually hit me. It really could have been a lot worse than it is. I'm fine but thank you. No worries." I lift my right leg up on the tailgate. Mile sets to work examining my leg, and working to heal it.

"Since we did just almost kill you, is it too much to ask your names?" The woman with pale skin, blue eyes, and black hair non so tactfully requests. This is where I decide to change the course of the future. There is no use to drabble on with a round of twenty-one questions. I already know everything that I need to make this decision. I'm sure I can steer this in the same direction faster. I introduce the group.

"I'm Jaiden; this is Lucas and Calli." I hiss as Miles cleans the rubble out of my leg with an alcohol swab. I should have remembered that. He places his hand over the wound. My knee itches. When he pulls his hand away I am still amazed that it disappeared. I look at Miles. "Thanks, Miles."

I look back at James to continue my speech when Kelly interrupts me. "How do you know Miles?"

I stare at her for a moment. Does she really not recognize me; at all? "Ah, we went to the same high school. Kelly. Daniel. Alexa."

"Oh." She turns around in a huff and goes back into the truck cab. We didn't run in the same circles, but we've had classes together. Enough that she should recognize my face a little.

Leah jumps to the ground beside me. "I'm Leah. I didn't go to your high school."

"Hi," I say.

"I'm Brad."

"Shawn." I recognize his face from a picture.

"Stephanie."

"Taylor."

"I'm James Ellesworn. Would you like to join us? I must warn you though, we are trying to go up against the rebellion and get the world back in order. We just came from a battle to take back one of the farms they were using as a headquarters. If you join us you probably will die." James jumps to his question. Though I don't know what causes him to jump to his question I do appreciate it.

I look at Lucas, then Calli. I nod, and they reciprocate. "Sure, sounds like fun."

"You have a weird sense of enjoyment," Leah tells me. "I like you." That's weird, but okay. Maybe, she doesn't understand my meaning.

"Sarcasm, but yeah we'll join you." I look from Leah to James.

"Alright then, welcome. Everyone pile in, and we'll get going." James says.

"Calli, do you want to ride with them or us?" I ask Calli. It might be better than being on the back of the motorcycle.

Calli looks at the truck, "I'll go with them. It'll be a great chance to get to know them better."

"You have your own ride?" A male asks.

"The jackets aren't just for show. We actually do have motorcycles. They're right around the corner." Lucas explains.

"We'll be right back." I walk over to Lucas and take him by the arm. I lead him to where we left the bikes.

"Are you sure we should go with them? We don't know anything about them." Lucas asks.

"Yeah, I've had visions of us joining them. James, he's like the Prime Minister of magic folk, and he's leading a resistance." I explain.

"Alright, but do you think it's smart to follow them, and not just go south by ourselves?" He still has doubts about this plan.

"Yeah. They were heading south anyway. If we don't like what we see, we can always just go off on our own." I reason.

Not that I would break off now. I know these people are with me when I find Dominique, so I obviously stay with them.

We reach our bikes back where we were ambushed by the ogre. I'm happy that my bag is still here. I put it on, and then go over to my bike. I throw my leg over my black Ninja. I find the key in my pocket, and place it into the ignition. I turn the key and make sure I'm in neutral before pressing the button that starts the bike.

Lucas starts his bike quickly after me. He leads the way back out to the truck. We slow to a stop when we pull up beside the truck.

I tilt the bike, so I can get my left leg on the ground. Lucas revs his bike up, and I see him nod his head.

The truck lurches forward, and James leads the way. Lucas rolls forward. I loosen the break and simultaneously rev the throttle, and bounce my left foot up a little.

We drive further south. The drive is snowy and peaceful, despite the destruction of every city we pass. I gaze down at my gas. I only have two bars left; though I wouldn't doubt if that turned into one in just a few minutes. My bike isn't going to last much longer. As if Lucas reads my mind, though I bet it is because he is running low too, he rips ahead of the truck and slows it down to a stop. I'd never take such sharp movements with all this snow.

I stop my bike and turn it off. No use in wasting what little gas I have. Taking the chance for a break, I put my kickstand down, and peel myself away from the bike.

I realize that both my hands are cramped and tingling. There is a chill in the air, and it has started snowing again. The wind has been blowing at me, making me sway a little on the highway. I have to lean into the wind a little more to compensate for the wind's strength. It's made me nervous a few times. Between the snow and the wind, I've figured I would crash a few times.

I don't want to lose any heat that has accumulated in my gloves. I stretch my hands in the gloves and massage through the material.

Lucas is at James' window. I better get over there so, at the very least, I know what is going on.

"I've only got about ten minutes left, which should be enough to get us to Airdrie," Lucas says.

"I'm at two bars. I should be able to make it there." I let them know. I don't know how long my gas will last. I might make it to Airdrie, but I might be able to make it to Calgary. That would mean ten minutes or a half-hour respectively.

"Just keep driving to Airdrie. You can jump in the truck if you run out of gas, or we'll be walking the rest of the day." James says. "We can get gas once we're in town."

"Great," Lucas says before walking away. James is already putting up his window.

I guess that's it then. I'm half disappointed that my break won't be longer. My legs are finally starting to feel normal, and my hands aren't as cramped.

Despite this, I jump back onto the bike, and we head off to Airdrie. Lucas pulls to the side to let James pass. James leads the way to the town. Just as it is in sight, he pulls off to the left. It's the first house before you enter the town.

The snow is built up on their driveway. I assume they had a dirt driveway because the pavement on the highway only has a light coating. I drive the bike into the snow. I go slowly to make sure the bike doesn't slip out from me, but I get stuck. I rev the throttle a little and lurch forward. I panic and hit the brake. I don't lock the tires, but the bike comes out from under me anyway.

The bike stops at an angle on its side, being held up against the inside of my thigh, and my grip on the handles. I try to stand the bike back up, but it doesn't move an inch. I contemplate letting the bike drop down, but I don't think I could manage to do so with the position I'm in.

I would scream for help, but I don't think anyone would hear me with the helmet on. I just wait and wait. But, no one jumps up to help me. People can see me, and they are watching me, but no one comes to help.

Okay, fine then.

Supporting the bike against my thigh, I turn the bike off. I grasp the handles and pull my leg over the bike. In the position I'm in, I can't put my leg on the ground. Moving my right hand to the bike seat, I try to push the bike up. I'm not strong enough.

Okay.

One, two, three. I jump backwards. The bike falls. Landing, I lose my balance, slipping on top of the bike. At least I don't injure myself.

I bring myself upright and walk towards the truck. The bike can stay where it is for all I care.

I remove my gloves. Both of my hands chill. Reaching underneath my chin, I undo the straps. Taking off my helmet sends a shiver down my spine. It's cold. I thought the drive was chilly, but all the heat retained in my gloves, and helmet is now gone, and I am freezing. My glasses fog up, and I can't see.

James comes back from the back of the house. "Come inside." He tells all of us.

I pull up the rear of the crowd. We usher into the cold house and straight down into a basement. There is a humming noise, followed by a light, then warmth.

An elderly man sits rocking in a rocking chair. His wife returns with blankets. She places them down on a wooden chest before she hands them out to their new guests. When she runs out she disappears into another room, and then shortly appears with more blankets for the rest of us.

She hands me a comforter. "Thank you." I unfold the blanket and wrap it around me until the only thing visible is my head.

"I'm sorry I can't do much more for you." She apologizes to the whole group.

James quickly refutes her. "We appreciate the respite, and the warmth you are providing us is more than we could have asked for. We shouldn't be here too long."

I wonder if James knew these people before the war. Are they supernatural beings? Are they just a trusting and caring couple? Either way, I am thankful for their hospitality.

People settle down. Sitting where they can, or finding a standing spot by the heater. Lucas is mingling with James and Miles, so I go sit beside Calli as my glasses slowly defog.

"How long have you been riding?" One of the men asks me.

"Just a few days," I tell him.

"But you're so tiny. That bike is too big for you." A girl states the obvious.

"Not a lot of shopping options in the apocalypse. You kind of get what you get." I joke.

Between chuckles, I catch the words 'Nikki's book' over in Lucas' direction. It peaks my attention so I look over there. It's a little dark to see anything more than a yellow glint, but I think I know that notebook.

Miles takes the book from James. "Maybe if we can decipher her vision book. We can get clues. She might have seen this coming. We just have to figure out what the poetry means."

Vision book?

"They have a vision book?" I ask the general group.

They look startled. No one wants to answer the question to a stranger. Or, maybe they don't know. Finally, Leah says. "Yes."

"Whose book is it?" I ask.

"Nikki Marshall's." She answers.

I bolt up and walk over to Miles.

 "Can I see that?" They look at one another, suspicious of me, and my intentions. They have all rights to be since they don't know me. "I think I know the person that owned that book, Nikki Marshall. I might have better luck figuring out what the words mean."

James nods to Miles, who hands me the book.

I open up the cover page. There inscribed on the cover is the name and handwriting I recognize. I watched her write it after she questioned my inclusion of a gift receipt. She had said she loved the book, wrapped in her favourite colour. She had no intentions of returning it.

Then she made me sign it. But, I was so nervous, I signed it backwards and upside down.

I flip through the pages to the back page. I show James and Miles the *From Jaiden* note. "See, I gave her this notebook." It puts them at ease.

One question burns in my mind. "How do you know this is a vision book? How do you know she had visions of the future?"

"The Marshalls have a long history of strong mental abilities, none stronger than the ability to see the future. They were trained to write it down so nothing was forgotten. Obviously, Nikki wrote what she saw down, but she put it in code." James explains.

I nod my understanding. "Her poetry. A disguise for her visions."

So Marshall was my dad's last name. That last name is my birth father's last name. I am a Marshall by blood. I am torn between elation and pain.

I should have known basic things like family traits and history. I should have been trained to write things down in a vision book. I should have been told about my visions as a kid and not been made out to be insane.

I read through a couple of poems in the beginning. I feel the pressure of a bunch of eyes on me. They make me want to hurry, but I don't want to.

I find the last pages she had written on. The words and tear smudges hurt my heart. They were obviously written after the attack.

Scouring the pages, I look for anything that could lead us to Banff in some sort of reasonable connection.

But, should I?

I toss back and forth. Would it be better to reveal that she doesn't have visions? That I'm the one that does.

If I tell them now, where we should go, will we change something? Making it never happen in the first place. Or, maybe we get a better opportunity to save her earlier.

It's so confusing.

It's possible to save her the way that we did. Just move a little faster and we could have her down before the ogre gets there.

It's possible that I said something on the original timeline to get us to Banff faster, and by delaying things we end up not saving her.

Maybe not. I don't know. I've never really tried messing with things like this. I don't know the rules. I should have been taught the rules.

Maybe they decide not to save her, because they find out she doesn't have visions of the future. She isn't any use to them as a human.

I should just leave things to happen as they should until the moment before.

"I need more time. I don't see anything that could tell us where she is." I admit.

"Then, how do you suggest we find her?" Brad asks me.

"We talk to people. Someone has to know where they took her or where they are going." In my head, I stick up my hand. Me! I do! Dominique is in Banff or will be.

I have to believe that somehow, sometime we make it to Banff; just in time to save her.

Chapter 58

We can't leave the farmhouse fast enough for my taste. Too many memories and all of them are bad. We make it out the door and stop about ten feet away in a patch of wet grass. I turn around and face the house one last time.

No one says anything. We stand around for a moment of silence for all who lost their lives over the battle, to those whose lives are still to be lost because we didn't accomplish anything real here, and to those who have lost their lives since the whole war started.

James breaks the silence by warning us, "Stand back." He rubs his hands together. Flame grows from the friction created and a little magic. He goes to the corner of the house and spreads the fire to the wood. Blowing on the flame it grows quickly; soon it encompasses the whole house. The white flame doesn't spread any further than the house.

We stay here, watching as the roof collapses. The fire eats away at the house until it becomes nothing more than ash in the wind and cinders in a pile. The fire goes out as the house is levelled.

James walks away. We follow him through the forest along the path made by all the traffic that went through here only a couple of days ago. Back we go to the abandoned farmhouse next door.

This place is buzzing with people more lively than our bunch. The people here must be excited. Having spent much time as the cattle in the demon's slaughterhouse, they seem enthusiastic about their freedom. A new chance at a life they probably believed was out of reach.

We are welcomed by applause, cheers, tears, hugs, and gratitude. There are some people saying things but I can't concentrate on them. The boards on the big picture window are broken; probably how the demons entered the house. Blood darkens the snow where someone must have bled out; the body is gone now.

Rayleen was taken during the attack.

A part of me hates that the reason Rayleen was kidnapped was because of me. When Darius had taken Rayleen originally it had been to give her to me as a gift showing his kindness, but Sandra is unpredictable. Sandra could have any excuse for why she took Rayleen.

I shake my head to try to clear it before I start thinking about why they took her and what they are doing to her right now. Crystal rubs up against my legs. She cries as she looks up at me. I pick her up and just hold her. The snow melts and seeps into my arms.

By the time I check back in on things around me, James is talking to the crowd. "Count this as a victory, a small victory, but a victory all the same. Yes, there were lives lost getting to this point, but we have also saved lives. We officially have taken back one piece of land from them.

You're free now. You can go where you want.

Some of us are continuing on; to go help others; take back more land; to kill Sandra and Darius; to try to bring peace.

Anyone is welcome to join, but we'll need a decision immediately."

People talk amongst themselves. For only a moment ,before a general consensus is shared by a gentleman. "We're thankful you freed us, but we're going to stay here. We can rebuild here. You are welcome back anytime."

James tells them. "Very well. I wish you luck. We must be on our way though." James turns to us. "If any of you would like to stay here this is your last chance. I will not make any of you risk your lives any more than you already have."

King Zircon nods to James, "That would be our cue. It's time for us to go back home. Good luck on your journey. Let us know when you need any help again."

"Thank you. Without your help, none of this would have been possible. Have a safe journey back." James walks to one of the pickup trucks and King Zircon leads the dwarves to the moving truck. Leah, Taylor, Kelly, Miles, Daniel, and I follow James. A few other people volunteer themselves to come with us.

I give Crystal to one of the people staying. I can't take her with me. She'll be too much responsibility. I don't want to try to take care of her too.

We all squish into the cab and leave the farm by going up a long driveway then back towards Leduc.

There have been so many people lost over since the war began. I do not even want to begin on the number of people in the world we have lost considering how many hundreds of people I have known to have died.

The further we drive, the closer I can see we are getting back to the city. Trees disappear and buildings appear.

It seems to be the calm after the storm. The roads are clear. Fires have died down. There are birds in the sky and animals in the street.

We turn onto the main highway going out of Leduc. We drive and drive. We bypass town after town. No one says much of anything. The weather gets slightly warmer as we go further. Snow layers become thinner.

James slows the truck down a bit once we get into another city, and rolls down the windows. "Does anyone hear anything or see anything?"

We stay quiet and just look at each other. Some look at our surroundings. Until finally Daniel says, "Like what?"

"Anything. Signs of people." James tells us.

"Maybe we can recruit more people since basically everyone abandoned us; your fault by the way," Leah adds.

"And, how is it my fault?" James asks defensively.

Kelly raises her eyebrow, "because you gave them a choice between living cozy at a farmhouse or the probability of dying trying to kill some big bad demons."

"It was not my decision to make. They had clearly talked about it beforehand." James has an edge to his voice.

I am thrown forward in my seat. Brakes squeal when James slams the brakes. Orientating myself, I get up from the truck bed and take a look around. To the right of the truck a golden blonde-haired girl is getting up from the ground.

A large grey-skinned creature runs towards her. She ducks and rolls out of the way of his swinging fist. The giant trips over his own foot. A man runs up and jumps on its back. He drives a blade into its neck; killing it.

Looking back to the blonde, I see another woman there helping her stand. The man yells, "Jaiden!" while jumping off the creature's back and rushing over to brace her in his arms. He pulls away only to look her over.

James is out of the truck cab and jogs over to the trio. Everyone else starts getting out of the truck. My legs could use a good stretching, as I'm sure everyone else could use it too. But, I decide to stay beside the truck and just stand here.

Chapter 59

I don't know what day or time it is.

I don't know where I am anymore.

I don't know why they don't believe me.

I don't know why they think I can see the future.

I don't know how much longer I can take.

Every inch of my body aches. Each patch of skin, every muscle hurts; I swear even my hair hurts.

I wish I could stop breathing; I feel like I'm getting punched with each breath.

Slowly, I open my eyes. My left eye stings and I'm sure it's swollen. Wait, is it even open? It's too dark in here to tell.

"You're awake. Listen. I don't have much time." A whisper enters my mind. Is it real? Am I imagining it? "Pretend to be their fortune teller, and you can stop this torture. You can buy yourself more time. More freedom. Show them they can trust you, wait for it, then escape."

The voice disappears as fast as it came. I want to call out for help but I'm not sure if that would be a good idea right now.

A blinding light turns on. It hurts even after I close my eye.

"Ready for round two? I was thinking it would be fun to make you watch as we do the same to the little brat." The feminine voice belongs to Sandra; she sickens me with how twisted her mind must be.

She wouldn't do anything to a child. Would she?

"I'll do it." Talking hurts. I barely hear the words come from my mouth. I'll do anything they want.

"Good. Let's get you cleaned up. Darius, please tell Mantei to come in here. We can't have our prophet dying on us." The voice is from a man I haven't met before, yet it seems familiar.

Chapter 60

I peek around the corner. The dark hall doesn't give much away. There isn't anyone there from what I can see, but my night vision is inferior to that of a vampire and a good portion of other supernatural beings.

They'd see me before I'd see them.

Dominique rushes forward as quietly as she can. Miles goes after her next. I follow, catching up on Dominique's right.

A small light catches my attention to my left. Before I can do anything Miles veers that way, and taps Dominique on the back as he passes her.

I follow them to a light coming from a crack between boards. Peering inside the dimly candle-lit room shows me what we might be looking for. There are people huddled together. Those who aren't are lying haphazardly around the room. I wouldn't imagine they are dead, yet.

Logically, it would seem weird for vampires to keep dead bodies when the blood would start going bad with their death, and no preservative methods.

I scan the room. A few people are walking around. These look like the guards.

Dominique moves beside me. I look at her. She points to the left. I look back inside and search the left side for what she was pointing to. There, huddled against the wall by herself is a frail little girl. She is dirty from head to toe. She looks like Rayleen. A rope is tied around her neck and the other end to the wall behind her.

"Let's go," Dominique whispers. I grab onto her arm as she tries to dash off.

"No. We should wait. We don't know how many of them there are. We don't know if Darius is here or not. We should wait, and watch for a couple of minutes."

"I'm not waiting." She insists.

I try to keep my voice down. "I'm sure you can take out ten vampires by yourself, but I don't think I can. Dominique, all we need is a few minutes. Nothing is going to happen that hasn't already happened."

"Okay." She says this, but she also starts off in the same direction. She turns around and puts her finger to her mouth to shush me. "I'm just going to look around. Find the entrance and people."

"Be careful. Don't get caught."

"Okay, Mom. Relax." She hurries off into the shadows.

I look back into the crack in the boards. "Stay here," Miles says beside me. I nod and keep watching.

Three large males come into the room. The ones already in the room talk with them for a moment before two of them leave. Maybe this is a shift change.

One of them walks over to Rayleen. He nudges her leg with his foot. She pulls her limbs even further into herself. She is scared.

He talks with a few others in the room. I don't know what they're saying, but they all start moving closer to Rayleen.

The one closest to her lifts her. His head dips down to the crook of her neck, and she screams. He's killing her!

Someone taps my back. I turn around.

I don't know her.

She lunges forward.

About Jacey K Dew

Jacey is an author and mom who was raised in Leduc, Alberta by her adoptive family.

She took inspiration from familiar locations to set the scenes. Asking the question, what if supernatural beings took over?

Jacey started writing stories when she was sixteen and continues to have a passion for creating tales. Writing across genres in whichever story needs to be told next.

Jacey can be found at a multitude of social sites under the handle @jaceykdew and her website hub jaceykdew.ca

Her link page can quickly sort you to social sites, merchandise and book shop, blog, fan club, and a few retail stores her books are available at.

You can also sign up for her newsletter on the links page to receive the occasional email about on goings, book releases, bookish news, discounts and freebies.

jaceykdew.ca/about/links

Subscribe to SuperData to immerse yourself in the Three Souls Universe. Choose between free and paid levels to customize your reader experience. Free to access forums, emails, customizable profiles, freebies, discounts, behind the scenes information, and Ask the Author discussions. Or, choose a paid subscription to add physical mailed items.

jaceykdew.ca/superdata

Other Books by This Author

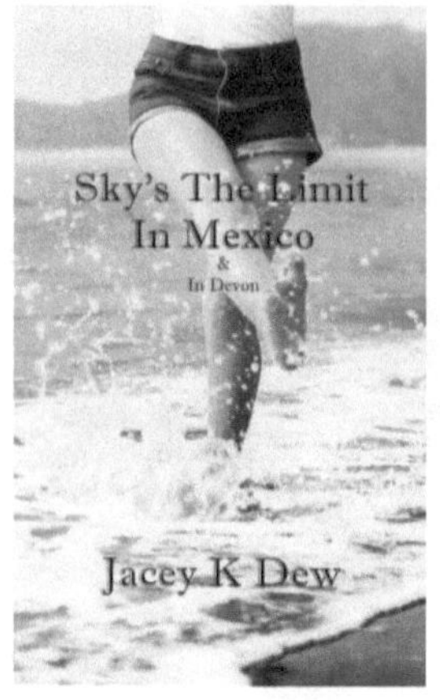

Vacation Romance

Skylar Bryson goes on the vacation of her lifetime. Tasting freedom and stepping out of her comfort zone while meeting interesting new people and gaining a different perspective. Will Skylar find more than adventure in Mexico? Once Skylar returns home her world is turned upside down. Will Skylar find her support system in her new companion, or should well enough have been left alone?

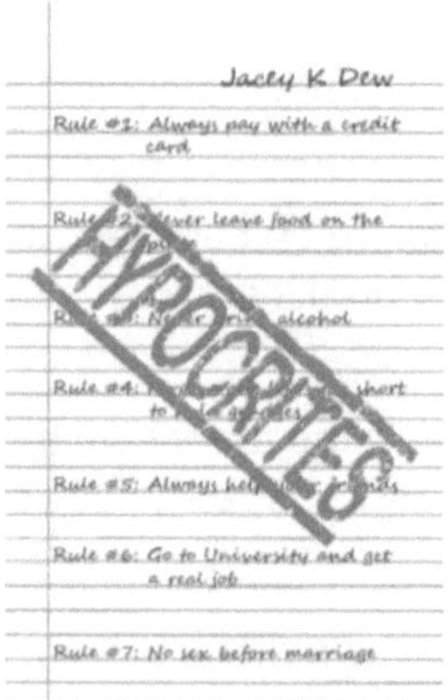

Coming of Age, Life Lessons Novella

Anna's parents had strict rules for life. Suddenly, at eighteen, her parent's deadly accident throws her life in turmoil. She has nothing more than her parent's rules to go by, but she soon learns that maybe her parent's beloved rules may be wrong for her.

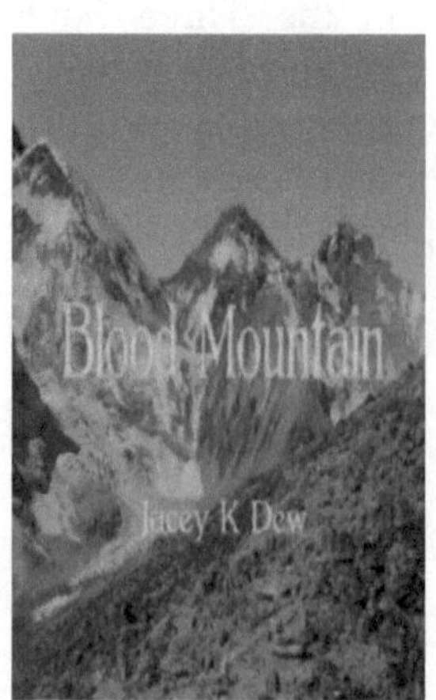

Small Town Drama Novella

She never thought she'd have to return to the city in the crux of a mountain. When her mother falls ill, Kara is beckoned home and thrust into the world she left behind.

9 781999 241452